FIDELIS MORGAN

# My Dark
# Rosaleen

Mandarin

**A Mandarin Paperback**
MY DARK ROSALEEN

First published in Great Britain 1994
by William Heinemann Ltd
This edition published 1995
by Mandarin Paperbacks
an imprint of Reed Consumer Books Ltd
Michelin House, 81 Fulham Road, London SW3 6RB
and Auckland, Melbourne, Singapore and Toronto

Copyright © Fidelis Morgan 1994
The author has asserted her moral rights

A CIP catalogue record for this title
is available from the British Library
ISBN 0 7493 15296

Printed and bound in Great Britain by
BPC Paperbacks Ltd
A member of
The British Printing Company Ltd

*Prologue*

# ROSALEEN

20.00 Wednesday 14 May. Having taken bedsit in Muswell Hill, await delivery.

Bell rings. Open door to two young men in leathers, balaclavas framing their faces. Both carrying motorbike helmets.

'Hi, there. We've got the goods.' Taller man holds up a six-pack of export lager. Shorter has a bottle of Scotch whisky and a plastic carrier bag which reads 'Happy Shopper'.

'Come in,' I say cheerfully and open the door.

Inside, the shorter man stands at the table and pulls some packets of crisps from the top of his plastic bag. He then reaches deeper into the bag and carefully extracts some short shiny sheaths of copper, a length of wire with insulating cover in yellow and orange stripes, two pint cartons of milk, and a larger squashy package tightly wrapped in white and red plastic which resembles a block of Italian mozzarella cheese.

'Super Ajax? Is someone thinking of scouring the flat?' I say sarcastically.

'It's industrial,' the short man says defensively.

'I know that,' I snap. 'I just wonder if that's the best you can get?'

'I don't do the getting, I just deliver,' says the short man, tugging a lager from the pack and pulling the ring sharply.

He flops into a grimy armchair and quaffs the beer. 'It won't be as powerful as it could be. You understand that?'

I hand the taller man a lager and a packet of crisps. 'You'll be here for a while,' I say, 'so you might as well enjoy the wait.'

He looks down at me, kindly. 'Sure?' he asks.

I nod, pick up the milk cartons and go to the sink, which is behind a strange wooden structure resembling a bar. I rip the cartons open and pour the milk down the plughole. I rinse them both out and come back into the main part of the room. I hand the cartons and a dishcloth to the men. 'Dry these out, would you?'

I take my glasses from my pocket and pull a tiny screwdriver from the table drawer.

After an hour I am done.

I place the two small devices resembling milk cartons into the plastic bag marked 'Happy Shopper'. Each is capable of blowing a car to pieces, of killing up to twenty people in a twenty-yard radius.

This is the story of a misfit. Don't worry. I don't expect your tears, much less deserve them. Tears have always been an embarrassment to me anyhow.

According to the papers I am 'the most wanted woman in Britain'. Well that certainly makes a change. Now that I have been taken and charged I suppose my wanted status has faded somewhat. I am being held on charges of terrorism although I am, and again I quote the press, 'a middle-class, middle-aged English housewife'.

I wonder how they know that. Who told them I was those things. 'Middle-aged' I suppose there is no quarrel with, though some time ago I heard a woman of sixty declaring that she was only just entering her middle age, so at forty-one, perhaps I am a borderline case.

How are these journalists so sure about me? I am not. I am in the dark. I always have been, really. Never knowing who I was, while all around me conspired in silence. If someone stopped me in the street and asked me to fill in one of those questionnaires I'd be stumped. Who am I? What am I?

I don't ask for adjectives here. There are plenty of those: cruel, cold, hard, bitter, ungrateful, unkind, irrational, sulky, sullen, spiteful, unloving, heartless . . . I could out-Roget a thesaurus of such epithets, I am sure.

Pure nouns are what I'm after. Class? Nationality? Status? Who do I belong to? Where have I come from?

In Liverpool I was Irish. At Catholic boarding-school I was a Liverpudlian working-class atheist; at Protestant school I was a southern middle-class Catholic. At university I was just clever (but then, cleverness is not always an asset to a woman). When I married an English Home-Counties-born-and-bred Protestant lawyer with perfect Received Pronunciation I found that I was Irish again, after all those years. Thick-Mick, Miss Bog-Irish, the Paddy with the heart of stone. Though, ironically, by now back in Ireland no one would see me as anything but upper-middle-class English.

So here I am, 'the enemy within'. Whatever the situation. It is only a tiny step from 'misfit', a person who cannot adjust to their social status, to 'enemy', a person who ranges themselves against it.

Believe me, if a person hears often enough that they are an outcast they will become one. Remember, next time you smugly squeeze someone out of your circle, that they have two options: they can take the honourable way, and have their revenge from a distance, proud to be different, thrilled to be the thing you made them – your enemy; or they can transform themselves, become so like you you forget why they were unacceptable, and as they become unrecognisable in their similarity to you, these chameleons will wiggle back into your clique, to attack from within.

But am I really either of these? I doubt it.

I am the sum total of centuries. I am my family. I am history. I am geography. I am phonetics, grammar, style. It all ends in a bare cell. Once it would have finished at the end of a rope. No more, unfortunately for me. Where did it all begin? How many centuries has it taken to lock me in these four walls, with only the odd fly for company?

HUGO

## 19 July 1588
## Santiago, Spain

Brother Hugo beat out the rhythm with his cane on the cobblestones as he dragged the boy along the narrow street. 'Salve, regina, mater misericordiae,' he sang. 'Vita dulcedo, et spes nostra, salve.' He crashed the stick down, and grabbed the boy's hair between his long, bony fingers. 'Sing, boy! Sing, in God's holy name, won't you?'

The boy's eyelids dropped down, and tears gathered on his black lashes. The priest clicked his tongue in irritation and continued to sing, walking along in time. 'Ad te clamamus, exules filii Hevae, ad te suspiramus, gementes et flentes in hac lacrymarum vallee.' He took a breath to prepare for the next strain, then spun round and faced the child. 'Again,' he hissed, crouching down so that his eyes were level with the boy's. 'Again!'

The tiny rosebud lips parted, and from them came an ethereal sound, more a breath than a song. 'Amen,' chanted the boy.

The priest gently held the boy by his shoulders. 'Amen, indeed,' he whispered. 'I knew there was a voice in there somewhere.' His eyes softened, and creased into a smile. He glanced upwards, past the hanging, timbered buildings to the dark, thunderous skies. 'Thank you, blessed mother.' He sang out again, quietly this time, still squatting before the child. 'O clemens, O pia, O dulcis virgo Maria.' He leaned forward, and tenderly kissed the boy on

9

the forehead. The boy parted his lips, and wiggled his tongue, then smiled coyly, jerking his fragile hand towards the priest's skirted lap. 'You want jig-jig?'

The Jesuit's firm hand clipped the boy smartly round the ear as he soared to his full height. 'No!' he shouted. 'Not jig-jig, you understand? No one wants your jig-jig any more. You must sing, do you hear? Sing to save yourself, body and soul. We don't ever want to hear about your jig-jig again.'

He seized the child's hand and strode forward, his cane cracking out its cruel rhythm on the wet street, his dry voice echoing in the cold morning air.

## 20 July 1588
### La Coruña, Spain

They had had no sleep. The thirty-five-mile journey from Santiago to the port of Coruña they had made mainly on foot. One advantage of being a priest meant that passing wagons did stop and offer him a ride, but Brother Hugo had declined all but one of them. He wanted to exhaust the boy. To break his body and thereby free his mind.

The boy's grip on his hand was still firm, his face a pale blank. What thoughts, wondered the priest, went on in that tiny, delicate head? It was less than a day since he had found him, called in from the street to a rickety wooden house in the slums of Santiago. An obese middle-aged man had had a heart attack. The priest went to hear his confession, and perform the last rites. A filthy fat woman, smeared with make-up, waited, hanging her head, in the doorway. There were other women in the house. The priest knew it. But he didn't get a glimpse of them. They would all be cowering behind closed doors now, listening, or maybe carrying on with their business, if they had no fear of God at all.

The fat man was naked, lying face down on an old broken bed. His blubbery lips were the only things that moved as he confessed his sins, his sexual debauchery, his lusts. Brother Hugo fumbled for his crucifix in the folds of his black gown. As he touched the floor his fingers felt

11

warmth. He stretched his hand under the bed, grasping the little arm, and tugged the boy out.

'That's the one who did it, Father. He's the one who killed me,' blubbered the fat lips. The woman in the doorway gasped and held her hand to her crimson gash of a mouth. 'It wasn't my fault, Father, believe me, I didn't know . . .'

The priest shot her a look.

From the next room a rhythmic knocking on the thin wall increased in time with the rising crescendo of a woman's groans. The priest closed his eyes and his face tightened. 'Don't you people ever learn?' he roared. 'Sell your own souls to the Devil if you must, but how can you expect God to forgive you for abusing a tender child like this?'

He snatched the boy into his arms and, violently shoving the woman out of his way, strode out into the street.

He bought some bread, cheese and olives and fed the child, quietly asking him questions. But the boy remained silent, gazing balefully up at the priest with his big dewy eyes. After an hour Brother Hugo still knew nothing about the boy. His mind raced. He could not keep the child with him. But to leave him would surely only send him back to that hell-house, or, if not that one, another. What the child needed was a new life, a new beginning. To start anew in a new world.

'That's it!' he exclaimed. 'We'll go to the sea. We'll find you a ship. You can sing your way to the New World.'

And they started their long walk to La Coruña.

Now, as they reached the top of the town they caught their first sight of the sea. Tall rigged ships jostled for space in the harbour, and more were anchored outside the walls of the port, their masts bristling on the horizon. The galleons' sails were furled, but against the cobweb of rigging fluttered a rainbow of flags: gold pennants with red crosses, white with blue, yellow or red stripes, flags emblazoned with elaborate coats of arms, white, depicting the Virgin Mary in sky blue, red flags showing the crucifixion, magnificent streamers and banners stamped with dragons, lions, and all nature of beasts, real and fabulous, in every shade and hue, rippling and whipping in the wind.

Along the dockside a crush of men jostled forward to take communion from a queue of priests. Sailors in buff jerkins and breeches, soldiers in browns and greens, aristocratic musketeers and captains in bright satin and velvet doublets, lavish with silk trimmings and slashings, some wearing gold and silver breastplates which sparkled even under the darkest skies, others in sumptuous cloaks which fluttered in the breeze, thousands of them, waiting to confess their sins. In their hands they held hats trimmed with riffling feathers. From their belts hung swords, and leather pouches, daggers and pistols.

Brother Hugo grasped the boy's hand tighter, and with his other hand excitedly pressed his wide-brimmed hat on to his head as the sea wind whipped up the alleyway.

'What a glorious sight! You're in luck, my child. If you can muster a few decent notes there must be one ship out of that lot that'll take you.'

The tall man and his charge started the steep descent, down narrow winding streets, singing as they went. When they reached the crowded quay the priest held his finger to his lips: 'Stay with me, keep your eyes down and your mouth shut, and shortly you'll be on your way to the New World, boy.'

They pushed through the soldiers and sailors and reached the line of priests as the mass came to a close. A squall of rain spattered down on them. The boy wiped the water from his forehead with a weary gesture.

Beside them a gnarled sailor spat on the shiny cobbles.

'They must be bloody barmy, the powers that be, ordering us to set sail again with this wind up. We'll only be driven back, like last bloody time.'

His companion slapped him roughly on the back. 'You wash your mouth out, Enrico, lad. Look, it's been so bad, things can only get better. Cursing isn't going to get the wind down. And there's a kid beside you, what's more, and a priest.'

The dark sailor spun round. 'Oh, I beg your pardon, Father. It's sea-nerves, you know. We always get a bit edgy before a long voyage.'

Brother Hugo covered the boy's ears with his hands. 'We have to protect the ears of the innocent, you understand, from impurity.'

The two sailors looked awkwardly down and smiled. 'I'm sorry about that. We do have a rule on board, Father,' added the Bos'n. 'Absolutely no swearing. My chum here would have been thrown in the bilboes for what he just said. I'd have put him there myself. It's my responsibility you see – discipline. Truly, Father.'

They glanced apologetically at the priest, then turned to go.

'One moment!' Brother Hugo caught Enrico by the arm. 'Do you need a boy on board? To sing the Salve, perhaps? This child sings like an angel.'

'Don't ask me, Father. This chap here's the Bos'n.' He pushed his companion forward. 'He does the hiring and firing of boys.'

The Bos'n's eyes swept up and down the child. 'He's not sick, is he? We've had a lot of sick'uns the last month. I've had to chuck a few of 'em off here. Send 'em packing, back to their homes.' He chuckled. 'We'd have kept the watch better ourselves. Little beggars were always puking up when they should have been singing out the hours.'

Brother Hugo put a reassuring arm round the boy's

14

shoulders. 'No. He's not sick. He's a tough little thing. Should serve you well. Very independent, aren't you ...' The priest realised he didn't even know the child's name, so in haste he gave him his own. 'Erm, Hugo. Very independent.'

'All right then, Father. If he's recommended by yourself ... He looks solid enough.'

The priest shook hands with the sailors, then pushed the boy forward. 'Off you go then, lad.' He tousled the boy's black curls. 'God will be beside you. Don't you worry. You'll be better off when you reach the New World.'

The two sailors squinted after the tall black figure as he slid away through the crowd.

'The New World?' said Enrico. 'What's he on about?'

'Search me,' replied the Bos'n, laughing. 'The next world, more like!'

The two sailors guffawed as they shoved the boy up the gangplank leading to the huge wooden galleon bound for England as part of King Philip's invincible Armada.

## Friday 29 July 1588
## At sea

'Feeling a little better after the storm, Father?'

The Bos'n smiled generously at the ship's priest, although he had little respect for the problems of landlubbers, especially their seasickness. It was just one more time-wasting operation, meaning he had to get the decks scrubbed down, and, as if that were not enough, they then rolled up with their viridian-green faces while he was doing his utmost to enjoy a meal of dried fish, olives and stale ship's biscuit.

The fat, pale priest flopped down on to a box and took a few deep breaths, throwing his face back to the sky. 'Well, the Lord has pleased to bring the sun out anyway.' He sucked in a lungful of sea air, and whistled it out again through pursed lips.

The Bos'n decided to change the subject. He knew from bitter experience that the very mention of the word 'wave' was enough to get them puking all over again.

'How's the Jesuit's little boy getting on, then?'

The priest mopped his brow with a large lacy handkerchief.

'Oh, fine, fine. Between you and me, I can't think why he was put forward as a ship's boy. He mimes, you know.'

The Bos'n chuckled. 'Mimes? How do you mean?'

'Well, he doesn't actually sing. Just breathes to the words. Still, he knows them well enough. Seems to know every

16

hymn there is. Mind you, I've never heard him utter a word in conversation either. He certainly doesn't talk to the other boys.'

The Bos'n felt uneasy. He, after all, had hired the boy. 'Ah, you know gromets, Father. Well, all children, really! Still, he looks pretty enough, though, eh, Father? Quite a little angel face. And if you're not up close, you'd never know he wasn't singing. He looks as if he's singing to me. Oh yes, he certainly looks as though he's singing. And he's very obedient, isn't he? Whenever I've asked him to do something, he's just done it. No questions asked. Not bad for a gromet . . .'

The priest was swallowing ominously.

'Excuse me, Bos'n . . .' He wobbled to his feet, staggered over to the rails and vomited into the navy blue swell.

The Bos'n sighed and looked across the deck to little Hugo. The boy sat, as usual, a few yards away from the other ship's boys. They were playing hand-clapping games, gathered laughing in front of the hour-glass which it was their task to turn every half-hour. Hugo looked into his lap, picking at the fabric of his breeches, and occasionally glancing over his shoulder at the hour-glass.

A group of aristocratic soldiers swaggered past the boys, the satins and velvets of their clothes rustling and the gold of their buttons sparkling in the afternoon light. Nearby a sailor swung down from the ratlines on to the deck. Losing his balance he toppled into an officer, and, grasping out, accidentally tore a golden tassel from the sleeve of his doublet.

'Sorry, mate,' muttered the sailor.

'Bloody hell!' grunted the soldier in reply, stooping to pick up the tassel.

The Bos'n was facing him when he stood up again.

'What's your name, officer?'

17

The soldier thrust his chin forward. 'Don Pedro de Castellote. What is it to you, my friend?'

The Bos'n looked him square in the eye.

'Swearing on this ship is punishable. Order of the Admiral, and the King himself. If you want a spell in the bilboes you can have one. But it might be easier not to do it again.' He tossed his head in the direction of the ship's boys. 'Particularly in the hearing of these children, who lead us in prayer.'

Don Pedro twirled his severed tassel in the air. 'Fine. You have your orders. I have mine.' He reached down to his black leather belt, pulled a delicately jewelled dagger from its golden scabbard and slashed off the matching tassel from his other sleeve. 'There we are now, at least my sleeves match again. Anyway, Bos'n, I'm ready for the battle, and that's the only thing I'm here for, so don't you worry about me.'

The Bos'n looked after Don Pedro as he strutted over to his friends.

'Wouldn't think about it, mate. We've got ourselves to worry about, and that's quite enough for me.'

Early that morning the Admiral of the Fleet had signalled to the ships to fall into formation, and now the fluttering Armada sailed in a huge crescent, said to be two miles from horn to horn. Hugo's vessel was the last in line, positioned on one of the horns at the rear of this huge floating moon of ships.

The priest tottered past the Bos'n, wiping his chops with the lace handkerchief and muttering apologies under his breath as he made his way down to the lower decks. Around the Bos'n, on the top gundeck, the common soldiers leaned against their gun carriages, or sprawled prostrate on the planked surface. The Bos'n picked his way across the confusion of bodies to the gromets. As he passed the hatches he could hear the rumble of hundreds of men's

18

voices coming from below. Tension was rising all over the ship. They had been at sea now for nine days since taking haven at La Coruña, and although they had spent a couple of those days becalmed, everyone, even those without a notion of navigation, knew that the English shores, and the ships of the infidel, would soon be in sight.

'Hugo, lad, how are you?'

The boy jumped to his feet, smoothed down the front of his clothes and smiled up at the Bos'n.

'You like the singing, then?'

The boy nodded vigorously in reply.

'You should join in with the others, you know. Go on. Go and have a game with them.'

The boy started nervously, wiping his hands down the sides of his breeches, and tutting his tongue against his front teeth. The Bos'n laid his gnarled hand on the boy's shoulder. 'It's all right, lad. You don't have to.'

Hugo seized the Bos'n's hand and showered it with kisses. 'Ay, ay, boy. It's all right.' The Bos'n squinted over the boy's shoulder at the hour-glass, and thrust the child forward. 'Quick, boy. The sand's run through. You'll miss the hour.'

Hugo jerked forward and swivelled the waisted hour-glass on its post. 'Four glasses done,' he sang, and the other boys leapt to their feet and joined him, chanting in harmony.

*'New one a-filling,*
*More sand shall run,*
*If God is willing.*
*To God let us pray*
*To make safe our way,*
*And Mary, Our Lady, who prays for us all*
*Save us from —'*

19

In the distance a cannon fired. Everyone on deck froze and turned towards the echoing sound. The men who had been basking in the sun jumped to their feet and leaned over the side, straining to see. The grumbling sound from the lower decks had swollen into a loud babble. From the watch-top on the mainmast the lookout yelled down: 'Land ahoy!'

The singing had stopped. The boys looked at one another wondering whether to continue with the Ave Maria. Officers crowded on to the decks, craning to see signals from the other ships, or hear orders via the lookout. The Bos'n pulled his hat down firmly and marched up to the Vice-Admiral's gallery to take orders.

Within minutes the vast white sails, with their red crosses to signal a holy war, unrolled. Cracking in the freshening breeze, they carried the galleons closer to their fate. Starting at the centre of the fleet, each ship fired a broadside, and on every deck of every ship the men fell to their knees and commended their souls to the Lord and his mother, Mary, the Star of the Sea.

'Ave, Maris Stella,' sang out the boys on every ship, and many men joined them in song.

> *'Dei Mater alma,*
> *Atque semper virgo,*
> *Felix coeli porta.'*

'Hail, star of the sea, kindly mother of us all, still always a virgin, happy gate to heaven.'

Hugo took a deep breath and pursed his lips, ready to mouth the words of the next verse.

The grey ridge of the Lizard Head rose ahead as the sun slowly sank behind them. As darkness fell the sails were taken in: they were too noisy and too easily seen in darkness.

Slowly and cautiously the Spanish fleet crept into the English Channel. All along the English coast the vast fires blazing out from hilltops were clearly visible from the galleons. But the Spaniards saw no English ships. Morning came. The Spanish fleet edged onwards. Afternoon, evening, and darkness fell again, with no sign of English opposition. At midnight a Spanish pinnace took in a small English fishing smack and interrogated its crew. From these four terrified Englishmen they learned that the English fleet had left Plymouth.

In the silent black night still they saw nothing. Four hours later the moon glanced out from behind the heavy clouds, casting its ghostly light on a thin line of white sails between the Spanish fleet and the land.

As the sun slowly rose over the smooth waters of the Channel, eleven large English vessels could be seen leeward of the huge Spanish fleet and forty more before them. On the Spanish decks the gun carriages were wedged and ready. Cannonballs stood in small pyramids. The rails were lined with musketeers, glittering in velvet and gold, their plumed hats riffling in the rising breeze.

'Get out of my way, boy!'

Hugo sprang backwards away from the gun carriage.
Don Pedro lifted his hand, signalling to the men to fire. A
burning stick was applied to the powder and shot, and the
huge gun jumped back a couple of yards. Hugo helped the
men roll it back to firing position.

'Reload,' barked Don Pedro.

The men scrambled to clean out the barrel and prime
the cannon to fire again. Hugo bent down to remove the
lid from the powder-box as a musketeer in black and silver
jerkin reeled backwards and hit the deck. His gun clattered
on to the boards, and slid towards the rails with the movement of the ship. Hugo spun round to help the wounded
soldier, grabbing the gun in his tiny hand.

'Leave him!' yelled Don Pedro. 'More powder! More
powder, boy!' He snatched the gun. 'Go on. More powder.'

Hugo scrambled down the scuttle, slid down the companionways, ran through each dark and crowded deck,
squeezing himself behind the cross pillars to avoid the
cannons jerking back after each shot. The booming of the
guns on the lower decks was deafening; Hugo felt thankful
to be assigned to the open of the forecastle's upper deck.
He dived down the scuttle to the orlop deck, deep in the
bowels of the vast wooden galleon. The stench from the

bilges almost took his breath away, and he retched as he ran deftly back along the deck. Wounded men lay against the sides of the ship, only a few planks between them and the cold waters of the English Channel. There were also scores of men here waiting for the call: the land soldiers equipped and ready to fight once they reached the shores of England.

Hugo slipped on a wet area of decking and crashed to the floor. A strong pair of hands gripped him under the armpits and placed him back on his feet. 'There you are, lad. Run for it!'

Hugo froze and looked up into the man's long, pale face. 'English?' he whispered.

'That's right boy. Run along, now.'

Hugo wiped his nose, and realised that his hands were red and sticky. He had slipped on a pool of blood. He scurried on, down the hatch to the holds and along the narrow gangway. Barrels lined one side, horses and mules were tied along the other. Eventually he reached the powder room, picked up his parcel of powder and raced back up to the top deck. The air was thick with smoke from cannons and muskets, and ugly black clouds hung heavily in the evening sky.

Don Pedro snatched the bag of powder. 'You've taken your time then.' He turned to the men and raised his arm. 'Fire!' he yelled, slashing his arm down again.

The gun carriage reeled back again with a roar. The blast threw Hugo to the ground. When he opened his eyes he saw Don Pedro lying flat on his back, his foot blown off. Hugo was smattered with the man's blood. He clambered to his knees, and bent over Don Pedro.

'Get me out of the way, boy. Come on, don't just stand and stare.'

Hugo tried to drag the tall man back to the mast, but with little success. He was thrown to the deck again, as the ship rocked in the rising waters. He heard a huge bellow from the lower decks.

One of the soldiers on his gun carriage limped back to help him with Don Pedro.

'We've had it now, boy. We're not only in the rear, but if I'm not mistaken that last blast means we're holed. We'll be captured. Sure as eggs is eggs.'

Hugo grabbed the man's breeches, and his small red lips started moving frenziedly.

The soldier bent forward trying to catch the boy's words. 'That's right, boy. Salve Regina, "To you merciful mother, we cry out in this valley of tears".'

'Fire!' groaned Don Pedro from the deck. 'Fire!'

Two divers shinned over the rail, armed with hides, planks and hammers, and slipped into the water to start work on the damaged hull.

The soldier and the boy returned to their jobs at the gun carriage. The rest of the fleet was getting further and further away; the enemy's ships getting closer and closer.

'Look!' The soldier pointed across to the main bulk of Spanish ships. 'The *Our Lady of the Rosary*'s turning. She's coming back for us.'

One of the larger galleons was indeed moving round within the Armada's formation.

Hugo was sent off again for more powder, and in the depths of the dark lower decks he saw the carpenters trying to repair a large hole in the ship's side. Soldiers formed a chain along the deck and up the scuttles, bailing out. The pumps were working flat out and horses were screaming in panic as the water swirled around their legs. Hugo waded boldly along to the powder room.

'Carry it above your head, boy. It mustn't get wet.'

Hugo grabbed the packet and made his way back up to the deck, where everyone's attention was on *Our Lady of the Rosary*. The ship had been damaged in turning. Caught up in the rigging of two other Spanish ships, her bowsprit and fore-topmast were broken, and now she drifted out of control.

A sailor hanging above him in the rigging yelled down to the soldiers: 'The Admiral's given orders we're to leave her to her fate!' The crew and soldiers on Hugo's ship roared their disapproval. *Our Lady of the Rosary*, after all, had been coming to their aid.

A triumphant yell from the lower decks indicated that the damage to their own ship was made good, if only temporarily. 'We're to go ahead,' the sailor shouted. 'To leave *Our Lady of the Rosary*.'

All eyes on deck were fixed on the other ship as it pitched and heaved hopelessly in the rising sea. As darkness fell heavily around them, their own ship slowly drew back into formation. They could just see the masts of *Our Lady of the Rosary* far in the distance as four or five English ships closed on it.

Gunfire was now pointless. The English fleet was far out of range. The decks fell silent in the cool night air, and a throbbing tranquillity crept over the galleon as it slipped on up the English Channel towards Lyme Bay.

Hugo crawled over to the rails and clung on, staring at the grey-topped waves as they crashed against the side, showering him with spray. He held out his hands, rubbing away the dried blood from the cracks in his palm. Near him a group of soldiers huddled under the shadow of their gun carriage, crunching their biscuit, sucking on their olives. Sailors hung from the torn rigging, tying loose pieces and splicing in new lengths of rope. The torn sails flapped helplessly in the freshening wind.

Hugo looked out at the shadowy cliffs of England. Silhouettes of Spanish ships glided alongside, sails catching the dim light. The wind gently ruffled his black curls. With closed eyes, he held his face out to meet the cool darkness. He could hear raised voices coming from one of the nearby Spanish ships. As he opened his eyes to follow the sound he was blinded, and instantaneously a blast thundered in his ears and threw him back against the mast. The deck was showered with splinters of wood and debris.

The voice called down again from the rigging: 'I don't believe it! It's one of Oquendo's ships, The *San Salvador*, the pay ship. Blown right out of the water.'

Everyone on the deck hung on to the rails and stared at the blazing hulk. The soldier who had helped Hugo drag Don Pedro to shelter put his hand on the boy's shoulder and said quietly to himself, 'Powder-store must have gone up. They wouldn't have had a chance.'

The men at the rail gasped as they looked down at the black waves scattered with charred corpses.

'They told us when we left that God was on our side. That He would protect us from the dangers of the infidel.' The soldier held Hugo's hand. 'He can't seem to protect us from ourselves though, can he?'

The boy's eyes rolled up to meet the man's.

'Either that, or . . . or . . .' The child desperately shook the soldier's hand, his tongue moving against his dry lips. The soldier crouched so that their eyes were on a a level. 'Either that, or I've a funny feeling He's deserted us.'

Hugo shook from head to foot, his small body racked with wild spasms, his mouth wide open in silent anguish. Then suddenly the boy's voice burst through.

'Fuck, fuck, fuck, fuck. Fucking hell. Bugger, bugger, bugger. Bloody fuck, bloody fuck, bloody fuck.'

# Night, Monday 8 August, 1588
## The North Sea

'Bring me more wine, boy.'

Don Pedro grabbed Hugo by the wrist as the child rushed past him. The officer was laid out on one of the lower decks, his back propped up against the hull of the ship. This area of deck passed as a hospital. All along the side lay wounded and sick men, crowded upon each other. The stench that rose from the bilges was overpowering, and the men had nowhere to relieve themselves but in the holds or, worse, on the decks. Dysentery had broken out on board. Wounds were septic, and in some cases gangrenous. And here, below the waterline, ventilation was poor.

'More wine, d'you hear? You've been confined to this area to make atonement, to serve those in need. And I personally am in need of more wine. So get it.'

Hugo shook his head, and tried to pull his hand away. The whole ship was on half rations. He could not provide extra wine for anyone, however much he tried.

'Don't be coy with me, you little ruffian. We all know you've got a tongue in your head now, and a foul one at that. So unless you're looking for more trouble, for insubordination this time, do as you're told.'

Don Pedro had been in the sick bay for a week; most of the other men had only come down that afternoon. Now the groans and shrieks of wounded men drowned out the dull sound of surf against the hull. The previous Tuesday,

Wednesday and Thursday had seen heavy action in the Channel south of the Isle of Wight. Then, on Saturday evening, the Armada had managed to drop their anchors in the relatively sheltered waters of Calais, hoping to be met by the vast armies of their allies under the Duke of Parma.

But the Duke was not ready. The short Sunday spent in the Straits of Calais had allowed some re-victualling, but events that night had driven the fleet out again into the range of enemy ships.

The sea was calm, the night still. The silence was broken only by the mournful strains of guitars drifting on the cool breeze from ship to ship, by the ghostlike hum of men singing, trying to drag their battered spirits back to normality.

A stir in the distant waters alerted the watch, who called that eight English ships were heading towards them in the black night. Suddenly two of the ships burst into flames, lighting the shining water, their guns firing across the still Channel.

'Fireships!' yelled the watch.

The English had launched unmanned ships, steeped in pitch, riding on the floodtide with the wind behind them, guns loaded, drifting blindly towards the Spanish fleet. Without warning the slow fuse would ignite and the crewless ship would burst into flames, careering relentlessly nearer and nearer to the Spanish. The tragedy of the *San Salvador* had shown what could happen when a mere spark reached the powder room, loaded with saltpetre, deep in the bowels of a wooden hulk. And now the wooden Spanish ships rested there on the sea like sitting ducks, unable to retreat, for the water was too shallow, with flaming uncontrollable infernos heading straight for them, belching fire into the night.

Onwards came the fireships, their sails billowing

flames, brightening the midnight sky and reflecting on the black seas a light redder than blood.

The Spanish command knew that with the tide and wind against them they could sail no nearer the coast without foundering on the shoals of the French shores. Fearing that the fireships were loaded with explosive charges, they desperately gave the signal to cut anchors and sail out into the Channel, to take up battle formation. There was no time to follow the normal procedures: the cables had to be cut, the anchors left behind on the seabed. Although the pilots cried out against the orders, predicting that it would be impossible ever to return to Calais once the fleet had lost their anchors, in panic the highest orders were obeyed.

At dawn, once out of the shelter of French waters, furious fighting started and by midday smoke hung so heavily in the air that the crews could not even see their own mastheads. Casualties were high. Some Spanish ships were seen with blood streaming out of their scuppers. By sunset the Spaniards were driven against the French coast and were again in danger of being driven aground on the sandbanks of Dunkirk. The order was given to take the wind and sail north.

As the wind started to rise, the smoke rolled back to reveal torn canvas, where any sails were left at all, the shattered hulls, the tattered spars and rigging.

'Hugo!' The fat priest snapped at the boy, and Don Pedro relaxed his grip on the child's arm. 'Come with me. I need help with the burials.'

The priest puffed his way up the companionway, the boy nimbly springing up behind him. As they reached the clear air of the open deck the priest turned round and hissed, 'We don't want those lewd ways of yours spreading on this ship. I won't have you holding hands with men in the sick bay.'

The child creased his face up in anguish, as though he would cry out but could not. His hands stretched out, pleading. The priest greeted his supplication by cuffing him around the ear. 'Don't you worry. I'm not fooled by your amateur dramatics. Get over there and help get those corpses ready for blessing.'

Hugo hung his head and crossed the deck to the long row of dead soldiers and sailors. As night fell, the bodies of men killed in action were to be dropped from the upper decks into the foaming swell of the North Sea. Hugo could no longer take part in the hymn-singing, or call the hours. His fit of swearing had seen to that. He was now confined to the orlop deck and the holds, far below sea level. A grown man would have been fined for such blasphemy, but Hugo had no money-belt full of gold ducats and escudos strapped round his waist. Hugo had not been paid when the fleet left Spain; he was a child and therefore worked for free. Now he had to work like a slave, doing all the jobs no one else wanted to do: scraping maggots from the wounds of injured men, swilling excrement from the decks, emptying pails of vomit, atoning for a sin he did not understand.

'Grab hold of this, gromet!'

Hugo ran over and took hold of the corpse. The sailor who had called him tugged his chin up to take a look at his face. It was Enrico, the sailor who had been with the Bos'n that day in La Coruña when Brother Hugo had unwittingly sent the child on this nightmare voyage.

'Agh, so you're the one who got himself into trouble. Lucky the Bos'n felt responsible for you, or you could have been going overboard with this lot, like. They've started hanging people for treason, I've heard, today.'

The first body tumbled down into the dark grey sea. The priest was behind them, holding his crucifix aloft and chanting at each corpse as its turn came to be tossed into the waves.

30

Enrico spoke again.

'You must know some other words though, lad. You mustn't keep all your worries in your head. What's bothering you? Would you talk to me? We all need a friend, you know.'

The boy looked at him from under his dark brows.

'I'll come down to orlop, if you like. We can go down into one of the holds. I go down most evenings after Salve. Sit with the horses, you know. No one will hear us there. You can tell me everything you want, like. Or nothing.'

The priest tapped Enrico on the shoulder. 'No chit-chat, please, sailor. This one's done.' He pointed at a shroud smaller than the rest. Hugo looked down, puzzled.

'That's right,' whispered Enrico. 'One of the gromets. Direct hit. Not much left of him now, like. It's safer down where you are, if nothing else.'

They picked up the small body and dropped it into the water. It fell, casting a mere ripple in the murky sea.

## Early September 1588
## At sea

Enrico had been coming down into the holds after Salve every evening now for almost a month. He would stand with the horses, stroking them, rubbing them down, talking to them. Shortly after he arrived he would catch sight of Hugo, slipping down the companionway, sliding round behind the wooden pillars and curling up in a dark corner. Then Enrico would talk, but only to the horses.

'Must be awful lonely with no one to talk to, stuck down here, never seeing the light of day, old boy. There, there!' He'd glance over to Hugo, then go back to stroking the horse, ruffling its mane. 'Ah, you're too delicate a creature by half to be here at all, aren't you?' He'd give the horse a pat on its behind. 'Pity of it all is you can't talk back. Wouldn't you feel better, old chap, if you could just give me a little neigh, just to let me know how things are going, like? D'you think you could set your mind to that, at all? Gets pretty dull for a chap to come down here night after night, talking to himself. They'd lock me up for it, you know, if we were anywhere else than on board this battered old barque. Ah well, as there seems little hope of a proper conversation, I'll put you in the picture about how things are going up there in the open air.'

Then, every day he would tell the horse about the progress of the Armada up the English coast, how the English fleet was creeping behind them like a dog.

One day he told how they had reached the coast of Scotland, and how, by all reckoning, the English fleet had turned back, leaving them to press on northwards without having to be always looking over their shoulders. He'd whisper thanks that they had been delivered safely from the battles. After all, they were here, and alive. They weren't wounded, they didn't even have dysentery, like those poor fellows up above, who were dying like flies every day. They hadn't been taken by the enemy, or drowned, or shot through. The time was full of hope, he said. After all, only a short time ago in the heat of the fighting, with the French coast looming behind them, and guns blazing before them, they had all looked only for death.

Sometimes he'd talk of the sea and the weather. 'Ah, you know it's the height of summer, old boy, but it could be Christmas. The chill on the air runs through your bones. The days are so dark, and the fogs so thick and ghostly that even the pilots have lost their senses. We're right out of formation now. Haven't seen some of the other ships for days. Don't know whether bad fortune's befallen 'em, or maybe they've just strayed away a bit, what with the fog and no sun to take readings, like. I wonder sometimes if we're not just going round and round in circles,' he chuckled. 'Round and round the North Pole.'

Orders had been given, he told the horse one day, to set sail nor'nor'east and make a course for the strait between the Orkneys and Fair Isle and then out into the Atlantic. 'Then,' he grinned and held the horse softly by its neck, 'then we're to go south. South, past Ireland, then south, south, south, and south again. Towards the heat of the sun and the love of God, and our friends and our families. And then God will bless us again, and we'll run before the wind and we'll be home again, on terra firma, home in our beloved Spain and out of this wretched English mess.'

Hugo stirred in the corner. Enrico surreptitiously glanced at him across the horse's back. He saw the child's lips move, and thought he heard the slightest of whispers.

'English mess.'

## Mid-September 1588
## At sea

There were English soldiers on board Hugo's ship, and more in other ships of the Spanish fleet. Catholics, exiled under the Protestant reign of Queen Elizabeth, they had joined the Armada to restore the old faith to England, to give the country back to King Philip II of Spain, the man who had been its king for four years after his marriage to Mary Tudor, Elizabeth's half-sister.

In between his turns of duty on deck, Enrico sought them out. The soldiers now had nothing to do but wait. Those who had not fallen sick and who had survived the battles spent most of their time sprawled out on the lower decks, singing, secretly playing dice – for gambling was forbidden, and telling stories. As time went by and the supply of food began to run down, fights began to break out. Men would challenge each other over the size of their maggoty biscuit, or the slimy dank green water which was all they had to drink.

'Water all around us,' went the cry. 'Water pouring down on top of us, water seeping in through the hull, so we can wring out the clothes we stand in. Water, water, water, all we see is water, and what do they give us to drink? Sludge!'

As a huge wave sent the ship heaving up, Enrico staggered back and stumbled across the legs of a huddle of soldiers. 'Sorry, sorry!' He bowed his head slightly towards the offended men. You couldn't be too careful at the moment, what with the tension on the lower decks. Having made contact, he pressed on. 'Do you know the English?' The men looked at him as though he was mad, and he realised that they had misinterpreted him. 'Not the enemy English. The men who sail with us. Our Englishmen.'

The soldiers looked at each other, then one spoke. 'They all copped it. The soldiers, anyway.'

'You mean there are others than soldiers?'

One of them sniggered into his lap. Enrico waited. 'Well, he is a soldier, but he fancies himself as a bit of a philosopher, and doctor and the like.'

'Too fancy for the likes of us. Too grand. He ain't content with sitting around with mere troopers. He's usually off do-gooding somewhere.'

Enrico grinned. 'I know the type. What's his name?'

The soldiers on the ground looked up at him and in unison and in fake English tones said, 'Jonathon!' They roared at their witty interpretation. 'Jonathon!'

Enrico found Jonathon trailing round after the ship's surgeon and part-time carpenter. The Englishman would hold the hands of screaming or semi-conscious men, and whisper prayers into their ears while the surgeon got out his saw and hacked their gangrenous arms and legs off.

Jonathon wiped his bloodstained hands down his jerkin as Enrico told him about Hugo, and that evening, after Salve, Jonathon went with Enrico down to the hold and talked to the horses. It wasn't long before Hugo joined them and sat in the deepening shadows under the companionway.

Enrico chatted with Jonathon, then faded out and let Jonathon speak English to his horse while he kept a veiled eye on the boy. Hugo cocked his head, then leaned forward, his hands resting on the deck, his haunches ready to spring back into the dark corner.

'Beautiful beasts! How did you get yourselves into a pickle like this, eh? Oh, mankind, what games you play with life.'

Jonathon crouched down, rooted in his pockets and pulled out a lump of biscuit. Hugo was coming out from the shadows, edging nearer and nearer to the Englishman.

'Like to share my supper with me, old boy?' He held the biscuit up to the horse's mouth. 'Not so appetising, I know. You'd be happier with a meadow full of lush green grass, wouldn't you, boy, under a pale blue canopy of sky?'

Hugo was now only an arm's length from the Englishman.

'But, like us, you can hope. For is it not spoken truly; if hope were not, heart would break. One day you and I will be free. In the goodness of our souls indeed we are already free, all of us here in this hold. For all good souls are free. Only the wicked are slaves.'

The child rested his tiny hand on the Englishman's sleeve. Jonathon turned his head, oh so slightly, and looked him in the eye. 'The horses are beautiful creatures, are they not?' The boy nodded. 'So big, so strong, so gentle.'

Hugo bit his lip and in a hesitating, small, cracked voice said 'English? English?'

Jonathon nodded. 'That's right. I'm English.'

The boy stretched his hands up to the man's bearded chin, and stroked it. He whispered in a high voice, speaking in Spanish, 'Are you an English bastard?'

Behind a horse, Enrico guffawed. Jonathon hesitated before answering. 'I am an Englishman.'

The child lunged forward. 'Are you my father?'

A huge crash on the companionway cut their conversation off. The boy scrambled back into the darkness. A team of soldiers invaded the hold, armed with sticks and ropes.

Enrico greeted them. 'What's going on lads?'

'The horses,' cried one. 'They've got to go.'

Enrico laughed. 'Where to, my friend? A nice swim, perhaps?'

'That's just about the size of it, yes.'

The men had already started leading the horses up the narrow gangway. Enrico grabbed the soldier's arm. 'What are you on about?' he demanded.

'Orders! Just obeying orders, that's all.'

Enrico bellowed at him. 'What kind of orders are those? You can't just throw a whole shipload of horses overboard in these dismal seas, miles from land.'

'They're drinking too much water, eating too much food. Get rid of them and perhaps we might all have a chance.'

'But — ' Enrico gasped.

'Orders are orders.'

As they spoke, the last horse was being bundled up towards the top deck. And in the thick dank fog around the ship, you could hardly hear the splash as the horses of Spain were bundled overboard, alive, whinnying and neighing, their eyes bulging in horror, left to drown in a foreign sea while the ships which had been their prison for three months took a bearing south.

On the open deck Jonathon found Hugo draped over the rail of the quarterdeck, tears rolling down his cheeks. He put his hand on the tiny shaking shoulders. 'That's right, my boy. Cry. Cry out as loud as you can.'

The boy turned and clung to the Englishman's legs. In the still sea below them the horses were splashing desperately trying to keep their heads above the swell. Some had already given up the struggle and their corpses floated on the calm waters.

'Come on!' Jonathon took the child by the hand. 'Let's not hang around here witnessing the ignoble death of these worthy beasts.'

Dawn was breaking as he led the boy down through the scuttle to the lower decks, past the soldiers sleeping and chatting, past the injured, the sick and the dying, down into the now empty hold.

He piled up some saddles and sat on this luxurious

throne, the boy on his lap, and he asked the boy questions. The boy replied, in a weak and hesitant voice, occasionally breaking off to cry as he told his story. How his mother had brought him up alone in Santiago. How she had told him his father, whom he had never seen, was an 'English bastard'. He spoke of his mother's kindness, warmth, generosity, beauty and poverty. And of how a year ago she had caught the smallpox, and how he had nursed her and fed her when no one else would come near. His frail body shook with grief as he told of her death. They had been alone in a tiny room, and he had sat there with her body for three days, putting blankets on her corpse because she was cold, shaking her, trying to wake her up when the landlord, holding a handkerchief to his nose, stormed in with a gang of men. He had taken her away, throwing the boy out into the street and locking the door behind him. He told how he had slept under the cold December stars until a big fat lady had offered to take him in. And then he told the quiet Englishman what had happened to him in the Santiago brothel where the Jesuit Brother Hugo had found him.

Beyond the barrels the boards creaked and the child sat up, alert. Jonathon peered into the black. The whole ship gently shuddered, and pitched up.

'The weather must be changing. It feels as though the wind's picking up again.'

Hugo slumped back against the Englishman's chest, and continued his tale. He blurted out in detail the revolting and degrading things he had done, finishing with the huge fat man with blubbery lips, who had suffered a heart attack as he thrust his small penis into the child's mouth. When he paused and looked up, Jonathon's eyes were full of tears. The child stretched out a hand and wiped his lashes, and Jonathon, leaning forward, kissed the little boy softly on the forehead. In return the boy gently wrapped his arms around his confessor's neck.

38

A voice barked out from behind the companionway. 'So this is where the action is!' Don Pedro stepped forward from the shadows, the gold braid of his black doublet twinkling in the dim light, a makeshift crutch under his left arm. Hugo sprang from Jonathon's lap and scampered away.

'I think they call it the English disease, don't they? Having relations with children of the same sex? I must say I always suspected all that poetry you're spouting must be covering the heart of a pansy.'

Jonathon's eyes blazed as he rose to his feet and crossed the hold towards Don Pedro. 'You are a very evil man,' he hissed. 'Well,' sneered the Spaniard, 'takes one to know one. Does one pay for this service, or do I just wait in line?' He glanced around. 'Where is our little Cupid? I hope you're not thinking of keeping him to yourself. Especially when I've already heard all the juicy details of the services he performs. Quite a wonderful advertising method, I must say. Certainly whets the appetite.'

Jonathon raised his arm and crashed it down on Don Pedro's neck, but the aristocrat's crutch helped him maintain his balance. The ship lurched and shuddered as the two men grappled, staggering along the row of empty water barrels, locked in each other's arms. Don Pedro managed to trip Jonathon, and knelt astride him, using one leather-gloved hand to pin him down by the throat. With his other hand he laid his crutch on the boards of the deck and pulled his jewelled poniard from its scabbard. Jonathon yelled for assistance, grabbing the Spaniard's wrist, his arm shaking with the effort of holding the man's hand away from him. The heavy roll of the ship grew thunderous, the hull pounding into the waves, its timbers shuddering and creaking as it smashed relentlessly up and down.

'What's going on?' Enrico called from the companionway. Jonathon shouted from the dark, 'He wants to interfere with the boy, Hugo, the gromet.'

'I think you've got that the wrong way round, English pervert!' Don Pedro lunged for Jonathon, lost his balance and rolled to the deck. Enrico edged forward, trying to keep upright as the ship rose and fell, his eyes not yet adjusted to the gloom. Jonathon had Don Pedro's arm pinned to the deck, the blade of the dagger pointing heavenwards. Glimmers of light in the hold danced upon its jewelled tracery. Enrico lunged down to snatch it. Suddenly the ship heeled to one side and all three men were thrown towards the hull. When they hit the wooden planks of the side Jonathon pulled his hand up from where it was crushed under the Spaniard's chest. It was dripping with blood. He rolled the Spaniard face up. The hilt of the dagger glistened in the dark. Its blade was deeply embedded in Enrico's chest.

On the gangway to the powder-store, Hugo, the little powder monkey and ship's boy stood shivering with fear. Silently he felt his way up a ladder to the orlop deck.

On open deck the sailors were struggling with a storm the like of which none of them had seen before. The wind sang as it whipped through the ratlines and the masts seemed to bend before it. The sails had all been taken in, but the strength of the wind broke them from their straps on the yardarms and now they flapped uncontrollably, ripping and tearing off, flying away into the purple sky. One sailor, trying to make good, had been blown from the rigging. Another had been washed overboard as the ship pitched and the bow was submerged before rearing up to lurch right out of the water. A large cannon that had broken from the ropes which secured it rolled for a while back and forth across the deck before smashing through the rail and plummeting into the sea. The mariners clung to anything solid to keep themselves from following it overboard.

Under the shadow of the forecastle the captain gave orders to the Bos'n to organise teams of soldiers to assist the crew to manage the ship in these lethal conditions. The ship was now pooping, a dangerous sailing condition, running before a hurricane force wind in a heavy following sea which was breaking heavily over her stern. Water flooded over the decks and poured down the scuttles and companionways. A muffled cry reached them from above. 'Land ahoy! Land ahoy!'

A group of sailors was immediately dispatched to drop the one anchor that remained since the two principal anchors had been cut in the retreat from the fireship attack at Calais. The Bos'n made his way below to gather a gang of volunteers from the lower decks to man the pumps. He sent some up top to relieve the sailors at the pump handles on deck while he led another group down to the hold to start bailing out. There he found Jonathon, his face smeared with blood, Don Pedro's dagger in his hand. His friend Enrico's corpse lay at the Englishman's feet.

'I did my best to avert this,' cried Don Pedro in the darkness. 'But it was never a good idea to have Englishmen aboard when we're at war with them. He's obviously a spy.'

With no ceremony or trial Jonathon was tied up and thrown into the bilboes in the ship's dungeon, a secure box amid the bilges in the very bowels of the ship. The heavy door was locked and barred behind him. He would be hanged in the morning, he was told: there was no reprieve for murder.

But Jonathon was the least of everyone's problems while the ship was being battered by hurricane force winds. For hours the crew fought the wind, the tide and gravity itself as the craggy coast of western Ireland loomed before their galleon, pitching, rolling and heaving out of control in the mountainous sea. The Bos'n led a group of sailors tugging at the midships wheel, trying, in a last desperate attempt, to turn the ship from its fatal course.

Others along every deck futilely slopped water into buckets and passed them along the chain.

All through the lower decks men were praying as they had never prayed before. The singing voices of the ship's boys, drenched in salt water and the sweat of terror, rose like larks in the air. The fat priest stood before them, clinging to the companionway rail, water pouring down on to his bald head, as his strangled voice yelled out the hymn to Mary, the Star of the Sea.

Below, Enrico's body floated on two feet of water. Still it tossed back and forth, slamming into the empty water casks lining the walls of what was once the stable, home to a score of horses, then pitching back to crash into the bare ship's side. Above him, on the stairs, a few rays of murky light glimmering around his head like a halo, crouched Hugo, his ankles submerged, his voice finally rising to join the chorus of prayer.

> *'Solve vincula reis,*
> *profer lumen caecis,*
> *Mala nostra pelle,*
> *Bona cuncta posce . . .'*

With a deafening crunch the ship lurched on to the rocks of Ireland, smashing and splintering into a thousand pieces. Like a tidal wave the water poured in, flooding the decks, sweeping men on its back and pulling them under. Soldiers, sailors and children grabbed hold of anything. Some were smashed to death against the craggy boulders, others sucked deep under the waves and tossed about like rag-dolls until they were washed up, limp and battered, on the shore. The injured and sick had no hope. Some drowned as they took time to snatch money-bags from the belts of the dead; the sheer weight of gold pulled them down under the tide.

## September 1588
## North-West Ireland

By evening a large group of survivors gathered on the short strand. Miraculously, almost half of the ship's complement had made it safely ashore, and now they sprawled on the sands, gasping with relief, tearing their tattered clothes to make bandages for wounded limbs. Hugo stood and breathed in the damp air. Some men near him had lit a fire and others were gathering sticks. In the distance he saw the Bos'n and another sailor dancing a jig of happiness to be alive. There were other soldiers and sailors he recognised too, and three of the gromets, tripping through the tide picking out splinters of the ship, broken spars and fragments of planking, for the fire.

The Bos'n called a brief meeting and a small group was sent off to find water and food. Darkness was falling, and the golden glow of the fire gathered a crush of men around it, the red light picking out the lines on their battered faces. Hugo's eyes darted round the circle. He could not see his English friend. Slowly he noticed that there were many others he did not see there. The priest, for one. Someone pulled out a whistle and played a soothing tune. Deep hoarse voices hummed along. Hugo squatted down as near to the fire as he could get, and gazed into the flames. As his eyes focused he saw, on the other side of the circle, Don Pedro, who was staring back at him.

'I won't sit in a circle with that blasphemer.' He raised

his arm and pointed at Hugo. 'The child. Over there. The impertinent one.'

The Bos'n led Hugo a small distance away and sat down beside him. 'Creep back nearer when he's had time to forget about you. There's enough men here to get lost in the crowd. But don't let him catch sight of you, all right, lad?'

Hugo nodded meekly. He had no desire to get any nearer to Don Pedro, ever. The man had taken his only two friends away from him. The Bos'n rose and strode back to the fire.

'What d'you think, Bos'n,' piped up a sailor. 'Maybe tonight we'll get a supper tastier than biscuits and maggots.'

'Whose side are they on anyway, these Irish?' growled an old sea dog.

'They're Catholic, like us,' snapped a nobleman, whose doublet had survived in beautiful condition, gold buttons flashing in the firelight. 'They've been fighting the English for years.'

'And what's their diet like, do you think?' asked a young soldier jovially. 'Do you think we'll get a paella?'

'And a flagon of best Jerez wine to wash it down,' laughed another.

The others began to join in the play.

'Maybe we'll be treated to roast suckling pig, basted in rosemary, with sweet red pimentos gently sautéed in olive oil . . .'

'Where are our food scouts?' pleaded a sailor. 'Why don't they hurry up. We'll all die of starvation at this rate!'

'Onion soup, with melted cheese,' murmured an aristocrat, rubbing his gold-trimmed doublet with gashed hands.

'Marzipan!' yelled one of the gromets.

'And nougat,' drooled another.

44

The flickering faces of the survivors of one of the largest ships of the Spanish Armada were lit up with happiness when, from the rushes of the shoreline the shadowy figures of local villagers loomed up behind them. The Bos'n looked up, smiling at the hesitant group of long-haired, bearded men dressed in long dull cloaks.

'At last,' he whispered, rising politely to greet them, 'the welcoming committee.'

The Irishmen looked down at the men round the fire, and cast their eyes along the beach where scores of the wounded lay in huddles, sleeping.

'Spanish,' explained the Bos'n slowly. 'Catholics. We are your friends.' He held out his hand.

Some of the Spaniards around him were gently climbing to their feet. An Irishman ran his fingers down the twinkling doublet of a soldier. He grabbed hold of a golden button and jerked it off, holding it up to the firelight, watching it sparkle. He shouted something incomprehensible to his friends, who gathered round to look. A Spanish sailor reached down and pulled the money-bag from his belt, plunged his hand in and pulled out a golden coin. 'For you,' he nodded, holding it out. 'For food.' He put his hand to his mouth and made chewing motions.

The bag was snatched from him as other Irishmen grabbed at the Spaniards' golden buttons and ripped them off in handfuls.

'Hoy!' Behind them the food-searchers were returning. In panic one of the Irish raised his great club over his head and smashed it down on the Spaniard whose doublet he had already torn bare of buttons.

The others followed their leader, battering their rough oak truncheons over the heads of the exhausted Spaniards, bludgeoning their brains out. Sprays of blood sizzled as they hit the flames of the driftwood fire. The Spaniards, wounded and weary, tried to escape, darting hither and thither in the moonlight, but were felled by the crowds of Irishmen who streamed over the hill and down on to the beach.

Hugo stood alone, unable to take in the truth of what was happening. Don Pedro, limping away as fast as he could, collided with the boy. As one of the Irish ran towards him he hauled the child up, using him as a shield. At that moment he was felled by a blow to the back of his head, and collapsed on the sand, bringing the boy down beneath him.

The wild Irish waved their clubs triumphantly over their shaggy heads as they ran amok. Down tumbled the Spanish warriors, tripping over the bodies of their friends to be beaten where they lay. Others, smashed from behind, fell on top of them until the sand was crimson and the pile of corpses was knee high. The Irishmen busily rifled the bodies of their victims, ripping clothes from their backs, grabbing their jewelled swords and daggers, tearing earrings from their earlobes and rings from their fingers, taking handfuls of golden coins from their money-belts and stuffing them into ragged pockets.

When they finally trudged off, dragging behind them cloaks full of stolen booty, the tiny stretch of beach was piled deep with Spanish dead, and the embers of the fire were growing pale in the light of the rising sun.

Hugo lay still under a mound of corpses, warmed through the night by the blood dripping from Don Pedro's skull. He stayed there for many hours, until the bodies above and below him had grown cold and stiff, and the daylight, which had crept through chinks between gory limbs and matted hair, had begun to fade. Only then did he edge forward until he could see around him.

Nothing moved but the bare gorse bushes which trembled in the wind. Everything was still. Everybody was dead. Don Pedro's face glared out at him from the reddened sand. Hugo shut his eyes and turned away. He was crawling along in the dark. Behind him he could just make out the black shadow of the shell of the galleon which had brought him to this bewildering country. It lay sideways, crushed against a great rocky cliff and swaying slowly in the swirling tide. The remains of its masts fingered the waves. There was more booty on board, and people would be back to find it. He had heard some of them today, screeching at each other from the rocky promontory.

On all fours he inched away from the carnage like a wild animal. He crawled further and further from the cruel sea which had brought him, the sea which had dumped him in this strange and barbaric land.

He crept under bushes and dashed across open spaces, for fear of being found by those savages. Under each bush he would crouch and listen, straining his ears for any sound, before breaking cover and running to the next shelter.

Suddenly the silence was broken by a distant rhythmic beating sound. He froze and hugged close against the bark of a tree. His eyes watered from the strength of his gaze, penetrating the dark. Eventually he made out a marching phalanx of men, muskets resting on their shoulders as they trudged towards the sea. Hugo was directly in their path. In a panic as the men got closer and closer, he darted out from his shelter, heading for a bush in a nearby hollow.

'Halt!' barked the leader of the marching men. 'Who goes there?'

The men stopped and looked about them, muskets poised for action. Hugo flung himself to the ground and lay in the grass, panting as though his lungs would burst, burying his face deep into the muddy soil, trying to disappear.

'Came from over there, sarge,' cried one of the men, pointing to the spot where Hugo sprawled.

'Careful now. May be a booby trap,' said the sergeant as the group edged forward.

A loud hollering broke the quiet of the night. It came from a small wooded area a few hundred yards ahead of Hugo. The soldiers spun round and threw themselves to the ground. Their muskets spat fire which lit the heath like lightning. The bellowing from the black woods stopped instantly. Hugo used the furore of gunfire to edge down into the hollow and covered himself with gorse.

The soldiers lay still for a minute or two, then their sergeant laughed. 'That'll give them something to think about for tonight. On we go. We'd better get to that wreck before the whole thing is gutted by those philistines.'

Hugo drifted off to sleep under the shelter of the prickly bush, but was woken by a rustling sound a couple of feet away. He froze, holding his breath, his eyes piercing the dark.

'Hugo?'

He lay still.

'Hugo? Don't be frightened. It's me. Jonathon. You remember? English.'

Tears of joy filled the eyes of the young Spanish boy as he stretched out his arms and replied. 'Oh, you English bastard!'

The man slid down into the hollow and under the gorse, then wrapping his strong arms around the boy he gently rocked him to sleep.

# CATHERINE

# 1906, County Down
## The North of Ireland

'Get out of this kitchen with those muddy boots, and the floor just freshly washed!' Cassie, the ruddy-faced cook, picked up a hazel broomstick and shooed little Catherine out into the yard with it. 'Go on with you, you little divil.'

The child, spattered in mud, ran a few steps before turning defiantly, hands on waist and shouting, 'I'll tell my daddy on you, and then you'll be sent off to live with the tinkers.'

'You go tell whosoever you wish, and I'm sure if you told your father you were wasting my time with your muddy boots he'd put the slipper to you.'

Catherine hitched up her skirts, in a final triumphant gesture. 'I hope the fairies come and take you in the night.' With that she curtsied as she poked her tongue towards the kitchen door, then turned on her heel and ran as fast as the wind in the direction of the stable block.

'I cannot be spoken to in this way by a mere mortal cook! I am a magical horse,' she muttered to the air. 'I have great mystical powers above ordinary men and women. The fairies know me by name!'

'Oh Catherine!' a nearby voice shrilled. 'It's Fairy Thistledown here. Let's pop down to the rath and have a little hootenanny.'

Catherine spun round and caught sight of her brother,

Brian, emerging from behind a barn, clutching his sides with laughter.

'You!' Catherine spat. 'You do not even merit a reply!'

'Really? What fine words from such a little girl. Isn't it about time you were growing up, and not bothering Cassie with your nonsense.'

'I can do as I please, as a matter of fact, and I please now to visit my colleagues in the stable.'

'Not that old wreck, Cuchullin? Rather you than me, with all his boring talk of the warriors and leprechauns and the fairies bestowing the gift of song upon the tone deaf.' Brian burst into a howl of tone-deaf singing. Catherine shouted to stop him: 'Indeed, I was not referring to my friend, Cuchullin, whose tales I find enchanting, but to my colleagues Napper Tandy and Wolfey.'

'You're too small by a good four feet, and they too tall by about ten hands to be your equals. You'd be better mounted on Puck, or even Molly. She's even your face.'

Catherine's eyes darkened. 'I'm friends 'tis true with both the donkey and the pig, but as for her features they're more alike with your own. Your eyelashes have both the same shade of yellow!'

Brian sighed the deep sigh of a very old man. 'I'm bored with you now. I'm too old to be mixing with six-year-olds. Even Mammy says so. I've book-learning to do.'

As he stalked off towards the main house Catherine stood for a moment and watched him go. It was a pity he was such a stuck-up prig, because, for all his yellow eyelashes, she wished he liked her and would play with her, for then she might be allowed to go riding up to the blue mountains, like he did. A droplet of rain touched her cheek. For a moment she stared up at the grey clouds; then she shut her eyes, letting the cold raindrops bathe her eyelids.

'Is it lost in a dream you are, my friend?' The throaty voice of Cuchullin, the old groom, gardener, stableman, odd-job man and nanny, dragged her from her reverie. 'Come on in here with you and join me in a cup of something hot and cheery.'

'Oh, Cuchullin, I'm wishing to have a small chat with my noble friends, Napper and Wolfey. Would they be willing to take tea with me this gloomy afternoon?'

Inside the stable Cuchullin had his own table and two chairs. In the corner a little stove served to keep the horses from freezing in the winter and to warm a small black kettle. The old man poured two cups of tea, and broke his scone into two. ' 'Tis a rare feast for two as close as we are,' he told her.

'Four! We are four.' She grabbed Cuchullin's scone, tore a piece from her own and went over to the racehorses. 'One day you'll take me off across the mountains to see the sea, won't you?' She held Napper Tandy by the face and kissed his nose. 'My honourable friend and liege lord.'

The horses nibbled the bits of scone from her tiny, fearless hand. 'One day you and I will gallop away from here, and never turn back.'

'Ach, you're not still going on about all that business, are you? Where in God's earth would you find a place as beautiful as ould Ireland?'

Catherine shrugged.

'I thought you loved the hills and the sea . . .'

'I have not been to the sea, I've only heard a deal of talk of it. And I think the sea and I would be tolerable friends.'

Cuchullin chuckled to himself. 'Ah, sure to God, listen to the tongue on you. You've the gift of the blarney all right. No doubt you'll be a poet, or write intolerable long and florid romantic novels that no one but the ignorant will read.'

Cuchullin was a tall, erect man, with white flowing hair, like snow, that fell profusely about his broad shoulders. He stood close to the huge horses, gently stroking their manes, while Catherine fed them. The scones finished, she rooted deep into her smock pockets, and eventually pulled out a large carrot. She grinned up at Cuchullin, a wicked glint in her eye.

'I stole it from the kitchen table while Cassie was grabbing the broom for to sweep me out of the kitchen! Would you like a bite?'

Cuchullin, who had lost both his front teeth in a brawl fifty years before, at the age of thirty, closed his lips tight before speaking.

'God be good to the soul of him that first invented the potato and the scone, because a man can masticate them without a tooth in his head, but as for a carrot, well, 'tis only fit for those with incisors like promontories.'

Catherine held the carrot steady while Napper Tandy nibbled. 'Cuchullin?'

The old man looked down at her.

'Is it true that leprechauns live up on the mountainside?'

'So I've always been told. Wee men with a great power of song, and they sing the most bewitching melodies in their little hovels, and caves and – for those who are small enough – rabbit burrows, and if you happen to be passing, or, even better, if you fall asleep lying on their little homes, you will awake with your head full of their heavenly melodies. Sure, that's how the "Londonderry Air" was first passed to mortal man. Some unknowing fellow fell asleep upon a fairy rath, and when his eyes were tight closed, out came a fairy orchestra and played him the tune, with a little leprechaun singing out the melody, and when he awoke he jotted the thing down, and there we are.'

Catherine was wide-eyed.

'Is that right?'

'As far as I know, that's the facts.'

'And these leprechauns live up the mountain?'

'That's right.'

'And how do you get up the mountain?'

Cuchullin rubbed his chin. 'Well now, for that you'd need a horse, I should think.'

'Could I ride Nap? If you come with me would you let me ride him?'

Cuchullin laid his hands on her tiny shoulders. 'Not yet a while, little one. You don't have the strength in your legs to control such an animal.'

Catherine wriggled out of his grasp and faced him, her eyes black. 'Then I'll walk,' she said.

Cuchullin shook his head and laughed. 'Now, even with your determination I think that would be out of the question.' He turned and took a pair of brushes from their hook on the wooden wall. 'Come on, now. Help me brush the ould fellows down.'

Catherine strutted to the stable door. 'No thanks,' she replied tartly as she reached up for the big bolt. 'My father pays *you* to do that. I have other things that need dealing with.'

She sidled out into the yard, leaving Cuchullin shaking his head and smiling.

The dining-room table was laid for dinner, and the whole household gathered around waiting for Richard Tate, Catherine's father, to say grace.

But Catherine was missing.

Through the Georgian sash windows, the greyish sun spilled its setting beams over the stable roofs, and touched the fragile glass.

'I saw her last playing nonsense games with Cuchullin in the stables,' piped up Brian, hoping for some reward for being four years older and wiser than his sister.

'Cuchullin?' Catherine's father looked at the old retainer, who merely shook his head.

'She left me about two hours ago. I had some work to

55

be doing, and she crept off to play somewhere else. You know how she is.'

Richard clenched his jaw and nodded.

The mantel clock ticked sonorously. Cassie smoothed her hands down her apron and looked at her feet. Catherine's mother, Brigid, looked over at her husband. Old Cuchullin looked through the window – the sky was almost dark. Brian looked longingly at the serving dishes piled high with home-grown food, the hunks of barmbrack, the greens, the potatoes topped with a melting piece of butter churned by Brigid that morning, the roast chicken sitting proudly at the end of the table, waiting for Richard's carving knife, and the jug full of steaming gravy.

'Has anyone any idea where she can have got to? She can't have taken a lift with Paddy's cart, can she?'

Cassie looked up to reply. 'No, sir. Paddy's cart comes on Tuesday and Friday.'

'She's probably only playing one of her games some-where on the farm, but I couldn't eat a mouthful until I know the child is safe. Will you come with me, Cuchullin, and we'll take a walk around the farm.'

Cuchullin had already taken the hat from his pocket and was screwing it on to his head.

'It's worse than that things could be . . . It's talking to me she was about going up the mountainside. She wanted to take the horse.'

'Do you think she's wandered up there?'

'It seems scarcely possible, but it's a strong little spirit she has.'

Richard pushed his chair in to the table. 'Let's go!'

'Can I come too?' Cassie asked, taking off her apron.

'No, Cassie, you stay here with Brigid to help in case the child comes in cold.'

'What about me?'

Richard smiled down at his son. 'You'd better sit down

56

at the table and force down a little of the food you've been drooling over for the last quarter of an hour.'

As Richard and Cuchullin closed the front door behind them, Brian opened his mouth, stuffing it full of buttered potatoes. Brigid sank on to a dining chair and sobbed into Cassie's skirts, 'God bring her back home safely.' Cassie stroked her mistress's hair, and muttered to herself, 'Ay, God bless and protect the little divil!'

Although the grey clouds hanging over the mountainside grew darker, Catherine spared no thought for how far she was wandering. It was only the soft rumblings of her stomach that made her remember home, and how far she'd walked, though her memory did not stretch to which direction she had come from. Never mind, she thought. I know that the sea is the other side of the hill, so if I keep walking up I'm sure to get there soon.

As the last of the light faded, a mist began to fall on the hills, and soon Catherine could not see more than a few feet in front of her. The granite boulders banged her ankles and knees as she walked, and her hands grabbed at gorse bushes when she was thrown off balance. She ached all over. Perhaps she should turn back. She was cold, damp and hungry. She knew now that she should have waited until someone would take her to see the sea. She should have asked Paddy to take her on the back of his cart, when he had deliveries to make to the folk on the other side of the hill. She longed for the warmth of the farmhouse, the smell of Cassie's stew, Cuchullin's rattly laugh, the smell of her mother's perfume, the strong arms of her father throwing her up in the air and catching her as she fell.

She stopped in her tracks: she would turn and head for home. She turned and walked in the opposite direction, the one she'd come from. Strange, she thought, it felt as

57

though she was walking uphill when she came, and still it felt as though she was walking uphill. She stumbled again, and badly gashed her hand on a sharp piece of slate. But though the tears pricked her eyes and her chin began to wobble, she would not let herself cry. There were worse things than this in life. She'd heard Cassie talking to the women down in the town; she'd heard her father telling her brother about being brave. But she knew she could be braver than he was. She dragged herself to her feet and marched on, head held high.

Suddenly a new thought burst into her head. What if the fairies found her and took her? Wishaw! She'd been a friend to the fairies long enough. She'd always left out bits of bread and milk for them by the farm's gateposts. She'd even smuggled bits of meat from the dining room in her skirt pockets and left them on the step before she went to bed. And they'd been gone in the morning too, so the fairies must have taken them, and they should be grateful to her. Maybe they'd teach her a new tune that would be famous, like the 'Londonderry Air'.

In the distance a dog set up a howling noise. It was a dog, wasn't it? Not a banshee?

She tripped, and her shoe came off. She got to her knees and groped around on the wet heather. She couldn't find the shoe, so up she got and limped on. Her stocking quickly tore and her bare foot was scuffed by the rough ground.

She could see nothing; the dark, the mist and tears blinded her. She began to sing, in a high, reedy voice. If she sang she would not feel so alone.

'The pale moon was rising above the green mountains,
The sun was declining beneath the blue sea . . .'

She stopped singing, and stood stock still. Through the fog, another voice sang on, a male voice, clear and strong.

*'When I strayed with my love to the pure crystal fountain,*
*'That stands in the beautiful Vale of Tralee.'*

She could see no one. But she heard a voice that seemed to giggle at her.

'Well, my little angel, what're you doing on the slopes of Luke's Mountain on such a wretched night?'

Catherine kept her mouth shut, but her eyes peered sharply through the fog. Still she could see so sign of the voice's owner.

'You've cut your hand too. And where's your wee shoe? Ah, dear me, what a sad, dotey, lost little thing you are. Come along now, let's get you warm.'

A strong pair of arms lifted her. She struggled.

'Don't be frightened, I'm only small meself, and these mountains are awful big for the likes of us. Hold tight round me neck, and we'll be home in no time.'

Still she struggled. 'I don't know you. I'm not allowed to go off with people I don't know,'

'Well I don't know *you* either, but I'm pretty sure you're not allowed to go off on your own up the mountains on a foggy night in November.'

Catherine gave his arm a good bite.

'Ah, for goodness sakes, leave off. I'll tell you what. You calm down a wee bit, and when we get home I'll show you me crock o' gold.'

Catherine stopped flapping and fighting in his arms. 'You're not . . .?'

'Now,' chuckled Hughie, 'that surely would be tellin'.'

A turf fire blazed in the open hearth. An old black pot bubbling with stew dangled over it.

Catherine sat on a cushion, gaping up at the little man. 'How old are you?'

'Well now, I've not an idea. No one ever told me, so I could be eighteen and I could be seven hundred and eighteen. What do you think? And anyway, for all that, how old are you, yourself?'

Catherine spoke as she gulped her stew. 'I'm six.'

She took another mouthful then asked, 'Why have you got see-through ears with lumps on them?'

Hughie's laugh cracked through the little room.

'And why have you got such a cheeky tongue on you? What's wrong with me ears? At least they're not like yours. I have individual ears, and that's the way I like 'em.'

Catherine smiled, and stuffed a lump of potato into her mouth. 'I like your house, but it's much smaller than Daddy's.'

'And if I'm not mistaken I'd be a lot smaller than Daddy too! What would a little feller like meself be wanting with a great mansion?'

'Oh no, it's not a mansion. It's a farm, just outside Kilcoo. Lots of us live there, animals too. Do you have any animals?'

'Lots and lots. I've got some chickens, and a moke, and a cow.'

'We have racehorses. Where do you keep your crock of gold? Is it buried on the mountainside?'

Hughie rose and went through a small brightly painted door to his other room. He turned and shot her a strict look from beneath his eyebrows. 'You stay there, now,' he ordered.

He pulled the door to after him, crawled under his bed, and fumbled about a bit. As his backside wiggled out again, Catherine, who had crept up to peer through the door, giggled. Hughie leapt up.

'Lookit, I thought I was after telling you not to come in here.'

'It's nice. Better than my bedroom. What a big bed!'

She gazed with awe at the bed, as well she might, for it almost filled the room. It was a red four-poster with gorgeous painting on the posts and the headboard. Gold curtains hung down, touching the pillows, and a black silk shawl embroidered with wreaths of flowers was slung across as a cover.

'Never mind about this, you were wanting to see me gold.'

Catherine's eyes were already open as wide as they could go. She bent down, her hands squeezing her cheeks, as he slowly lifted the lid of an old Spanish chest. Inside she could see old, crackly, dusty papers and a small leather pouch. Hughie pulled this out by its drawstring.

'Go on, little one, open your hands.'

The large gold coins glistened in the candlelight, which spilled in from the living room.

'So you really are a leprechaun! I knew you were when I heard you singing.'

Hughie beamed. 'I'm whatever you'd like me to be.'

'Do you know any good songs you could teach me so I can be famous?'

'What is it you're doing now? Is that silent singing, or are you just yawning? I can almost see down into your tummy. You've a fine pair of tonsils on you anyway.'

Catherine put her hand up to cover her mouth, and the coins fell to the floor. Hughie started to gather them up and put them back into the drawstring purse. 'What's your name, titch?'

Her eyelids drooped as she tried to speak through another yawn. 'Catherine Tate.'

He picked her up from the floor and placed her gently on the bed. 'Well, goodnight, Catherine Tate. It was nice to meet you.'


Cuchullin gathered a group of men from the village, while Richard rode up the hill on Napper Tandy. It was one of Cuchullin's men who found the sleeping girl, curled up in a red blanket by the farm gateposts. When he shook her and woke her, she looked mournfully up to his relieved eyes.

'Oh, no!' she said. ' 'Twas never only a dream.'

Catherine pulled hard on the reins as she leapt over a groyne on the beach. The old horse's hooves spattered the rising tide and they galloped on against the rising wind. She bridled him in, and they turned inland at a trot. 'Once more up the hill, Nap, old boy.'

Since the night seven years before when she had been lost on the mountain, she had mastered the riding of a horse, even one the size of Napper Tandy, now retired from racing. She could ride up the mountain and sit at the peak to watch the sea, and see quite clearly the Isle of Man and beyond to the Cumbrian Hills.

She would sometimes trek all day round the lower slopes searching for Hughie's tiny cottage. The trouble was that there were so many that could be his. She would sit outside, at a polite distance and watch for anyone to come in or out. She saw many people go through many doors, but no short men with transparent ears. Her family had laughed at her tale, but there was the problem of the red blanket; allowing that she had wandered off and strayed back and fallen asleep by the gateposts, how had she come by the blanket? Brian was now eighteen and off at university, so she only had to put up with him in the holidays, but he didn't trouble to spend as much time insulting her as he once had. Which was just as well, for now that she helped her mother in the dairy, and Cassie in the kitchen, baking the daily barmbrack, preparing vegetables and mixing up the scraps for the hen food, which was left to bubble away on the range when the household food was not, she could always have spiked his meals.

Napper Tandy stepped lightly over the loose shale as they headed down now to the seaside town of Newcastle. The streets were quite animated for an ordinary Thursday morning. Men stood around in small groups, shaking their heads and scratching them. Some leaned against the walls of the public house nursing glasses of porter, and laughing. A boy not much older than Catherine gave Nap a firm stroke as he passed. 'What a beauty!' he cried after them. 'Will it be racing over at Downpatrick you'll be going?'

Catherine wheeled the horse round to face him. 'He's a bit old for that, I'm afraid, and I a bit young. But I'd like to go and watch. How do you get there?'

'I'm going meself, as are most of the folk loitering here this fine morning. Hang on and I'll get me brother's old nag and we can ride there together.'

The smell of mown grass and turf turned up by the horses' hooves mingled with the scent of tobacco smoke. Catherine had never before seen so many people gathered together. Huge white tents flapped in the breeze. Inside them were bookies, bars, and food stalls. Outside there were stalls selling eggs, hats, sticks, chocolate and baked potatoes. Against the wooden rails at the edge of the enclosure, men and women huddled together selling goats, donkeys and horses.

'Will you be having a little flutter?' The boy's teeth seemed to sparkle in the sun as he spoke.

'I don't know what that is.' Catherine bit her lip. She didn't like to look a fool.

63

'You put a bit of money on a horse, and when it romps home you double it or more.'

The strains of a small fiddle band spun through the air. 'I've only sixpence, will that do?' she asked.

'Ay, certainly 'tis a start. Now we'd better make our choice in the first race.'

Catherine bet her sixpence and her horse came last. Between races she and Colm wandered the course, taking shots at hoop-la, listening to the ballad singers. The field was packed with people: lords and ladies in their coaches, city folk down from Belfast for the afternoon, farmers, gypsies, tinkers, local villagers, holidaymakers from New-castle. A young gypsy girl grabbed her hand as she pushed through the throng.

'Let's be seeing what mother fortune has in store for you, my little one. I'll tell you your destiny for sixpence.'

Catherine drew her hand back. 'I don't have it, I'm afraid.'

The gypsy woman screwed up her eyes and scrutinised her. 'I'd have thought you were born with a silver ladle between your lips.'

'I sneaked away to come here . . .'

'It's a lot of that you'll be after doing. Cross the sea. And your children will be born with wooden spoons in their mouths, if they're lucky.' She cackled to herself as she swayed off into the crowd. Catherine pulled herself up, and made after the girl. Colm stopped her.

'Ah, don't bother with her. She always gives a bad fortune to the ones who don't give her the money.'

They stood silently for a few minutes near a row of stalls. 'Come, come! Gather round and play at the Wild Bird's Nest. Come now, lords and ladies, put the ball where you like, shove it down where you fancy! You play and I pay!'

The ball clattered around the gaudy wooden board. 'Ah, there we are. The feather wins again. And so poorly backed too . . .'

64

Colm took Catherine by the arm. 'Come on, we'll take a spin.'

'That's it sir, give the young lady a turn at the board! Just nominate your colour, sir. Quick, while the ball is still rolling.'

The ball stopped.

'Thank you sir, and the green wins again. The lucky Irish green.'

Colm and Catherine turned and moved silently off towards the paddock. Behind them a couple of old men played on at the Wild Bird's Nest: 'One down, two down, any more or any other? Then off she goes again.'

'There's no point in those games really. They weight the ball, or magnetise it or something. No one ever seems to win anyway!'

'Really?' said Catherine. 'And what's the fun in that, for anyone? There's no point in anything unless the same rules apply to all.'

Colm smiled.

'Now, there's a fair piece of philosophy for you. If only the rest of the world took your side. It's what they call the survival of the fittest. Which horse do you fancy is the fittest then?'

'Well, I'll be having the one with the magnet in his ears. The tall chestnut. He'll do.'

The chestnut won, but she had not bet. In the penultimate race she chose a black mare, and Colm said that if it came in, though he'd laid out, they'd share the takings. They won a shilling, and Catherine got her sixpence back.

'I like this. It's fun!' She looked hard at Colm. 'You must be younger than my brother, but you don't treat me as if I was an addlehead. Why is that?'

'Why does he treat you like that, you mean, or why do I treat you like this?'

'Anything.'

65

' 'Tis the gold that glistens nearest to us that seems like dross, while we venture across the high seas in quest of the tawdry.'

' "Tawdry"? Now that's a good word. What does it mean?'

'Trumpery.'

'And a second, but I don't know that one either.'

'It's something showy, but not worth the having.'

'Like a diamond necklace.'

'Well, I suppose there's some as might think that was worth the having, but I don't know that it'd suit me so well. What do you think, now?'

Catherine laughed as he posed around, mimicking the walk of the English ladies climbing into their coaches.

'I think diamonds aren't worth the having except you'd be meaning to be selling. They say that the necklace on Lady Pembroke's neck is worth about twenty of our houses down in Newcastle.'

They pitted their double sixpences against each other on the last race, and both lost.

'But we had the pleasure of the moment, do you not agree?' Colm said.

'Oh, Colm,' Catherine bit her lip as she spoke. 'It's the best afternoon I've ever had. I wish I knew more people like you, but we live so far from anyone.'

'Ah, get along with you! Let us have a ride on your nag, and you can ride mine home.'

Colm gave Catherine a leg up on to his mare and then pushed through a small crowd that had gathered around Napper Tandy, who was tethered to the outer fence.

'Clear the way now chaps. I must be making me way home.' He had put his foot in the stirrup when a rough voice behind him yelled out, 'Give you a fiver for him!'

'No thank you, kindly, but 'tis not me own to be giving away.' The voice bellowed louder: 'I hope you'll all be me witness, when I repeat: I'll give you a fiver for him.'

Colm tried to edge the horse back, but too many people stood in his way. He made another attempt to mount, but a man held him by the leg.

'Did you hear, my friend, or are you deaf? He said he'd give you a fiver, and will you be refusing him?'

Catherine steered Colm's horse into the crowd. 'Listen to him, can't you? It's not his horse. It's mine. And I'm not selling.'

'Now that's a likely story if ever I heard one. A little girl barely out of nappies owning a great beast like this!'

The rough man's friends roared out at his wit. He turned back on Colm, and gave him a crack across the back of the head. Catherine screamed: 'Leave off him, you brute! It's *my* horse, do you hear? He's called Napper Tandy, ask anyone round here, they'll recognise him.'

Another of the louts broke away from the crowd and lurched towards her. 'A nice nationalistic name there. So if you're the owner I suppose you must be one of these Papish rebels to be giving a horse that sort of a name.'

'I don't know what you're talking about, but I advise you to leave us alone, or . . . or . . .'

'Or!!!' The mob shrieked back.

'Or my father will go after you all.'

To the drunken men this seemed the funniest thing she had said so far.

Colm had managed to mount the horse, though his jacket was torn and his nose bloody. 'Come on, Nap, come on,' called Catherine.

The men parted as the horse moved. The ruffian shouted out again: 'I believe in these parts it's agin the law for a Catholic to refuse an offer of five pounds for his horse.'

'Who said I was a Catholic?'

The man pulled open the boy's shirt and tore a gold crucifix from his neck. 'If you were not a Catholic, why would you be wearing this Papish trumpery?'

'But it's not my horse, you fool.'

The man reached inside his jacket. 'So you're refusing my offer?'

Colm kicked his heels in. 'Come on, Nap!' He leaned forward into the horse's mane. Catherine got the other horse off to a canter, leading Colm and Napper Tandy. The crack of a gunshot rang out behind her. She pulled up the horse and looked round as Colm slouched forward. The horse took two more steps, then crashed to the ground. Horse and boy were dead.

'Let's get out of here!' she heard as the gang started to run in different directions. From other corners of the field people, alarmed by the shot, ran forward to help, and stooped around the prostrate figures. Catherine jumped down and ran to join them. 'It's Colm O'Hannon!' cried a voice. 'God rest his soul.' Women wailed as the men pulled the body from under the horse.

'It's those bloody gun-happy Volunteers it was,' a woman yelled, 'down from Belfast for a day's trouble.'

Catherine stood behind the crouching figures, looking down. She had no tears, just a dry, aching throat. When she spoke her voice came out high and quavering.

'What am I to do? Oh, dear God, it was my fault. What am I to do?'

A head below her turned and stared coldly up into her eyes. 'Would it be Catherine Tate, from Kilcoo?'

She noticed that the man's transparent ears had little lumps on them.

'It looks as though once again it's escorting you home I'll be,' he said.

The tiny wooden trap rattled along the old dirt road. After a few miles Hughie started to whistle a jaunty little tune. Catherine sat slumped in the corner with her face in her hands, as she had done for the whole journey.

'Stop that,' she muttered. 'How could you?'

'Stop what?' enquired Hughie.

'It's not the time for whistling.'

'Lookit, it's never the time for whistling, is it? Tell me a time when all's right with the world? And then tell me a place where music's not the thing. We have it at weddings *and* at funerals.'

'Not jolly music like that. That boy's dead, and it was my fault.'

'Oh, you're taking all old Ireland's troubles upon your little shoulders now, is that right? Most certainly it's a tragic thing that happened today, but it's not the first and not the last tragedy we've seen in these parts. It's to say that death becomes a sort of way of life. We live in dangerous times, but dangerous times are always with us. The best thing for us all to do is to be as quiet and as small as we can be. Give a shrug, let it go. Life's for the living, for it's a long time we are dead. And if you're worried about the style of me music, I'd like to refer you to the funeral music they have in the southern parts of Americkay. It's all rocking in the streets they are over there, I'm told.'

At last Catherine broke into racking sobs.

'I just didn't know what to do. It all happened so quick.'

'Ah, me little girl, you're still the very young baby you were when we last met, lost on the hills in search of something over on the other side. And what do you think you'll be finding on the other side, eh? I'll tell you now. Only the same thing again parading as something else.'

Catherine looked up and bit her lip. 'My folks don't know I was at the races. What am I going to say? I told them I was going for a ride. Oh God, how'll I explain about poor old Nap? What will become of me?'

'And how the Lord's anyone going to explain to the

mother of that poor wee boy, and him only a few months older than you yourself?'

Hughie tethered his horse at the gateposts of the farm and led Catherine to the kitchen door. 'I'll tell your folks what happened. They've no cause to be cross with you.'

He left her in the yard as he marched into the kitchen. His work done, he was shown out through the front door and departed without bidding Catherine goodbye.


After the funeral of Colm O'Hannon the Tate household returned to the farm. Catherine gathered up her skirts, ran up the stairs to her room and, turning the key, put herself into retreat from the world. At first she sat at the window, gazing out at the hills. Soon she began to hate their purple gloom, and could no longer see the magic in the rising mist or the sparkling dew. She shut the curtains, lay on her bed and turned her back to the light that still crept in through the cracks.

Her father, not knowing any other way, stood outside the door knocking, telling her she was being silly. She must shake herself out of it. She must eat. Her mother sometimes joined him, and sometimes came alone, usually in the evening, begging Catherine, in her sweet and light voice, to let her in so that they could talk. Neither of them got any response.

When she had been in her darkened room for three days, Brian, back from Dublin for the holidays, sat all afternoon on the floor in the corridor outside her door, playing jigs on his penny whistle. After a while she spoke quietly through the door, telling him to go away. He played on. She shouted, banged on the wall, and finally opened the door a crack and hissed at him to leave her in peace. He pushed his foot against the door and grabbed her by the wrist.

'Come on downstairs, and eat. None of us can rest while

you're at this caper in your room. Face up to things, Cath, there's nothing to be done in your room that's going to bring back Nap or the boy. But don't go killing yourself into the bargain. Mother's quite grey-faced with it all.'

Once he had got her out of the room he snatched the key and locked the door from the outside so that return was out of the question. He led her into the kitchen. Cassie, seeing them come in, discreetly exited, 'to see to the hins'.

Catherine spent the rest of the day sitting in the kitchen talking to Brian, and to Cassie when she tactfully returned to chop and stir and carry the huge black iron pans from the draining board to the range.

Catherine was up early the next morning, and threw herself into helping her mother with the work. It was the first time she'd ever really worked on the farm. She spent the long days of the next few weeks working in the dairy, milking the cows, sieving whey, churning butter, hanging out cheese in muslin bags. She occasionally met Cuchullin over tea at the kitchen table, but never would she set foot in the stable, or join her old friend for his stable-brewed afternoon tea. When Cuchullin came into the dairy and started on one of his tales of Finn McCool and Deirdre, of shipwrecks, of heroes and fairies, she would tell him she'd heard it all before; it bored her stiff, she had work to do.

'I'm too old by half,' he would mutter in apology. 'I'll be off to meet my maker one of these days, and to gallop with Napper Tandy through Elysian fields.'

The mention of the horse brought a flash from her black eyes, and she would pointedly ignore him until he moved on. He soon gave up his visits to the dairy.

It was Cassie who found him, one grey Tuesday, slouched down by his stable stove, the kettle boiled dry, his parchment skin seemingly ironed out, his gnarled hands lying, palms up, on the floor, and the glimmer of a smile playing on his blue lips.

One of the big barns was cleared out for the wake. The hustle of the day's preparations was an effective antidote to the blood-chilling and numbing grief of bereavement. Catherine's father and brother, together with some farm workers, moved chairs and tables and drove out to the town to pass around notices of Cuchullin's death and to buy loaves of white bread, barrels of beer and bottles of whiskey. The women worked flat out preparing food.

Catherine opened the barn door and slid inside. Her mother rushed forward and guided her out through the huge door.

'Catherine, acushla, go and play outside for a while. We'll give you a call, darling, when we need your help.'

Catherine lingered. 'Why can't I help now? I have to do something. He was my best friend.'

Brigid put her arm around her daughter. 'Look, darling, it's going to be a very late night for us all. Go, see if your father needs a hand.'

Behind her mother, Cassie stood solemnly holding up a white sheet. Catherine shifted from foot to foot. 'I'd prefer to help you, Mother, if it's all the same.'

'No, no, darling. We're doing just fine in here.' Brigid had edged her daughter out into the courtyard.

'Please, Mother, you must let me do something to help.'

Cassie came out behind Brigid. She held out a basket

and said, 'Well now, here's something needs doing. Why don't you go into the fields and gather me some flowers. We'll want to have a bit of prettiness around the barn for this evening.'

Catherine took the basket. She plucked at the strips of willow as she replied. 'I know what you're doing in there. I'm not a child any more. He was my friend. Please, please let me help.'

A tear ran down her cheek into the corner of her lips. She swallowed audibly. 'I don't mind seeing him dead. I feel so bad because I blamed him for everything that day at the races. I have to tell him I'm sorry, Mama. I have to, you see.'

Catherine's voice broke into dry sobs as she spoke, but when Cassie tried to stroke her arm, she shook her off. 'If I can help you wash him and prepare him for tonight, at least I'd feel as if I'd made some amends.'

The two women exchanged a glance.

'Please. Please . . . You have to let me help. You just have to.'

Brigid put her arm round her daughter's waist, 'Now, sweetheart, you must tell me if anything upsets you, or if you change your mind and want to stop at all.'

Cassie rolled up her sleeves and picked up a bucket from the doorway as the three women went back into the barn. Brigid kissed her daughter on the cheek before removing the sheet from old Cuchullin's body and starting the delicate job of washing the corpse.

'Well, you see, the ould fellah went from the first shop, where they'd given him the price of sixpence, to the big shop up in Newcastle, and asks *there* for the price of a shroud . . .' Paddy, the grocer with a cart, was holding a group of villagers in rapt attention with his yarns.

'And do you know what the chap says to him?'

The group solemnly shook their heads. Paddy sat back in his chair and raised his eyebrows as he went on: 'Ninepence. Ninepence for that very same item that the first shop had cited him sixpence for. Well, now, the ould fellah was wanting to be knowing the reason for this inflationary pricing. So he leans on the counter, like, and asks straight out: "Now, these here shrouds are ninepence, and I could buy the same item down at O'Connell's for only sixpence." He looked the shopkeeper straight in the eye, now. The same shopkeeper just shook his head as he replied, "Oh, yes, he'll sell you a shroud for sixpence all right, but it's your money you'd be after throwing down the drain. A shroud from O'Connell's is an inferior shroud. Why, the knees would be through it in a week!" '

The crowd at Cuchullin's wake roared their approval. A woman leaned forward. 'Now, can anyone tell me this?' she asked. 'A shroud is like a white dress with strings on it, am I right? And it fastens at the back, does it not? And that fastening is a loose one?'

Another most knowledgeable woman piped in her piece: 'Oh, no, the shroud covers at the front, but barely meets at the back, at all, at all. There's a six-inch gap round the back.'

'Right,' the first woman crowed. 'Then tell me this: what are we all going to look like now when the trumpet blows on the Day of Judgment and we all rise up from our graves? – we'll all be running around with bare backsides!!'

The crowd screeched hysterically at the idea. Catherine sat quietly amongst them. She knew they could not have loved old Cuchullin as she had, or how could they share such hilarity, with his corpse lying only a few yards away, on a door resting on two trestles? He was laid inside his coffin, a clean white sheet draped over him. She glanced towards him, and the tears again pricked her eyes.

She looked down at the plate on her lap, picked up the sandwich and tried to take a bite, but her mouth could not open, so she put it back on her knee.

Paddy was on to another of his tales.

'And he leaned up on the bar, intimate like, and axes the barman for two pints of porter. "Now, Michael," says the bar-keeper. "What for would you be wanting two pints of porter a little chap like yourself?" Now, Michael looks him in the eye, and smiles at the barman while he replies. "No, sure it's not for meself they are. It's the one for me and the one for me brother, Sean." Now our barman was rather taken aback with this piece of information, so he comes round the bar, like, and puts his arm round the fellah, in a comforting sort of a way, you know. "Now, Michael me ould son, are you forgettin'? Yer brother Sean's been dead and buried these three weeks." And a tear comes into this ould Michael's eyes. "No, no, you're wrong there, sure, for he's outside on me cart." And you know, what he told him was right. The poor sod had missed his brother so much he'd gone and dug him up, and his dead corpse was indeed sprawled across a cart outside the door of the pub, awaiting his pint of porter!'

His audience gasped and shook their heads, tutting away for some minutes between bites of sandwich, gulps of beer and the odd chuckle. Catherine got up and went out into the courtyard. She'd had enough of this. If this was a wake in respect of the dead, it was not her idea of it. She felt worse now than when she had woken up this morning and remembered that Cuchullin was dead. She took a deep breath of the night air, and walked over to the gate. Leaning on the white gateposts she gazed up at the sky. One thought kept coming into her head: how much she wanted to talk to Cuchullin about it all. For a split-second she thought she'd write him a letter, then realised that death had no address. She stamped her foot in the dust in fury, and the tears came. When she had cried herself into some sort of tranquillity she wandered over to the stables. She'd feel near to him there, anyway. Nearer than she did in the shadow of that horrible white-draped box. The catch was not on the stable door and she inched it open in silence. She could hear murmuring inside: low intense voices in a heated discussion. She froze, and listened.

'. . . ah, but they can put it through a third time all right, and so what? The House of Lords will put the axe to it, just like they did the other times.'

'Well, now, if we want Home Rule how do we fight such mighty institutions as these? Look what they did to poor old Guy Fawkes.'

'I think we must be careful.' It was her father speaking. 'For myself, I'll put money into the cause. Then when things are better organised I'll see what else is to be done, and only if the worst comes to the worst will we have to use force.'

'Ah, but they're using force already. Look at how they killed that boy Colm, and it was your own daughter with him, and your own horse killed.'

Catherine leaned forward and the bolt of the stable door slid out of its catch. The talking stopped. After a few seconds it began again.

'It's just the bolt dropping. Look, English top-nobs are pouring money into keeping the Ulster Volunteers in a position of power — '

'That bloody Rudyard Kipling's just given them £30,000.'

A whistle of amazement went round the group. 'Well it's the last time I'll be reading one of his books!'

'Joxter, me laddo, you've never read a book in all your life, you spalpeen!'

'And I've heard they've got more than a hundred thousand men drilling . . .'

'Have they got arms then?'

'Well, they used guns to kill Colm, didn't they? Ach, the

polis and the rest let them smuggle in guns without batting an eyelash. The sods are armed to the teeth, and there's no one out there with even half a mind bent on stopping them, and that's the way they'll keep hold of Ireland.'

'Well, maybe Joxter's right, maybe the only way is to form our own volunteer force to counter them. We are at war. At war with the Ulster Volunteers and with England.'

A murmur of approval ran round the stable.

'Anyway, lads, let's call it a night now and get back with the others. But keep your eyes and ears open.'

Catherine tiptoed across the yard and slid back into the barn before they had a chance to come out. Paddy was in the middle of another morbid story. She skirted the large circle of chairs around him, went to the big table and pretended to pick at the food. Her mind was racing. What was her father up to? What was all this talk of guns and war? The barn door opened and a couple of men slipped in and joined Paddy's group. She didn't turn. She didn't want to know who they were. That way she'd not be in trouble if she saw them again.

Suddenly her father was behind her, putting his arm around her waist.

'Come on, you little darling, you're looking very tired. Are you all right in yourself? It's a sad day we have to say goodbye to old Cuchullin.'

Catherine couldn't look up.

'Here, have a sip of this. It'll warm you, and help you sleep.' He handed her a glass of whiskey. 'Just a sip, mind, it's hot stuff.'

Catherine drank and the spirit ripped her throat. She winced. Her mother smiled across the table at her. 'You look very tired, acushla, go on up to your bed now. It's been a long and dreadful day.'

'Your mother's right, darling. Slip on up to bed, and we'll see you in the morning.'

77

Catherine looked into her father's eyes. She wanted so to ask him what was going on, but knew she'd be fobbed off with some wild explanation. She turned and made her way to the door.

'Goodnight!' the cry went up as the wakers saw her go. 'Sweet dreams!'

But her dreams were not sweet. They were a jumble of images of horses and guns, her father, and corpses under white sheets, their backsides proud to the world. And behind her Cuchullin, pushing her on to see more.

Just after dawn she awoke with a start, and realised that, in all her preoccupation with her father's involvement with the gunmen, she had not taken her last farewell of Cuchullin before they nailed the coffin down.

Brian came up from Dublin and took over care of the stables. The summer of 1914 was hot and dry. Hired men sweated it out, bare-chested in the fields.

Catherine's mother was not well. She was thin and pale and had a hollow, dark cough. She could no longer work as she once had in the dairy. Cassie gave Catherine some help, while occasionally her father put in some hours between doing the men's wages, accounts, overseeing the farm work, and taking animals to the fairs for auction.

One afternoon Catherine had been working heavily, alone, for some hours when he popped his head round the door of the dairy. 'Brian not in here?' he asked.

Catherine went on stuffing the thick butter into its shaping blocks as she replied. 'Not seen him all afternoon. He's probably over with the horses.'

Richard strode across the courtyard. He pulled open the big door and walked out of the bright sunlight into the stable's gloom.

'Brian?'

There was a sudden rustling in the corner, where Cuchullin had had his stove.

'Are you in there?'

'Here, Father!' Brian bounced round the partition, an inane smile on his face.

'What's going on? I thought I told you I needed someone to oversee the big meadow this afternoon, while I sit in the office and pay the extra men.'

He pushed past his son into the darkest corner. 'So what's going on?'

Cuchullin's stove, never lit since his death, was piled high with books. Papers lay on the straw, an inkpot, pens; it was a little study of Brian's own.

'And is this why it takes you twice the time even old Cuchullin took to do anything you're asked? Is it in here snuggled up reading books you are?'

'I can't do stable work all my life, Daddo. Wasn't it your idea I went to university? Surely you want me to finish my studies, and bring credit to you?'

Richard Tate shuffled from foot to foot. 'Of course I do, son. But this farm will be all yours one day, and it's time you were pulling your weight and getting used to the responsibility of it. Your sister works harder than you do.'

'Then put her in charge of the farm. Did you not hear me just now, Daddo? Exams don't just pass themselves. Work has to be done first – book work.'

'And what good is book work going to be to a farmer?'

Brian looked grimly at his father.

'What good at all? It's wasting my time I am, either way. If I work like the devil on the farm all holiday I'll fail my exams for sure, and have wasted these years, for I'll leave without the degree. But if I get my degree – what's the point of that, if it's just a farmer I'll become?'

'Are you mocking me?' Richard Tate took a stride towards Brian, who stood his ground.

79

'No. But sometimes you presume on a person. I'll make my own mind up how I'm to lead my life. I won't have you do it for me.'

Brian sidestepped his father as he marched out of the stable. Richard shouted after him, 'Then find me someone to help out! I can't manage this whole place on my own. I'm at the end of my tether.'

Standing in the yard, Catherine heard the whole scene. As Brian hurried past her, she sidled into the shadows of the barn door. 'I can do it Daddo,' she whispered. 'I know how to manage horses.'

Richard forced his way past her into the sunlight. 'What in God's name do you know about anything?' he shouted. 'You're just a silly pig-headed little girl. It's a man I'm needing. Someone with a bit of strength.'

After her father had slammed his office door behind him Catherine took off her apron, and for the first time in months, saddled up one of the smaller horses, climbed on its back and rode out into the hills.

People from all around marched like shadows up the dark mountainside. The sun had set, the day's work was done, and the night was about to begin. It was Midsummer's Eve, and tonight was the night of fire.

Once upon a time in Ireland, on the eve of the feast day of Saint John the Apostle, a sacred fire was lit with much ceremony on the eastern promontory of Howth, north of Dublin. Along the coast, every village in sight of that hill had its own fire, and when the people saw the flame burst forth on Howth hill, they lit their own fires. The next villages saw them blazing, and lit theirs, until the whole country was encircled with a cordon of fire.

On Midsummer's Day, the eve of the feast day of Saint John the Baptist, fires continued to be lit in memory of that ceremony, and over these sacred fires the traditional fertility rites of ancient times were still performed, with dancing and singing and drinking, until the grey light of day broke on the far-off hills of England.

At the end of the night's revelries every young man would take a lighted stick from the fire and run home with it. The man whose stick was still ablaze as he stepped over the threshold brought with him a year's good fortune.

Catherine saw the orange glow on all the mountains; the black shadows of people gathering round. She could smell the roasting meat and hear the murmur of anticipation. She reined the pony in, and changed her course. So what if she stayed out all night in this crowd? Would anybody even notice? She hated the atmosphere at home anyway.

Along the side of the dust track gypsies and tinkers were out in force, sitting in gangs round their own little fires. Children staggered around, half-gnawed bones gripped in their fists, faces glistening with grease. A dog bowled along beside her, leaping up and yelping with excitement. She kicked her heels in and gathered speed. She was going to make a night of it.

When she neared the largest bonfire she tethered her pony at a safe distance. Pushing her way through the throng, she soon worked her way to the front and stood so close to the fire the heat of the flames burned her cheeks.

A couple standing next to her, their arms flung carelessly round each other's waists, offered her a swig from their bottle.

'What is it?' she enquired politely.

'A wee drop of the hard,' said the young man. 'To keep you warm.'

'Oh, I think I'm in no danger of getting cold here, thank you,' she replied.

'Just take a small mouthful,' added the woman. 'For the crack!'

She'd heard Cassie and Cuchullin talking of doing things for the crack, and if ever she felt like a bit of crack it was tonight.

'Thank you, I will.'

She took a swig and handed the bottle back. The back of her throat took the first shock, then down and down until it hit her stomach and she did feel an inner warmth.

A band of fiddlers, pipers and drummers struck up a sprightly jig and the front line around the fire joined hands and started to dance round and round. At the end of the first tune the dancers sidled into the shadows and new contenders took their place.

Catherine leaned against a tree, breathing in the balmy, smoky night air. Far beyond her she could see the dull glimmer of the Irish Sea. She turned and gazed again at the blaze. She wandered closer to the band, spread out her skirts and sat down among a group of village women who were singing along.

> 'From Bantry Bay up to Derry Quay,
> And from Galway to Dublin Town . . .'

She smiled to herself, and hummed along, watching the young men pulling their girls to them as they danced around the fire.

> 'No maid I've seen like the brown colleen
> That I met in the County Down . . .'

How she longed to be older.

An old woman held out a large chunk of bread and a slab of cheese. Catherine took it gratefully and munched as the band jigged on. A small boy near her was pushed forward by his friends, and stood nervously a few feet from the circumference of her skirt.

'Would you be wanting a bite?' she asked, holding her sandwich out for him.

He looked down and kicked up the dust with the toe of his boot. 'No, I was just wonderin' . . .'

'Yes?' she smiled back.

'If you would dance with me a while.'

She threw back her head, laughing, as she clambered to her feet. It wasn't quite what she was looking for, but it was a start.

When the smaller fires had burnt low, the serious games began. Young men took it in turns to leap the flames. Others crowded round looking on, clapping rhythmically and hollering as the men sprang into the air and landed again on the other side, dust rising from their boots. A young woman had taken the stopper from a huge bottle of beer, and the contenders swigged from it between leaps.

Catherine recognised some of the young men as harvest workers from her father's farm, so she cheered them on slightly louder. It felt good to be on someone's side. At some distance a clear tenor voice rang out from behind a sloping gorse:

> *'I could scale the blue air,*
> *I could plough the high hills,*
> *Oh, I could kneel all night in prayer,*
> *To heal your many ills!*
> *And one beamy smile from you . . .'*

The girl with the beer handed it to one of the men and skipped off towards the voice. An old woman standing near Catherine whispered to her neighbour, a large woman wrapped in a bright red shawl: 'That Rosalind MacFarlan! She's touched! She thinks he's singing for her!'

'A likely scenario!' hooted her friend.

Catherine turned and asked them if they knew who it

83

was that was singing. The women laughed together in reply, 'Don't you be skippin' after him too.'

'That's big Johnnie Morgan, back from Americkay,' added the red shawl. 'The girls are all after chasing him.' The old woman leaned in towards Catherine, intimately. 'They've got it into their mithered heads that he's come home because he's made his fortune, but how could he? He was just a steward on a ship . . . !'

The red shawl dived in for the kill: '. . . and what's that but a waiter decked up in a bit of gold braid!'

They cackled again as the beautiful voice drifted over the hillside towards them.

> '. . . My true,
>     My Dark Rosaleen!
>     My fond Rosaleen!
>     Would give me life and soul anew,
>     A second life, a soul anew,
>     My Dark Rosaleen!'

Catherine turned to the two old crones again. 'But isn't that girl called Rosaleen?' she asked

The women shrieked with laughter. 'No, no! Rosalind! Rosalind!'

'Agh, truth, she thinks it's for her, and he's such a card he'll play up it is her he's singing about.'

Catherine turned to look towards the voice, but the old woman tugged her arm and pulled her round to face her. 'But the Dark Rosaleen is Ireland,' she said. 'That's what he's come back for. Ireland.'

After a while watching the boys leap the small fire, Catherine slipped off through the crowd. Above her, around the huge hilltop bonfire she could hear excited cheers. Someone was going to try to leap this fire, although the flames still spurted into the navy blue sky.

She could see the silhouettes of men struggling against the firelight.

'Hold him back, he's drunk.'

'Leave hold of me. I am not drunk.'

She edged closer to them. A group of about four men scuffled about at the dusty edge of the bonfire.

'Ah, leave off. If he wants to set his pants alight let him! It's his own pants they are.'

The voice came from just behind her. Catherine turned round: beside her stood Hughie.

'Good evening Miss Tate. Absconding from home again, are we?'

'Do you follow me around, or something?'

Hughie smiled. 'What a rare conceit! 'Twould be fun, if I only had the time.'

Around them the crowd gasped. A tall dark man in mid-air was skimming the top of the flames. He landed on the crackling pieces of tinder on the other side, smoke coming from the seat of his pants. He grabbed someone's beer flask and poured it down his back.

'I hope it's not brandy!' he yelled to the crowd, who were still clapping. They clapped louder, and cheered. He spoke to the couple whose flask he had snatched: 'I'll buy you both as much as you can drink tomorrow for lending me that to douse meself with!'

He bowed to the crowd, his white teeth sparkling in the fire's light, his black curls flung back behind his ear from which hung a small gold ring.

'Is he a gypsy?' asked Catherine.

Hughie shook his head. 'No, he's just a great big baby, who'll never grow up if he lives to be ninety-three.'

The fiddle band further down the hill were playing sentimental ballads. Hughie and Catherine wandered down to sit by them. 'You mustn't be giving your folk all this anxiety, you know,' he told her. 'Lookit, I know they're

85

pretty quiet, not like all the folk from the village. But they love you, and want the best for you, like any pair of parents in the universe.'

'Maybe I should go home now, then? I can't bear it though, I'm enjoying myself so much.'

Hughie looked out to the sea. 'Ah, we'll all be going home soon. Look, the sky's whitening at the edges. Come on with you. Where's your transport?'

He walked her to the pony. She climbed into the saddle and thanked him for being kind to her again.

'Ah, nonsense!' he said. 'You're an old friend of mine, aren't you? Off you go.' He gave the horse a slap on the backside and it started off down the hill. Catherine turned. 'Where is it that you live?'

Hughie called after her, 'Now wouldn't that be telling!'

On the hillcrest a voice boomed out: 'So now grab your sticks, and stand by for my signal.'

Catherine heeled her pony to a canter.

'And go! God bless you all!'

A stampede of men waving burning twigs descended the hill in all directions, leaping boulders and bushes. Some stumbled, cursing, as the fire on the stick was doused.

Catherine slowed her horse, so it wouldn't be startled. A voice sang out beside her, 'Come on gal, will you try to outrun a poor man, with your fancy horsewomanship? Be my pacemaker.'

'What's that?' yelled Catherine.

'You just keep up a steady rhythm, and keep me running nice and fast.'

The man held his stick in one hand and a stretch of the rein in the other as they raced through the village street. 'Where are you going?' she called.

'I don't know. Just keep on going the way you're going and we'll be right.'

86

Within minutes they were at the white gateposts where Hughie had once deposited her in the early hours. She reined in. 'This is where I live,' she announced.

'Fine!' said the man. As he looked up she saw the earring and realised it was the man who had leapt the giant fire. She laughed, 'Have you run all this way with a hole in your pants?'

He smiled his widest grin. 'You're a scamp! Where's the way in?'

Catherine gasped. 'You can't come in here,' she said.

'Why on earth not?'

'My father would kill me.'

The man laughed up at her. 'Now who's getting the wrong idea. I just want somewhere to put this.' He held up his twig, which was still alight.

'Aren't you taking it home?'

'No, it's for you.'

'But won't they be expecting you to bring it to your own home?'

'And what home's that? I don't have a home round these parts. Come on, gal, where shall I put it?'

She jumped down from the horse, left it standing in the yard and ran with the man to the kitchen door. 'Here,' she opened the door. 'What do we do with it?'

'Burn it, of course.' He strode across to the range, opened the lid and dropped in the burning stick. 'Now I'll be off to me bed.'

She followed him out to the courtyard, to put the horse in the stable. 'What's your name?' she called after the man as he darted out through the gate.

'John Morgan', he replied. 'The man from the sea.'

# 24 June 1914
## County Down

'Well you certainly know how to put the tin lid on things, my girl.'

Cassie was scrubbing the floor when Catherine finally came down the next morning.

'There was a right to-do here last night, and you missing as well.'

Catherine, floating with the tiredness of only a couple of hours' sleep, sat down at the large wooden table. 'Why, what happened?'

Cassie stood up, untucked her apron, wiped her hands down it and sat down beside her.

'Your father and your brother continued their little argument until it got so loud that your poor mother climbed out of bed to find out what all the ruckus was about. And what with your father shouting and your mother crying, and all the horses and even the hens started joining in you could have heard the cacophony over in Newcastle town, I shouldn't wonder. And the upshot was this: Brian packed his bags and has gone back to Dublin to do some work, as he calls it, on those books he's always got his nose stuck into. And, lucky for you, no one even thought to wonder where you might have got to. And then I suppose they all thought you'd gone to bed. I took the liberty of locking your room until they'd all gone to bed themselves, so if they enquired there they'd think you had one of your moods upon you. I knew you'd not be back early from the fires.'

Catherine bit her lip.

'Thanks. How did you know that's where I'd be?'

'Oh everyone knows everyone else's business round here, as you know. And when Armageddon was raging here at the farm I took myself off for a little walk and bumped into my old friend Willie Corcoran, the old grocer's man from Kilcoo, and he said he'd seen you heading off up the hill with the mob.'

Catherine was silent.

'Well, how was it? And who walked you home?' Cassie asked.

'No one.'

'No one in a pair of size twelve boots, by the look of the marks on my floor this morning. I noticed they walked in the door went to the range and straight out again, so I suppose he dropped the stick off without any argy-bargy, am I right?'

Catherine was about to tell all when Richard Tate burst in. 'There you are,' he snapped. 'It's bad enough your brother's gone off, shirking his responsibilities, without you sitting in here chatting when you should be working in the dairy.' He turned to go out but at the door poked his head back and said, 'And I might be reminding you, Cassie, that you're paid and given board here in exchange for work, not sitting gossiping with my daughter.'

He slammed the door after him; both women pulled a face at each other before hurrying to their work.

A few weeks later things at the farm were very different. The harvesters from the village brought with them terrible news. Great Britain had declared war on Germany. In the late post Catherine received a letter from Dublin. It was from Brian, asking her to try and make their parents understand that he had not gone to Dublin to spite them, but because he wanted to do the right thing. He was not cut out to be a farmer, he declared, and was setting himself up with respectable qualifications for another job. She had not finished reading it when a great commotion in the courtyard brought her to the dairy door. A horse and trap had arrived, and Brian jumped out, with all his suitcases.

'Wait there,' he shouted up to the coachman. 'I won't be long, and I have to be on that train back to Dublin.' He ran past Catherine and into the kitchen. She followed. 'What's happening?' she cried after him.

'I've come to wish you all goodbye. I've taken the shilling. I'm in the army. I sail for Liverpool tomorrow.'

Brian went in and sat on his mother's bed. Catherine joined them.

After about half an hour, he kissed his sister on the cheek and his mother on the forehead and took his leave of them.

'I'll just say goodbye to the old man, and then I'll be seeing you when I come back on leave. Farewell, you two darlings.' He clicked the door shut behind him. Brigid sobbed into the sheets. Catherine didn't know what to say or do. She just sat quietly stroking the blanket. She felt nothing.

Brigid rested her hand on Catherine's and said, 'You'd better run along. I'll be all right.'

As Catherine walked towards the kitchen, she heard muffled voices raised in argument coming from the front parlour, a room that was never used except to receive visitors. She crept along the hall, listening.

'. . . Ireland . . . England . . . Irish . . . Collusion . . . Germany . . . the enemy . . . England . . . Home Rule . . . Can't beat 'em . . . reward . . . Ireland . . . the only way.'

As usual her father and brother had found something

to argue about. Sometimes she thought that men could never seem to get along with each other but were always picking fights. All this politics drove her mad. What had Germany to do with them, or England, and so what about Irish Home Rule? Life on the farm wouldn't change, would it? Everything would shamble along, whatever went on across the Irish Sea. Who cared about it all? Politics, politics, politics! Just a silly boys' game. She went out, into the fresh air, and sat down on a stool in the courtyard.

Soon Brian, red-faced, strode past her and climbed into the waiting coach. 'Goodbye, then,' she called.

He looked straight ahead and bid the coachman drive on. He did not even turn for a last look at the farm or his sister, as she leaned against the gateposts waving goodbye to his back.

The strange silence that fell over the farm lasted for days. No one knew what to say. Cassie cooked and cleaned without her usual chorus of sentimental songs, slightly out of tune. Richard stopped shouting at anyone who crossed his path. Catherine stirred the curds in a sort of silent fury, and from the sick Brigid's room came only the sound of her hollow cough.

Regular letters came from England while Brian did his brief training, and when he was out in Flanders letters still got through.

Many local men were also in Europe and both the village, Kilcoo, and the big town, Newcastle, had a quieter air. A steady stream of telegrams arrived, announcing injuries and deaths. Lights burned all night in houses mourning lost sons and husbands. There could be no funerals and no proper wakes: bodies were buried where they fell on foreign soil.

Every now and then a handful of uniformed men would

return for a week or two's leave. They seemed to have changed too. They spent much of their holiday propping up the saloon bar, knocking back as much drink as their stomachs could hold.

It was almost two years before Brian came back, unannounced, on Easter Sunday, 1916, bringing with him a friend from his brigade. Brigid, who was a little better, was sitting in the kitchen plucking chickens; she covered him with feathers when she jumped up to hug him.

Catherine flung her apron on to the dairy sideboard, and skipped into the kitchen to join them. Brian's friend clicked the heels of his boots. 'My word, Tate, you told me you had a sister, but I thought she'd be just a baby, not a blushing young beauty like this,' he said.

He took his cap in his hands, bowed, then took Catherine's hand and kissed it. He looked her straight in the eye. 'Thomas Salisbury, very pleased to make your acquaintance.'

At dinner, Brian told them of the state of the trenches, how many men died of hunger and thirst when the supplies couldn't get through, of the gas attacks which had left men blind and scarred, of the unbelievable noise and dirt and squalor. Thomas told the family how Brian had been commended for bravery in the face of battle. Brian blushed and changed the subject to the taste of the good old Irish potato, which he'd missed so much.

'When things got very bad I'd just turn off my brain,' he said, 'and dream of Cassie's stew, of the smell of the stables and the flax in the fields, the sight of the hills. Oh, it's grand to be back.'

Later the two soldiers went into the village to take a drink with other soldiers home on leave. Catherine watched them stroll out of the gates. She liked the sight of men in uniform, but it was a pity it was such a horrid colour. Brian should have joined the navy, he'd have looked so dashing in navy blue, and as for his friend . . . Now, there was a handsome fellow. How well the navy uniform would have set off his beautiful blue eyes. He was so tall, slim and . . . that funny accent. She'd never realised that English people spoke in those quaint tones. Very masculine, it seemed, very forceful.

Catherine spent Easter Monday climbing the hills with her brother and Thomas Salisbury. It was a glorious spring day. That evening, dinner was a grand affair with three courses, and even wine, which Brian had bought in town.

Afterwards Catherine lay in her bed smiling to herself. Mr Salisbury was a very nice chap. When Richard started proposing toasts, 'To the end of the War', and the like, he had insisted on proposing a toast himself, and had toasted her. It had embarrassed her and she hadn't known where to look as they all raised their glasses and drank, but now, in the dark warmth of her bed, it thrilled her. She closed her eyes and tried to sleep – but how could anyone sleep on such a night?

After a couple of hours she heard noises in the yard – footsteps and whispers, the bolt on the barn door opening and then closing. She climbed out of bed and knelt down by the window. She could see nothing out of the ordinary. But after a good ten minutes she saw the barn door open slowly and a hunched figure scamper out, run across the yard and tiptoe into the kitchen. Her heart thumped. Were they being burgled? She listened at her bedroom door. Nothing. She grasped the handle and slid it round, easing the door open a crack.

The corridor was very dark and it was hard to make anything out. Catherine froze as a dark figure glided past her bedroom door. At the top of the stairs the figure stopped. She could hear the faintest of whispers. The first voice was her father's: 'What on earth's happening? What's going on? It's the middle of the night.'

'It's Joxter, sir. He's been wounded.'

'Joxter? How on earth?'

'You'd better come down and see for yourself, sir.'

The two men made their way downstairs. Catherine grabbed her dressing-gown, determined to follow. She watched from the window until she saw them go into the barn, then, just as she was about to go down, the barn door opened and three figures came out, crossed the yard and went into the kitchen. The light went on. Catherine crept down and listened at the kitchen door.

'Oh, I was lucky to get away, at all, sir. Lucky I was indeed. There'll be executions, you mark what I say. They'll be making examples of the ones they catch. Ouch!'

A tap ran. Footsteps crossed the room. The stove lid was opened and closed again.

'So tell me this' – it was her father again – 'I suppose this is the famous organised rebellion you were all telling me about. I don't know what you think you're all playing at. Running around with guns isn't going to do anyone any good. People will get hurt.'

'Oh, no, sir, you're right, sir. It's a shambles it was. There's people dead. And the security forces are out for blood. With me arm the way it is, I think I'll be easily associated, so I'd best keep low for a few days at least.'

'Agh, he was only trying to do what's right for us all, sir. We're all after wanting Ireland for the Irish.'

A chair scraped on the stone floor.

'There are ways of getting things. And this is ridiculously ill-timed.'

'Sorry, sir. It just seemed right at the time.'

'Yes, yes. Look. Sleep in the barn, if you can. Tomorrow do some work on the outer fields. Mid-morning make out you've hurt your arm with the tractor or something. Come

94

to Cassie, she'll bind it again. That way no one will know. Now boys, if you don't mind, I'll be getting back to me bed.'

Catherine hurtled back up the stairs and into her room. Standing on the landing, wrapped in his dressing-gown, was Thomas Salisbury. 'What's going on?' he asked.

Catherine was at a loss. 'I was just getting a glass of water,' she mumbled.

He laughed. 'Well, where is it, then?'

'What?'

'The glass of water.'

She glanced back towards the kitchen, stammering out her reply. 'Uh, I drank it down there. I'm fine now. Best get back to bed. We'll be getting up before we know where we are.'

Behind her, the kitchen door opened, flooding the corridor and stairs with light.

'What's going on here? A party?'

Her father laughed casually. 'It's the wine I think. We're all parched.'

The soldier looked down at Richard Tate, who shrugged genially in return.

'I'll be down to have a glug myself, if you don't mind,' said Thomas. He marched down the stairs, passing Catherine and Richard as they silently made their way back to their beds.

Brian, Catherine and Thomas spent the next afternoon riding up the mountains. Cassie had prepared them a small picnic lunch, which they ate perched in a sheltered spot overlooking the sea.

After a short time Brian decided that he wanted to ride down to Newcastle, and gallop along the strand. He was feeling too restless to sit eating and chatting. Thomas gave him a leg up and patted the horse to see it on its way: 'See you later, Paddy, my lad.'

'Have a good picnic!' called Brian.

The horse shambled down the rough hillside. Thomas and Catherine stood and watched it go. 'Why do you call him Paddy?' she asked. 'That's our grocer's cart-man's name.'

'Oh, it's what we call all the Irishmen. And the Welsh are Taffy, the Scots, Jock. It's just an army thing, I suppose. If your name's White you're called Chalky, and if you're a Clark you're Nobby.'

She was puzzled, but said it must be a jolly thing to have such camaraderie.

Thomas agreed, but went on to tell her dreadful tales of blood and rats, what it was like to sit in a trench for days in the wet silence waiting for something to break the deadlock. He told her of the fear when the dark yellow fog of mustard gas rolled along the top, and, if you were unlucky, down into your trench.

She felt very sorry for him, and tried to imagine Brian sitting beside him.

He described the smell, the filth, the noise; how you went on firing, even though the man next to you was dead, or worse, dying. 'And we're fighting for you. You, and all the other women and children. So that you can go on living a good life, a free life. It'll all be worth it when the Hun is smashed down, and peace in Europe is restored. I'm proud to be doing my bit for England and all the English people.'

He took a deep breath and bit into another large doorstep of barmbrack.

'Well, this certainly beats bully beef and iron rations spattered with mud and blood!'

Catherine was not going to let his previous remark go unchallenged.

'But we're Irish. I'm Irish, you see, Thomas. Brian's Irish.'

'Ah, yes, but that's just a technicality. Actually you're as English as I am. This place has belonged to England for centuries.'

He sat silently chewing, looking out to sea, then continued, 'The only difference is there's no conscription in Ireland, I believe.'

Catherine shook her head. He smiled at her. 'But plenty of volunteers, like your brother. It's just a shame that so many of the Irish seem to think it's their place to be stabbing us in the back.'

The sandwiches had already turned to dust in Catherine's mouth. She sipped at her lemonade. 'I'm sorry, I don't understand you,' she said quietly.

'These Republicans, you know the types. I think they hate us English.'

Sometimes she despaired of her father. Why did he have to be on the wrong side at a time like this? Catherine shifted uneasily. Maybe Thomas suspected her father? Was he trying to get things out of her? She couldn't bear it. She'd found a friend and here she was feeling guilty because of her father's cloak-and-dagger nonsense.

'I don't hate you. I think you're grand. When all this war is over, you will come back, won't you? Please?'

He lay back on the grass, his blond hair bright against the dark green grass, and gazed up into a sky which matched his eyes. 'Who knows,' he said. 'Maybe I won't make it back at all.'

He turned and leaned on his elbow, looking up at her. 'But if I do make it, I promise I'll come back here for you.'

He pulled her down and brushed her lips with his own. 'There now! Look what you've got me doing. I'm meant to be looking after you. I am sorry. Don't take it the wrong way, will you?'

Thomas jumped up and started cramming the picnic

things back into his saddlebag. 'Let's get back now,' he said briskly. 'Brian will be home soon.'

Alan Bird, the new farm manager, spent his first day giving the farm offices a lick of paint. He put up lists and charts, tidied the desk, then worked out rosters and details of employees and temporary farm-hands. He spent a whole afternoon interviewing for a new groom. A stream of men, cap in hand, queued outside the office door then shambled through the gates and back to the village.

Brian and Thomas sat with Catherine watching them, having bets on the men's chances, and on whether their demeanour would change after their interviews.

'This new chap'll do wonders for the place,' cried Brian. 'What are his plans for you and the dairy, do you know?'

Catherine shrugged. 'Ah, no one tells me anything.'

'Only because you're always running off,' Brian laughed. 'Did you ever tell Thomas about the time when you were as tall as a blade of grass and went off to sing with the leprechaun choir?'

Catherine chucked a towel at her brother. 'I'll thank you not to go spoiling my reputation with your friend, or I'll go stamp on your whistle.'

Both men roared with laughter, Catherine knew not at what. When they quietened down, Thomas changed the subject. 'You didn't tell me you played the whistle, Paddy!'

'Oh, yes, he's a devil on the penny whistle. Oh play for us, Brian, go on,' Catherine urged.

The farm manager popped his head round the office door. 'I'm awfully sorry to spoil the party, but would you mind keeping the noise down a bit? These poor fellows are nervous enough as it is.'

They pulled faces of apology and moved into the kitchen to get under Cassie's feet. Soon the kitchen was spinning with Brian's tunes. Brigid sat at the table and clapped while Cassie and Catherine tripped around it with Thomas. As evening descended Richard joined the party, singing the odd song or two, and opening a bottle of whiskey.

When the party was in full swing Cassie heard a sharp tapping on the frosted glass of the door. She opened the door and Alan appeared. 'I'm sorry to interrupt the dancing,' he said, 'but I'd like to introduce the new groom.'

He ushered in a tall man in a long black coat. The man held high his dark head of curly hair. 'Hello folks,' he said. 'I'll not be keeping you from your little shindy. See you tomorrow.'

He waved and followed Alan out into the yard. Cassie whistled through her teeth as she closed the door. 'Well, fancy that!' she muttered. 'Wee Johnnie Morgan.'

Catherine was scarlet. 'Oh, this dancing is awful hot work!' she cried. 'I think I'll have a long glass of water.'

Brian picked up the whistle. 'I should think he'll keep your horses well, Da. He's certainly a big strong fellow.'

'Let's just say he couldn't look after them as badly as you did.' Richard laughed and topped up everyone's glass. 'Mind you,' he added, 'it's Alan I'm pleased with. I think everything's going to change for the better now that he's in charge.'

Thomas noticed that Catherine had gone very quiet since the farm manager's brief entrance. He slapped Brian on the back. 'Come on, Paddy, me lad, let's get the dance going again. Let's eat, drink and be merry and dance . . . for tomorrow we go back to defend our country.'

Brian put the tin whistle to his lips and the dancing resumed.

As the first streaks of dawn broke in the sky, Brian and Thomas left to return to their regiment.

But life on the farm was, if anything, more lively than usual. The huge form of John Morgan could be seen lifting bales of hay and straw from barn to stable. He took the horses out, one by one, to get the feel of them. During his tea break in the kitchen, the sound of Cassie's laughter could be heard right out in the dairy. Catherine longed to know what was going on, but didn't dare make an appearance in case it came out that she had already met the new groom.

At lunchtime, when she failed to appear at the table, Alan came into the dairy to check everything was all right. 'Oh, I've just fallen a little behind. I'll be in later,' she said, looking down into the curds as she stirred.

'And by the way, what would you be doing at the weekend?' Alan asked.

Catherine couldn't think what he wanted.

'Nothing in particular, as usual, I expect,' she replied.

'Well in that case, I was just wondering if you would like to come out with me. There's a little dance going on up at Castlewellan, and I've got tickets. Your father said he wouldn't mind, in fact he thought it a fine idea. Well, that's as long as you agree, of course, so . . .'

'Why not?' said Catherine. Why not indeed? She was sixteen. She smiled to herself. So, she'd got a date with the new manager, and was going to her first dance.

'I'll give you time to get ready, then, and wait for you. Just give me a shout.'

When he had gone, Catherine flopped down on to the stool by her side. She still had the problem of the groom. Of course now that she was practically going out with the manager she had some protection, at least. She was frightened that this John Morgan, whom she had been naive enough to let take her home, would be over-familiar with her. After all, she was the daughter of the house, and her father was virtually the squire.

She glanced across the yard to the stable. The top of the door was open so he was probably inside, back at work. She took off her apron and went over to the kitchen, but froze as she opened the door. He was still there, sitting at the table. Cassie was at the range, chatting to him. He jumped up when he saw her. She jumped back. This was it, she thought: within seconds her escapade would be exposed.

'Ah, well, Cassie, old love. I'll be getting back to me work now,' he said. As he strode past Catherine he touched his forelock with his finger and thumb.

'Good afternoon, Miss Tate. I'm delighted to be working on your father's estate.'

He gave her a slight bow, and closed the door behind him. Catherine was relieved and mortified. Was he trying to make a fool of her, or had he just forgotten her?

'You're in late, my girl. What kept you?'

Catherine hesitated before replying. She wasn't sure how far she could confide in Cassie. Especially now that it turned out that she too seemed to know John Morgan from before.

'Alan just popped in for a chat,' she explained. 'He's asked me out with him on Saturday.'

Cassie beamed and gave her a hug.

'Ah, me little darlin', you've grown up so fast! Well, he's a nice chap anyway. Dependable sort. And quite a catch if you compare him to most of the gormless spalpeens you find around these parts.'

Catherine was going off him by the second. She bit furiously into her bread and cheese. Well, things could be worse. At least that sarcastic specimen of a groom hadn't asked her out and really put her on the spot. Anyway, she was finally going out to see some life. And she was going to make the most of it.

# 1917
## County Down

At the dance Catherine realised many things. One was that there was not that much fun to be had in being escorted, because you were immediately protected from everything that looked as though it might be fun. It was rather like being a yoyo. You could wander off for the odd dance with a stranger, but you always had to come back to the fellow who'd brought you. The problem was, this was the only way to get out. It was quite out of the question for a young lady in her position to go out dancing alone.

The next morning she felt so depressed that she decided to take herself off for a ride. When the groom was well out of sight she stole into the stable, saddled up a horse and trotted out of the yard heading for the hills.

She galloped the horse until she felt that she could breathe again. They sped past bushes and trees until they were well up the hill, then she let the animal slow down until he was walking, occasionally stopping to graze at the short green grass. A hundred or so yards away, near a small dilapidated whitewashed cabin, a man was toiling with some sort of wooden implement in a tiny field, which was more stone than soil. He bent over, woollen hat pulled down over his head, fiercely attacking the ground until he had worked it into something useful. Then he stood for a moment, leaning on the long wooden handle. He wiped the sweat from his brow, and stooped again to his work.

Catherine walked her horse over to get a closer look. The man went on scraping at the ground. She coughed. He paid no attention.

'Hello?' she said tentatively. 'Excuse me?'

Hughie looked up from his work.

'Ah, yis. Miss Catherine Tate. How can I help you?'

Catherine jumped down from the horse. 'I knew it was you,' she cried. 'I just couldn't work out what you were doing.'

Hughie opened the gate. After tethering the horse, she came in. 'Well? What were you doing?' she grinned.

'Just working on me farm.'

Catherine doubled up with laughter. 'No, really? What were you doing?' she asked again.

'I'm not in the habit of telling lies, me girl. This little patch is my farm. There's the front garden and the four fields. And I can manage it all meself.'

Catherine looked around. Still she wasn't sure whether or not he was joking.

'Would you like to join me in a wee cup of tea?' he asked. They walked across the field to Hughie's little house. It was much smaller than she remembered it. One room deep, one room high, and two rooms wide. Catherine even had to bend down to get through the front door.

Inside it was cold and bleak. The fire was burning, and a pot hung over it from a chain in the chimney; but it seemed to give out no heat. Catherine wasn't sure whether it wasn't warmer outside than in. She sat warily on a rickety wooden stool. How had she ever thought that this place was so warm and romantic? How many days had she wasted riding round the hills trying to find it? She wrapped her arms tight around herself to keep warm, while Hughie arranged kettles, pots and cups. He opened the range, pulled something out, plopped it on to a plate and handed it to her. She took a bite, winced and spat it out.

'What is it?'

'Potato bread. If you don't like it I'd be thankful if you gave the rest back, it'll do for me supper.'

Catherine gave him the plate.

'Why don't you have proper bread?'

'I didn't think you'd grow into such a little snob, Miss Tate, if you don't mind me saying.'

Catherine glared at him, unable to think of a reply and trapped inside his horrid little hovel. She tried to humour him.

'It's a long time since I've been here, isn't it?' she said.

He nodded.

'Would you show me your Spanish doubloons?'

Hughie cackled. 'Is it kidding me on you are? Lookit, that's me own private, secret box, and I'm not after showing it to all and sundry.'

Catherine stood up and noticed that she now towered over little Hughie. 'I'm not staying here to listen to your rudeness. I'll skip the tea, thank you.'

Hughie stood between her and the door. 'Excuse me, Miss Tate, but I'd advise you to mind your manners,' he said firmly. 'Just because I'm poor is no reason to think you can lord it over me. My little box is worth more to me than all the money on God's earth. It's been passed down through the generations, like your own farm. And for all your family's wealth, that doesn't make you a better person than I am, at all. I'm just trying to offer you the hospitality of me house, and the least you could do in return is treat me, for these few moments, as an equal. That, you will discover, Miss Tate, is the secret of good manners, whether you're a king or a tinker.'

Catherine tapped the end of her horse whip against her thigh. 'If you don't get out of my way, I shall set my brother on you.'

Hughie sighed. 'At least credit me with a little intelli-

'gence,' he said. 'I know your brother is too busy fighting Germans to have the time to sort me out.'

'Well I wish you were there instead of him!'

'I'm not so stupid as to get myself involved in that ridiculous bloodbath,' shrugged Hughie. 'And anyway, as you can't fail to see, I'm a good foot too short.'

He stood back and opened the door.

'I hate you!' Catherine screamed as she ran past him. ' I hope I never have to see your ugly face again.'

Out in the minuscule front garden she turned back. 'And anyway,' she spat out, 'there's a groom who works for my father, and he's twice the size of you, and he'd defend me. I know he would.'

Hughie slowly shook his head. 'You wouldn't be meaning wee Johnnie Morgan, by any chance?' he asked.

Catherine smirked as she replied, 'I thought you might have heard of him. Well I'd just advise you to watch your lip in future.'

She marched over to her horse. As she rode past the front door she could see Hughie watching her, his hands on his hips. He appeared to be rocking with laughter.

She was leading the horse back into its stall when a voice boomed out behind her: 'And where have you been with that?'

She spun round. It was John Morgan.

'I believe your father employs *me* to look after his horses – not you – and how am I to do that with you sneaking them out of the fields and riding them up rough mountains that they were never intended for?'

'Whoever said I'd gone up the mountain?'

'I don't need anyone to tell me where you go. I know, remember.'

So he did remember her. What a big grinning pig he was, standing there, holding the reins.

'I think,' snapped Catherine, 'that if you ask my father, he'll say that I can do what I like with our own horses.'

'I already have spoken to him, Miss, and he agrees with me. In fact he said when you returned he would like to have a word with you.'

Catherine glared at him with steely eyes. What was wrong with everyone today? Why were they all against her?

'Well, Miss, if you don't mind getting out of my way, I'll just take the old nag out for a bit of a spin. Just to check him over, you know.'

He leapt up on to the horse's back and said, 'Your father is waiting for you in the farm office.' He pulled his forelock as he rode off. 'Ta, ta, Miss Tate.'

Catherine slouched over to the office where her father sat, grim-faced. Alan lurked in the background.

'You're back, at last,' Richard said.

Catherine shrugged as her father went on,

'There's only one way to run a farm, and that's for everyone to co-operate. You're not a six-year-old any more, and I'd be grateful if you stopped behaving like one.'

'But . . .'

'No buts, Miss. You can apologise to John, and then please find something useful to do. I'd like double the output from the dairy today, if you have to stay up all night doing it.'

She changed, went into the dairy and started work. About half an hour later, Alan came in.

'I'm so sorry about that, Catherine. I rather agree with you, in fact, and I certainly think that groom fellow has a bit of a nerve reporting you to your own father.' He hesitated, then continued, 'But on the other hand we do have to do what your father says . . . it is his business.'

106

Catherine was relieved that not everyone on the farm was in on this conspiracy, and that she might even have an ally.

'Anyway . . . I just thought I'd pop in and let you know.' Alan was on his way out again, when he turned with another postscript.

'Oh, and by the way, I had a wonderful time at the hop. It makes a man quite proud to be seen out with a beautiful girl like yourself.'

He opened the door adding, 'And, um, if you fancied it at all, maybe you would like to come out to tea with me on Sunday. I could take you to the Slieve Donard if you like. You know, a really posh tea.'

Catherine smiled.

'You're on.'

Alan slid out into the yard, closing the door behind him.


Catherine's outings with Alan continued on a regular basis, and she made a point of avoiding John Morgan when possible. When it was impossible, she determinedly averted her eyes. Even so, she couldn't help noticing that he seemed to smirk at her antics, and sometimes she thought she caught him exchanging looks with Cassie, as though they were having a private joke at her expense.

She tried to enlist her mother's support, but Brigid insisted that he was good at his job, a hard worker, strong, and cheerful. She also pointed out that he was particularly kind to her, in a way that no other farm workers had ever been. Apart from running little errands, on sunny days, when she would sit looking mournfully out of her bedroom window, he would call to her and then stride up to her room, gently pick her up in his muscular arms and carry her downstairs. He would arrange a chair for her out in the courtyard, wrap her tight in blankets and lay her head softly upon a pillow, so that she could have company and sunlight, the things she missed most about being ill and bedridden. He amused her too, she said, by singing her favourite songs in a strong clear voice as he rubbed down the horses in the evening. She loved to lie and hear the old Irish ballads floating in through her bedroom window on the crisp evening air. And didn't he have a lovely bright smile?

So it turned out that Catherine's only ally was Alan, who agreed that John Morgan was just too smug for his boots.

In midsummer 1917, just before Brian was due home on leave, a telegram arrived announcing that he had been killed in battle. His body, it said, would be buried where he fell.

The rituals that provided practical work for the bereaved and helped to soothe the mourners after a death were impossible. The family held a vigil, drew the blinds three-quarters down and left the lights burning all night, but because Brian's body was lying, shattered, in Flanders, there could be no wake, and no funeral. Their grief was intensified by unease and a sense of unfinished business.

The vigil lasted a fortnight. One day soon afterwards, when the shadow of death still lay over them, Catherine came into the kitchen for tea, and found her father in the middle of an intense conversation with Cassie and John.

'That's right. Well, Sir Edward Carson, the man who's already given us enough trouble with his Ulster Volunteers, has put forward this plan, and it's got support from many English ministers, and looks as though it'll go through all right.'

John Morgan shrugged. 'Isn't he the lawyer who hounded Oscar Wilde into ignominy?'

Catherine was reminded of her childhood. 'Wasn't his mother Lady Wilde, who wrote all those books about the fairies?' she asked.

John Morgan continued as though she had not spoken.

'No second and third attempts needed! This one'll go through first time, I suppose?'

'I think there's no doubt.'

Cassie topped up everyone's tea as she poured Catherine a cup. John Morgan shifted in his chair.

'So are you telling me that if the English give Ireland the Home Rule they promised us, it's not going to extend to us up here?' he asked.

'Correct. Carson's plan excludes the north-east quarter of the country. We here in County Down will remain under British dominion,' Richard explained.

'But they promised us,' Cassie blurted out like a child. 'They said Home Rule was a fact, that they were just holding back because of the war. Sure, but they can't go back on it now.'

'Oh yes, Cassie, but they can. Their word counts for nothing. I think we've learned that by now.'

Catherine wasn't interested in this talk, but because of the atmosphere felt she could not just get up and go, even though she had finished her tea and had nothing to say. John Morgan stared down into his cup as he spoke.

'So, up to a few miles from here the folks will all be Irish, but we will still be English, and ruled from London.'

Richard grunted his assent.

'What irony, then,' John continued, 'that the Mountains of Mourne, the most Irish of landmarks, will be English.' He looked grimly towards Richard. 'I'll bet you're furious that your son was killed fighting for them.'

There were tears in Richard's eyes as he said, 'That's the point, you see. He didn't think he was fighting for them at all. Brian thought he was fighting for us, for a united free Ireland. He thought that because they'd promised us independence, the least he could do was help them in their troubles. Anyway . . .' his voice cracked, 'the boy kept his side of the bargain.'

He covered his face and cried. Cassie got up and put her arms round him. Catherine, embarrassed, sat at the table, squeezing her hands tightly together, trying to think of an excuse to get out of the room. Cassie clucked as she stroked Richard's back. 'There, there, Mr Tate. Brian was a sweet boy. We all miss him so.'

John Morgan rose to his feet.

'I think, maybe, sir, that you should have a little drop of whiskey.'

Cassie nodded and indicated the cupboard. John opened the flask, poured out a shot and handed it to Richard. 'If there's anything that I can do to help . . .' he said.

'That's fine, John,' Richard muttered. 'Let's just carry on as normal, shall we.'

John picked up his cap and went quietly out into the yard. In the kitchen they could hear his boots clacking across the cobblestones. Soon his voice swirled round the courtyard in song.

> 'All day long, in unrest,
>   To and fro, do I move.
> The very soul within my breast
>   Is wasted for you, love!'

Richard's tears dropped into his glass. John sang on.

> 'The heart in my bosom faints
>   To think of you, my Queen,
> My life of life, my saint of saints,
>   My Dark Rosaleen!'

The handle of the hall door rattled softly and then opened. There, leaning heavily against the architrave, stood Brigid, who had been unable to walk unaided for over a year. Her face was as pale as her nightdress, and her voice came out in an intense whisper. 'I have to be with you all . . . I've not got long.'

Richard and Cassie rushed to help her to a seat by the stove. The groom's sweet tenor voice still wafted in from the yard:

> 'My own Rosaleen!
> To hear your sweet and sad complaints,
> My life, my love, my saint of saints,
> My Dark Rosaleen!'

Catherine jumped up and moved towards the yard door. 'I'll tell him to be quiet, shall I?' she asked.

'No, darling. I don't want any fuss.' Brigid struggled for breath. 'Anyway, it's beautiful music he sings.'

> 'Woe and pain, pain and woe,
> Are my lot, night and noon,
> To see your bright face clouded so,
> Like to the mournful moon.'

Richard stood beside his wife, stroking her straggling hair. She lifted her heavy head and motioned to Catherine, 'Come here, dote, and hold my hand.'

Catherine moved across the room. Her senses were numb. She felt as though she was part of a dream. She knelt on the floor, clinging to her mother's hand.

'Look after each other, my darlings,' Brigid said. The grip on Catherine's hand tightened.

> 'But yet will I rear your throne
> Again in golden sheen'

Brigid winced and then smiled a weary smile. 'That boy sings like an angel,' she whispered.

>   ' 'Tis you shall reign, shall reign alone,
>     My Dark Rosaleen!
>     My own Rosaleen!'

'I love you, my darlings.'

Brigid closed her eyes, and relaxed her grip on her daughter's hand. Her voice came out like a sigh: 'I am going into the light.'

As the rich voice drifted through the evening mist, Brigid's last breath mingled with the warm air from the stove, and her frail lifeless body seemed to shrink into her chair.

>   ' 'Tis you shall have the golden throne,
>     'Tis you shall reign, and reign alone,
>      My Dark Rosaleen!'

# 1921
## County Down

'It's funny, but, you know, I feel that I never got to know either my mother or my brother.'

Catherine sat in the stables with John, helping him polish the saddles.

'I loved them both, of course, but . . . I don't know . . . I just never knew them.'

'What about your father?'

'I've made a resolution to try and please him more. I know I drive him mad. Look I've already done a day's work and now I'm in here helping you . . .'

The top of the stable door swung open, and a fair head popped over the top.

'Hello? Anyone at home?'

John stood up and greeted the man.

'Can I help you?'

'Yes, I'm looking for the Tates. Do they still live here?'

Catherine stood up and pushed open the bottom of the door. 'Thomas Salisbury!' she exclaimed. 'My God, what are you doing here?' She undid her apron and slung it over her shoulder. 'Come and see my father.'

'Hold on, hold on! Let me have a look at you. My goodness, what a beauty. I suppose you've been snapped up long ago. Are you married?'

'Ah, don't be an eejit. No one round here'd ask me. I'm still as free as a bird, I'm glad to say.'

'Thank God for that then. I'm back here for a while and it'd be nice to have your company for my days off.'

Catherine opened the kitchen door and called out, 'Cassie! Cassie! Look who's come back! Brian's friend, Thomas.'

Cassie had her head in a cupboard. She closed it and turned round. Catherine couldn't help noticing that her expression changed violently when she saw Thomas, but she asked, 'Well then, Thomas, would you be joining us in a cup of tea?'

Thomas pulled out a chair and motioned to Catherine to sit. He sat down next to her as Cassie brewed up and hovered behind them.

'I'll just pop out and get your father in for his tea.'

Thomas looked after Cassie and said, 'Where's she off to?'

Catherine laughed. 'She probably wants to let us have a few moments alone. You know how romantic she is.'

Thomas picked up a chunk of bread and took a bite. 'I'd forgotten how delicious bread was over here.'

The door opened and Richard came in, followed by Alan.

'Thomas! This is my manager, Alan. Thomas was a good friend of my son,' Richard told Alan. Thomas rose and shook hands all round.

'So are you here for a long stay, Thomas?'

'Well, Richard, I'm stationed here for six months, with an extension, depending on the circumstances.'

Richard gulped his tea, and said, 'Good, good. Let's hope we can see a bit of you.'

'Well, I can't stay long today, but now that I've renewed the friendship . . . I'll be seeing you again.'

After he had gone Richard spoke to Catherine in the office. 'I want you to be very, very careful with that young man.' Catherine couldn't believe her ears.

'Why?' she asked. 'I thought you liked him.'

'Catherine, you couldn't have failed to notice his uniform.

The man is a Black and Tan. And there's no messing with the Tans . . . either way.'

'Oh Father, why do you go on so? No one really cares about these things. What are we meant to do? Ignore him?'

'Quite the contrary. We keep our eyes and ears open and our mouths shut. But whatever we do, we keep him at a safe distance, do you hear me?'

Catherine slouched out into the yard, where John Morgan was sweeping up. He looked at her. 'Do you remember what you were just saying about pleasing your father? Well, I'd stick to it if I were you. Do as he tells you.'

She swung round at him, her eyes flashing. 'And what would you know about anything? You don't even know him —'

He grabbed her by the arm and hissed into her ear, 'Listen, little girl, it's not only you I'm thinking about. There's a lot of people who live and work here, and any trouble you stir up will affect us all.'

Thomas Salisbury picked Catherine up from the farm gates in his division's Crossley tender. He had sped past her in it one day when she was out walking and stopped to make the arrangement to take her out. She had agreed keenly, inspiring a whoop of delight from Thomas's fellow Tans.

It was her first trip in a motor car, and she loved it. He drove her very fast along country lanes, swerving round horses and little ponies and traps. He drove her out through Newcastle and miles along the coast road. Eventually he stopped outside a small tea shop and led her inside, where he treated her to a very nice tea. He kept their outing short, as she had explained she was busy, and within a few hours he dropped her back at the farm, tooting his horn as he drove back to his billet.

She smirked at John, who was scowling from the stable,

115

and swung past him into the dairy.

The following morning John took Catherine into town in the trap. She had shopping to do, and he was to pick her up from the market-place at midday.

She picked up the messages, then had a short browse around the milliner's and dressmaker's shops. When the clock struck the hour she made her way along the High Street and back to the Square. She tossed her packages on to a bench and sat down beside them, looking round for John and the trap. He was late, as usual.

Around her, crowds of people jostled at stalls selling fish, and cheese and vegetables. An elderly woman asked her to move her parcels so that she could sit down. The woman scrutinised her face and asked, 'Did I not see you yesterday?'

Catherine shook her head. 'I doubt it.'

'Sure, I did. I know that face. I'm seldom wrong with a physog.'

Another woman, standing by a lamp-post, shifted from foot to foot and joined the conversation.

'Come on now, dear. Sure, 'twas you, sitting up in the front in that big motor car with the young uniformed gentleman?'

Catherine was beginning to feel uneasy. A crowd seemed to be forming around the bench. She could no longer see anything but coats, bags and skirts. She stood up.

'I'm sorry, I'm late. I have to go. Excuse me.'

She tried to push through the group of women, but they were crushed firmly together and were not going to yield. Women now pressed against her on all sides.

'Please let me through!' She knew her voice was out of control.

A grey-haired woman beside her pulled off her hat and threw it to the ground. Behind her she heard a muffled clicking noise and tried to turn, but someone was pulling her by the hair.

'What's wrong?' she implored. 'Will someone tell me what is happening here.'

116

A woman was grasping her tightly round the waist and another lifted her skirts, while people seemed to be smearing something hot on her legs, and hands and neck. All over, hands were gripping her, rubbing her. They pulled her hair and squashed against her cheeks. One woman suddenly grabbed her face in both hands and spat on her: 'That's for your boyfriend, the Tan.'

Catherine started to wipe her face: it was sticky and her fingers came away black. She reached up to her hair which was not only matted with tar but seemed to have been hacked away at random.

As suddenly as they had attacked, the women melted away into the market-place crowd, leaving Catherine alone by the bench with her crushed pile of parcels.

The clock struck the quarter. She gathered her things and started to run. Hoots of derisive laughter followed her. Behind her the clipping sound of horses' hooves pursued her. She gathered speed, dropping parcels, and stumbling on the cobblestones.

The trap pulled up just ahead of her. John Morgan leaned back and pushed open the door. 'You'd better get in,' he growled. 'And keep your head down.'

Catherine threw herself into the trap and burst into tears. John jumped out, picked up her parcels, slammed the door and climbed back on to his perch.

'Here!' He took off his cap and tossed it over his shoulder at her. 'Put that on your head.'

He stared at the road, and never once turned to look at her during the homeward drive.

'I don't know what happened,' she sobbed. 'They just came for me.' She pushed the hair out of her eyes. 'Oh, no!' she gasped. 'My hair. They've chopped off all of my hair. What am I going to do?'

John spoke in a low, sarcastic tone, just loud enough for her to hear.

'I suppose you'll have to grow it again. But you can't say you weren't warned.'

She hung her head, looked down at her blackened clothes, stuck with feathers, and was silent until they got home.

Catherine was lying on her bed, wondering what she could do, when there was a knock on her door.

It was Alan. He spoke quietly: he had seen her come in and wanted to help. She let him in.

'Look at me,' she wailed. 'I've tried to wash this stuff off my face. It just won't come . . . and my hair . . . what am I to do?'

Alan put his arm around her. 'Now first, sit down. You're probably in shock. I think it's tar on your face. I'll rush down and see if I can find some meths and we'll have that clean and beautiful again in no time.'

Catherine sobbed.

'It's all right. Calm down, calm down! Do you have a pair of scissors?'

She backed away from him.

'No. No more, please! Look what I look like already.'

Alan bit his lip, thinking. An idea came.

'Now just hold your horses. You stay here. I'll be back in a few minutes. I'll knock once, then twice. All right?' He went to the door. 'It'll be all right. I promise.'

Some time later he returned with some meths and a long silk scarf, which he had bought for her imminent birthday. He cleaned her face then wrapped the scarf gently round her head, and styled it like a turban.

'There you are!' He stepped back and admired his work. 'You look like a most elegant lady going out to a ball,' he said.

Catherine looked at herself in the mirror. 'But I can't waltz around like this all the time,' she complained.

He spoke to her very gently, almost as though she was

a child. 'No, I know.' He hesitated. 'But you could cut your hair into a style, a short style. It's the new fashion. You'll be all the rage.'

She didn't know whether or not to believe him.

'Don't worry, Catherine, I'll stick up for you. It must be awful to be attacked like that just for seeing an old friend ...'

Suddenly she felt him change, become even softer and kinder. 'I'm awfully fond of you, you know. I really am,' he said.

She wasn't sure now if she should burst into tears, or laugh hysterically. The latter seemed nearer, but still she couldn't help liking someone who took her side at a dreadful time like this.

For the next week Catherine did her best to keep out of the way of the farm-hands. Who knows, maybe their wives, sisters or mothers were part of the group that had set on her. But it was impossible to avoid Cassie or John Morgan. Cassie was very subdued in her presence, while John Morgan annoyed her by making jokes, asking her were her ears feeling the draught, and would she like to borrow some hair from the horses' tails? One day her father called her into the parlour, a room used only for receiving visitors on formal occasions or business. She sat down. He stood.

'I've asked you in here today,' he started, 'because you are almost twenty-one, and there are important things to be decided.'

She shuffled in her chair. She was not prepared for a lecture. Her father continued.

'As you probably realise, you are my only living relative, and as such my heir. I am a successful farmer, but I'm getting on in years and I must be sensible about what is going to happen to this place when I am too old to manage it.'

This was worse than she could have imagined. He was

119

going to make her learn how to take over the farm.

'I have drawn up my will, and in it I have left the farm to you and your heirs, just as it came down through my family for centuries. My only worry is that you are a bit on the wild side. You need a controlling influence.'

That was going a bit far, she thought, but decided to let him finish.

'Now, Alan, as you know, is a very good farm manager. He's really got the hang of the place, he's dependable, honest, steady. I would feel very happy if I could guarantee his position here.'

Catherine shrugged. 'That's fine with me.'

Her father walked towards the door.

'Good. I am going out now for a little while, but Alan would like a word with you,' he said. He opened the door, put his head out and called, 'Alan! Would you come into the parlour now please?' He turned round. 'Now, Catherine,' he said firmly, 'think hard before you make any decisions. But know that whatever you decide, I will be behind you.'

He left the room, leaving Catherine wondering what on earth this was all in aid of. Of course Alan could go on running the farm. She certainly had no intention of taking it all on if she could avoid it.

While she waited to find out what Alan was to contribute to this coming-of-age debate, she opened a jar on the table, took out an icing-sugar mint, and popped it into her mouth. With two more in the palm of her hand, she wandered back to the armchair. Alan was taking an almighty long time to come down an extremely short corridor. She flopped down into the chair, flinging the mints into her mouth.

Alan came in and shut the door behind him. He looked very, very solemn. Catherine tried and failed to swallow the sweets. She decided to put one in the hollow of each cheek, hoping it didn't make her look as though she had mumps.

'Catherine!' His voice was hoarse.

120

'Alan!' The sweets made her sound as though she had a cleft palate.

He was nervously stroking his hands down the front of his trouser-legs. He looked as though he was about to milk a cow. She knew she'd better leave off thinking about the sweets, or she might laugh and accidentally send it flying across the room like a bullet from a gun.

'As I believe I have already told you, I am very fond of you, Catherine,' he croaked.

'Yes, thank you, Alan,' she said, to her own surprise. She knew it was hardly an apt reply.

'Well, you see, I'm coming up to thirty in a year or two, and it's about time I was settling down and finding myself a wife.'

Catherine began to panic. He was going to leave, and she'd have to look after the farm without him.

'I don't want you to go away,' she blurted out. For some reason he smiled at this.

'That's all right, Catherine. I won't, if you'll have me.' She had managed to work one mint into the hollow under her tongue, ready for a surreptitious chew. Suddenly Alan threw himself on to his knees. 'Will you marry me?' he said.

She gulped and the mint was stuck half-way down her throat. She swallowed. 'I'm sorry?' she said.

'You won't?'

'Won't what?'

'Marry me.'

Catherine's mind raced. He was very sweet, after all. And there were hardly thousands of rival suitors killing each other for her love. And of course it would be quite prestigious to be Mrs Somebody. Everyone who worked on the farm, including that John Morgan, would have to toe the line if she was the owner's daughter and the boss's wife. She looked at Alan down there on the floor and felt sorry for him, his forehead all wrinkled up with anxiety.

121

'Why not?' she said.

He jumped to his feet.

'Is that a yes? Oh, Mammy, what a turn-up!' He leant towards her as he said, 'Would you permit me to take a little kiss?'

'Oh, no,' she spluttered. 'One second and let me swallow the other mint.'


'So, anyway,' she was bragging at the kitchen table, 'we're to be married next year, and the engagement party's to be after the weekend.'

'When'll that be, Monday night?' John Morgan nursed a large cup of tea.

'That's the plan,' smirked Catherine. 'It's my birthday at midnight, too. A double celebration.'

'Thank the Lord for that, then. I won't be here to get in your way.'

'Oh no,' Catherine crowed, 'of course you're invited. We're not snobs here, you know. All employees will be invited for a glass or two . . .'

John scraped his chair as he rose. 'No, I'm off. Didn't your fiancé tell you? I've given in my notice. I leave this place for good on Sunday night.'

Before Catherine could gather her thoughts to reply, he was gone. Cassie cleared away his cup and sat down beside her. 'I didn't think he'd stay here as long as he has,' she said. 'It's too quiet round here, it is, for the likes of Johnnie. He's one for the high life, you know. Always dashing off somewhere or other, America, France, London . . .'

Catherine was silent.

'Agh, you little divil!' Cassie held Catherine's hand, which lay clenched on the table. 'You've not changed a bit since you ran off to join the leprechaun orchestra! You're still the young pup with your head in the clouds, you are.

Don't you worry if he's not around. We'll all pull together and give you the darlingest engagement party that's ever been seen this side of Luke's Mountain.'

Alan took Catherine up to Belfast to chose the ring and to buy an evening gown for the party. When they returned to Kilcoo late that night, they were told that John Morgan had left them a present, to be opened at the party. He wished them the best and hoped they would be lucky with their next groom.

'So that's that!' snapped Catherine, tossing the package on to Alan's desk.

'Yes, I suppose it is,' laughed Alan. 'Good riddance, eh!'

The weekend was filled with frenetic and exhausting activity. The barn had to be cleared out to make a dancing space for all the farmworkers and local tradesmen, and in the big house rooms that had not been used for years were aired, chimneys swept, mirrors polished, shutters eased open, floors waxed. On the morning of her party, Catherine roamed from room to room. She had lived in this house all her life, but until now had never realised quite how big it was, or how beautiful. She pictured herself holding lavish balls and soirées. She unlocked the grand piano and plonked on the keys. How she wished she could play. She remembered her mother playing when she was very small, her father standing behind the piano stool, singing. What had happened to all that? Since she had been about ten it had been all farm, farm, farm.

She crept back to her bedroom. The dress was laid out and necklace and bracelets lay sparkling on her dressing-table. Guests had been invited from far and wide. Many she had not seen since she was a child; friends of the family. Then there was Alan's family. What on earth would they be like? She'd have to circulate, chat to everyone like a real hostess. What a thought. She wished she could sit with Cassie all night.

For a while she perched on the windowsill, gazing out. She watched Alan cross the yard from the kitchen back to his office, carrying a tray of tea. Cassie was so busy with the party food she obviously didn't want him under her feet. For the first time she noticed that Alan had a very peculiar walk; as though he had a fragile ornament, a plate or something, down the seat of his pants. It made her laugh. Four farm-hands carried long planks into the barn to make up a table for the food. She could hear hammering. Everywhere people were doing things. She felt quite left out. She'd tried to join in, but was always shushed away and told to rest. How could she rest at a time like this?

She went down and loitered in the yard for a while. Alan saw her and yelled jokily that if she had nothing to do she might like to take all the horses out for a trot, seeing as there was no groom to do it.

'Your father's just been telling me about you and the pixies! Bring me one back if you find one!' He creased up with laughter and went back into the office.

Catherine turned on her heel, opened the stable door, saddled up the biggest horse and took it out into the yard. She threw herself on to the saddle and trotted out through the gates, without turning round. She could hear Alan's voice yelling after her: 'I was only joking, Catherine. Catherine!'

He bellowed her name, but she was going, and no one was going to stop her. 'Leprechauns anyway, not pixies,' she muttered. 'Quite another breed.'

She rode out across fields, jumping hedges, and then made her way up the hills. She rode straight to Hughie's cabin, stepped up to his door and rapped urgently upon it.

Hughie showed her in.

'Is it inviting me to yer party you are?'

She flopped down silently by the stove.

'That's right, sit yourself down. You won't be wanting a cup of tea then?'

Catherine looked down, nervously wringing her hands.

'Well, aren't you the woman for surprise visits! I hear you're making a spatchcock of that manager lad . . .'

Tears started rolling down Catherine's cheeks.

'Agh, come on now, quit yer blubbering. I've not the energy to think of compliments for yer; I've been up since the shriek of day — '

'And I suppose you think I've been lying in bed all day,' she snapped, 'resting my head on feather pillows and sipping champagne . . .'

'Whoah, whoah! Slow down to a gallop, would yer. It's all too much to take in. Here am I, quietly minding my own business, when in screeches the human whirlwind called Catherine Tate, throws herself down into my best chair, and stares at the floor; and she about to be shouted from the treetops as the fiancée of the year.'

Hughie pulled out a chair next to her, picked up a flask and two glasses from a shelf behind him, and sat down. 'Now, shall we have a slurp of whiskey. A sort of celebratory drink for you,' he said.

She looked down, her chin quivering.

'Agh, come on now. A finer drop than this never went down the red lane . . .' He took a slug. 'Well, if you're not going to talk, maybe you'll drink up.' He sipped at his glass. 'Lookit, why do you think you've agreed to it all then, if you don't want to go through with it? Tell me that. Is there someone else on your mind, maybe? Perhaps you'd prefer to be running off with that pretty soldier boy, is that it?'

'Who said there were any problems? Everything's fine, as a matter of fact.'

'Well then, as a matter of fact, what are you doing up

here? Why would you be wanting to sit in what you consider a hovel if everything's so jolly down in your little palace?'

'I am about to get engaged to a very nice, efficient, orderly man, and together we will run my family's farm and . . .' She burst out crying again. 'Oh, I wish I was dead.'

Hughie laughed. 'Here you are. Have another drink. A bird never flew on one wing. I'll tell you what I think. I think that you should go back to your daddy, thank him for the party and just ask if he doesn t mind delaying the announcement of the engagement for a bit. You'll come round to it soon enough. You'd be mad not to.'

Catherine looked up at him, her eyes full of hope. 'Why's that?'

'Oh, he's a good enough quiet type. Just the one to let you have your own way, I should think. If you got yerself hitched to anyone a bit spirited it'd be fireworks, sure enough. Do it, girl, if you want to live to a happy old age.'

He took her by the hand and led her outside, facing down the hill.

'All that green land, all those beautiful meadows, and the fat cattle grazing upon them, those roofs – do you see the roofs of your farm, over there behind those trees? – it's all yours for the taking. Do you understand that for centuries people have died over land as fine as that, and it's yours, all yours, if you take the fellah's ring and wear it and call yourself by his name. Of course it's all yours anyway, but I think it'd be an awful aggravation to a soul like you to have all that work and responsibility on your plate. Look at it, girl. That land is fertilised with human blood, with the bodies of Catholics and Protestants. Sure, lass, it's the richest pastureland in the world. You can't run away from that.' He turned and stared into her eyes. 'Can you?'

Catherine took the long way home. She walked along the

strand at Newcastle, throwing stones at the breakers that crashed in from the Irish Sea.

'Catherine!'

It was Thomas Salisbury, standing by the railings with a group of Tans.

'Oh, Thomas, hello.' She moved quickly towards him, speaking quietly, hoping none of those awful women were around spying on her. 'I can't talk long, actually, I really shouldn't be here at all. I'm just taking a bit of a breather. I'm getting engaged tonight. It's all very hectic . . .'

He grinned as she clambered up the steps to join him.

'So who's the lucky fellow? Do I know him? No wonder you've been keeping your distance. You should have told me you had a beau.'

She peered around her. 'Yes, yes,' she said nervously. 'Alan, you know, the farm manager.'

She shuffled anxiously along beside them, heading for the town centre, and said, 'My horse is just over there, so I'll be running along. Grand to see you again.'

As she darted off one of the Tans grabbed her by the arm. 'Look out, ahead!' he shouted.

All of them dropped into firing positions. Further up the street a man had lobbed something through a window and was now running away.

'It's the Constabulary!' screamed Thomas. 'That was intended for us.'

'As usual,' hissed a voice behind her.

As the windows blew out, Catherine was thrown to the ground. The Tans stampeded forward over her, shooting randomly into the Square. Ordinary shoppers ran here and there, diving into doorways, throwing themselves under benches. Catherine saw a little girl fall on the pavement, hit by a stray bullet. Instinctively she ran forward, grabbed hold of the child and dragged her to the shelter of a doorway.

Gunfire still rang out round the square. She stood up,

snatched a handkerchief from her pocket and waved it high. 'Hold your fire!' she cried. 'There's a child injured here. She needs help.'

She found herself eye to eye with Thomas. His gun was pointed at her.

'For God's sake, Thomas,' she called. 'Put that down and help me.'

He didn't move.

'She's just a little girl, Thomas. She's done nothing to you. Help me, will you.'

'Put your hands up,' he shouted.

She laughed. 'Don't be stupid, Thomas. Stop being like this. It's me, Catherine.'

'Put your hands up.'

'I'll do no such thing. You put that gun down, now, and help me get this child some help.'

She turned back to the girl, who had crawled, sobbing, to the mouth of an alleyway, and bent down to help her.

'Stand up, I say,' Thomas shrieked. 'You bloody Paddies are all the same. You just won't take authority. None of you can be trusted.'

He fired. The shot sparked as it hit the wall above her head. She turned and shouted at him, 'How could I ever have thought that you were a friend of mine!'

As he raised his gun to shoot again, she was pulled from behind and stumbled into the alleyway. Someone held her tight by the wrist and pulled her along at top speed. She could still hear shooting behind her in the Square.

As they turned into another street she saw the girl who had been on the ground, jogging up and down over the shoulder of the black coat of the man who had saved her. He glanced round. 'Come on, gal, get a bit of speed on!' he urged.

It was John Morgan.

They came to a halt at a doctor's surgery. Inside John presented the child to the doctor and explained, 'She was wounded by the Tans. It's just a graze on her leg.' He dipped into his pocket and dropped a handful of cash on the desk. 'This should cover anything that needs doing. Now I have to be off, I'm afraid. I've to get this gal to her engagement party, and then I've a boat to catch.'

'Can't you come to my party?'

John Morgan shook his head. 'Do you not listen to a word I say? I'm off tonight, sailing the high seas, to a new life.'

Catherine pulled at his coat, stopping him from walking ahead. 'But you can't go, you just can't!'

John peered into her face. 'Why on earth not?' he asked.

'Well,' she stammered, 'you tell me why you've got to go, first.'

'Agh, look around you, gal. What's left for any of us here? You were there in the Square. There'll be no end to these troubles, not up here in the North. No man can serve two masters, and that's what we're meant to do. Look at what happened to you, that day with the women. Whatever side you take, you'll have the others agin you. And there's no hope of not taking sides. Somehow or other it always works out that you're on one side or the other. There just aren't any fences to sit on round these parts.'

He laughed as he took the reins of the horse from her and tied them to a tree. He threw his coat on the ground and motioned to her to sit with him. 'Tell me now, could you have walked past that wee girl? If you could, then this is the place to live. If you couldn't, get out. That's my way of looking at it.

'Agh, lookit, this stuff's been going on for centuries. And mark my words, they can talk and talk, but all I see is that it'll get worse. They tell us now that Ulster is to be part of Britain, that we're all British. Well, they can keep Ulster,

I'm going to have a bit of real Britain. I don't want the scrag end of it. If I've got to have it, I'll have the real thing, thank you very much. We'll always get the dregs of it up here. So I'm off to England. If you can't beat 'em, join 'em.'

'But what about me?' Catherine was desolate.

'What about you, lass? You're marrying and settling down and running a farm.'

'I'd do all that if it was you I was going to marry . . .'

John Morgan lay back, his black curls resting in the fallen leaves, and roared with laughter. 'What would you like me to do, then – storm into the party, knock your fiancé to the floor, throw you over my shoulder and stride off into the sunset with you?'

Catherine bit her lip and shrugged.

'Why not?'

John Morgan sat up and put his head in his hands. 'D'you know, of all the women I've ever met, I've often thought that you're the only one with enough spirit for me,' he said.

Catherine could hardly breathe.

'But,' he went on, 'and it's a big but – your father is hardly going to let me marry you, with you heir to all that land and all, and anyway, I don't want to be tied down. I'm going to Liverpool, tonight, on the midnight ferry from Dun Laoghaire. I don't see any other way.'

He stood up, pulled her to her feet, and threw on his coat. 'Here,' he said, 'I'll give you a leg up. You'd best be getting back, they'll all be waiting on you.'

His hand was on the reins as he ran along beside the horse. He picked up a stick and held it out before him. 'What does this remind you of?' He had to shout so that his voice could be heard above the horse's clatter.

'Saint John's Eve!', she yelled back. 'When I first met you.'

When they reached the gates he pulled the horse to a halt. 'So, I'll be saying goodbye,' he said.

130

She bent down and stroked the back of his head. 'Good-bye, then, you big bully!'

He held her face in his hands and kissed her on the lips, then, handing her the twig he had carried home for her, he slapped the horse onwards, and ran off in the opposite direction.

'You little divil, where've you been? Lord, haven't we all been going frantic wonderin' where you'd got to?'

Cassie stood in the kitchen in her best party dress. 'There's been trouble in town,' she continued. 'We were frightened you'd got caught up in it.'

Catherine gripped her stick and shook her head.

'No. I just wanted to go for a ride.' She made her way to the stairs. 'I'll go up and change. They'll all be arriving in a minute. If you see Daddo, would you send him up?'

In her room the dress lay where she'd left it. She took off the clothes she'd worn for the afternoon, poured a basin of water and washed her hands and face. As she was drying herself she heard her father's footsteps galloping up the stairs.

When he came in, Catherine asked him to sit down. They sat on the bed, either side of the dress. Catherine began by asking her father whether he'd mind delaying the announcement of her engagement to Alan. 'I just don't feel ready, yet,' she said.

'You are twenty-one years old, Catherine. What I wonder is when you'll ever be ready to join the adult world. You can't always go gallivanting around pleasing yourself, you know. You have to toe the line, and fit in with other people. Anything else is just selfish.'

'I just thought I'd like a bit more time . . .'

'Oh, yes, I'm sure you would. But what of all the time you've already had? Why didn't you come to me before now? There are already people downstairs, and more arriving every minute. If you'd really changed your mind about things I know you would have come to me before. You've never been afraid of speaking up. So all I can deduce is that, quite understandably, you're feeling nervous. All young people get nervous when they're on the threshold of a new life. The only thing I can say to help is that you'll feel better when it's all over and done with.'

'But what if I wanted to marry someone else?'

'Oh really,' he sighed, 'allow me a little intelligence. Who on earth could you marry around here?'

He picked up the twig, which lay on her pillow, and tossed it into the waste-paper basket.

'The rubbish you pick up! Now get ready and come downstairs as soon as you can.'

He left her alone with the dress.

She stared at it for a few minutes, then stood up and threw it over her head, stretching out her arms and sliding them into the sleeves.

A lone seagull screeched above the dock at Dun Laoghaire. John Morgan leaned over the side watching the sailors tugging at ropes. The wind was high. Swirls of smoke from the huge funnel behind him swooped down and made his eyes water.

In the distance a church bell chimed the first stroke of midnight. The ship's engine roared and the ropes were released from the capstans. Two young lads grabbed the wooden gangplank, and pulled it away.

John Morgan pushed away from the deck, as a cheer from inside the ship signalled the opening of the bar. He didn't hear the call from the shore: 'Hold it, Jack! One more to go aboard.'

He didn't see the lads throw the gangplank over as far as it would reach, or hands reach out from on board to catch the young lady as she jumped.

132

# ROSALEEN

I wish I could sleep. I wish, when the light burning in the centre of the ceiling all day dimmed and I lay on the hard bed and let my eyelids drop and veil my eyes, that the pictures I see would stop coming. I can start peacefully enough. I can start by thinking of green. Green hills.

A burst of glass. A flash of light. Wind sucking the skin from my face. Sound banging my eardrums into my skull. A sparkle of gold. Blood running from my head and draining into the dust. A child's eyes wide open.

I sit up, gasping for air.

I think of all the others. Children, mothers, fathers, brothers, lovers, friends. I still feel nothing for them. God help me.

What god?

I don't know how long I have lain here in this cell, or how long till I am next dragged along the echoing corridors to that dusty little room and interrogated.

SAY NOTHING, SIGN NOTHING, SEE NOTHING, HEAR NOTHING. This is what they drum into you in the organisation. They have no need to tell us to feel nothing. If we felt anything we could not do it, I suppose.

SAY NOTHING, SIGN NOTHING, SEE NOTHING, HEAR NOTHING. There's little need to instil such dicta in me. It should be taught instead to all young girls before embarking on marriage. For that is where such instructions are really necessary.

SAY NOTHING: when he comes in late, when he smells of booze, or perfume, when he forgets your birthday.

SIGN NOTHING: don't become a director of his company, swear affidavits that you were with him if you weren't, let him oversee your parents' wills, or the deeds of your joint home.

SEE NOTHING: the dent on his car, the lipstick on his collar, the tranquilliser he slips into your morning coffee,

HEAR NOTHING: when he tells some mystery caller

that he's got away with it, when he tells you he's doing the accounts and spends the whole evening in another room curled up cooing into a phone.

I should be sorry that he is dead. But I am not. It is my greatest achievement. I should have done it years ago. Should have thrown a toaster into his bath, dropped paraquat into his gin and tonic, knifed him to death in his sexually sated sleep, when he lay beside me dreaming happily, having fucked us both on the same evening. No doubt if I had done it properly in its own time I would still be sitting in a cell, but so many others would not be dead as a result of my efforts.

When they questioned me they didn't go into my family life much, which surprised me. The inquisition had three stages. I was led from the police cell, my face bruised, some of the cuts still raw from the beating given me in the van which rushed me from the airport to the police station. I was thrown into a room and left there. People shouted obscenities through the door at me during this time. The first gang who entered shouted at me until their skin glistened with sweat. They held their faces right up to mine so that when they moved their lips tiny bubbles of their spit would make my eyes flicker. It was a useless technique to try on me, even at the best of times. But that day I couldn't have talked anyway, even if I'd been tempted. The muscles of my jaw were clenched shut: a crowbar could not have prised them open wide enough to slip a straw between my teeth.

These so-called crack psychological forces haven't a clue. The 'dumb insolent' don't respond to accusations. When a nun used to hiss at me that I was a sinner, disobedient, a troublemaker, the only emotion it aroused was determination: determination to be exactly the thing I was accused of being. If everyone calls you a troublemaker you might as well be one. It acts almost as an inspiration; the mind answers back, 'Trouble? You ain't seen nothing yet.'

And when these people accuse you of being a murderer, and you happen to be one, what can you do but sit there and face them out.

The second bunch were hilarious. They sat with folders with my name on them, 'dossiers' they called them. You'd think they'd spent their whole life at the pictures, studying how to be quiet but forceful, their stern faces only just covering a welling sympathetic heart.

'I'm a Catholic myself,' whispered a baby-faced fellow, when his partner went out and left us alone for a well-staged moment of intimacy. 'And my parents are Irish too. I think the troops should get out.'

I lifted my eyes to scan his boyish looks.

'Do you have a guardian angel?' I asked, winding him up.

'Oh yes,' he said gravely.

'I clearly don't,' I replied.

My third batch of interrogators smashed into the room as though drunk. They snapped and growled around me like rabid Dobermans.

After a while two vast beefy women came in and stripped me. They made me bend over as they performed what they described as an intimate search. The men stood behind them and made remarks about my private parts. When the women finished whatever it was they were doing they ordered me to stand, and left me there naked. One of the men hissed out, 'If you don't talk we can get your family.' To my surprise the women stiffened. The men didn't realise they'd made a tactical mistake.

'Too late for that, isn't it?' I said calmly. 'I got them first.'

I remember best the smell. Oilcloth and gas. There were other things too which, if I think of them hard enough now, bring it all back. Dandelion and burdock, fizzing in a glass, with its brown foam and a tang of liquorice catching in

137

your nose before you sip; blackcurrant tarts from Sayers, with the indigo juice streaming down your chin if you weren't fast enough to catch it after the first bite; lino with a brown parquet pattern; the relentless cold, draughty even when sitting hunched up next to the kitchen fire (cosy, my parents called it); armchairs with bent wooden arms and rough lumpy cushions; tiger nuts and liquorice sticks; beige china hot-water bottles. Things I loathed. Things I loved. Things I was ashamed were part of me. All of them are Liverpool. And yet Liverpool was the place I never seemed to be allowed to belong to – except once when, Saint-Peter-like, I renounced it.

I don't know whether the memories help or if they make the whole thing even more painful. What's the point of thinking now? There isn't one. But what else do they leave me to do? The walls around me are magnolia. My least favourite decorative tranquilliser. You can see the bricks and mortar beneath, they saved on plastering. The floor is lino. No, not lino. Lino I know well, its smell, its texture, the way it cracks at the corners. This is the modern alternative – vinyl. The bed is small, hard and has a rough, grey blanket and a pillow. There is a low toilet in the corner, and ahead of me in the door is a large hole with a metal grille through which eyes peer from time to time. The grille sometimes goes back and a string of abuse is hissed through. Sometimes a gob of spit lands on the floor with the sound of a distant clap. And I am left alone all day with nothing to entertain me but my thoughts. And, quite frankly, I would rather put a stop to those now, if only it was possible.

Recite from memory:

'The Erne will be strong in flood, the hills be torn,
The ocean be all red waves, the sky all blood,
Every mountain valley and bog in Ireland will shake
One day, before she shall perish, my Roisin Dubh'

I did it. I did it all. Everything they accuse me of. More, if possible. They can put me down for as long as they like – I don't want freedom. I wish they'd bring back the rope and put me out of my misery. They'd do it soon enough if I was a pit-bull terrier and had bitten the hand that fed me. I wish my uncle was alive to talk sense into me. Or better, I wish I'd listened to him in the first place. Him and his Harry Stootle.

Crying is the one physical activity left to me. But old habits die hard. My instinct is to fight like hell the moment I feel the hot wellings in my throat, the tightening of the lips, the stabbing warnings in the eyes. However strong my urge to let the tears go, I have to work to overcome it. I think of things to dam them up until they burst so hard against my skull they can only spill out, like milk boiling up in a pan.

Better remember more of that Uncle Hughie stuff, how I never did understand, or care, who this Mr Stootle was that he was so keen for me to read, not until it was too late, and I stood there alone in the ruins of his tiny house, the furniture broken all around me, the little china that was left behind smashed on the floor, the bookshelves empty, pages littering the floor, blowing out of the door, the wooden bed torn down and great chunks of it lying singed in the fireplace.

The scene of the crime. Not the only crime by any means, but the crime through which I killed myself.

Switch memories. This is too dangerous.

Back. Back.

The *Jolly Roger* was a pirate ship in Liverpool. It sat on a lake in Sefton Park. Because my grandfather was a pirate, limping round Everton with a black eye-patch and a stump instead of a hand, it was easy to get me along to the William Brown Library to look up the pictures. I wish I had seen the ship for real, but the scratchy pictures looked very impressive to my child's eyes. Hitler got the ship before I was born. It sank, there in the lake, during the war. If it had survived I would have seen that it could never have housed my grandfather as it was only about ten foot tall. But the photographs gave me a thrill, and stirred some dark yearning deep down, lurking in my blood like a time bomb.

Because he could only provide me with other people's brown pictures of the pirate ship, my grandfather gave me practical evidence of a life on the ocean wave by taking me for rides on the ferry to New Brighton. In that magical fun-land on the Wirral he'd buy me sweets and comics, which I wasn't allowed at home. And orange squash. I drank deep quaffs of that illicit drink, enjoying the deceit and the complicity much more than the taste.

My mother told me not to listen to his blarney. The nearest he'd ever got to being a pirate was working as a steward on transatlantic liners. She never did explain to me how, if he was not what he claimed to be, he had managed to assemble everything necessary – the patch, the limp, the parrot. He had also lost one hand, but I felt sadly cheated because he did not have a hook. I was forever pestering him to get one; he'd just smile at me. I think now that if there was somewhere in Liverpool that he could have bought such a thing he would have done so, just to please me. Sometimes in cafés, if I went off to the lavatory I'd return to the table and find him sitting there with a fork taped on to the end of his arm, so that it emerged from the end of his sleeve where his hand should have been. He made no reference to it, simply sat and ate his dinner with it. And if I watched him, which I did, naturally, he would tell me it was rude to stare, and go on shovelling the food on to the fork and into his mouth.

Sometimes I'd go back with him to his small room in a rooming house in Everton, and he'd have his parrot recite poetry to me before taking me home to the gloomy house where I lived with my parents and my grandmother. He would never come inside the house, partly because my mother didn't like him, but mainly because my grandmother lived there. I didn't understand. He stood there outside on the pavement, and tears would well up and roll down his nose. I thought he cried because he didn't like saying goodbye to me. But of course it wasn't that at all. I represented a loss to him which was much more important.

I betrayed him too in the end. Would I, I wonder, have done so if I had known the truth?

I don't see why not. I seem to have injured everyone else in my life, whether I cared for them or not.

When they tell you life begins at forty don't believe a word of it. It's just that when you reach forty you suddenly realise you only live once. A youth misspent cannot be made better. There is no second chance. And as you understand this you also find yourself hurtling towards a certain death, losing your looks, losing your figure, losing your brain cells, and know that there's nothing to be done. Time does not ever give us a second chance.

> 'Far have we journeyed together, since days gone by.
> I've crossed over mountains with her, and sailed the sea.
> I have cleared the Erne, though in spate, at a single leap,
> And like music of strings, all about me, my Roisin Dubh.'

They tell me to start thinking of my defence. They won't listen when I say I don't want one. They can do with me as they please.

The key goes in the lock and the door opens. Two wardresses enter. They always come to me in pairs, like policemen up the Scotland Road on a Saturday night. The tray is plonked down in the middle of the floor.

'Lunch,' snaps the blonde one (whom I think of as the Colleen Bawn), and wipes her hands down the sides of her uniform as though the tray was covered in slime.

If they brought back the death sentence and it was like it always was in black and white films – 'Prisoner, you have less than a day to live. What do you want for your last breakfast?' – it would be one Sayers blackcurrant tart, and a glass of dandelion and burdock. I look down at a plate of slops. Left-overs fried up together, not unlike the suppers at convent.

'You think you're so clever, don't you? So superior.' She wrinkles up her nose and spits down into the tray. 'Scum!' She looks at her partner, 'the moustache', satisfied, for the moment anyway, and they leave me alone again.

God, the wardresses here make me laugh. They call me the usual names relating to murderers but when they run out of those they say 'you snooty bitch', and remark that I have no call to be looking down my nose at them. It feels more to me as if I look up at them through my eyebrows. 'Dumb insolence' they called it at school. The more sorry or guilty I felt the more insolent I seemed.

It's pride, really. I just didn't want them to see how miserable I was. The tears were there, but I could never, like my grandfather, let them spill, warm and salt, on to my face, not if anyone could see me, anyway.

My poor old grandfather, who was so scared of my mother and her prim ways. Though in all fairness it should have been the other way round. She should have been terrified of him. Who he was. What he knew.

Everyone said my mother was a saint. The way she looked after my grandmother all those years, fed her, washed her, put up with all the scenes. Now I see it was just a deal. She only did it in return for the thing she'd got from her. And from guilt too, I suppose.

Grandmother's room had a Prussian blue roller blind which rattled in the breeze. Maybe it should be called the draught, rather than the breeze, for breeze suggests a pleasant gust of air soughing through an open window.

142

The window was always shut. The blind was always drawn. The room was always dark, even though it was the nicest room in the house and looked out on to a tree (something of a rarity in that part of Liverpool). My grandmother wanted it kept like that, and no one dared to disobey her.

Through the panelled door, playing on the landing, I would sometimes hear her as she burst into song. She sang in a raucous way, weird and tuneless. Sometimes I'd hear her crash things across the room. Then my mother would run up the stairs with a dustpan and brush, slip in through the door, gently click it behind her so that I saw nothing, and take a torrent of verbal abuse.

Once when my father took her off to hospital for an X-ray (I rather hoped they'd keep her in and I could have her room) I sneaked into her room and gingerly inspected everything. It was very stuffy and the smell made me feel a bit sick. I pulled on the acorn-shaped piece of wood which dangled from the bottom of a length of string and the blind snapped up, sunlight spilling in for the first time in seven years. I knew it was seven years because she'd been in this room ever since I was born, and I was seven, almost.

It was all quite tidy. The dressing-table had a lace cloth laid out in front of the mirror. Resting on it were a beautiful silver hairbrush and comb. I ran the brush through my curly hair. Bored with this end of the room, I looked under the bed. A china chamber-pot, a big brown pottery hot-water bottle. Same as the view under my own bed. On the bedside table was a magazine. The cover showed a photo of Charlie Chaplin. Covering his eyes were two sea-shells. I had some sea-shells myself which I'd picked up one day in New Brighton with my pirate. I approved of hers, which were very white and even. I put them down and turned to the drawers. Boring, boring, only clothes. Same in the wardrobe. On top was an empty suitcase. On top of that a rather old-fashioned hat.

I heard the taxi pull up and dashed to pull the blind down and make my escape. The string had caught up and rolled round the blind. I climbed up on the stool at the dressing-table and fumbled with the string. The key turned in the front-door lock. I tugged and managed to make it click down on the third pull. I shoved the stool back into place and scampered out of the room, then took up a stance, dawdling innocently against the banisters and indifferently leaning over to watch my father as he carried the old woman up the stairs.

'It's too bright! You're not taking me to Blacklers are you? I hate shopping there. I prefer the Bon Marché.' She looked very angry. I was glad I was safely behind the wooden rail.

'No, Mammy, no worries. We're home now.' My father looked up at me. 'Get the door, would you, sweetheart?'

I dashed across the landing, pushed the door open and got myself quickly out of range.

'Thanks.' He strode past me. 'Run along downstairs, would you, and fill the kettle. I'll be down in a moment to put the gas on for you.'

When we'd made the tea and my father had poured out three cups, there was a knock at the front door.

'I'll get that. It'll be the rent man. You take up your grandmother's tea, there's a good girl.'

I gingerly picked up the cup, determined to engineer the entire operation without letting one drop spill into the saucer. I wanted to make an impression on her. I knocked, let myself in, and entered the room. She sat in bed, propped up with pillows. Her head lolled against the brass bedstead. Her eyes were closed. I thought she was dead. 'Grandmother?' I whispered hoarsely.

Suddenly she erupted in a violent fit of coughing. I jumped out of my skin and almost all of the tea was now in the saucer.

She looked down at me kindly. 'Oh, dote, there you are

144

now. I gave you a fright, did I not? It's the cough, you know, they're worried it's TB, but I can tell you now it's only a cough. Believe me. I know my own body.'

I handed her the cup and saucer. 'I'm sorry. I've spilled some.'

She looked down at the tea and laughed. 'Oh, dear me, yes, so you have. Ah well, no matter. You're only small after all. How old are you?'

'Seven', I said. 'Almost.'

'Ah,' she replied. 'And what is your name?'

I'd lived in the next room all my life, so I knew she knew my name, but to be polite, as it was true we hardly ever actually talked, and maybe she'd forgotten (my mother told me that she had forgotten things) I announced my name with pride. 'I'm Rosaleen,' I said.

She screwed up her face and looked at me intently. I held her gaze, and swallowed.

She seemed to grow before me, as though she was a balloon being blown up by someone hidden under the bed. 'You're not Rosaleen,' she shouted. 'I know who Rosaleen was. She was my daughter. And dead. Dead! You're not my daughter. You're not my Rosaleen. You're an impostor.'

'But — ' I stammered.

She shrieked and dropped the tea all over the covers. I could hear my father's feet striding up the stairs. I was rooted to the spot. My father's hands were firmly around my shoulders and he swept me from the room. 'That's all right, darling. You go down and drink your tea. She's a bit upset after the X-ray, that's all.' And he disappeared into the room and stayed there until the old woman was asleep.

'Clear the top, there, darling, would you?' My mother's hands are holding the tray. The room is gloomy. The only

145

light spills in from cracks at the sides of the dark blue blind. On the bedside table lie the magazine with Charlie Chaplin on the cover, and the two white shells.

I timidly emerge from the folds of wool and reach out for the shells. My grandmother is too busy eyeing the tray, the plate of fish and potatoes and peas, to notice me. Using both hands, I pick up the shells and step back. My mother moves towards the little table.

'No!' shrieks my grandmother. 'Cover his eyes! Cover his eyes! I can't stand him looking at me, accusing me of stealing the man from him. We would have been rich. We'd have all been American millionaires. Put them back, put them back!'

I stand paralysed, each shell-gripping hand raised before me.

'Put them down, Rosaleen, if that's what your grandmother wants.'

I can't move.

My grandmother frowns at me. 'She's an impostor,' she tells my mother in a matter-of-fact way. ' I don't know why you put up with her.'

My mother scoops an arm under the tray, and with her free hand unlocks my fists and replaces the shells. She then passes my grandmother the tray, and takes my hand. 'Give us a shout when you're finished,' she says.

We leave the room. My mother says nothing to me.

A few days later, when my father is at work (after leaving the navy he worked in a radio repair shop in the city centre), my mother leaves me in the kitchen playing with some Plasticine. 'I won't be long,' she says. 'I just have to run up to the shops. You sit quietly in here.' She puts a guard in front of the fire. 'And don't touch this.'

She goes out through the back door. I watch her pass through the yard and into the jigger. I give her a few minutes in case she has forgotten something and has to return. Then I go out into the hall and listen. All is silent. I creep up the stairs, carefully avoiding the one that creaks. I hover a while on the landing, holding my breath. I take the doorknob in my hands, twist it round and gently push open the door. I stand and face her, eye to eye.

Neither of us blink, or speak, or breathe for some moments. I lean forward and speak clearly at her, my hands on my hips. 'I'm Rosaleen,' I say. 'I'm Rosaleen.'

She holds the sheets up for protection.

I hold my thumb to my nose and bounce up and down. 'I'm Rosaleen! I'm Rosaleen!' I laugh. I stick my tongue out and wiggle it.

Before I can think, she has thrown back the sheets and leapt out of bed, and is lurching towards me with her bony hands. Terrified, I jump backwards and stumble out of the door. I trip on the landing carpet, a thin runner held down with dark metal clips, and land on my backside.

She is there in front of me, gripping the banister, wobbling on her shrunken legs. I scamper down the stairs, taking them in twos and threes and run forward to the front door. I reach up to the Yale lock. It is too high. I cannot reach it. I turn and freeze. She sits on the stairs, her hands flat out on the wooden edges, and comes down, step by step. Thump! as she hits the fourth step. Thump! as she hits the fifth. I jump for the latch. It is no use. I dash into the front room. I grab a small stool near the door and drag it to the front door. Thump, thump, thump! She is four steps from me as I clamber up on to the stool, grasp the lock and pull. Thump! The door will not open! Thump! The stool is in the way. Thump! I leap off and throw the stool down with a clatter. Thump! I tug at the door and race into the street and scream at the top of my voice.

The next-door neighbour, Mrs Braddock, and a woman from over the road ran out to me, put their arms round my shoulders and wiped away the tears I had not noticed.

147

'There, there dear! Come along, what's wrong?'

'Here, Doris!' shouted Mrs Braddock, from the front door. 'It's the old girl, she's fallen and hurt herself.'

Doris patted me on the shoulder. 'You did right, kid, getting us in. Poor old thing. She's not all there, is she?'

Together the women helped my grandmother back to bed. Mrs Braddock sat with me till my mother got back, and then told her how brave I'd been, saving my poor grandmother like that. I kept quiet.

There is a mosquito on the ceiling. It hangs there quivering above my head. How fabulous to have company. Maybe I should kill it and keep up my image.

I rise from the bed, stepping gingerly over the untouched tray. They have put out that I am on hunger strike. I am not. I was always a little fusspot. I will not eat anything with a dollop of phlegm for sauce.

I rap on the grille. I know from experience that this is a lengthy procedure. I wait and rap again. About five minutes later the grille slides back.

'Yes?'

'May I have something to read?'

I can see only her mouth, her curling lips crowned with a downy moustache, her nicotine-stained horse-like teeth. 'Like what? *Bombers' Weekly*?'

'One of the philosophers. Something Greek? Plato, Aristotle.'

She slams the grille back into place. I can hear her feet in those sensible lace-up shoes receding down the corridor. I throw myself back on the bed and stare up at the vibrating mosquito. If he, or she, stays here might I ever be able to classify this creature as a pet? But of course the mosquito will have the best of the bargain. For it will suck my blood and leave only a hot red burning patch in return. I never had a pet of my own. Even in the sphere of animals I lived vicariously.

'I swapped him for you,' said my grandfather, thrusting a wad of birdseed into the large shiny cage. 'He's my baby, aren't you Jake?'

'Did he go to school?' I asked.

'Old Jake? Lord no, darlin', he's a little natural, ain't you boy? He trained at the University of Life. He was a plane-spotter in the war. Did his duty on the streets of Bootle and even saved an old woman's life after an air raid.'

I screwed up my face. 'You make things up,' I said. 'He's just a bird.'

'He might be just a bird to you, sweetheart, but he's one of my oldest friends, and you've got to be loyal to your friends, you know.'

He had taken the bird from its cage and it sat on his lap, pecking seeds from his open hand.

'Why do you talk in a funny voice?' I asked.

'What's so funny about it? I don't see you laughing.'

'It's not like everybody else though, is it?'

'There, I beg to contradict you, lass. For no two people talk in the same voice.'

'But yours is all singy,' I cried.

'That's because I'm Irish,' said the Pirate. 'You are a Liverpudlian and Jake here is Polynesian and he speaks with quite a different accent.'

'Everyone's a Liverpudlian, though,' I said proudly.

'Everyone in Liverpool. You wait till you go to France, There's not many Liverpudlians there, or in Timbuktu either for that matter.'

The bird cocked his head and said very clearly 'Upon the Ocean Green'.

My grandfather clapped his hand on his knee, which

made the bird flap his wings. 'There now, I knew he'd get it. "Upon the Ocean Green",' he repeated, enunciating each syllable. 'I'm after teaching him a song so he can sing to me at night, when I lie alone here in the dark. And together we go back and are young again.'

'The priests are on the ocean green, They march along the deep,' squawked the parrot brightly, then closed his eyes and tucked his head under a wing.

'There now!' cried my grandfather. 'We've tired him out with our blether.' He lifted him carefully back on to his perch. 'How about a cup of tea, for Bos'n?'

I nodded enthusiastically. I loved to take tea with my grandfather for he would always amuse me.

He plonked a battered old hat on his head and made for the big black kettle. When he had brewed up he sat and solemnly poured out two cups. As I drank my tea he placed his saucer on the table and tipped some tea into it from the cup. He then raised the saucer to his lips. 'Oh, my,' he jumped back. 'Too hot for me.'

He put the saucer down and fanned it with his hat, while I giggled at him. He had another try at the saucer and sucked in the tea with a slurping noise. 'Aagh!' he sighed. 'That's better all round. Sure, your mouth is paved.'

Next time tea was served at home, I tried this trick and received a clip around the ear from my mother: 'You'll have to stop going round there if that's the way he's going to carry on, encouraging you to behave badly.'

Do children really need to be encouraged to 'behave badly'? Bad behaviour is so exhilarating that everyone should try it.

The mosquito has now moved and is hovering above the lavatory. It's warm in here at least. I wonder if the mosquito might like my lunch, or as my parents would have called it, my dinner.

Keys rattle in the steel door. I sit up.

'Still on hunger strike?' says the Colleen Bawn, glancing down at the untouched food. 'A lot of good that'll do you.' She picks up the tray. Behind her stands the large woman with the downy moustache and the long yellow teeth. 'Here's your book,' she says flatly, and she tosses a paperback on to my bed as though it is something filthy. 'I couldn't find any of your philistines or whatever it was. We don't have much call for foreign books. You can have what everyone else has.'

I look down at the cover. A Mills and Boon romance. She must have seen my face flicker with disappointment for she starts justifying the book. 'It's a good one, actually. Gripping, you know. Better for you than all that political stuff.'

I gather that she is attempting to be nice to me for some reason, so I try to be graceful in my acceptance of the book. 'Thank you,' I whisper.

'No need to be sarcastic,' she drawls. 'If you don't want it I can always take it back.'

'No, no,' I cry. 'I look forward to reading it.'

When they have gone and locked up after them I flick through the flimsy book, and read a few passages about panting girls and gruff dark men. I smile to myself. Old Harry Stootle would be turning in his grave. What use romance to still the mind? How could such a work help me come to terms with my tangled life? I drop the book on to the cool floor, take a few laps round the cell, then lie down upon the bed and close my eyes.

My father had a brother. He was a policeman and lived somewhere in the Pennines. No one talked about him much. I only remember meeting him once. I was about nine. He was in Liverpool on special guard because of a royal visit or a ship launch, drafted in to supplement the local force. He came to see his mother, my grandmother.

My father welcomed him in, and my mother, who had never met him, made tea.

I stayed with my mother and watched as my father and his brother did a lot of back-slapping and laughing in the hall. My uncle was in uniform, dark blue, the silver buttons glinting in the dark hallway. He wore a policeman's helmet with a little silver knob on the top.

I peered out of the kitchen as they climbed the stairs together, making noises of planes and bombs dropping. They went into my grandmother's room and I could hear nothing. 'Come on, daydreamer,' said my mother. 'Put these out on a plate, would you?'

She handed me a paper bag full of Eccles cakes, called flies' cemeteries by the children who played up our alley. We took all the tea things and laid them out on the sideboard in the front room, which was odd in itself. My mother called upstairs, then poured a cup, and laid out a plate for my grandmother.

'You wait there,' she said as she left the room, 'and don't touch the food till we're all here.'

My uncle came in and shook my hand. He'd taken off his helmet and hung it in the hall. 'You're little Rosaleen, then,' he said in a higher voice than the one he used for my parents.

'Yes,' I replied. 'Would you like some cakes or sandwiches? Only we can't eat them till my mother's back.'

'No, no. Let's wait.'

He laughed and sat down. My parents came in, served and sat on the sofa.

'You're a good lad, Al, most people would have put her in a home.'

My father tensed up. 'We couldn't do that. She does no harm.'

'I remember that hat though, don't you?' said my uncle.

'On and off,' laughed my father. 'Wasn't it always going into hock?'

'Oh, ay, that and the bloody radio. Do you remember that radio?'

'I should do,' my father said as he took a bite of sandwich. 'I took it to bits about once a week.'

They both laughed again.

'I don't actually think she ever wore the hat, did she?'

My uncle held his chin and squeezed up his face in thought. 'No, Al, I think you're right there. I'll have another of those Eccles cakes, please.' He dropped the flaky cake on to his plate. 'See much of the old man?' he asked.

My father tensed again. 'He takes the child out. He won't come round here. He doesn't want to upset her.'

'How's he doing?'

'Fine. Fine.'

My mother took the teapot round again, and the three of them talked about Liverpool: how this shop had gone, and that bomb site was still there, how the city centre had lost its heart. When it was time for my uncle to go we all crowded into the hall as he took his coat from the stand and put it on. He reached up for the helmet, hanging upside down by its strap and gasped, 'What the . . . ?'

As he pulled the helmet down we were all splashed, and the front of his uniform was drenched.

He raised the helmet to his face and sniffed. 'It's piss,' he said in a very high voice. 'It's bloody piss.'

'Oh, no.' My mother pushed past him and ran up the stairs.

'I thought you said she couldn't walk?'

My father was brushing down his brother's uniform with a large handkerchief.

'Bloody stupid cow,' said my uncle.

I decided I hated him.

*

Without thinking, I find myself getting off the bed and reaching under the bed for that Mills and Boon. Romance is bad for the soul. Of that I am certain. Maybe the sugar-sweet billings and cooings of the windswept maiden on the cover will give me an overdose and cure me, for the moment at least.

I spend a mindless hour reading about an idiot girl and her vile boyfriend before the door rattles open again.

'Dinner!' calls the Colleen, 'but only if your ladyship is in the mood of course.'

She puts down a tray a with a dollop of mashed potato and a sausage drenched in gummy gravy forming the centrepiece. There's also some bread and butter (or is it margarine?) and a mug of pinkish-grey tea.

Moustache points to the book, lying on my pillow next to the indentation left by my head. 'There, I knew you'd like that one. It's one of my favourites.'

Fat chance of anything like that happening to you, I thought, surveying the furry, wrinkled upper lip with its dark stubble. We're told that if we are captured we should try to think of our interrogators and our captors as primitive people doing a war dance; imagine them in a large floppy hat, or in animal sexual positions. The floppy hat idea is too upsetting, but the war dance and bestial sex between these two brings a giggle to my throat.

'Your solicitor will be here in the morning. The trial's very soon, you know. You don't have time for laughing now.'

They puzzle me, these lumbering, stupid women, knotting their eyebrows together to feign intelligence. Don't they realise I have my whole life for laughing now. What else is there to do here in this dismal cream room, unless it is to cry.

They lock up with a theatrical display of rattling keys, and leave me alone with the sausage. They've forgotten to spit this evening. I stir some gravy into the mess of potato, and raise a forkload of it to my mouth.

Not hungry, funnily enough. Just the smell makes my stomach turn. I put the tray down and walk round and round, my evening stroll.

The lights go dim. It's like being in a bar as cocktail hour begins. The bulb gives an odd, shaky sort of glow, not unlike candlelight.


Dusk. A cottage. Windswept. Warm. Cosy. I'm eight years old. Accompanying my father on a business trip. He is at his sales meeting at an electronics show in Belfast, and I am at his uncle's house waiting for him to collect me.

We watched the sun set through tiny windows.

'Turn on the light then,' I said, moving closer to the fire, which spilled an orange glow across the room.

My father's uncle rolled up a piece of paper, and after holding it to the flames, crossed the room and lit a pair of candles on the dresser.

'No, silly,' I chuckled, 'the real lights. Where's the switch?' I leapt towards the front door and fumbled with the hangings around it.

'This is the only switch I've got,' he said gravely, holding up the paper and blowing it out.

'But what about the electric switches? Or do you have gas? Is that a gasolier?' I pointed at a bracket screwed to the wall over the fireplace.

'No, silly,' said my great-uncle. 'That's just a hook for hanging things out to dry. Herbs, onions, you know. Sure, we've no need of such new-fangled notions up here.'

'No electricity, no lights!' I marvelled.

'Agh, we've lights enough now haven't we?'

The next day when my father brought me back to make my farewell I handed my great-uncle a present. 'It's almost electricity,' I said pompously. 'You just put batteries, which are electric things, inside, and look . . .' I pressed the on-switch and a beam of white light spilled out of the long shiny silver torch. 'Very useful,' I added, 'and modern. This is the twentieth century,' I said. 'You have to join in.'

My great-uncle turned it on and off a few times, and then shone it in my face. 'Got you!' he exclaimed, and gave me a peck on the cheek.

'You have to change the batteries when they run out. It's quite simple,' I explained.

'Come along, now, we'll be late.' My father grabbed my gesticulating hand, and dragged me towards the door.

'They're easy to find. You just ask at the shop.'

My great-uncle stood smiling and nodding his head.

'You'll do that, won't you now?'

He just laughed.

Every birthday since I was born, this man whom I hardly knew sent me a ten-shilling note. I put them in a post office savings account. After giving him the torch I used his birthday money to send him batteries. I kept this up, even when I was away at school. I hated to think of him sitting there all alone in the dark.

I was sent off to boarding-school at eleven because I won a scholarship. I climbed on to the train at Lime Street and was placed care of the guard. Although my throat ached and my tongue pressed hard to the roof of my mouth, I could not let those tears out. My mother stood on the steamy platform wiping her face with a huge handkerchief of my father's. The more she cried, the more impossible it was for me to join in.

I sat reading a book for the long journey to London. The guard would pop his head into the carriage from time to time and say cheerily, 'Why, you're a little bookworm, aren't you?' And I would nod back, then look down again at the blur of letters swimming through the film across my eyes.

I was met at Euston, a black filthy station with pillars, by a Universal Aunt who took me across London on a tube train to Waterloo where I was left with a small shivering group of girls dressed in the same red and green uniform. A nun asked me for my name and ticked me off her list. Other girls were accompanied by fathers in long soft coats, and mothers in furs and hats. They all spoke like cats. I loved the radio and knew a BBC voice, but this was something else. It was hard to understand the words they squeezed out of their orange-lipsticked lips. And their daughters replied in incomprehensible little snaps of sentences: 'Take care of Tigger for me. And keep the tack in order'; 'Remember to send me some tuck'; 'Send on my lax stick, it's frightful using spares.'

Other girls squealed with delight as they recognised each other. I stood alone outside the circle. The nun shook my shoulder. 'New girl, are you all right?'

'Yeah,' I nodded.

The station announcer told us on crackly speakers that the train was on platform thirteen, and we all shuffled towards it, the smoke puffing out before us weighed down by the sharp autumn air.

On the train I stared out of the window. Because it was dark I could only see the reflections of the other girls sitting beside me, fuzzy through the condensation.

The school itself smelt of polish and candles. Garishly painted statues with night lights at their feet stood along each corridor. I shared a dormitory with seven others. It was called Saint Theresa of Lisieux, 'the little flower'. Across the corridor was Saint Maria Goretti, who we were later taught was a child rape victim. At the far end of the school lay my name-saint's room, the most impressive of them all, Rose of Lima, a South American woman who spent her whole life thinking up bizarre punishments for herself, and offering up her pain to the Lord.

I undressed in silence, picking up (by observing the

157

others) that you had to undress and put on your pyjamas under your dressing-gown.

After lights out I lay in bed in the dark, watching shadows moving in the hall outside the open door. Some time later a nun glided into the room. After she pulled a curtain round the end bed I could hear the rustling of her clothes as she undressed, and the creak of the springs as she got into bed. Her breathing changed, and she started to snore. Only then did I let out the tears that had boiled behind my eyes since breakfast time.

'Marmalade, please,' squeaked a girl at my side.

I reached out and handed her the bowl.

'Could you pass me a knife,' I said in return, pleased to have an excuse to make contact.

'I'm sorry?' The girl turned and looked over the top of her glasses at me.

'I asked if you would pass me a knife.'

The girl glanced briskly around the table, her lips tightly holding back a smile. 'Would you just say that again.'

Sorry that the girl not only wore glasses but was hard of hearing, I spoke loud and clear: 'I just asked if you would pass me a knife.'

The whole table seemed to be holding their napkins up to their faces, their cheeks bulging out and their eyes sparkling. Then they all busily found things to do, frantically spreading butter and giggling as they stirred sugar into their cups of tea.

Coming back into the dormitory after breakfast to make our beds I found a confab, which broke up as soon as I entered the room. A girl with red curls stepped forward, holding out her hand for me to shake.

'Hello, you're the new girl Rosaleen. I am Cynthia. I'm your form captain.'

158

'Hello,' I replied.

'I've just made out the term's tidying rota. Would you read it aloud, please, so that everyone can be sure who's doing what for today.'

I took the list and read clearly. 'Monday: Clare – Dormitory; Sarah – Bathrooms; Vanessa – Changing room; Daphne – Classroom.' The whole room seemed to be quivering with delight. I could see their elbows digging into one another, feet pressing down on each other's shoes. I handed the list back to the form captain.

'Thank you,' she said. 'Now you'd better get a move on and make your bed before Sister Van Den Berg comes in.'

There was a desperation in the way the others were tugging up their sheets and plumping their pillows. One wiry girl in plaits ran out into the corridor as a bunch from another dormitory strolled past on their way down to class. Although she whispered, the excitement of her voice carried her words to me as clearly as though she had spat them right in my ear, and they vibrate in my mind to this day, shining as brightly now as when I heard them that morning, penetrating my ear as sharp as an arrowhead.

'Get the new girl to talk. It's hilarious! She's *common*! She says *bath*!'

Short A, you understand.

I knew I'd gone red, so bent down and pretended to get something that was bothering me, a piece of grit, a splinter, out of my sock.

The first lesson was Grammar. When the teacher asked me to give a list of nouns I rose and, gripping the desk lid so hard that my knuckles burst from my hand like snow-capped mountains, spoke loud and clear, keeping every A short: 'Bath, path, class, brass, plaster, outcast, nastiness, blast.' I sat down.

The teacher, a middle-aged woman who came in from a nearby town to teach English and history, frowned at me.

'You're new aren't you?'

I nodded.

'Are you trying to be clever?'

I looked her in the eye. 'I believe I am clever, or I would not be here.'

The girls around me rustled in their chairs.

'Was that a swear word I heard?'

'Which word do you mean, "outcast"?'

'No,' she replied. 'The last word.'

I smiled, delighted to be so easily misunderstood. 'Blast, you mean. It's what happens when you let off a bomb. I'm sorry if my northern accent has distorted your understanding of my use of English.'

Flustered, she moved her attention swiftly elsewhere, and did not address me again for many weeks.

For the next month I spoke only when spoken to. I listened hard to the other girls, and never, while I was at school anyway, said 'bath' (or any of those other words) with a short A again.

I think of the East Lancs Road. I was fourteen, riding my bicycle with the parish priest Father Songster alongside me. He was young and handsome and English and did a party piece of singing songs from the shows – Ivor Novello, Noël Coward and the like. He wore a suit and a dog-collar, no long skirts for him.

'She's looking very pale,' he said to my mother, on one of his dreaded visits to the house to bring communion for my bedridden grandmother. 'I'll take her out.'

My mother beamed, and I got the bike out.

'Hold on,' he called and pulled in at a lay-by. He turned his collar round and pulled a silk cravat from his pocket, which he put on, and suddenly he wasn't a priest any more. 'Let's walk for a bit, shall we?' he said.

Well, I'd been brought up to do as I was told where priests were concerned.

He walked me to a bomb site, now grassed over, with tall weeds growing as thick as a hedge.

'Hot, isn't it?' he exclaimed as he sat and pulled off his jacket and rolled up his sleeves. He patted the ground beside him and I dutifully sat. Before I had time to straighten my skirt he'd rolled on top of me and was pressing his tongue into my mouth. My eyes boggled, scouring his face for some explanation. His eyes were closed and one hand was fumbling with my blouse, the other searching up the inside of my skirt. I managed to do something with my legs that made him flinch, then I scrambled to my feet, dashed for the bike and pedalled home like a maniac. I swear I could have won the Milk Race that afternoon.

The next time he was due I made sure to wear protective clothing – jodhpurs and wellingtons. My mother gave me a strange look, and I knew it would be useless to put on a mac as well; after all, it was August. Father Songster arrived with the ciborium and his incense-swinging choirboy, went upstairs to the darkened room and gave Grandmother communion, while my mother knelt on the floor and prayed. While the choirboy packed the holy equipment into a small case, my mother whispered, 'See Father Songster out, would you, Rosaleen,' and I took the dreaded journey down the stairs. I reached up for the latch on the front door as he slipped his hand under my arm and cupped my small bosom. I jammed my hand down and thrust it into my jodhpur pocket. He slipped his hand in there with mine. There was something crinkly with it. A piece of paper.

As the choirboy reached the landing he whipped his hand out and pulled the door open.

'Come along, Stephen. See you next week, Rosaleen. You are a good child.'

When I got into bed that night I pulled out the note and read it.

'I am lying in the presbytery, totally naked, thinking of you. Father Songster. XXX.'

Horrified, I shoved it in the toe of my wellington, jumped into bed, and prayed to be pure in mind and body.

The following week the note read: 'I love you, you temptress. FS', and another: 'To think of you makes me hard.' The exact meanings weren't always utterly clear to me. I thought of hard then as being something rather good in a man, like Charles Atlas, all glistening and ripply and brown. But I had a feeling even that wasn't quite right for a priest.

When I went back to school I hid the notes under the piece of wood at the bottom of my bicycle's front basket.

Unfortunately, unknown to me, Alma, a girl who lived next door and was probably my best friend, found them and gave them to her brother.

One evening at half-term she called for me to go to the pictures. As usual we took the short-cut through the cemetery, past all the Chinese graves. From behind a monument four boys appeared and blocked our way. They wore paper bags over their heads, with eye-holes torn out, and stood on the path, their arms folded, like a paupers' fancy-dress interpretation of the Ku-Klux-Klan. To my surprise, Alma thrust me towards them.

'Go on, hussy, defend your shame,' she said.

I turned and laughed at her. It was obviously a game that I didn't know yet.

The tallest boy stepped forward, lifted his arms and said, 'You Mary Magdalene!'

I was very puzzled at this appellation, and could think of no suitable response.

'The silence of shame!' he continued. I recognised the voice: it was Alma's sixteen-year-old brother. 'The silence of guilt.'

162

'I'm sorry,' I giggled. 'What exactly am I supposed to do?'

'Confess,' said another lurking boy. Then the other two spoke together, like the congregation at mass.

'Confess!'

They surrounded me now.

'You've been trying to tempt the priest with your Mary Magdalene ways.' Alma's brother reached into his pocket, pulled out Father Songster's notes and threw them on to the pebbled ground.

'Read, harlot, and repent.'

I stooped to check that they were the filthy letters, and hastily explained. 'Oh, no, that was nothing to do with me. I didn't do anything. I think it's all disgusting, that stuff. Especially from a priest.'

One of the boys was now behind me and he pulled at my hair. 'It's always the woman who tempts the man.'

I realise now that I spent longer being tormented that night because I had nothing to confess. I could have made things a lot easier for myself if I had just made something up. Anyhow, I did not manage to get to a film, but instead spent a few hours in Anfield cemetery having my hair pulled and being spat on, though the boys found this difficult with paper bags on their heads.

When I sneaked in, in the dark, having spent half an hour up the jigger tidying myself up, my mother asked what the film was about. I said: 'the war'. With films of the early 1960s this subject never needed further explanation, and in the unlikely event that you were pressed you could chose either black and white or colour, which explained the whole film, for in black and white there was usually someone with a missing limb and the English won. In colour everyone had a very impressive set of teeth and the Yanks won.

I had already privately given up being a Catholic at the time of this encounter with the third degree, though in moments of desperation I still prayed, I just couldn't get

163

out of the habit. For the sake of peace and quiet I also trudged off each Sunday to mass and took communion and went to confession where I said the same every week: 'I have told lies, I have been disobedient.' Although I think only the second of those was true.

The reasons for my new-found agnosticism were all-embracing. My horror at the sexual advances of the priest started the doubt and the tin lid was put on it one day at school when I received a tear-stained letter from my grandfather, in his wobbly handwriting, telling me that Jake, his parrot, had died. I was very upset, not only for myself, but because my pirate had lost his pal. The nun who sat at the lunch table, where letters were dished out alongside pudding, asked if I had had bad news. I said, 'Yes, Mother. My grandfather's parrot has died.'

She laughed and said, 'Oh, that's nothing. I thought it was something that mattered.'

Thinking that she was tackling the subject from the theological perspective, and trying to cheer me by reminding me of the afterlife, I lifted my chin and said 'Yes Mother. No need to be upset. After all, I'll see him again in Heaven.' Her face clouded over and she replied in a mat-ter-of-fact way. 'Oh, no you won't. Animals don't have souls. They don't go to Heaven.'

I lay in my bed that night, thunderstruck. What on earth was the point of a Heaven with no animals, only beastly humans, and worse, hundreds of thousands of nuns? I don't need their Heaven, I decided. I want to be with my friends, and they're all likely to be in hell.

Lying here in this bleak room I know that on Judgment Day, if anything happens at all, I will certainly go down, not up.

How I wish that, if I am to be alone, it could be in the dark.

I curl up under the grey, coarse blanket and sleep. My dream is as usual a nightmare rush of confused images: crumbling stone, a house in ruins, myself hurtling down a steep, rocky hill in a battered car with no brakes, a baby crying, an old man holding out two hands wrapped in paper. 'Mutt and Jeff!' he shouts at me. 'Mutt and Jeff!' Blood soaking into the dust.

I wake, as I do each morning, with my hair stuck to my face, sweat running in cool dribbles down my neck and the small of my back.

When I came home from school for the Easter holidays I visited the Pirate. His room seemed bare without Jake. The cage was gone, and nothing was in its place.

'It's quiet without him, isn't it?'

He looked at me, and, although he smiled, I could see the sadness shining in his one eye.

'No, no, darlin', I've got two little birdies who come in whenever I want them.'

His hand was splayed out on his knee. He rolled it into a fist, and then held it up to me. Two fingernails were covered in white paper caps. 'Mutt and Jeff,' he said. 'There they are.' He waved his fingers about, then shut his hand into a fist again.

'There you go!' he said, flicking his hand towards the open window. He spread his fingers again and the white caps were gone. 'They like the sunlight.'

I inspected his hand. It was empty. 'How do you do that?' I asked.

As I spoke, he flicked his hands again, and they reappeared. 'That's better', he said, to his fingers. 'It's only polite to stay long enough to be introduced to my bos'n. Mutt – ' he wiggled one white-tipped finger. 'Jeff – ' he shook another. 'Be pleased to meet the honourable partner

165

of my travels upon the briny.' Both fingers bent down, coyly into his palm, then flickered and, as his eyes darted towards the window, the paper was gone.

'Ah well,' he said. 'Nothing lasts for ever. Cup of tea?' He was up and limping over to the kettle.

I get up and go to the door. All seems still, although it must be morning as the lights are back at full strength. I rap on the grille.

'Anyone there?'

Silence.

'Hello! Good morning, Buenas días, Buon giorno, Bonjour.' I kick the door a few times, but it is so thick it makes little noise, so I resort to further tapping on the grille. Suddenly it slides open and I am eye to eye with a wardress. I don't recognise the eyes. These are bulbous bug-eyes, with red lashes and tiny pupils. From the eyes you'd think she was on something. Cocaine, heroin.

'What d'you want?'

'A cup of tea, please,' I say. 'And toast.'

'What d'you think this is, the bleedin' Savoy?'

She slams the grille shut.

I poke around at last night's tray, but cannot face the cold mug of tea with its white skin, or the brown gelatinous mess on the plate.

I briskly wash and clean my teeth.

The door rattles open and two new wardresses appear, Bug-eyes and friend.

Bug-eyes is tall and thin, and looks as though she'd be more at home in a Noël Coward play than in a uniform. Her partner squints out from the fringe of a clumsy Mary Quant bob in brown and grey.

'There's your tea,' says Bug-eyes. 'Grab the tray, Miss Hart. While she's got her hands full.'

166

Miss Hart, the Bob, dives down and with a balletic wobble swoops up the tray to her flat chest.

'Well done, Miss Hart.'

The strange couple walk backwards, keeping their eyes fixed on me. If I didn't know better I'd swear I was on *Candid Camera*.

'You don't have to be a bomber to be Irish, you know,' murmurs the Bob, who, to my surprise, has a mid-Irish accent, Mullingar or thereabouts.

'I'm not Irish,' I claim, and hesitate. 'Well, only half anyway.'

'Your solicitor will be here shortly, I'm told,' sneers Bug-eyes. 'Much good may it do you.'

'Bitch!' hisses the Bob.

I take a step towards them, just to see what will happen. They both take a step back.

'Come on, Mrs Lancaster, let's leave the bomber to her conscience,' says the Bob in her singy Irish voice.

'If she's got one,' snarls Bug-eyes.

They back out of the door and lock it behind them. I stand, amazed, and drink the hot, tasteless tea.


'All Irish girls line up beside the lockers.'

A shuffle of girls make their way across the cloakroom, and nuns walk up the row, smiling and pinning on each shoulder a large floppy bunch of shamrock.

Mother Flynn does a count.

'Right. Any half-Irish girls here? We need one to make up the team.'

I know both my parents are English, so I can only qualify as a quadroon-Irish. I am jealous. The Saint Patrick's feast day is a grand occasion here at school. No lessons. A raucous hockey match and a grand lunch with soda bread and onions chopped into the mashed potato. This dish

167

they call 'champ'. It is delicious. In the evening various girls, some of the nuns, and even an outside teacher or two, put on a concert of Irish songs and recitations. Some of these are quite funny: 'Paddy McGinty's Goat' about the tribulations of the owner of a naughty goat; some sad: 'The Mountains of Mourne,' about a poor man who comes to London and whose innocence is abused. A pretty senior with long blonde hair recites a poem. Girls turn and nod at me during this one, as it is about a girl with my name.

> 'Tis you shall reign, and reign alone,
>   My Dark Rosaleen.'

I find the whole thing very embarrassing. I do not like being looked at. Heads turn among the audience in front of me, girls in my own row lean forward, waggle their heads and leer.

> 'Over dews, over sands
>   Will I fly, for your weal:
> Your holy delicate white hands
>   Shall girdle me with steel.'

A wit, sitting next to me, picks up my hand and waves it along the row. Utterly humiliated, I snatch it back.

> 'At home, in your emerald bowers,
> From morning's dawn till e'en,
> You'll pray for me, my flower of flowers,
> My Dark Rosaleen!'

Several rows of girls around me are by now convulsed with laughter.

> 'You'll think of me through daylight hours,
> My virgin flower, my flower of flowers,
>   My Dark Rosaleen!'

Anne, the girl beside me, is laughing so hard her seat is shaking mine. Another girl in front of me has had to lower her head to hide the tears rolling down her cheeks in delight. Anne wiggles harder, and squeaks. 'Oh God,' she hisses under her breath, 'I think I'm going to wet myself.' On stage the blonde senior drones on.

> *'The Judgment Hour must first be nigh,*
> *Ere you can fade, ere you can die,*
> *My Dark Rosaleen!'*

'Oh God, oh God!' wiggles Anne. 'I am going to wet myself, I am.'

A burst of applause drowns her anguish.

'Oh, no,' she twists herself frantically, 'I *am* wetting myself. I am.'

As the applause dies down there is a clattering sound from the chair next to mine, as the urine hits the wooden gym floor. Now I am the one laughing. I shiver and shake and finally explode with a howl. Mother Flynn, my form mistress, stands at the end of our row. She points her finger at me. 'You! Rosaleen! Out.' She jerks her thumb towards the gym door. I shuffle past all the girls and out.

'Just because you can't be part of our celebration is no cause to wreck it. You are determined to be a troublemaker and have just made a spectacle of yourself. You tried wilfully to ruin a girl's performance. I have no alternative but to put you into detention for the weekend. You are also gated for the rest of term.'

Detention was no punishment to me. It gave me the peace and quiet I yearned for, and as for being gated this was a meaningless punishment unless your parents wanted to come and take you out on a Sunday. Mine, thankfully, lived too far away, and could not afford the train fare.

To my surprise, when I came out of my detention I had

become a hero. And from that day I was a popular girl. People said I was 'a hoot' and 'a brick'.

I was fearless. If there was a dare, I would do it. I was transformed. No longer the cringing child I was at seven, clinging to my mother's skirts as she took lunch into my grandmother. Though I suspect the bad seeds were already sown, even then.

I came to the conclusion that a 'troublemaker' was a good thing to be. It allows you to breathe right to the bottom of your lungs. It's trying to join in that is the stifler, the thing which brings out the worst in everybody.

Once I had managed to shuffle off the ignominy of being 'common' I joined the civilised club and became nothing more than a barbarian.

My mother had shown me 'common' people round Scotland Road. I thought then that they had an accent, and that I did not. I now realise that everyone has an accent, but that it actually counts for nothing in the study of their souls.

The door is thrown open. Four wardresses rush in and pull me up from the bed. Two hold my arms, the others propel me from behind. I am thrust into the corridor. Women scream obscenities at me through their grilles. At the end of the walkway a prisoner on her hands and knees with a bucket and scrubbing brush leaps to her feet and applies the brush to my face.

We walk on. Doors are unlocked before me, and locked behind me. The air is shrill with the screaming of my fellow inmates.

I am brought to an interview room to see the solicitor. There is a mirror on the wall, and before I sit I notice that I still have the remnants of a black eye and a swollen lip. Half of my face is tinged yellow.

'Oh dear,' I say to him. 'Must have walked into one of those kitchen cupboards again.'

He looks across the table at me. 'You have kitchen cupboards in your cell?'

So, they have not got me a solicitor with an enormous IQ! This fellow is nowhere near the class of my husband. I doubt he could get you off even if you were Mary Poppins and accused of an axe murder. This pleases me.

'I did it. I did everything. I killed them all. I made the bombs. I delivered them sometimes. I am a terrorist bomber, a murderer — '

'Really, please stop,' he says in an ineffectual little voice. 'This will get you nowhere. I should explain, I have been allocated this job, because by law you must have representation. I am not sympathetic to your cause, or your actions. I am only here because I am paid to give you a fighting chance to defend yourself.'

'I don't want to defend myself.'

He shuffles his papers. 'Well, it's not quite as simple as that, I'm afraid. Your, erm, partner, is putting up quite a fight over in Brixton.'

'That's up to him, isn't it.'

'Really, you must be serious.' He fiddles with his ballpoint pen. 'Now, you have me for two hours today. I suggest you tell me what happened.'

'I can't talk about what happened, I'm afraid. I can't bear to think about it even.'

The wardress hunched up against the wall, the Bob, yawns loudly and raises her hand to her mouth. The little man bristles.

'Do you mind, Miss, I am having a serious meeting with my client.' The Bob shrugs and lets out a weary sigh. 'If you want me to get you put on report I shall do so Miss – ' he waits for her name. The Bob straightens up in a half-hearted way. My solicitor turns to me as he speaks. 'Thank you.'

He pulls out a clean sheet of yellow paper. 'Now, if we're not going to discuss the incident, maybe you can tell me some other things about yourself. Where were you born, and when?' He coaxes my life from me. He may be a mousy little man, not a flamboyant lawyer in the manner of my husband, but that helps, and I am grateful to have someone to talk to. I have been alone in my cell for weeks now awaiting this trial. 'I am cruel and cold and without a heart,' I say. 'I deserve to die for the things I have done.'

My mind flies back to sports day 1962. I have gently persuaded my parents not to come down. They have suggested that it was about time they put in an appearance, to keep the side up.

By now I am an accepted member of the school. The other girls have all forgotten I once said bath with a short A. While no one can see my home, for all they know I live in a detached house, surrounded by rolling lawns with a stable full of ponies. My absent parents could still be a cat-voiced woman with orange lipstick in a mink coat, and a tall man with a grey moustache in a pin-striped suit and bowler hat, or a long camel cashmere coat.

I wrote back a chummy letter telling them how hardly any parents ever turned up for sports day, how it would be a waste of money, how the trains home would be so difficult, how I longed to see them, but why waste such precious moments on a silly sports day. I got a letter in return agreeing with all my 'sensible' points, and enclosing a pound note, with which I was to treat myself.

The morning came, and the school buzzed with activities. The ground-floor classrooms were cleared for art and crafts exhibitions. The gym was filled with tables, and I volunteered to lay these with tea things. Other girls set up floral displays and polished floors and windows. Outside, the smell of newly mown grass mingled with the sounds of a mobile loudspeaker system blaring out Sousa marches and a man going 'One two, one two'. Crocodiles of girls carried the classroom chairs down to the sports field and arranged them in neat rows. Lunch was early, and the excited noise in the refectory sounded like an aviary when a fox has got inside.

Through the open french windows we could hear the Sousa come on, and the gravel drive rustle with the sound of tyres drawing up, footsteps crunching along the path towards the field.

A bell was rung and we rose and said grace. The sporty people filed out to the changing rooms for pep talks and whatever else they got from the games mistresses. I joined the crush of mere observers in the senior cloakroom. A pair of nuns was streaming us into rows, by form, and starting with the junior school we started filing down to the pitch. I ended up at the end of my form's line, sitting in the middle of a row, towards the back. All around me girls were subtly waving at parents who sat on the other side of the pitch. I threw back my head and let my face soak up the sunshine. Next to one goalpost was a small rostrum covered in bunting, where the Mother Superior sat with some of the governors. Four of them gave short speeches. The parents and school laughed politely at their feeble puns, and at the end clapped.

At the far end of the pitch a handful of girls were limbering up and falling into start positions. When the bang of the starting pistol ricocheted through the woods behind us they dashed off and ran round and round till one of them won. The same sort of thing went on again and again while I drifted into a daydream.

I started to inspect the glum-looking parents. They looked a tight-spirited crew. I was shaken from my reverie by a thump in the ribs from the elbow of my form-mate, Susan.

'Look!' she whispered without moving her lips. 'Look!' I searched the pitch. Nothing remarkable. Then I heard the senior to my right hiss to her left. 'Oh, my Lord, look, it's a tramp! Here! At sports day!'

This would be fun, I thought, as I scanned the area they both seemed to be looking at.

Sitting, grinning at me, the elastic from his black eye-patch pressing a ridge into his long curly white hair, his earring glinting in the afternoon sun, was my grandfather. I looked down into my lap. I appeared to be winded, and took deep breaths to keep my equilibrium.

'Oh, my, Rosaleen, look! He's waving at *you*!'

I glanced up. He held his good hand up: two fingers were capped with patches of white paper. He wiggled them and the paper disappeared.

My cheeks burned, and I could not swallow. I tried to shake my head at him, to stop him making such an exhibition of himself. After a minute or two he gave me a wink and pulled a face to indicate that he understood. The girls around me suddenly clapped. I jumped. Another race had come to an end. I joined my hands and feebly tried to make them create a sound, then gave up and flopped them back on to my lap. After this I kept my eyes resolutely on the races, and watched each winner go up to the rostrum and pick up her prize. I did not look across to that section of the crowd again.

When the last race is run and the prizes all awarded the two groups either side of the pitch are allowed to mingle. Girls rushed forwards and hugged mothers, fathers, brothers, sisters. A group of prefects and volunteers, mainly foreign girls whose parents were not going to leave their embassies in Bangkok or Moscow to watch a gaggle of large-thighed adolescents running round in circles, filed up the hill back to the main school building. I rushed to join them. I met eyes with my grandfather as he stumbled across the field, trying to run despite his bad foot; he was waving his hand frantically. He thought I had not seen him. I hurried along, so that there was no hope of his catching up with me.

Once in the safety of the school I dashed to the gym and offered my services as an extra waitress. The nun in charge was astonished, but handed me an apron and told me to serve tables in the quarter of the room by the doors to the hall.

I stooped around with trays of tea and cakes (baked the day before by the domestic science class), grinning hideously at the patronising parents and their daughters.

When I looked up to sweep a strand of hair from my eyes, I saw him again. Now he was standing in the corner of the gym, talking to a nun who was pointing across at me. He smiled at her and shook her hand. This made her laugh. He limped across the gym, stooping obsequiously to parents, who stared at him.

He pulled up a chair at a table for four, occupied only by a mother and her daughter. 'Do you mind?' he asked with a small bow. Doubtfully, they shook their heads. The nun in charge tapped me on the shoulder and pointed at his table.

I walked slowly towards him.

'Hello there, gal! Sure that old nun by the door's a cracker. She's an Irishwoman, like meself.'

My face did not crack. 'Can I help you, sir? Tea and cakes?'

'That's right, Bos'n, and make it snappy, eh?'

I shot him a cold look. 'Certainly, sir.'

He pulled me down by the sleeve. 'Don't worry, I get it. You've to pretend to be a real waitress. I'll play along, if you wish.'

I walked away without comment, fetched the tea and cakes and laid them before him, without a smile. Removing my apron, I went to the nun in charge and got permission to be excused as I had a headache. I walked through the swing doors to the hall, ran up the back stairs and into my dormitory, where I washed my face, and then sat on my bed, relieved that I had not been found out.

After half an hour I heard the crunch of tyres on the drive outside my window. I sat on the radiator and watched girls kissing their mothers goodbye and cars speeding down the drive and away. Many girls stood across the way, leaning on the fence and waving till the cars vanished out of the main gates.

Then I saw him again. He was weaving in and out of groups of girls in the drive, who parted as he approached. I saw the moment when he gave up looking for me. He held his head down, and brought his hand up to wipe his cheek. I could have thrown open the window and called down to him. I did not. He limped away along the the drive, occasionally looking back, until a car stopped and somebody leaned out of the window. They obviously offered him a lift to the station, for he tipped his hat with two fingers, and when he had climbed into the back door and pulled it shut behind him, the car whooshed down the drive and away.

I never saw him again.

A week later, my mother, not having heard from him since he had made the trip down to my school in the south, went to visit him at his Everton flat. She found him sitting in a pool of urine, unable to move. He had had a stroke, the doctors said, probably a few days before, on the Sunday morning. He was taken to hospital, but died later that night. When the nuns told me a year later that I was possessed by the Devil, I am sure they were right. But is it fair to blame the Devil for my own ignorance and cruelty?

*I killed him* as surely as though I had put strychnine in his tea, or stabbed him through the heart with a kitchen knife.

I was allowed home for the funeral.

176

We gathered in the bleak cemetery at Ford, on the outskirts of the city. It was warm but cloudy.

The family was all there: my parents, my uncle, my great-uncle, my grandmother – the dead man's widow. She had chosen to wear the large hat I had seen on top of her wardrobe. No one could persuade her that it was not the right occasion for such an Eastery piece of apparel.

I did not cry, but I burned inside with horror at what I had done to my friend, the Pirate.

'Salve Regina, mater misericordiae; vita, dulcedo, et spes nostra, salve. . .'

The priest droned on and we all gazed grimly at the coffin as they lowered it into the crumbling hole in the ground.

'Ad te clamamus, exules filii Hevae, ad te suspiramus, gemente et flentes in hac lacrymarum valle . . .'

Sighing and mourning in this vale of tears, I thought, my mind now automatically translating the Latin as he spoke. We all stooped and took a handful of earth then stepped forward and dropped it into the grave: my father, my mother, me, my uncle and my great-uncle. My grandmother hesitated. We looked at her, frightened there would be one of her scenes.

She dropped the soil, and it trickled into a pile at her feet. Hurriedly she fumbled inside her cardigan, thrusting her hand right down into her dress. My father stepped forward. My great-uncle held him still. My grandmother produced a large twig, singed at one end, from her breast. She held it up, as Lady Macbeth might have wielded her dagger, then fell to her knees and dropped it gently into the grave.

Again my father and his brother made to hold her back, but were again restrained by my great-uncle. 'Let her say goodbye in her own way, boys,' he said quietly. She was whispering softly to the soil-strewn box. I doubt that any-one but me heard her words.

'Acushla, you ould divil!' she cried softly. 'Keep this to remember me by. Forgive me, my darling. Wait for me. I will come to you. And you were right. The hat is a marvel, is it not?'

When she stood up she shook, and her face was shining with tears but, to me at least, she seemed to glow with strength. Her sons took her arms and supported her as she took a step back.

She laughed during the rest of the service, and as we walked towards the cars which were to take us back home, my uncle pulled a face and screwed his finger into his temple. My great-uncle turned sharply to him: 'Mind your manners, boy. This is a lady.' He moved forward, took her arm and led her to the car, as though she was a duchess. He looked haggard. I don't know whether it was the awfulness of burying his brother, but I suspect it had more to do with seeing *her* again.

Afterwards my parents discussed how the strain of the funeral had finally proved too much for her, that she had finally 'gone', and was now as 'mad as a hatter' (which, as she had worn that gay floral hat to the churchyard, seemed to afford them much mirth).

But, for a split-second, as she rose from the grave, I had caught her glance. Struggling wildly with the turmoil in my own conscience, as our eyes met in warm recognition I knew that at that moment she became sane.

# HUGO

Jonathon and the boy had travelled together for about a week. They kept under cover, preferring a longer route with trees to open fields. They fed themselves on wild mushrooms, blackberries and sorrel leaves, and drank water from the many streams they crossed on their journey. While they walked Jonathon talked to the boy, pointing at things and speaking in English and sometimes Latin. It was important that the child could understand some words in the languages they were likely to encounter in this country. Gaelic was spoken too, but Jonathon knew nothing of it.

'We must find a monastery,' said Jonathon. 'The monks will give us shelter and food, and at least there we shall be safe. No law can override the right of sanctuary.'

Hugo nodded and gripped the Englishman's hand.

The wood was dark, its floor carpeted with a thick layer of crispy leaves. They travelled by night, and slept by day. Now that the trees were getting barer it was safer this way round.

From the shelter of tree trunks they could now and then see small villages, rows of houses fashioned from straw and mud. Cattle grazed all around the hillsides. In the dark these habitations glowed with the light of large communal fires. The savages, their hair hanging in matted locks upon their scrawny shoulders, danced drunken dances around the flames. Hugo and Jonathon crouched amid the gorse and watched. The boy shivered.

'Friend or foe?' sighed the Englishman. 'If only we knew for sure we could go and warm ourselves beside them.'

Hugo shook his head.

'Quite right, old man. Better safe than sorry.' Jonathon reached into the lining of his doublet, and pulled out a leather purse. He handed it to the boy. 'Here, you take care of this. You may need it more than I do.'

Hugo backed away, shaking his head. Jonathon pulled open the boy's doublet and shoved the bag inside. 'You can give it back one day. It will be safer with you. You are keeper of the purse, all right?'

Hugo fastened the buttons and pressed the purse down into his waistband.

They turned and walked back into the shelter of the trees. There was a fluttering nearby, and a crackle of broken twigs. Hugo flung himself to the ground and Jonathon crouched beside him. They stayed very still. Another crunch. Hugo caught sight of a leg protruding from behind a tree only feet from where they were. He gasped and crossed himself. 'Ave Maria,' he muttered. Jonathon gripped him and held his head close, his eyes searching the darkness.

A dark voice spoke quietly to them from the tree. 'Spanish?' it said. 'Friends! Shipwrecked?'

Jonathon replied. 'From the Armada, yes.'

Ten or so shadowy figures emerged from the wood. They stood there in the dark, naked and bleeding. Jonathon and the boy stood to observe the strange sight.

'We were wrecked some miles north of here, and have since been cruelly robbed and beaten. They took even our clothes.'

Jonathon answered them. 'We too were wrecked many miles to the south-west. The survivors were cruelly massacred on the beach.'

'There were hundreds of survivors from our ship,' cried another of the naked men. 'They surrendered to an English platoon. We were separated from the others.'

'They were the lucky ones. At least they will be prisoners of war. Fed and clothed, and exchanged in some deal,' spat out another. 'They'll see their families again, and lie once more in the Spanish sun.'

'Where can we go?' asked the first Spaniard. 'We know not who is our enemy.'

'We are heading for a monastery which I have been told lies near here,' Jonathon said pulling off his cloak and jacket. 'Take these. We have been lucky too. We are alive.'

The strange group marched on through the night. The moon rose and faded with the dawn. Rain started to fall, a mere drizzle, but cold and closing the visibility to a distance of only a hundred yards or so. As the light grew, they climbed up a dark hill, reaching the brow as the sun spilled out, melting the mist. Jonathon pointed down. 'There it is.'

Below them, nestling in the shadows of the hill, lay a grey stone building, with a cross for its weathercock. The sun threw warm rays across its tiled roof. The men grouped tightly around him, crossing themselves and murmuring short prayers of thanks.

'Remember, we're not safe until we are inside. Let's keep our wits about us, and go down quietly,' Jonathon told them. 'Come along, boy.' He heaved Hugo up into his arms and carried him at his side, resting on his hip. The men strode down the hill, their eyes still scanning the horizon.

They walked up the drive, a large kitchen garden burgeoning with cabbages and carrots to either side of them. Jonathon let Hugo slide to the ground before lifting the large brass knocker and clapping it firmly against the heavy oak door. The men waited in silence. Jonathon banged the clapper down again.

'Maybe they are at prayer,' he said. 'Matins, or lauds.'
He turned the heavy handle and the men piled into the
stone hall.

They stumbled on towards a door at the far end. 'This
must be the chapel,' muttered one of the naked Spaniards.
'Look at the carving.'

'Why are they not singing?' murmured another.

Their leader pushed the door open. They all stood and
gaped at what they saw. The altar was smashed into lumps
of stone, the pews hacked up, thrown into a pile and burnt.
The smell of smoke was still strong and acrid, making
them cough. The stations of the cross had been torn down
or daubed with white paint and the stained-glass windows
were knocked out. But the worst sight that met their eyes
was the bodies of ten men, hanging from the iron window
gratings.

'Spaniards!' cried one of the men.

'That is Don Carlos,' gasped another, pointing to a body
dangling in a red velvet doublet.

The leader turned to Jonathon. 'These are the men we
told you about before. This is how the Lutheran English treat
their prisoners of war. These men are all from our ship.'

'These are the survivors,' cried another with scorn.

The group retreated to the empty hall.

'What are we to do in this country of living hell?'

Jonathon grasped the boy's hand. 'It is not all like this,'
he said. 'This is a beautiful land.' He stroked the child's
hair. 'We will reach safety.'

'How? How? How?' one of the Spaniards was shrieking
with panic. 'We have escaped the death of battle, the death
of the cruel sea and the wild savages, only to be murdered
by heretics in this godforsaken land.'

Jonathon spoke softly, but firmly. 'We must continue
northwards. There are noblemen there, in Ulster, who will
receive us and help us back to Spain. First let us eat some

of the food from this garden. Then – back to the woods and hills.'

The Spanish leader spoke. 'We will let down the bodies of our compatriots and lay them near the remains of the altar. I hope God will forgive us if we borrow their clothes. The dead surely can have no need for shirts and breeches.'

Only three of the Spaniards elected to follow Jonathon. The rest decided to go back to their ship and see whether they could make any of the landing vessels seaworthy.

After three nights' walking Jonathon, Hugo and the Spaniards were woken from their midday slumbers by cattle wandering in the wood. This was a strange sight. Cows preferred the sunlight. While they debated what it could mean they did not hear the footsteps behind them.

'Thou Spain,' said a voice.

They spun round. An old woman emerged from the leafy bushes. She was a rough savage of about eighty years. She leaned on a gnarled stick, her gummy mouth drawn into a mockery of a smile.

'Spain?' she cried again. 'Thou Spain?'

Jonathon nodded. The woman stumbled towards them. Jonathon made signs to her, telling her they had been shipwrecked and needed food and shelter. She shook her head and waved her arms. She pointed out of the wood, down the sloping hillside. 'No go,' she said. 'Bad. Bad. Sassanas.' She mimed out what they took for a warrior, or soldier. 'Spain . . .' she ran her bony fingers along the line of her throat. 'Kill. Kill. No go. Sassanas. Bad, Spain . . .' she mimed the cutting of throats again, pointed at her cows, and again banged her hollow chest to indicate a soldier. 'Sassanas. Take. Steal.' She shook her head and pointed to the darkest corner of the wood. 'Hide.'

Jonathon made more signs to her, asking where they

185

could hope to find friends. The woman nodded and pointed into the wood. She drew mountains on the ground with the point of her stick, then held up five fingers, and mimed sleep. 'Five days' journey,' whispered a Spaniard, 'over the mountain.' She stamped out her drawing of a mountain and swept her stick across the dust again. She drew out a tall tower with turrets.

'O'Neill,' she cried with a grin and smacked her lips into a kiss. 'O'Neill.' She spat on the floor. 'Sassanas.' She made the kissing motion again. 'Spain.' She pointed at them all. 'Thou.' She slapped her wrinkled hands together and shook her own hand. 'O'Neill.'

Jonathon bowed to her. 'Thank you,' he said, indicating his heart. The men all bowed to the old woman and turned towards the distant mountain. Hugo pulled at Jonathon's breeches. 'Jonathon,' he murmured. 'Wait.'

He ran back to the woman, dug deep into his pocket pulled out a golden coin and thrust it forward. The woman's eyes lit up. She gave the kissing motion again and, taking the coin, made a cross in the air before the boy. He waved at her, then turned on his heels and caught up with his countrymen.


On the second night their walk led them within smell of the sea again. Gulls swept overhead, screaming raucously. When dawn broke they found themselves on another rocky promontory. The wreck of another Spanish galleon lay below, reduced to a couple of masts swaying in a bay full of loose timber and floating bodies. They passed on.

At dusk they were parallel to a beach black with ravens and choughs perched upon the bodies of their country-men, tearing at the carrion flesh with their sharp beaks. The Spaniards kept their eyes on the fields ahead. When the boy tired they took it in turns to carry him. On the fifth night they reached the mountain and by dawn they were safely inside the castle commanded by the great O'Neill.

When they were washed and clothed they were led into the great chamber on the second floor of the tower. A huge fire blazed in an open fireplace and an oak table groaned under the weight of hundreds of metal and wooden dishes laid out to feed the soldiers and noblemen and their Spanish allies. Steaming pans full of cabbage, carrots, and broth were laid before them. Plates were piled high with oatcakes and slabs of butter.

'I must apologise for the welcome you have received in our country,' said O'Neill from his ornately carved oak chair at the head of the table. 'But, as you see, it is dangerous for us to keep you.'

Jonathon acted as interpreter for the whole group. 'We only want to get back to Spain,' he said. 'Please help us to some ships which can rescue us.'

'We play a double game with the Sassanas,' said O'Neill. 'They will come after you. If they find you here we will all be in danger. The Sassana Queen loved me once. I am the Earl of Tyrone by her hand, brought up and trained for leadership in the City of London.'

A servant walked round the table and poured liquor into pewter vessels.

'Uishce beathadh,' cried O'Neill. 'The water of life.'

They raised their tankards. Hugo spluttered and coughed as the fiery liquid drained down his throat. The men laughed.

'Maybe the little man would prefer something more familiar.' O'Neill clicked his finger at one of the waiting servants. 'Wine for the boy,' he snapped.

As the servant rolled a barrel on its side and pulled the

187

stopper to release the crimson liquid, Hugo read the stamp on its side. 'Santiago,' he muttered.

Jonathon shot him a look. The barrel had clearly been taken from a wrecked Spanish ship. Even their friends were not above looting.

'The boy is tired,' Jonathon stood up. 'He dreams of home. Can we place him in the women's care?'

O'Neill made a sign to one of his servants and Hugo was carried off up the winding staircase to the women's quarters.

'He's so lovely,' giggled a thin woman.

'Look at those black eyes . . .'

'The eyelashes! See how long.'

A group of Irish women gathered round Hugo and fingered him as though he was a pet. 'We have lots of gorgeous sweetmeats for you,' they told him.

Hugo felt ill at ease being swept away from Jonathon and thrown among these chattering women in their grand room hung with tapestries, the floor strewn with rushes. But at least it was warm: in a cavernous fireplace a peat and log fire blazed. As well as spinning wheels and armchairs there were benches, tables and in the corner a harp. The small windows let in little light, but the centre of the room was welcoming enough, although the corners were dark and shadowed. Some of the women gathered round the fire were spinning, while others pulled pieces of cloth on to their laps and started stitching them with rich swirling patterns.

'Does he not talk?' laughed one young girl.

Another fingered his hair, and ran her hands across his shoulders. 'It will be like having a monkey. We can dress him in lovely costumes.'

'Do you think he's a gypsy?' asked a small fair woman with green eyes. 'He has the swarthy look.'

188

'All Spaniards have a swarthy look,' a tall woman replied tartly.

'Not that learned one. What's he called?'

'Jonathon' they called in reply.

'English,' whispered Hugo. 'He English. My father.'

'He talks, he talks!' the fair woman said and thrust her hand out to the boy. 'What is my fortune? Tell me my fortune.' The women gathered tightly round the boy.

A low voice behind them shattered the circle. 'Leave the child alone.'

Hugo saw a woman sitting alone in the shaft of light spilling in through a slit window. She was dressed in green, and her long red hair flowed down over her white shoulders. Hugo shrank back. She frightened him with her cold dark voice, which had silenced the gaggle of women around him.

The fair woman stepped forward. 'Erin, there's no need to spread your bitterness to this little innocent.'

Erin held her hollow face high. 'And what exactly is your definition of innocence, Dearbhla?' she sneered. 'I'm sure not one of you could recognise it if it shone upon you in full light.'

Dearbhla took the boy's hand. 'Don't listen to her. She's a witch anyway.'

The circle of women closed around Hugo, sheltering him from Erin's steely look. He huddled close to the roaring log fire, but from time to time could not resist peeking sideways to watch the lone woman in green.

As night fell they wrapped him warmly in a blanket and laid him upon a wide bench littered with ornate cushions. Hugo slept.

In the deep of night footsteps clattered up the spiral stone staircase leading to the ladies' chambers. A burly man swept in.

'Hide the child,' hissed the soldier. 'There are English

189

here. They are checking for Spaniards.' The man left. Only three of the women rested within this chamber, Erin and two others. The two, in a panic, picked up Hugo and bundled him behind a curtain. Erin sat still in her corner.

The door to the chamber opened slowly and an Englishman in a red jacket entered. The two women were guiltily sitting by the fire doing nothing. Erin remained in the shadows. Two more red-jackets followed the first.

'Pardon me, ladies,' the first Englishman said. They began to poke about in the room. As one drew near the hiding place, the two women sprang up and made forced conversation. It did not confuse the soldier. 'What's this?' he called, pulling back the wall curtain. Hugo blinked, his mouth open and dry with fear. The soldier bent down and hauled the boy up. 'My oh my, a little Spanish brat.'

As he fingered the child's face, Erin rose and stepped into the light. 'Do you mind,' she hissed. 'That is my boy. And if you must know, he is half English; left me as a present by one of your friends some years ago.' She strode across the room and pulled Hugo out of the man's grasp. 'Perhaps you'd like to find him for me. Tall. Dark, like the boy. Name of Morris. Or so he told me.'

The English soldier backed off. 'Sorry, sorry, er, madam. No need to look at me like that.'

'You surprise me with your arrogance, soldier. You are in the castle of the Earl of Tyrone, dubbed so by your own gracious Queen Elizabeth. Don't lower yourself by grubbing about trying to tell us that we are your enemies. One day you may need our help.' She turned her back on the men and wrapped Hugo up again. 'You're cold,' she said softly. 'Come sleep on the wide bench, near the fire, my little darling. Sleep, acushla, sleep.'

The other women stood trembling by the hearth as the Englishmen left without a murmur.

When the echo of their steps upon the stairway faded

and was gone Erin spoke softly into Hugo's ear. 'Fight like with like. If they threaten you, you threaten them.' She touched his brow then swiftly withdrew to her dark corner, and hummed a weird and haunting melody until the boy was asleep.

Hugo spent two weeks exploring the castle. There were noisy rooms, which the Spaniards and Jonathon shared with a hundred or more of O'Neill's men – the kerns, sturdy footsoldiers, and the gallowglasses, vast men with axes. There were more Spaniards here too, all survivors from wrecks.

Sometimes, to escape the cacophony, Jonathon walked with him up to the ramparts to look down on the green fields and the sparkling loughs. 'Those are the Mountains of Mourne,' he told Hugo, pointing at a row of blue hills in the distance. Beyond lies the sea, England, Scotland.'

They walked round the top of the tower.

'That is south,' said Jonathon. Leinster, Munster and the Pale.' He continued round. 'West. Connaught. The Atlantic. The New World.'

'Spain?' asked Hugo. 'Where Spain?'

Jonathon laughed, and moved back to the southerly position. 'Far, far away, over land and over sea.'

'I hate the sea,' sighed Hugo. 'I hate.'

Jonathon rested his hand on Hugo's shoulders. 'Yes,' he said. 'I know.'

At night Hugo stayed with the women. Sometimes he would cry and scream in his sleep, and the women took it in turn to tell him stories. Although they tried hard to interest him, and told him cheerful tales of pleasant happy folk, only Erin's stories spun round in his head, and he begged her for more.

She asked him to tell her of the things he had seen since

he left Spain, and then she told him legends concerning those things.

She told him the mysteries of plants and animals he had passed as he trudged from the ship. Of the seals, their round bald heads bobbing on the waves, that came rolling up the sands to bask in the sun. Creatures who sang mournfully each night, she said, for they were the souls of drowned men. 'And that is why it is so unlucky to kill a seal, for who knows but it may have been an old friend. They have magical powers,' she whispered into his ear, 'and can transform themselves into women and return to the land. Sometimes they even marry or have families. But they can never be happy on land, and in time the sea will always claim them back, the seal-women. These wretched creatures,' she hissed, 'can never be content, for their sea longings are land longings and their land longings sea longings.'

She told him how the choughs he had seen scavenging the beaches were once nothing but plain black crows, but that they spent so much time pecking at the corpses of the dead in battle, and wading in their blood, that God had given them a pair of red legs and a red beak.

The whitethorn tree she said was the fairies' tree, and woe betide the person who tried to chop one down. The elder on the other hand, was a tree of evil, for the cross on which Christ died was fashioned from the elder. If you fell asleep under an elder you would never wake, or if you did, you would have lost your senses.

Dearbhla snapped at her. 'Stop it can't you? Don't you see how you terrify the boy?'

'I enchant him,' Erin replied and hummed low until Hugo slept.

Two weeks after their arrival at the castle, a messenger arrived and was taken immediately to the presence of O'Neill. The men were coming from mass, which was celebrated each day in the great chamber, when the Spaniards were summoned to the earl, who told them a ship was waiting to the the north-east, to take them to Scotland and thence to the Low Countries and home to Spain.

Hugo jumped up and down. 'To Spain!' he cried. 'Me home, good, good.'

O'Neill continued. 'You will leave on horseback with my men as soon as you can muster.'

The Spaniards buzzed with excitement.

'I will send gallowglasses to guard you. You will ride day and night and set sail as soon as the tide is right. God bless you all.'

Jonathon accompanied Hugo to the women's chambers to fetch his heavy cloak. Erin stood waiting in front of the fire. 'You are leaving us, you men of Spain?'

Jonathon nodded, picking up the cloak and fastening it around the child's neck.

'You cannot take the precious child. The English think that he is mine,' she insisted.

Jonathon laughed. 'And the Spanish think that he is mine.' Jonathon pushed the boy forward. 'Say goodbye, Hugo.' Hugo stood looking up at the witch. She stooped and kissed him, whispering in his ear, 'Come back to me, boy. Come to me when you are a man.'

Hugo stepped back into Jonathon's grasp. 'Me go Spain,' Hugo burst out with pride. 'Come, we go.'

At the door Jonathon turned and bowed to Erin. 'Thank you for taking such care. The boy is indeed precious.'

'Come come,' Hugo bounced up and down at the head of the stone stairs. 'Me happy. Me go ship. Spain.'

Jonathon took a step forward, took his hand and they started down the stairs.

'His Spanish gold!' cried Erin suddenly. She ran across the chamber holding up Hugo's leather money pouch.

Turning quickly, Hugo saw the woman hurtling towards them, and he pulled away from Jonathon. As he did so he lost his footing and stumbled. He grasped for the rail, but his nails only caught at the cold stone wall as he fell, twisting and turning, his small body crashing down each tread, and ricocheting from the circular wall, down, down, till he lay sprawled and still on the lower landing.

Jonathon and Erin clattered down after him as the voice of a guard echoed along the corridor: 'All Spaniards heading for the ship come straight to the stables.'

'Don't move him!' cried Erin. She knelt on the damp flagstones and ran her fingers along his crushed limbs. 'His leg is broken,' she announced. She wiped her long fingers across his bloody face. 'And there is a deep cut above his eye.'

The trembling child opened his eyes and looked up at Jonathon. 'Don't leave me. Me go Spain. Me stay with you,' he pleaded.

'Last call. Come now or we miss the light,' rang out a distant voice.

Jonathon looked along the long corridor.

'No go, English. I am your friend. You need. Lift me.' The boy struggled to get up but his leg hung loose and he could not move. He bit back the pain and tore at Jonathon's leggings. Jonathon stared down at the boy, blood mingling with the tears on his cheeks. 'I couldn't carry you. Not on a horse, through mountains. It would hurt you. I cannot hurt you.'

'No, no,' cried the child. 'You hurt me if you go without me, please, English. Please.'

The clacking of horses' hooves rang out from the window. Jonathon said gently, 'I must go. You keep the purse for me. I will come back for it, one day.'

'No!' shrieked the child.

'I promise. I will come back.' He looked Erin in the eye.

'Keep him well.' He swept his cloak across his shoulders and ran swiftly along the long corridor and out of sight, the boy's cries ringing in his ears and drowning out the clatter of his own footsteps.

## 1598, Tandragee Castle
## near Armagh, Ulster

Hugo stood on the leads of the castle looking out across the green hillside and countryside beyond, his shaggy hair riffling in the soft wind, his long matted fringe hanging over his eyes like a visor.

'My lord is calling upon you.' The small boy who had come up behind him had to tug at his cloak to catch his attention. Hugo turned. 'Is it another raid?' he asked.

The boy shook his head. Hugo followed him down the narrow stone staircase and into the great chamber.

For ten years Hugo had lived in hope that he could get back to Spain, a country he could now barely remember. Unlike the others in the castle he could spend hours alone almost in a trance. He did not join in the long drinking bouts of the night, always keeping himself ready for the call. There had been envoys from Spain, bringing weapons and ammunition, wine and money, blessings from the Pope. But there had never been a message for him, and ships leaving for Spain left without him.

Erin, called the Witch, had nursed him well after his fall, and had then mysteriously left the castle. He had not seen her since.

One rare day when he was eleven he had heard Spanish voices echoing in the courtyard and seen envoys from the Spanish king bringing in trunks full of documents. He had even been called into the great chamber to help interpret, and stood in thrilled trepidation believing that these Spaniards had come to take him home. When they had turned to leave he had started to go with them, and every-one in the room, men and women, Irish and Spanish, shook with laughter, chucked him under the chin and he was packed upstairs to the women's quarters again, where he sat in the dark staring out at the courtyard until he saw the Spanish mount their horses and gallop away without him.

Shortly afterwards he had watched men unloading crates of guns and bullets, and heard talk that the King of Spain was at this moment getting a crown of gold ham-mered out at a blacksmith's shop in Madrid to crown O'Neill King of Ireland. Strange instructions spread through the castle at Dungannon.

Men wandered from room to room dismantling the inner wooden structures of the castle by day, and as night fell everyone set to work destroying the outer walls, taking the fortress down, stone by stone. By dawn it was gone, and its inhabitants were riding off to other strongholds nearby.

'The English were on our doorstep,' he heard the sol-diers laugh. 'I'd like to have seen their faces as they drew up their troops for the assault!'

O'Neill had destroyed his own castle rather than let the English have the pleasure of doing it.

Three years later Hugo had watched the gallowglasses and kerns go off to fight alongside the Sassanas, or English redcoats, to defeat rebel Irish lords, enemies of O'Neill and the English alike.

Within months O'Neill had been declared a traitor by the English, and the soldiers who had fought alongside the men he knew were now sent to fight against them again. He didn't ever understand what they were fighting about. All he knew was that loyalties in this land swung back and forth and that O'Neill's men were always fighting someone, and that no one could tell who it would be from one day to the next.

'Good day, boy. Hugo isn't it?'

Hugo nodded to his lord.

'Our master, O'Neill has asked for you.'

Hugo shifted uneasily from foot to foot. 'The great O'Neill does not know me, sir. I spent some time at Dungannon when I was a tiny child, that's all. In the company of the women, I was. I only ever saw him from a distance.'

'You are the child from the Armada, are you not?' The lord peered down at him from under his matted white fringe.

'Yes, my lord.'

'Then you are the man. This missive calls you tonight to meet with O'Neill and Red Hugh O'Donnell. Arm yourself, in case of bandits, and set out instantly. I will have the scrivener make you a map.'

When Hugo arrived at the designated house later that evening he was ushered straight up to the great chamber where a huge table was laid out with whiskey and wine. A group of men huddled around the fire, and Hugo heard a voice speaking in Spanish. His heart beat. It was Jonathon, come to take him home.

The men pulled away from each other and turned to greet him. He scanned the faces.

'Welcome, boy. We need your services.' O'Neill stepped forward and poured him some wine.

A dark man in a gold-trimmed doublet addressed him in Spanish. 'I am Captain Alonso Cobos, envoy of His Majesty King Philip.' Hugo's heart sank. Jonathon was not there at all, only a small group of Spaniards and the great earls of Ireland.

'An armada from Spain, landing where you yourself

came ashore today, at Killybegs. We need six thousand men,' said O'Neill, 'and money and arms to equip another ten thousand.'

Hugo translated. Cobos wrote the figures down in his notebook then pulled the large parchment map towards him. 'I think there will be no problem with that,' he said.

The men rose, and Hugo stepped back as Cobos passed him. 'Thank you, boy,' said O'Neill. 'You may go. In the morning you will return to Tandragee. Give my best wishes to your lord.'

Hugo bowed and left the chamber behind a serving boy, who led him through many winding corridors and up some stairs. 'Where are we going?' asked Hugo, who knew that the sleeping quarters for men of his degree were always on the lower floors.

'There is someone here who wishes to speak with you.'

The servant knocked at a heavy wooden door, and pushed its iron handle. The door swung open with a creak. The room beyond was dark but for the flickering light of a tallow candle. Hugo stepped in, and the boy closed the door behind him.

'Welcome, boy,' a mellifluous voice said from a dark corner. 'I had to see how you'd grown up, acushla agus asthore machree.' Erin stepped into the light. Her long red hair seemed to glow. 'Come, sit.' She pulled a stool from the side of her harp by the wooden armchair.

Hugo stepped back. He had not seen her since he was nine years old, and she had terrified him then.

'Handsome,' she murmured, 'as I knew you would be.'

'I don't know ...' Hugo stuttered. He was greatly struck by her presence. It was as though she had cast out an invisible rope and twisted it around him, pulling him forward. He stumbled into the chair.

'Have you heard again the singing of the seals?' she hissed.

Hugo shook his head.

'Or encountered those witches in disguise, the stoats, creeping snakelike through the woods and hills, poisoning the milk within the cow?'

'No,' Hugo whispered.

'Danger is nearer at hand for you, I think.'

Hugo held up his hands. 'I am well looked after,' he said. 'I am learning to fight with my lord's men, and soon one will come from Spain for me and I will go home.'

'And their land longings are sea longings, and their sea longings land longings,' she sang in a dark voice. She stretched out her arm and stroked his cheek. 'Take care, acushla. You have a pure soul. Keep looking over your shoulder, for black is white and white is black, and the days ahead are scarlet with blood.'

She pulled her hand back and tugged a ring from her finger. It was gold and green, two snakes entwined.

'They say there are no serpents in all Ireland, since Saint Patrick drove them out with his rod. He cursed the salmon from Lough Derg and turned the heathen women into mermaids, obliging them to sing for ever in Tir So Thuinn, the land under the waves. But two snakes survive. You and I. If you are in need, send for me by that ring.'

Hugo held the ring and peered at the inscription within its circle. 'What does it say?' he asked.

'Acushla agus asthore machree. The very pulse and delight of my heart.'

Erin rose from her stool and strode across the room. 'Go now.'

Hugo followed her to the door.

'And don't forget, Hugo machree. Keep looking over your shoulder.'

The castle rang with the voices of men. Hundreds of hired soldiers slept in each corridor. In rooms on every level the pipers were warming up their instruments, the soldiers pulling on armour, the gallowglasses sharpening their axes. Musketmen primed their guns, and shot was handed out.

Since the night Hugo had interpreted for the Spanish envoy, Cobos, the King of Spain had sent two armadas. Both turned back when overwhelmed by tempestuous seas. Some arms and money had got through, but no men. Now King Philip claimed poverty. He could muster no more ships to help the Irish. Four and a half thousand English soldiers were now marching towards them through the ruined town of Armagh, with its hilltop cathedral shattered and roofless and its many burnt-out churches, and setting up camp by the riverside north of the city.

Hugo and the Irish soldiers took to the woods and passed stealthily along, always keeping the English army in their sight. The August sun beat down on their shoulders when they came out into the open. Along the ridge of a distant hill they could now see the slender line of O'Donnell and his men. They had timed their rendezvous perfectly.

As the first gunshot rang out across the valley the Irish swept down. Hugo ran, grasping his arquebus in sweaty hands. He crouched behind a gorse bush and raised the gun. He looked down the sight and aimed. Terror rushed through him. The memory of the gunfights he had witnessed on board ship racked his brain. He caught an English soldier in his sight, and froze. He could see his face. This was no good. He knew he could not fire when he could see a man standing before him, a being with every right to live. He lowered the sight and pulled the trigger. The bullet hissed through the ankle-length grass and hit the boggy ground. A spray of brackish water flew up around the Englishman's feet. Hugo reloaded, and crept further down the hill, running, bent low along the line of the river.

He fired many shots into the water, or sent them whistling like snakes past the ears of the enemy. His compatriots dashed around beside and behind him. He saw them fall. Pikemen made a rush and hoisted English bodies backwards, staggering into the bloody water.

A group of English mounted soldiers tried to rush them, but were dispersed. A shout went up from one division of the English: 'The Marshal is dead!' The news spread general confusion among the English troops. O'Neill and his men capitalised on it, storming into their midst and wreaking havoc.

Hugo ran with them, gasping for breath, mud dripping from his chin, blood sprayed across his cheeks. His foot caught. Was it a rabbit warren, or the lair of a stoat? He fell forward and his head banged hard against a rock. He panted now, as he pulled himself up again with flashes before his eyes and smoke filling his lungs. He pulled at his gun, brought it up to eye level to get a view and found himself eye to eye with a soldier in a red jacket. His finger slipped along the trigger as the Englishman quickly raised his own gun. Hugo looked into the man's eyes. He pulled at the trigger, but could not fire. A loud blast rang in his ears as his vision exploded into red.

He heard singing, and the gentle music of a harp; dark haunting melodies that wrapped him up and soothed the endless pain. When he opened his eyes the singing stopped.

He was in a tapestry-hung room, lying in a wooden bed strewn with woollen blankets. In the fireplace logs crackled. Erin gazed down at him.

'They said you had no chance. But I knew you'd come back to me, avourneen.'

Hugo struggled to speak, but she hushed him. 'No.

Don't. The bullet took much of your jaw. You must not speak. I will tell you all.

'You were carried home more dead than alive. But men speak of your heroism. How you moved deep into the fray.'

Hugo moved uncomfortably in the bed.

'I know. I know, boy. Black is white, and white is black, remember? Still, whatever the truth within your head, you will be rewarded for your deeds. And I would say, you should not refuse. For what is a stretch of land in exchange for a beautiful face? You have paid dearly so that the Lord of Ulster can celebrate a great victory over his enemy. You were not there to fight for your own sake, were you?'

Hugo reached up to feel his face. His once rounded cheek was now gaunt and pulled tight across his cheekbones. His brow felt much lower and hung heavily over one eye. He could feel now that his mouth pulled tightly down on one side.

'I used herbs and honey and spiders' webs,' Erin crooned, 'and the skin which was blown apart grew together again. You still have the ring, I see.' She held his hand in hers and stroked it. 'I am glad of that. You have been here with me now for six weeks, waking and sleeping, crying out in the dark terrors of night. The leaves are tumbling from the trees now, and winter is on her ruthless way. I have been told that you are to be granted lands in Down, near the sea, under the shadows of the Slieve Donard and the mighty Mountains of Mourne. Farmland, good for animals, and crops of wheat and barley.'

She bent over him and wiped a tear from his now craggy and hideous face.

'Don't cry, little one. With land you can be happy for you can work with life, instead of courting death.'

At this Hugo started to sob. Erin gazed down at the shaking body of this eighteen-year-old boy.

'They say it is a great thing to be a hero. And you are one, Hugo. Not in the way they think you are. But I know you as though you are a part of myself. I know that you were never allowed to be a boy, and now you are a man.'

Erin bent low and ran her fingers through his black hair. He felt the warmth of her breath touch his lips like gossamer silk. He threw his arms around her neck and pulled her down, kissing her face wildly as he sobbed. She gently rocked him till his tears dried, and he slept again. Then she lit the candles round the small room and sat by him, quietly reading in the flickering light.

When he was well enough, Hugo rode out to see the land. 'It's of little value, in an area that everyone seems to have forgotten exists,' said the man riding beside him, a gruff steward. 'But it's a great honour to have been given anything at all at your age.'

Hugo looked at the man. 'I did not expect anything. And I have agreed that I will pay my lord as long as I stay there. I hope soon to return to my country.'

The man on the horse laughed. 'And what country, pray, is that?'

'Spain,' said Hugo briskly.

They rode in silence for some time.

'There's no dwelling place, you understand. You will have to get that built. It is only a small reward.' The steward pulled his horse to a halt and waved his arm. 'There. The four green fields.'

Hugo looked up behind him at the purple-shadowed mountains, and down again at his fields. 'Do I stay here now?' he asked.

The steward guffawed and his horse kicked, startled at the crack of his voice. 'Where? Under a fairy ring? You can't sleep down a rabbit warren, can you? You boys!' He gave his horse a jab with his heel, and they trotted down the hill to the boundary of Hugo's new fields. 'There is a village to the north, called Killocony, and a small town across the hill, down by the shore, Donomawe. You'll find lodging there, and men to help you. You have money?'

Hugo nodded. His earnings from fighting, translating and working within the castle were all in his saddlebag, with his clothes. The other men spent their wages on whiskey and ale, but Hugo did not like the taste of the local drinks, and preferred to spend his evenings alone with a book.

'I'll see you to an inn. Then, should my lord need your services, we shall know where to find you.'

They hitched up the horses and stooped through the low door into the small inn on the strand. A girl with long golden hair stood at the bar, chatting to some drinking men. The room was full and smoky, and smelt of beer.

'Could my young friend have a room for a month or two?' the man asked.

'Certainly, sir,' beamed the girl. She glanced at Hugo and failed to suppress a cry. Hugo's gloved hand flew up to cover the wounded side of his face.

'Injured in the great battle at Yellow Ford', said the man. The drinkers all held out their hands to touch the hero. The serving wench, still unable to conceal her horror, forced a smile. 'For one of O'Neill's victors we should make a room, whether we had one or not,' she leered.

Hugo closed his eyes and took a deep breath.

'You must be tired,' she said. 'I'll take you up.'

Hugo worked hard throughout the winter months. He hired some local men, who dug foundations and felled the trees, sawed and strapped the timber, until he had built a small house with stables, room for a dairy and a large kitchen which opened on to the paved yard.

He bought cattle from a local fair, and offered board, lodging and whiskey money to anyone who wanted farm work. Soon the house was full, and everyone busily working. At night the yard echoed with the sound of men's laughter, and the cackle of the two old women who worked the dairy.

By day Hugo worked in the fields, as evening fell he would visit the dairy and sample the milk and cheese.

'You should be finding yourself a wife, nice boy like you,' smiled Kitty, a rosy-faced woman with no front teeth, as she scooped out a yellow spoonful from one of the large cheeses.

'We can dream,' said Hugo, taking a bite. All young women stayed clear of the place. They could not bear to look upon his twisted face. He handed the spoon back and smiled. 'Very nice. I shouldn't want for a decent meal if I married a full-blooded woman like yourself.'

Kitty laughed. 'What you need is a round-hipped young lass who'll give you bonny children.'

Hugo turned and walked to the door. 'Ah well,' he sighed, 'maybe one day.'

'What a shame,' he heard Kitty whisper to her friend Sally as he pulled the door shut behind him, 'I'll bet you he would have been the handsomest lad around these parts.'

'If he had a face, you mean,' quipped Sally and they dissolved into manic laughter.

For two years Hugo built up his farm, and managed to keep the workers happy. He paid promptly, got high prices for his goods at market and regularly sent fealty money to O'Neill. He rode out alone sometimes to Donomawe, the town on the sea, his hat pulled low across the bad side of his face. Other days he would gallop inland, leaping brooks and hedges, to the Ulster border and beyond.

The English garrison, he knew, had retreated after the

206

great battle, and most were forty miles south, safe within the Pale, the English settlement of Dublin and surrounding counties. In the nearest town one day he stopped at a tavern for some food. He kept his hat on, and took his plate to a table where sat a priest.

'May I join you, Father?'

The priest did not look up from his book. 'Mmmmm, yes,' he murmured.

Slowly the tavern filled, mainly with gallowglasses of the local lord, on border duty. Hugo sat with his back to the room, picked at a chicken leg and mopped up the gravy with a chunk of wheaten bread. Two giggling girls hovered by the table behind Hugo and asked the priest if the spaces on the bench were free.

'Mmmm,' he grunted again, and the girls sat down. Hugo slouched low over his plate.

'You're not from round here, are you?' asked one of the girls. 'No, no,' mumbled Hugo. The girls could not see his face, and now it was too late to let them see it gently.

'Why won't you look at us when we're talking to you?' said one, in a flirtatious tone.

'I prefer not to,' said Hugo.

'Very nice I must say,' sneered the girl. 'Are you a spy for the English, or what?'

'Show us your face, show us your face,' chanted the girls. The priest turned sharply to Hugo. 'Are you a spy?' he demanded. He snatched the hat from Hugo's head. Before Hugo had a chance to cover his skull-like scars the girls had jumped up screaming. Men from adjoining tables sprang to their defence, grabbing Hugo and strapping his hands behind his back.

'You'd better come with us,' snarled a burly man in brown. They bundled Hugo out of the tavern and up the road to the big house. When Hugo had explained his position to the local lord he was let go, with apologies.

So as not to encounter any more strangers he decided to take the sheltered way home, through the woods and across the hill.

After he had ridden for an hour, he dismounted to give the horse a rest. Sitting against the trunk of a large tree he watched the steam rise from the horse's back. Suddenly he heard a crackling noise behind him. Footsteps. He sprang to his feet and peered through the dappled light. Through the darkness he could make out the forms of about twenty men. They seemed to be crouching, crawling towards him on all fours. They were so thin they were little more than skeletons, their skin stretched across their bones as tight as a drum, their eyes hollow. Their legs were too weak to support them and their clothes hung in rags. They crept forward, occasionally stopping and holding out an arm, partly in supplication, partly to keep their balance.

'Food?' groaned one, in Gaelic. 'Food, please?' His voice was like a ghost crying out of his grave.

Hugo walked slowly towards them. As he came closer he noticed that their mouths and lips were stained green: they had been reduced to eating grass and dock. 'English?' he said tentatively.

Fear came into the men's eyes.

'I will not hurt you, I swear,' said Hugo holding his palms towards them in a gesture of peace. 'I speak English. It is easier for you.'

The front skeleton nodded painfully. 'English soldiers,' he whispered, 'left behind, and unable to get past the gallowglasses, back to our garrison behind the Pale. Since the great battle we have wandered scratching for food. Some among us have died of famine fever, we alone have survived.'

'That's almost two years,' said Hugo. He looked at these men, and wondered whether it had been one of them who shot half his face off that August day.

'We were lost in the retreat, cut off. We tried, like you Irish, to use the shelter of the wood, but this is a strange country and one tree looks much like another.'

Hugo pulled the cloak from his shoulders. 'Huddle together under this,' he offered. 'I will go down into the town and buy you food and clothing.'

He remounted and galloped off down the hill towards the town. It was almost dusk when he returned, his saddlebags bulging.

He dipped the bread in milk and handed out pieces to the men. He washed their green faces with a damp cloth and helped them into the rough woollen clothes he had bought.

'You will still be weak. Stay here and I will return tomorrow with more food. When you are stronger you can make your way south to your people,' he told them.

The leader of the Englishmen took his hand and kissed it.

'God has sent you, sir. We thank you.'

Hugo tossed his head stiffly. The gratitude of others made him uncomfortable. 'I will be back tomorrow,' he said.

The next morning he set out early from his farm and by midday was with the men again in the woods, doling out food.

'I have brought enough, I hope, to last you about a week. By then I am sure you will be able to fend for yourselves.'

As he got back into the saddle one of the men touched Hugo's leg. 'We don't even know what we are fighting for,' he said. 'At home in England we have wives and children. We would rather be there than here.'

'I know, I know,' said Hugo. 'I know how it is to be among strangers.'

He wheeled his horse round and walked it gently under the stooping boughs towards the light. Before him the sun

lit the green hill with a white luminous glare. He bent to
clear the last low branch before the open ground. He raised
his head and came eye to eye with the priest who had sat
opposite him in the tavern the day before. He reined in his
horse and halted.

'Nice day for a picnic, yes?'

Hugo stared down at his grinning face. 'Yes.'

'Lots and lots of food too. You must have a hearty
appetite.'

Hugo nodded.

'Or friends, perhaps. Maybe you have a group of weird
girls with you who secretly like the sight of your twisted
face?'

Hugo calmly stroked the mane of his horse. 'Time is
passing, Father. I must be getting back to my farm. It is a
long ride.'

'Aaah,' sighed the priest in a honeyed tone, 'of course.
You are so busy, you live so far from here, and yet you
come all this way to eat your lunch. It is a hard mistake,
you know, to think that with a face like yours you can pass
unnoticed.' He turned and looked down the hillside at a
cluster of small trees and gorse bushes. 'I brought some of
my friends up here too. Come out, come out, my friends.'

A gang of gallowglasses and two horsemen emerged
into the light and strode over to Hugo and the priest.

'So,' grinned the priest, 'now that we are all met, why
don't we go into the woods and meet *your* friends, eh?'
Without waiting for a reply, the ruffians ran past Hugo
into the darkness of the wood.

Hugo turned and yelled, kicking his horse to reach the
shelter of the trees first. 'Hide yourselves!' he cried. 'In the
name of God, hide yourselves.'

The two horsemen were ahead of him; the
gallowglasses, their heavy axes balanced on their wide
shoulders, ran beside his horse, unhindered by the low

branches. He could see the English, gaunt in their Irish clothes, trying with feeble arms and legs to climb the trees. One was simply crouching, grovelling at the ground, trying to pull dead leaves up to protect himself.

He looked up at Hugo with horror. 'We thought you were our friend,' he howled. 'We thought you were our friend.' His words were cut off by a gallowglass, who kicked him to the ground and struck his skull with an axe.

Other axemen gripped their wooden handles and swung so that the silver blades caught the light before they fell, crushing bone, splattering blood, severing limbs.

Hugo dropped his reins. 'No!' he screamed. 'No! They can be no harm to anyone. No. No.'

Hugo's horse whimpered and stood still. Hugo sat, hands at his side, his body trembling, as the Irishmen killed and mutilated the starved English soldiers before his eyes. He held his face in his hands and sobbed. 'It is my fault. I have brought this about. May God forgive me.'

'May God forgive you indeed, you helper of heretics,' the priest snapped as he held Hugo's bridle. 'I think you'd better step down here. You will not be riding anywhere today.'

Hugo was bound and marched into the town where he was taken to the big house and thrown into the dungeons. He lay prostrate on the wet stone floor with his eyes shut. His guards spat at him, and made much of his deformed face. He did not know time, for there was no window. Food came at irregular intervals; sometimes he thought he was given none for two or three days. But he was sure that when it was delivered it would always come with a kick or a punch.

Perhaps I will be here till I die, he thought. No one knows who I am. I have no one who could miss me or search for me.

Months later a great rattling of chains from the staircase presaged the arrival of another prisoner.

211

'It is the year of Our Lord 1601,' the man told Hugo. 'I've been brought here as a suspected spy. People in this town are very edgy. It's what comes of living so near the Pale.'

'You seem very easy about being here,' suggested Hugo.

'I shall be out soon. I work for the O'Neill. Friends saw me taken, they will make sure I am released.'

Mindlessly Hugo toyed with the serpents coiling around his finger. The prisoner watched him.

'Strange kind of ring,' he said. Hugo looked down at it. 'Yes,' he agreed.

Late that night the keys rattled again on the stairs, and the other prisoner was released.

A day or two later guards hurriedly came in with buckets and soap, washed Hugo down and gave him new clothes. They had only just finished when he heard voices on the stairs. As the guards crushed back against the bars of his cell to let the visitors pass Hugo could hear ingratiating male laughter. The guards bowed and left the visitors by the dungeon.

'Acushla agus asthore machree,' hummed a low voice. Erin stood in the shadows on the other side of the bars. Her hand reached through and stroked Hugo's damaged cheek. 'Why did you not send for me?' she asked. She turned to the local lord. 'Get this lock undone, at once. This is the man. He is a hero of Yellow Ford and a friend of the O'Neill. He will be returning with me. His services are urgently required to help negotiate for the new treaty with Spain.'


Candles flickered all round the room. Worried-looking men were gathered round maps spread out on the large table, while others stood in huddles gesticulating and arguing quietly.

'We have an envoy from the new King of Spain, Philip

III,' bellowed O'Neill. 'He has news that a new armada is shortly to be launched, to come here and save us from the English tyrants. We have been making plans now for a few months.'

Hugo looked blankly at him. After the massacre of English soldiers he had witnessed he was not interested in taking sides. In this country, it seemed clear to him, no one was right; everyone was wrong.

'So I shall take you to meet the envoy and we can set to work making our lists.'

O'Neill strode out of the room, Hugo following quietly at his heels. They arrived at an inner office in the tower and went in as the scriveners and negotiators rose to their feet in the presence of the great O'Neill. Hugo could see the familiar ornately decorated velvet doublet of the Spanish emissary. He was shuffling papers on the table as he rose.

'Take a seat beside me, boy,' instructed O'Neill.

Hugo sat. He looked across the table and his eyes alighted on the Spaniard. He froze. 'Jonathon?' he whispered.

The envoy looked up and their eyes met. There was no flicker of recognition.

'I'm sorry?' said the envoy. 'Have we met?'

'Can we press on,' said O'Neill. He held out a map. 'It is vital that the landings take place at either Limerick or Waterford, and no further south . . .'

The scriveners scratched away at pieces of parchment with feathered quills. Hugo muttered his translations in Spanish and listened hard to the replies of the envoy.

After an hour, O'Neill called for some refreshments, while the papers were read over to him. Hugo moved round the room, looking carefully at the envoy until he was close enough to whisper without being overheard.

'Do you not remember me, Jonathon?'

The envoy scanned Hugo's drawn face.

Hugo murmured so softly that he was practically mouthing the words. 'English bastard?'

The envoy's eyes searched Hugo as though trying to memorise every detail of a loved one he would never see again.

'Can it be you, Hugo? They told me you were dead. At the great battle.'

Hugo's breath came in gulps. Jonathon looked up at the young man with half a face. He lifted his hand and held it an inch or so from Hugo's great wound. 'What have they done to you?' he whispered.

'I knew you would come for me,' said Hugo.

The door was flung open and a mud-stained messenger hurtled into the room. He knelt at the O'Neill's feet.

'My Lord,' he panted. 'I bring news from the south. I have ridden with the wind these five days to tell you that a Spanish fleet with over three thousand men has landed on September the 21st.'

The messenger stayed there catching his breath, as a cry went up from all in the room.

'Where?' growled O'Neill. 'Where? We must move instantly.'

The messenger licked his lips. 'Kinsale,' he hissed.

'Kinsale!' went up the cry of dismay. 'But that is at the other end of the country. The far south.'

'Yes, sir,' gulped the messenger.

Chairs scraped as everyone rose.

'Call a meeting of the great council!' O'Neill yelled at the messenger. 'Send out watches to the English to see whether there is any troop movement. There is no time to be lost.'

As the castle rang with cries and instructions, and the courtyard clattered with horses, Hugo and Jonathon sat alone in Jonathon's room.

'I still have those pieces of eight,' said Hugo.

Jonathon laughed. 'Can I have them back?'

'No,' laughed Hugo. 'They are miles away from here, near the sea in County Down, on the land I told you I'd been working.'

'How can you be sure they'll still be there?' asked Jonathon. 'You've been away from the place a mighty long time. And when it comes to gold most people will stop at nothing.'

'I buried them,' said Hugo. 'I buried them where no one would dare to dig for them. In a stoat's lair on the hillside.'

The great lords of Ireland and thousands of men, variously marched south through Roscommon and Galway, through the Delvilsbit and Slieve Bloom mountains, across the counties of Limerick and Cork, through Westmeath, Offaly, Leix and Tipperary, through bogs and forests, over mountains and along valleys, picking up men as they went. They crossed the River Sluir to arrive on the outskirts of Kinsale, where the English held the Spanish army in siege, in November. By the time they set up camp, winter was well established, and a heavy ice made slippery the thick carpet of snow.

Hugo and Jonathon had ridden together. They were lucky. Few horses were brought and most men had marched the whole way. Once they arrived they could do nothing but wait.

Just after four o'clock on the morning of Christmas Eve the whole Irish army marched from their separate camps the six or so miles to Kinsale for the assault. The night was stormy, thunder rolling and lightning illuminating the way ahead of them, sparkling on the axeheads and armour, and striking the tops of the spears.

'We are almost there,' said Hugo. 'Almost back at the ships which will take us home.'

215

Commands spread along the musketmen to prepare their guns, and the darkness was lit by hundreds of striking matches all over the hill.

They marched farther south. In the bleak light just before the dawn Jonathon looked over his shoulder along the long lines of men and realised that many divisions had become detached; some had marched too far, some had pulled up too early. When the march was called to a halt Jonathon hissed across to Hugo. 'O'Donnell's men are not with us.'

They watched together as a horseman galloped up the hill to take stock of the situation and race back with information. O'Neill's men were ordered to march back the way they had come to rally with O'Donnell. As they turned a row of English musketeers appeared on the hilly horizon and, with a thunder of hooves, from behind them the English cavalry stormed down the hill.

Both groups skirmished for some time in the boggy ground. 'Where are the Spaniards?' cried Jonathon, a thought which was racing round the field.

O'Neill's small cavalry prepared to charge. As the chief horseman raised his hand to give the signal, a large bag of gunpowder accidentally exploded nearby and the horses ran in terror in all directions. Jonathon and Hugo were separated. In the rout that followed the English troops stormed into the central area and divided the Irish companies further. Many men, whose nearest experience of battle was a night cattle-raid, took to their heels.

Hugo galloped through musket smoke, and roaring cannon fire towards the town of Kinsale. He passed soldiers fighting in single combat and leapt across mounds of Irish dead. The English army was small, but well trained. The day was over for O'Neill. The Spaniards held the only hope. When he reined in his horse to stop the jar of the paved streets of the town, he looked around for the

Spanish army. The streets seemed deserted. By the harbour he saw them.

'What is happening?' he called to a group of men stretching and tearing at lumps of bread. They had clearly only just risen.

'We are waiting for the call,' yelled back the Spaniard.

'The battle is in full flight,' cried Hugo. 'They are waiting for you.'

The Spaniards looked around shiftily. 'We heard gunfire,' said one. 'But it seemed so distant.'

'There's been no signal,' shouted another.

Hugo galloped further into the town. He found a group of noblemen and desperately explained to them.

'O'Neill did not arrive at the rally point, so we came back,' explained a tall man in a purple and silver doublet.

From beyond the city limits the cacophony of gunfire penetrated the sleepy snow-covered streets. One of the Spaniards perked up. 'Should we inform the commander?' asked the purple jerkin.

Before long the Spanish army was marching out of the town. Hugo waited behind, near the ships.

'That was the rally signal, you see, that volley of gunfire,' said the ship's victualler, sitting on a box in the harbour at midday.

'No,' said Hugo grimly. 'I know what that was. That was the English way of announcing a triumph.'

Away from the water he heard the clacking of hooves on cobbles. A minute or two later a handful of Irishmen leapt from their horses and spoke to the victualler, who shook his head. He spoke only Spanish.

'I can translate,' suggested Hugo. 'What do you want?' Hugo recognised the leader: it was Red Hugh O'Donnell, the second lord of Ulster.

'All is lost,' O'Donnell said. 'I am leaving this country for Spain. Is there room for me and this handful of men on your ship?' Hugo looked up at him before starting to translate. 'But you are the leader of your people. How can you leave them?' O'Donnell glared down at him. 'Translate, scar-face. There is no future here now, for anyone. It will be bloodshed till Doomsday.'

Hugo waited for Jonathon by the ships. Nine days later the Spanish commander signed a surrender and his men started boarding for the voyage home. O'Donnell was hiding on board. Jonathon appeared on the eleventh day, looking weary and grey. He smiled when he saw Hugo sitting on a barrel at the harbour. 'Ready for another sea voyage?' he shouted.

Hugo nodded.

'Best to get out now,' Jonathon added. 'I'll have a word with someone and get you on board.'

Jonathon spoke to the Spaniards. After about an hour he came back and told Hugo that he would almost certainly get on, but they had to wait for their whole complement; he should wait till the orders were given to sail, then be ready to board instantly.

Hugo sat in a nearby inn while the Spaniards loaded food and water, carrying barrels and bales up the rickety gangplank. A strong atmosphere of frustration could be sensed among the Spanish troops and sailors. They had sailed so long ago and had never seen action, despite being almost starved out by the English, and now they were due to return home, having surrendered without firing a shot.

At dusk on the feast day of the Epiphany, the twelfth night of Christmas, sails were set and orders given to sail with the tide. A few stragglers had dribbled through the town and on to the waiting ships. Now, one by one, the galleons were hauling up their sails and turning in the bay before heading out into the open sea. The Spanish captain made Hugo wait on the shore even though it looked sure that there would be room for him.

Hugo heard the priests start chanting the prayers for the start of the voyage; could see the gromets, so small, grouped under the mast and singing beautifully. The older boys ran up rope ladders, clinging to the sheets, hanging from the quartermasts and unfurling the sails. Jonathon stood at the top of the gangplank; Hugo at the bottom. Four men had gathered at the top of the plank to pull it back on board. The captain came over to the rail and spoke to Jonathon, who yelled down to Hugo: 'Come on, boy.'

Hugo raced up the ducked board and leapt on to the deck, and the men instantly pulled the plank up behind him. One of them stood up and turned to Hugo to welcome him aboard. The man screamed. Many men turned to see what was happening; seeing Hugo's face, they crossed themselves. A noble on board turned indignantly to the captain. 'This is the face of death!' he shrieked.

'It is an omen,' shouted another, 'that we will all meet our deaths before we reach Spain.';

'How can we rest easy when we have to face the sight of this man, half-human, half-skeleton, day after day?'

The men were beginning to riot. Jonathon tried to subdue them, but his gentle voice was soon shouted down.

'You are English, anyway. How do we know you are not a spy?' hissed a fat man with a long beard. Jonathon spun round, 'Say what you wish to me, but the boy is a hero, for God's sake. Let him be.'

The fat man lunged at Jonathon and a scuffle broke out. No one seemed to want to fight with Hugo – they dared not touch him. Instead their wrath fell on Jonathon. Hugo ran forward and tried to pull them off. The nobleman kicked Hugo away, and he skidded across the deck. Jonathon pulled himself up and drew his sword but a crewman grabbed him from behind, while another wrestled the sword from his hand and darted towards Hugo. Jonathon lunged forward, stretching out for his sword. The crewman had Hugo up against the ship's rail: he pulled the sword back, ready to run it through him. As the ship took the swell of the open sea Hugo pushed the man and he lost his balance, staggering backwards, the sword flailing in mid-air, as he tried to regain his footing. At the same moment Jonathon dashed forwards and his neck took the full force of his own sharp blade. Blood pumped from his arteries and he slumped down, holding the neck wound, his eyes on Hugo, who was gripping the rail.

'Jump!' he cried. 'Jump, Hugo. Save yourself at least. ' He tried to speak again but only emitted a long gurgle.

Hugo threw himself forward to try to save his dying friend. He took a step, his foot slid in the growing pool of red, and landed face down, his hands now sticky with Jonathon's blood. As he raised his head Jonathon slumped forward. Hugo stretched out and grasped Jonathon's fingers. They gripped his hand and then flickered as Jonathon died. Hugo squeezed the hand tighter. 'No!' he cried. 'No, no, no!'

'Good idea of his,' said a voice behind him.

'Let's put him over.'

The men gripped Hugo and pulled him into the air. He still clasped Jonathon's hand.

'All right. Save time with a burial,' growled a voice behind him and Jonathon's body rose parallel to his own. Together they flew through the air and hit the water. Hugo tried to swim, holding on to Jonathon's body, but the current soon swept the corpse away, and in the darkness of the January morning, Hugo drifted slowly back to the Irish shore.

His journey back to Ulster took him two years. Since the

fiasco at Kinsale the English army was in control almost everywhere, and, where it was not, the fields were burned and trees pulled down to starve the people out and take away their cover.

Famine stalked the land from north to south. On his way Hugo heard terrible tales: of a group of children under ten who were found alone with the remains of their dead mother, whose flesh they had been living on for weeks; of old women who lured young children into their hovels then killed them and cooked their bodies. Stories of a desperate nation. O'Neill was still the hope of the people, and even he, Hugo heard, had been driven into the woods when the English had razed his home to the ground and smashed the ancient coronation stone into tiny pieces.

Hugo trudged northwards still, picking berries where he could find them, drinking from streams. Everyone he passed on his way had the same ghostly transparent look.

When, exhausted and starving, he finally reached the Ulster border, he heard that O'Neill had submitted to Queen Elizabeth, but she had since died, and O'Neill was now in London suing for clemency from the new English king, James. In the summer Hugo arrived at a village near O'Neill's camp in Fermanagh. The sun burned his paper-thin skin, and feeling weak he sank down under a bush to sleep until the evening's cool permitted him to continue his journey.

He awoke when someone roughly shook him. He opened his eyes, but could not see for the glare.

'Are you from around here?' a serving man was saying 'You need food, work?'

Hugo sat up. 'Yes. Yes I do.'

Behind the servant a woman was slowly climbing down from her horse. 'Who is it, Donnel? Have the fairies taken his brain?'

'Eaten his face off, more like.'

Hugo saw the skirt of the woman quickly swish nearer. Donnel stepped back to clear her path. Hugo looked up and came eye to eye with Erin. She swooped down and cradled his face in her palms.

'My poor starving boy. I thought you had returned to Spain,' she said. She stood up and issued orders to Donnel: 'Carry him on your horse. We must get some food for him, and fresh clothes. There's no time to waste.'

Hugo fell back with weakness and relief. Donnel bent low, scooped him up in his arms, and carried him to Erin's home nearby. 'It appears that fate has decreed you stay here in Ireland,' she told him. 'You still have those four fields, acushla machree.'

Hugo dipped a chunk of bread into his soup. His mouth was still too sore with ulcers to chew anything rough.

'Have you lost my ring, boy?' Erin was stroking his long bony fingers. Hugo shook his head.

'It became too big, so I hung it around my neck. Here.' He pulled it out from under this shirt.

'Don't feel you have to agree to this out of gratitude, please,' said Erin, 'but, if you would like it, I would like to stay with you, to marry you.'

Hugo studied the face of the woman who had once terrified him, and knew it must happen. She was the only person who recognised him for the outsider he felt he was; the only person in whose presence he felt at peace. The only woman who appeared not to see the scars on his face.

# 1607
## County Down

They settled down in the small house in a quiet corner of County Down, and worked the four fields.

When they arrived they had found the place deserted, the wooden house destroyed, the fields charred and barren. The local villages were like ghost towns, so many people had died during the famine.

'The burning will be good for the soil,' said Erin, surveying the scene.

They chopped wood and made themselves a small cabin. From the beach they fetched baskets full of seaweed which they dug into the ground, and the following year they produced a bumper harvest. Always they worked side by side – Erin was not afraid of heavy work – and once the fields were seeded, ready to overwinter, it was she who started to build.

'Stone,' she said. 'It must be stone, then they can't just blow it down, and it will outlast us both, and our children and our children's children.'

'But the troubles are over now,' said Hugo.

'The troubles,' Erin picked up her hammer and brought it down, shattering a large stone into many workable pieces, 'will never be over. Of that I am sure.'

That night, as they sat in the warmth of the glowing peat fire, a horseman galloped up to their door.

'I come from the O'Neill, and the Lords Tyrconnell and

Maguire,' he said, steam rising from his horse. 'Do you have, or know of, any children with six toes on one foot?'

Hugo laughed. 'Is this some foolery?'

Erin came up to the door behind him and addressed the messenger. 'Wish my lord a peaceful and successful voyage.'

The messenger seemed perplexed.

'Tell him that we send him our blessing, but we know not of any such children.'

When the messenger had ridden off Erin swept inside, running her hands through her long hair. 'We must stay calm,' she said, ' and be prepared for what must follow.'

Hugo shook his head, puzzled.

'Such a child is sought for a charm against a bad sea voyage. O'Neill and the great lords are leaving us.'

'I don't understand,' whispered Hugo, remembering the face of Red Hugh O'Donnell on the harbourside at Kinsale. 'This is their country.'

'And we are on O'Neill land. If he goes into exile, we will have a fight on our hands. So now we have no leaders to protect us; they are leaving us, lambs to the slaughter.'


Heavily pregnant, Erin rode with Hugo to plead before the English Deputy. 'We must play a double game,' she warned Hugo. 'Always fight like with like. Don't be surprised if you hear me lie.'

They stood together in the council chamber before a panel of linen-ruffed Englishmen scratching away with quills and pulling at their trim beards.

'Surname?' barked the clerk.

Hugo looked at Erin: he had never been given a surname, nor needed one.

'Muirgean,' she said. She turned to Hugo and muttered, 'Child of the sea.'

'We have a smallholding in south Down,' said Hugo.

'A reward for us, after my husband received wounds in the battle of Clontibret, your honour, fighting alongside the English to suppress the wild rebels.'

The judges looked up at Hugo and seemed impressed. How were they to know that he had lost his face at quite another battle, fighting the English?

'We are not bound to upkeep any promises made by Tyrone,' said one juror, a man in a green doublet, 'or any of his cohorts. They are nothing to us but base-born, contemptible creatures, outlaws.'

'If you refuse to give up your land, you understand that the law allows us to hang you?' added another.

'And that is why we have ridden all this way, my lord,' murmured Erin, humbly. 'I am late with child. We trust in the great beneficence of the English court in helping us through this difficult time.'

'To be frank,' said the man in green, 'we are not inspired to generosity, quartered as we are in this barren, uncouth and desolate land, only fit to confine rebels and ill-spirits.'

'One wonders, sir,' said Erin slowly, 'if you harbour such thoughts about our country, why you are keen to take it from us.'

The lord laughed at this, but the man in green tightened his lips. Before he had a chance to speak, Erin started to pant, quietly as though she was trying to suppress it. The lords looked worried.

'I am sorry, sir,' she bowed her head and gripped her belly in both hands, 'but the child pains are upon me, and I do not know what I am saying.'

'Our plan,' said a kind-faced man, 'is to plant the North with civil people of the Protestant faith from England and Scotland, to bring civilisation to the wilderness.'

'We will welcome such neighbours,' gasped Erin. 'If my lords will excuse me. My husband paid fealty to the

O'Neill, and we will gladly pay fealty to the English king.'

Erin swooned upon Hugo's shoulder. He put his arm around her waist and moved as though to help her from the chamber. 'Please, no,' she whispered hoarsely. 'I will remain here until the lords have given their judgment.'

The Englishmen looked at each other in panic at the idea that this savage woman might give birth in front of their eyes. The green man stuttered, 'I am in no mood to uphold the petition, petit . . .'

Erin stared him in the eye, panting the while. Her look was dark, intense and unblinking.

'Petition . . . upheld,' he said finally, looking round in surprise as though the words had been pulled from his mouth against his will.

'Hurry, husband,' said Erin, gripping Hugo's arm, and the pair made their way from the court.

A week later she gave birth to their child.

'These Sassanas,' she explained, 'are terrified of nature, and of women. Nor do they like the sight of a scarred face. All those things were worth making use of to keep our land. And, they're happy with anything if it brings them a profit.'

Over the next thirty-four years Hugo and Erin witnessed a stream of homeless and dispossessed people passing through their village. Many stopped off and worked at their farm. The Protestant settlement had been successful in that there had been no bloodshed after the initial troubles, and the settlers were peaceable enough. The new English landlords provided money for drainage schemes and built mills and roads. Luckily Hugo and Erin lived in a quiet corner of the country, made slightly inaccessible by its position, surrounded by mountains on one side and the coast on the other.

They had four children, three boys and a girl. The eldest boys, Sean and Patrick, were working on the fields from an early age and their sister, Mary, grew up to the lowing of the cows at milking time, and enjoyed sitting with her mother and watching the warm milk spurt into the wooden buckets. The youngest son, Jon, was born with weak and crooked legs, and he spent most of his time with the women.

Patrick married Kate, a pretty girl from Newcastle, and they lived in a small house there with their baby and Kate's brother.

One October evening, while Hugo and Erin prepared hot water to wash the boys down after a heavy day's planting, Patrick came panting into the kitchen.

'Armagh's been taken, and Dungannon. Armies are on the march I can't just sit here and rot,' he told them.

Erin stood, shaking by the fire. 'What do you mean?'

'The news has only got through, but from here to the Derry the Irish are on the march, the Protestants are on the run, and I am going to join them. Sean too.'

Hugo faced the young man. 'Stay here. Blood spilt only leads to the spilling of blood.'

Patrick turned on him. 'It's all right for you, Father. You had your adventures. You had the chance to fight and be a man. What sort of life is this for us, cooped up in this dismal corner, playing with horses and cows and planting crops? That's women's stuff.'

'Then maybe women have more sense,' hissed Erin.

'We knew you wouldn't understand. Both of you are happy to sit and take whatever anyone throws at you. You just pay these ridiculous tithes and rack rents with no complaint, even though we all have to work like slaves just to keep skin on our bones. Sean has already saddled the horses. We'll see you when we've won our country back.'

'What about Kate?'

'Kate can please herself,' said Patrick, as he strode out of the room without a last look at his mother, who had sunk tearfully into a chair. Hugo passed his hand across her grey hair and made his way into the yard, but he only caught the sight of dust rising as the horses galloped out of the gates and into the lane.

Rumours came to the farm with every messenger-boy sent to buy a pail of milk or a bushel of wheat: thousands of Protestants had been massacred, others were driven naked from their homes which were then burned out so they could not return. Shiploads of Scottish settlers were daily fleeing from Belfast; civil war had erupted in England and driven the King out of London, and Puritans were slowly taking control of the country. At Portadown the Irish, they were told, had driven over eighty English and Scots women and children off a bridge and into the River Bann, where they were left to drown while the Irish used them for target practice. Any who swam to the banks were, while gasping for breath, coldly clubbed to death.

'No good will come of this,' said Erin to Hugo.

'But we may win,' Mary said, looking up from her sewing.

'Not "we",' snapped Hugo.

'No one will ever win this way.' Erin looked her daughter in the eye. ' "We" will pay in blood. You wait and see.'

The uprising grew, and a large Scottish army was dispatched by the new Puritan government. The Catholics, old English settlers as well as the Gaels and Ulstermen, joined together to repel them.

Sean returned, triumphant, after three years. 'We've driven most of them out,' he announced. 'Now all we must do is finish them off. When the Scots army marches south against us from their winter quarters we will strike. We are fighting under Owen Roe O'Neill, who's just back from Spain. And the Spanish know something about fighting.

228

They wouldn't be cowed by a lot of braying fools in red jackets.' Hugo gasped. Sean bent over his mother and kissed her forehead. 'Don't worry. We'll win. Just see.'

Erin raised her face and spat at her son. 'Don't bother,' she said. 'I don't know that I like winners very much.'

When Sean had stormed off, Mary came in with Jack, Kate's brother, who had helped them out over the years that Sean and Patrick were absent.

'Jack and I are to be married,' she said, 'if that's all right with you.'

She could see that her parents had both been crying. Jack stood shyly by the door while she crouched down and held her mother's hand. 'Don't worry,' she sighed, 'we won't leave you, will we, Jack? We want to stay here and give you grandchildren and live in peace.'

When the news of the great Irish victory at Benburb reached them Mary was large with child. A few days after the little girl was born, Sean and Patrick returned to the farm.

'You see,' crowed Sean, 'all your predictions were nothing but superstition. It's all fairy-ring stuff. It was all right for us when we were children, but these are times for men's tales.'

Crippled Jon sat eagerly in his wicker chair, and, next to him, Jack was rapt. Mary, baby at her breast, was eager to hear Sean's stories.

'The battle began just before dawn,' he began. Hugo rose from his fireside seat, and shuffled out into the yard. Sean tossed a look over his shoulder. 'Jealous, you see. His lot never won.'

Erin walked slowly towards the table. 'Nobody's won anything . . . yet.'

Sean sighed. 'You older generation are such pessimists. So where was I?' He turned back to address his sister and her husband.

'Dawn, the battle commences.' Jon wriggled in his chair so that the wicker creaked. 'If only, if only I was strong and could have been there with you . . . ' he murmured.

'Dawn,' repeated Sean. 'Rows of men, striking their matches, each man striking six or seven, so that the enemy thought there were many more of us than there were . . .'

Erin found Hugo leaning against the gateposts in the moonlight. 'I have failed all along the way,' he said.

'No.' She put her arm round him and laid her head on his shoulder. 'You lived the only way you could. You were always very brave.'

'I was a coward,' said Hugo. 'Always a coward.'

She lifted her face and kissed his chin. 'It is far braver not to kill.'

Hugo froze and looked down at her. 'What do you mean?' he said hoarsely.

'When you fought at Yellow Ford you shot at the air and the mud. You did not shoot at men.'

'How do you know that?' said Hugo, hardly breathing. 'You used to say I was a hero.'

'So you were. It would take a hero to face the barrel of an enemy gun and not fire his own.'

'But . . . ' Hugo looked down at his wife, her long white hair cascading over her shoulders.

'I told you when you were just a child, those years and years ago. I know you, acushla agus asthore machree. From the sea you came, just as I did. We are only lent to this world.' She reached up and stroked the salt from his cheeks. 'Sometimes I feel such a howling in my heart. You mustn't be afraid of your own children or allow them to upset you. They will learn in their own way. Just as we did.'

She was quiet for a moment, then moaned again in her haunting dark way. 'For their sea longings shall be land longings, and their land longings sea longings.'

230

They stood together in the blue light and kissed before going back into the glowing kitchen.

Three years later the English beheaded their king. Sean and Patrick, with Jack who was inflamed by tales of heroism on the field, joined the Irish army and headed north to meet Cromwell's army which had landed at Belfast. But this time fortune shone her light on the English side. The Irish army was quickly dispersed.

As the Commonwealth army marched south, they burned and looted, taking their revenge for the terrible massacre of Protestants some years before. Sean was killed in the field. Jack managed to make his way home, but Patrick was captured.

'He's to be transported to the New World,' said Jack, who heard the rumours from Catholics fleeing from the docksides at Belfast. 'They're loading droves of them on to huge ships. They're going to start a new life there, they say.'

What they didn't say was that the thousands of men and women crammed on to the ocean-bound ships were heading for a new life as slaves: they had been sold by the British government to plantation owners in the West Indies.

'Not in your mouth, darling,' laughed Mary as the baby picked up a stone and licked it.

Hugo and Mary were sitting on boxes in the yard in the warmth of a July afternoon with the baby, three generations together. Jon, who had been carried out in his wicker chair, occasionally rolled the little coloured ball for the baby. Jack was out on one of the horses, riding into town to see that his sister, Kate, was all right, and Erin, now very frail and in her early eighties, was asleep inside.

When they heard the hooves coming up the lane, they expected to see Jack. Instead four young men climbed down from their horses and strolled nonchalantly into the yard.

'This a farm?' asked a blond boy dressed all in brown but for a starched white collar which fell round his shoulders like a little cape.

Hugo nodded.

'Can we get you anything?' asked Mary, holding her hand up to her forehead to cut out the sun's glare.

'Some milk, please,' grinned the boy. 'We're hot and thirsty.' His friends stood behind him, nodding. 'I'm Captain Tate. We serve in the Lord Protector's army.' The boy looked around him. 'All yours?' he asked.

Hugo nodded again as Mary swung into the dairy to fetch the milk.

'This your heir?' asked Tate, pointing down at the baby.

Hugo smiled. 'Yes. I suppose so.'

'Anyone else here at the moment?'

Jon chipped in. 'No,' he said. 'Why? Can we help you to anything. Are you lost?'

'Oh, no,' said the captain. 'We know where we are.'

As Mary returned from the dairy with a tray full of wooden bowls of milk, the boys advanced on the child. Captain Tate picked up the baby and held it out to the others. 'So little,' he said. 'What a shame.'

The three boys advanced, holding clubs. Hugo jumped up and ran towards them. Mary stood, frozen. The clubs swung up in the air, and down on the baby's head.

Jon, with untold resources, threw himself from his chair and on to the ground and gripped one of the boys' legs. The boy kicked and Jon was thrown into the shadow of the house. Mary dropped the tray and screamed.

The boys dashed back to their horses. Captain Tate turned at the gatepost. 'Nits make lice,' he called, climbed on to his horse and galloped away laughing, with the others.

Erin, hearing Mary's scream, rushed into the courtyard to find her husband crouching on the cobbles nursing the child's battered body, her crippled son crawling through puddles of milk, and her daughter silently shaking as the milk ran in rivulets around her feet. Her child's blood mingled with it, turning the white pink.

The old woman, in her youth called a witch, ran to the gateposts and cursed the murderers of her grandchild. 'May death hound you. May your lands drip in blood and your children and their children down the ages, generation to generation, live lives haunted by the spectre of this killing of an innocent child!' she cried. The wind blew down from Luke's Mountain and carried her words along the valleys and green fields for miles around.

Erin prepared a hot drink with whiskey, honey and herbs, and watched over Mary as she slept. Jack sat in the kitchen, gazing at the flames licking the chimney back. When Jack's head fell forward in a restless, drunken sleep, Hugo got up and went to the door. 'Where are you going, Father?' asked Jon.

'I know how things go. This is not the end. The beginning, rather. There are things that must be done. I saw it once when I was a child, and now it seems our only option.'

'Please let me help you.'

Hugo paused and looked at his son, a man in his early thirties trapped for ever in his wretched chair.

'It's heavy work,' he said, shaking his head.

'And you are an old man, now, Pop,' Jon replied.

Hugo laughed as he helped Jon up and walked him out into the moonlit yard. 'I'll give you string,' he said. 'You make everything carriable, by any of us.'

From the stable Hugo brought out a pick. He started at the back of the house, far from his sleeping family.

Hugo climbed a ladder and levered off roof tiles, then tossed them down to Jon, who laid them out in small piles and tied them into small parcels. When he reached the timbers he was stuck: his arms were not strong enough to saw them through.

'Help me up there,' said Jon. 'One thing I have got is strong arms.'

Hugo looked down and both men started to laugh at the thought. Jack staggered out into the yard.

'What the devil's going on?' he whispered.

By dusk the next day Hugo and his family had dismantled the main part of the house. Then, stone by stone, they filled small carts and saddlebags with the grey bricks and carried them up the mountain. Jack, Mary and Hugo walked the mule up and down, carrying armfuls of their house with them, while Erin and Jon loaded up down in the valley.

They picked a secluded spot with stony thin soil. 'No one could ever want this,' said Hugo, surveying the bleak landscape. 'We'll build here.'

When they had put together their house, Jack and Mary came to Hugo and Erin and told them that they were going to move off. There would not be room for them all in this tiny place. They were going to try to leave the country, move to the New World or France. This country had too many bad memories for them, and held no future. Jack's sister had a friend, Rose, who would come up and make sure they were all right.


Some weeks after they had gone, Hugo took the spare hunks of rock, still stacked in a pile beside the walls of the single-storeyed house, and walked the hillside dropping

234

them in straight lines. Jon sat at the door and watched him.

'What are you doing, Pop?'

Hugo looked across at his son.

'We had four fields down there. So we will have four fields up here.'

'But . . .'

'Yes, I know. We had luscious green fields stretching as far as the eye could see. Fields that could hold wheat that would grow as high as a mule. Here we'll get an inch of grass if we're lucky. We can have chickens, a goat. We'll survive.'

Jon toyed with one of the pieces of timber stacked against the low frontage. He pulled out a pocket knife and whittled away at it. 'You're Spanish really, aren't you?' he said.

Hugo nodded.

'So I'll make you a present, you and Ma, from this spare wood. I'll carve you a beautiful four-poster bed, and paint it with Spanish patterns in red and green and gold, like the stuff you talk about on those ships.'

'You stay there!' chuckled Hugo.

Jon shrugged. He wasn't going anywhere.

Hugo darted into the cottage and came out with a leather pouch.

'Why I kept hold of these I don't know,' he said. 'You can't spend them here.'

He spread a handkerchief on Jon's lap, pulled the drawstring of the purse and emptied the Spanish pieces of eight into it. Jon whistled softly through his teeth. He picked up one of the intricately stamped coins and looked at it closely. 'They're beautiful,' he said. 'I'll make you a little Spanish chest too, to keep them in.'

'They're for you,' said Hugo. 'And your children.'

'Children?' said Jon, looking down in embarrassment.

'Agh, I've seen the way that little girl Rose looks at you.

I've caught her blushing when you radiate her with one of your smiles.'

Jon shifted and the wicker chair rustled.

'You're a good-looking man, you know, Jon. And a decent woman isn't going to be put off just because you've weak legs.'

Rose came out of the cottage with a chair and Erin followed her. 'There's you two,' the girl said with a sweet smile, 'always hatching some plot or other.'

She helped Erin into the chair, wrapping a blanket around her legs, then sat on the grass at her feet and sighed. 'I love it here,' she said. 'I'm so fond of you all.'

Erin smiled and placed her hand on the girl's shoulder. 'And we're fond of you too,' she smiled.

'I get so frightened down in the town.' Rose hesitated before speaking again. 'It's a long way up and down, too,' she blushed. 'I don't suppose I could stay up here, on a pallet, anywhere?'

Hugo glanced at his son, who had turned a darker red than the girl herself. 'Jon was going to be speaking to you about that,' he said, glancing at his son. 'Weren't you?'

Jon was fiddling with the pile of gold coins on his lap. He picked one up and sent it spinning in the air, sparkling and catching the sun as it went. Hugo stretched out his hand and caught it.

He laughed.

# CATHERINE

# 1921
*Liverpool*

Liverpool. England! Who'd ever have thought it would be like this. Catherine had always imagined a world of gents in dapper suits, and elegant ladies dancing at balls. The smoke! And the darkness of the streets, lined with blackish red terraced houses. She'd never seen anything like it in her life.

She scuttled along the pavement, stepping off the kerb now and then to avoid children playing hopscotch with hunks of chalk and pieces of brick.

It was midday, but it seemed as gloomy as an autumn evening. The wind blew pages of a torn newspaper up gloomy Silvester Street, Bootle. An eddy of dust at Catherine's feet caught a dried-up leaf and dispersed as another strong gust whistled up from the Mersey docks. An old coal cart with sides painted 'J. Edwards, Fazakerley' heaved past. The coal man, seated high up, held the reins in one hand and yelled down at her, 'Good luck, kid! It's lucky to see the coalman you know, on yer way to church.'

He gave her a wink and a wave before clicking his tongue at the horse and clopping past her.

She could actually see the church ahead of her now. A gloomy red building fronted by cast-iron railings, it blended curiously well with the rows of terraced houses on either side and opposite. Under an old overcoat she had picked up at Paddy's Market the morning before, she wore the white party dress she had put on that strange night a month ago in Ireland.

John had got her a room in the same boarding-house he lodged in; the only one in the street without a sign in the window stating shamelessly, 'No blacks, no children, no animals, no Irish.'

When she first found him on the ferry, he had picked her up, twirled her round and treated everyone in the bar to a round of drinks. Later in the night he led her out on to the deck to watch the play of moonlight on the waves. He held her in his arms. 'I don't need to give you the moon,' he said. 'It's there for free for anyone to enjoy. But now you've thrown your lot in with me, gal, I'll give you everything it's in my power to give.'

She had been ecstatic.

The ecstasy had worn off somewhat just before dawn, when the ship berthed at Liverpool in the pouring rain. But Catherine's heart was still high as she and John stepped down the gangplank. They walked arm in arm down to the Pier Head in the cold grey light, then sat on a bench underneath the overhead railway and talked. When the stalls started opening up John bought them both a cup of hot tea, and then, with rain plastering his hair to his forehead and dripping from his chin, got on his knees and proposed. She accepted.

That night, alone in her dingy room, she crouched over the small coal grate and wrote to her father. It was a long letter, full of apology, and explanation and love. In reply she received a letter from her ex-fiancé Alan, telling her that as far as her father was concerned she was no longer his daughter, and to 'desist from any further correspondence'. 'Desist' indeed. Whoever wrote words like that to people they'd once been engaged to? Thank goodness she hadn't married him.

She wrote again, this time to Cassie, whose long letter back told Catherine that her father would not allow anyone to mention her name. He did not want to know what had become of her or the infamous John Morgan. Cassie was very sorry. She sent them both much love and luck.

Catherine was desolate. John suggested she go back home and make it up with her father, and not marry him at all, or at least put it off until she had thought about it for a month or so. At this Catherine became even more determined to press ahead with the wedding, father or no father. Who needed to be given away anyway? Given away, indeed. What was she – a parcel? She wiped the farm and everyone on it from her mind.

And now here she was on a cold, damp Liverpool morning, making her windswept way to the church. John was, she trusted, waiting for her at the altar, having rustled up a few friends from the docks, where he had a job as a stevedore, to act as witnesses. She was determined not to be sad at having to walk up the aisle alone, and now was more irritated than upset at her father cutting her off. He would come round, eventually.

A rosy-faced fat woman stood on her front step grinning at Catherine, as she hoiked up her skirts and jumped over a puddle where a handful of cobbles were missing.

'Come along, lass,' she said. 'It's not right to have no one to help you to church.' The woman shouted back through the open door: 'Susan, keep an eye on the little ones, would you. I've got to go to the church for a bit.' She stood up, unwrapped her apron, tossed it over the threshold, grabbed a hat from the hooks by the door and walked along with Catherine.

They turned into the church gate, climbed five stone steps and entered the wooden doors.

'Is he there?' whispered Catherine.

'Who?' replied the woman.

'John', hissed Catherine, 'my husband; to be, that is.'

The woman took a few paces along the stone passage-way and looked to the right into the almost empty church. 'A tall handsome fellah, with curls and an earring, is he?' she asked.

Catherine gasped with relief. 'He's there. I knew he would be.'

The woman smiled and helped Catherine remove her coat, then hung it on the coat-stand by the door.

'I'm Gertie, by the way. Gertie York. Now I'll be off. You don't mind if I sit at the back and watch, do you? I love a wedding. It's wonderful living right next door to the church.'

The woman shuffled off into the church. 'Good luck,' she whispered. 'You look lovely.'

Here was a wedding to remember, thought Catherine. Walking to the church, escorted by a total stranger, and going up the aisle alone.

She stood at the back of the church and smoothed her hands down the front of her dress. She counted six people in the pews, including Mrs York. She took a deep breath and stepped forward. Behind her a clatter of feet echoed on the stone flagstones, then someone grabbed her elbow.

'Slow down to a gallop, would you now. I'm barely after getting me breath back from the dash up from the ferry.' Catherine stared down in amazement at Hughie, her leprechaun from the hills.

'What on earth are you doing here?' she gasped. 'Did Cassie send you?'

'No questions, my little girl, aren't I here to show a tiny bit of support for an old friend.' He winked and held out his arm. 'I've just popped over for the afternoon, and we'd better get along, for I've a boat to catch in an hour. Come along there, the wee boy will be thinking you've run off with a Chinaman.'

'But . . .'

242

'No buts, unless that is you've changed your irascible mind yet again.' Hughie nodded towards the altar piece. 'Well now, look at that, will you. They've painted up the church just like me old bed. Isn't it a pretty sight!'

Catherine looked at the gaudily painted altar and suppressed a smile as Hughie took a step forward. Together they stepped up the aisle towards John Morgan's beaming grin.

Despite a perfectly legible marriage certificate, their landlord was not willing for them to move into one room together.

'Overcrowding!' he said. 'There are laws.' And that was that.

So while John was at work, Catherine marched the streets looking for accommodation. Eventually she found them a 'Scotch house', a quarter of a terraced house, but with one wonderful thing – their own front door. And within this tiny space she created them a home.

She sat in it, day after day, hearing the neighbours quarrel and brawl through the thin walls, gazing for hours out of the window, watching children playing and people coming busily to and fro. Twice a week she'd see Jack 'Fazak', the coalman, rattle past with his worn-out horse, and they'd exchange a few words, about the weather usually or something else that neither of them cared much about.

She began to pine for the open spaces, for the green fields, the blue mountains and the sea. She missed the company on the farm, where there was always someone to talk to. Here she was surrounded by people, but had only the flimsiest of conversations with them: 'How's your husband?'; 'Hear there's a new liner coming in today from America, that'll keep them busy'; 'Butter's rather dear these days . . .' She thought she'd go mad.

Sometimes as the afternoon dragged on and the sound

243

of her own fingers tapping on the windowsill began to drive her mad, she would scoop up her shawl and let herself out of the back door, stepping briskly into the yard. She skipped down the jigger at the back, past the dustbins, and muddy children screaming at each other, and walked lightly out into the Scotland Road. When she reached the Pier Head she bought a ticket to ride on the ferry and spent the afternoon going back and forth across the Mersey to Seacombe, sitting on a bench at the prow of the ship and enjoying the salt wind whipping her face for the half-hour round trip; sometimes she went as far as New Brighton and felt she was almost at sea again.

On such a day she returned to find John stoking up the small stove, to boil some more water for a wash. 'Agh, you've been out on the high seas again, have you, my little banshee!' he greeted her.

He picked her up in his grimy arms and kissed her.

'Oh, John, now lookit, you'll have me all filthy like yourself.'

He lifted a lid from a pot on the stove. 'I've peeled the potatoes. Who do you know with a husband like that, who'll get his hands wet in the kitchen?'

'Sure, *you* taught me to cook.'

'I had to, didn't I, or I'd have had to live on bread and butter for the rest of me days.' He pulled a stool up to the table. 'So there's potatoes. What else shall we have?' They scraped the carrots together.

'Well there, an interesting thing happened to me today,' John told her. 'I was loading a car on to the American liner, and the fellah who owns it is hanging around all impatient like as we lower it, and as we're swinging the thing over to drop it on the deck, he pulls me aside and tells me he wants a word with me.'

'Oh no! What had you done wrong?' Catherine asked.

'No, gal, it was nothing like that at all. The fellah pulls

out a card from his coat, with his name on it, and a lot of addresses in Americkay, and says to me "I like the look of you, sir, you have physique. I can find you very good work in California, in the movies." Now of course I just laughed him in the face, but he says, "No, sir, I do not joke. I am a scout for Mr Charlie Chaplin, an Englishman, like your-self." Well, I didn't disabuse him of that, and he continued, "And you, sir, are the kind of man I have been sent over to find." So how about that!'

'Was the fellow drunk, or what?'

'No, no, I think he was the real thing. Who'd be rich enough to have a huge car like that to bring over on the boat from America?'

'And will you be taking him up on this offer?'

John laughed. 'I shouldn't think so for a moment.'

Catherine grabbed John's sleeve. 'I don't think I'm feel-ing too well'.

'Oh acushla, you're very pale. Come and lie down.' He picked her up and carried her to their bed, where she slept fitfully.

It was a few months after this day that John came home and announced that he was going to throw in his job at the docks and take a job on board a transatlantic liner as a steward. Better money, he said, and easier work.

'And I suppose Mr Charlie Chaplin's friend had nothing to do with this decision?'

John shook his head, but muttered, 'Well, now you mention it, it wouldn't be a bad idea, would it?'

'So having dragged me over here to live in this sty, you're now going to dump me while you go off in search of fun.' John tried to interrupt but couldn't get a word in. 'They warned me, you know, they warned me that you were undependable, flighty. I don't know why I never listened. They were right. I should have stayed there and married Alan. I'd have had a better life than this.'

She had run out of steam. She stood and faced him, defiant, her hands on her hips. John just raised his eyelids and said quietly, 'That was your decision. Not mine.'

He sat down and opened the evening newspaper, cracking the pages loudly and holding it up so that he could not see her. He could hear her though, as she crashed around.

After about an hour of this, John tried to break the ice. He followed her around until he was near enough to put his arm round her shoulder.

'It'll be better all round for both of us if I'm bringing home decent money, you know, gal. And if I did have a little spell in the fillums, and came back a millionaire, that would be a bit of all right, don't you think?'

Catherine simply shook his arm away, pursed her lips and started busily taking the clean crockery from the drainer and washing it.

Later, when John had given up his vigil and gone out to the pub for a drink, Catherine quietly and calmly packed all her belongings and walked down to the dock where she caught the night ferry for Dun Laoghaire.


It was dark by the time she started climbing the mountain. She was miserable and exhausted. Her appearance at the family farm had not provoked the welcome she had hoped for. There had been no tearful reconciliations for the prodigal daughter, just tight-lipped insults from that hateful Alan, and her father walking away and slamming the door behind him when he caught sight of her. Cassie had shaken her head and told Catherine there was nothing she could do. Minds had been made up, and the atmosphere of the place was not the same since Catherine's wild departure. Cassie said she'd like to let Catherine stay the night with her, but that Alan had given strict instructions that she was to be sent on her way by dusk at the latest.

When Catherine reached the tiny house on the mountainside she began to be afraid. There were no lights on. She rapped at the door. No reply. Next time she pounded, calling out Hughie's name at the same time. When this got no response she walked around the house and peered into the tiny windows. All she could see was blackness. She tried the door handle. The door opened. She walked into the living room and fumbled around in the dark trying to find a candle then flopped into an armchair in the darkness, and waited.

She woke as the door burst open and a rowdy group of men stumbled in. They struck matches and lit candles and burst into a roar of laughter.

'Hey, there, Hughie! Now here's a big secret you've been keeping from us!'

Hughie pushed through to the front and stood before Catherine, his lips set. His friends laughed on.

'You weren't after telling us about your beautiful new girlfriend, you old rogue!'

'She's no girlfriend of mine,' hissed Hughie. 'She's my sister-in-law.' He bent down to Catherine, pulled her up by the arm and led her towards the other room. 'You'd better be getting some sleep. The bed's warm enough, I left a warming-pan in it. In you go. I've company. I'll talk to you later.'

He handed Catherine a candlestick and closed the door on her. She sank down on to the ornate bed and sobbed. She lay gazing at the candle throwing bursts of golden light on the posts of the bed, making the red redder, and the gold brighter, and thought back to the altar at which she had married John almost a year before.

When the men left shortly before dawn Hughie threw open the door and coldly called for Catherine to join him. 'I know you didn't sleep. You'd better come and explain yourself,' he said.

'I'm so unhappy' she cried.

'I'm not in the least surprised at that,' he muttered. 'What in God's name are you doing here?'

'My father wouldn't listen to me, wouldn't let me home. He kept shouting "As you've made your bed so shall you lie", so I had nowhere else to go but here.'

'Whoa, whoa, slow down to a gallop, will you now. What I really want to know is why you're not at home with your husband.'

'Oh him. *That* home,' sighed Catherine. 'He doesn't love me. I don't know why I married him. Thank you by the way for telling those fellows I was a relation. I don't suppose it would have looked so good if people thought I was staying up here with you alone all night.'

Hughie sat cross-legged on the hearth and looked solemnly up at his friend.

'So he's not told you then . . .?'

She did not respond, and Hughie shook his head before going on. 'John Morgan, you see, is my little brother. You are my sister-in-law. I'm Hughie Morgan, did you never think of that?'

'I've never known your name,' said Catherine. 'It never seemed necessary.'

'And did you never think why I turned up for the wedding?'

Catherine whimpered, 'I thought it was because you liked me.'

'Oh you little thing! Of course it was that, but the wee boy had written to me about how upset you were to have no one there, and I thought I could cover for you both. I knew it would make him happy if you were happy, you know, although I knew nothing could make up for the loss of your father.'

Catherine stared into his eyes.

'But how can you be his big brother, you're so . . . you're . . . '

248

'Small, deformed, ugly as the Devil, yes I know. You'll fall over laughing when I tell you the truth of it, which is that we're not only brothers but we're twins. I'm only a minute or two older! But the thing is, the big fellow was always greedy, and back there in our mother's womb he scoffed enough for two, and I was born like this. From the age of ten I looked like a little old man, and now I still look like a little old man, even though I'm only a year or two older than you, and when I am an old man at last I'll look me age, and there we are.'

Catherine held her hand out. 'So I've lost the family I had, but I've got new family now.'

'Now, now, now. Let's not be getting sentimental. I think you'd better start explaining what you've done to my brother, and why you're here and not there.'

She told him everything, while he sat and listened, making no comment. When she had done he made her a cup of tea and told her that after she'd had a sleep they would wire her husband and then he would help her on her way back home to Liverpool.

'I'm not feeling too well,' she said as she climbed into bed.

'Of course you're not,' he replied as he tucked her in. 'You've been up all night for two days running, and had a few shocks along the way. You'll feel better after a kip.' He drew the curtains against the dawning sun, and left her alone. He was woken from his own slumbers in the armchair, some hours later, by her screams.

In Hughie's florid four-poster bed, that afternoon, as the last rays of the sun streamed in from the brow of the blue mountains, Catherine gave birth to a baby girl.

Hughie made his way down to the village when night fell, and roused Cassie, who came back with him to look after

249

Catherine. The next morning he wired John in Liverpool and sat the whole afternoon at the post office awaiting the reply. When they shut up shop he climbed the hill, knowing the telegram would be brought up by the postmistress's son if it came in overnight. Secretly he hoped that John would be on the boat across.

He met Cassie at the gate.

'They're both doing fine,' she beamed, and lowered her voice as she continued: 'The whole thing's a mystery to me. Why that stubborn father of hers still refuses to see her I don't know, allowing that insinuating little bookworm Alan to lord it over us all.'

Hughie shook his head. 'And then there's the puzzle of how the girl got to be nine months pregnant and never noticed anything was up,' he said.

'Oh, you hear of such things, Hughie. Remember that woman in Dromore, a few years back. She was a schoolteacher as I remember, so you'd think she'd know about the birds and the bees, suddenly drops a baby in the middle of a history class. Thought she had indigestion from the awful school lunch!'

'Didn't it show?' Hughie whistled quietly through his teeth. 'The girlie here didn't at all. You'd never have suspected a thing.'

'Lying sideways, that's what happened. The baby must have been lying sideways. Most women blow up like balloons, but some just don't. Mind you, you'd have thought she'd have noticed something.'

'Agh, but there now, she was always the same. Never saw anything but what she wanted to see, and to tell truth, it wouldn't surprise me if she was ignorant of the facts of life altogether. Did you ever tell her about them?'

'Of course not,' said Cassie, 'that was hardly my business.' She paused and screwed up her face. 'But your brother now, you can't be telling me he doesn't know a

250

thing or two. I imagine he knows how babies get conceived.'

'Ay, ay, it's a mystery all right. But where the divil is he?'

When there was still no word next morning, Hughie went into Newcastle and used the telephone to try John's employers, the Mersey Docks and Harbour Board. They only told him that John Morgan, stevedore, had not turned in for work that day, or the day before. Hughie then contacted the local church, and arranged with the priest to go round to their Liverpool house and make some enquiries. Hughie would phone back after an hour.

The news was not good. According to neighbours, when John had come home and found his wife gone, he had called on everyone asking them where she was, with tears in his eyes. Then he'd gone to the pub and come out rolling drunk. They'd heard him crashing about in the room in the night, and since then no one had laid eyes on him. The priest had peered through the windows, and there was no sign of him.

Hughie came out of the dark little post office and sat down on a bench on the strand. He gazed out across the Irish Sea. 'Oh you pair of stubborn fools,' he muttered, and held his face in his hands. A wave crashed on the groyne, and spattered him with spray. He jumped up. 'That's it!' he cried, and raced back into the post office.

It was two weeks later when John Morgan bent low to enter Hughie's tiny home on the mountainside. Hughie had found the only liner to have left Liverpool that day, and had sent a telegraph via the ship-to-shore to the ship's purser. He had passed it over to John half-way across the Atlantic ocean. He had been transferred, after complex organising, to a ship going in the opposite direction, and from Liverpool came directly to Northern Ireland. With

him he brought a bottle of whiskey, a bunch of flowers and
a huge teddy bear with a label round its neck which read:
'Teddy came to visit, and thought you looked so nice he
decided to stay, love Daddy.'

# 1926
# Liverpool

'Mammy! Mammy! Look at my drawing of Daddy.'
Little Rosaleen stretched up a damp piece of paper for her
mother to see. Catherine, new baby in one arm, looked
down cursorily as she stirred the pot on the stove.

'Lovely, darling, lovely!'

'I'll start a new one now. I'll paint baby Ossie. I think
he's funny, like a frog.'

'That's right, darling.' Catherine reached out for the lid
and clattered it on to the bubbling saucepan. She wiped
the condensation from her brow and swung through the
kitchen to the living room. It really *was* a living room, for
they all lived, ate and slept in it.

'Oh, now look at all this mess,' she complained. 'What'll
your father say when he gets in?'

'Oh he doesn't mind, Mammy, at all, at all. Don't you
worry. I'm going to paint Ossie purple, I think. And I'll be
painting you green and red. Because that is what you are,
usually.'

A clattering at the door and a rasping voice through the
letterbox announced the arrival of Gertie and a handful of
her ten children.

'Catherine, love, it's Gertie. I've brought some clothes
for you.'

'Rosaleen, open the door would you?' Catherine raised
her voice. 'I won't be a minute there, Gertie.'

'Hello scamp!' Gertie tousled the child's hair as she piled in with her own gang. 'Now, now, calm down, won't you. Remember you're not at home now.'

As the York children gathered around the table to inspect Rosaleen's drawing Catherine wiped a stray piece of hair from her furrowed brow. 'I don't know how you manage Gertie, really I don't,' she said.

'Agh, it's no problem. I love the little rascals. They're no bother. It's when they start growing up you get the problems. Dave, he's eighteen now, and lives round the corner in the shop he works in, but, oh my, he gave me lip enough when he lived at home.'

Catherine looked at her friend and realised for the first time that she must be younger than forty. She looked much, much older.

Gertie stretched out her chubby hand and stroked the baby's fine red hair. 'There's a handsome little chap, eh? Who's a little champion.' Without warning Catherine burst into tears.

'Ah, there now, there now.' She turned to the children piled around the table. 'Susan York, come here and mind the little one for a moment.'

A gangly girl of about thirteen ambled over, gently took the crying baby, and sat quietly singing to him in one of the armchairs. Gertie put her arm around Catherine, walked her through to the kitchen and sat her down on the little wooden chair by the stove.

'Well, the dinner smells lovely. I'll just pop the kettle on, love, and we can have a nice brew.'

That done, she crouched beside Catherine and took her hand and said, 'Now then, what have you to cry about, you beautiful girl?'

'Everything!' Catherine gasped through her sobs. 'What is my life?'

'Agh, what are any of our lives if it comes to that.'

'But you don't understand. There must be more than this. There must be.'

'Any more would be enough to give you indigestion I should think, kid. You've got two lovely healthy children, a clean little place to live, and a big devil of a husband, who doesn't come home unconscious with drink every night and beat you, or pawn the children's clothes for tobacco money like many of the scallies around here. I should say you're laughing.'

Catherine hung her head on her chest. 'I want something else, though.'

Gertie laughed. 'And you'll get that soon enough, I should think. Look at me. I've ten little something elses, and I love every hair on each of their heads.'

'Oh, yes, that. I've already another on the way. I found out this morning, and the baby not yet out of nappies himself.'

'Catherine, Catherine. That's no reason for tears. You should be laughing to think how God has blessed you with such lovely children. Look at that Rosaleen, she's a real bobby-dazzler.'

The door crashed shut, and they heard John's voice joking with the assembly in the living room. 'And here comes the biggest child of them all,' sighed Catherine.

Gertie took a hankie from her pocket and dabbed at Catherine's tear-stained face. 'He's a lovely fellow. And you know it too.'

John's frame filled the doorway. 'And there you are, two of the most beautiful women in Liverpool.'

He stepped in, holding the baby in one arm. 'How are you keeping, Gertie? You're looking blooming.'

Gertie chuckled. 'And you don't look so bad yourself, you old rogue. Now I'll just be gathering up my brood and we'll be off back to Silvester Street for our tea.' She kissed Catherine on the forehead. 'Goodbye, kid, let us know if the clothes are no good. Bye, John. Take care of that pretty woman of yours. I think my lot have worn her out.' She pulled a hat out of her pocket and put it on, calling out for the children as she left and clicking the door shut behind her. John crouched down on his heels and looked up into Catherine's face.

'Well, look now, my beautiful girl's been crying.' He stood and lifted her from the chair, then sat her down on his knee, the baby still gently held in his other arm.

'What's getting you down, acushla? I don't like to see you cry.' The baby let out a sudden wail. 'Agh, there's the two of you at it now. Come on, little Ossie, me lad, don't you go encouraging her.' The child screamed harder.

'I can't stand it, John. Day after day, scrimping on everything, never having enough money, never being able to go anywhere.'

'Come on, gal, we get by all right. I've a job. We've a house. We have food in our bellies.'

'And I've another babe in mine.'

John looked hard into her eyes and wrapped his arm tighter round her waist. 'Well, isn't that the best news I've had all week! It's funny, I must have had a premonition, because I knew you'd be wanting a little something. Rosaleen, sweetheart, fetch me in the box I brought home with me, would you darling.'

Rosaleen's squeaky voice called back. 'I'm busy, Daddy, making you a painting.'

'Agh leave off your painting for a moment, gal, your mammy's in need of a hug.'

Rosaleen, four years old, thin and dark, staggered through the doorway with a box half her own size.

'That's a good girl. Now because you're awful clever at doing things why don't you untie the knot for your mammy, and then help her open it.' He kissed his wife on the cheek. 'That's for you, acushla, something mad to help brighten up the days.'

Catherine bent down to help untie the parcel and Rosaleen lifted the lid of the box. Catherine lifted out a large hat. 'Well, what the — '

'Put it on, why don't you?'

She stood before the little mirror hanging over the sink, laughing as she tied the ribbons. 'Whatever are you after buying me this for?'

'For nothing but being beautiful. Every beautiful woman should have a nice, pretty hat to wear on important occasions.'

'Important occasions! And what will they be, I wonder. Being taken to court for not paying our rent maybe?' She carefully took off the hat and placed it in the box. 'The problem is, you see, John, we barely have enough money to buy shoes for the children, without you spending a fortune on a silly hat. It must have cost a week's wages.'

John laughed. 'Don't you go worrying yourself.'

'But where did you get that sort of money, John? And why couldn't you have just brought the *money* home and we could have spent it on things we really need?'

'Agh, God, I thought you needed a treat, something a bit different, you know.'

'But we're not different, are we, John? We're just the same as every poverty-stricken person in this godforsaken city. How are we different from Gertie York and her family, from the McBrides down the road, from the Sharkeys, the Roaches, the Rooneys? We're all just like ants crawling around so busily all our lives until we die. There must be more to life, there must, John, there must.'

'Well, I don't know about all that. As me brother's always saying, we've got one foot in the grave and the other on a banana skin. We can only live for the present, and try to laugh at fate.'

'Take the hat back. Get us somewhere decent to live. We can't go on stuffed up in the one cluttered room when the next one comes along.'

257

Rosaleen tugged at her mother's skirt.

'The next what, Mamma?'

John bent down and picked up the little girl in his empty arm. 'Your clever old mother is going to bring us another little brother or sister for you to play with,' he told her.

Rosaleen peered up from under her heavy black brows. 'I hope they can talk better than Ossie. I want someone to talk to.'

John wiggled her about in his arm. 'Agh, go along with you, kid, don't I talk, talk, talk to you till me tongue needs bandaging. Now, let's the three of us give your mother a great big hug.'

John stepped forward and gently laid his head on his wife's shoulder. 'What'd any of us do without you, acushla, eh Rosie, gal?' Rosaleen stroked her mother's hair, with her purple- and green-stained hands. 'We love you, Mamma.'

After supper John tucked the children into their bed, and sat up holding Catherine's hand. 'I hate to see you unhappy, gal. It'll be a fine thing to have another little face around the place, so don't you worry. We'll manage.'

'Oh John, don't you see? I want more than just to manage. I want to breathe again.'

They stayed there in silence for some time. Then Catherine climbed into bed, and slept. John sat up alone, his head in his hands, as the firelight caused shadows to dance around the room behind him like leprechauns.


When Catherine awoke in the grey dawn, she reached out her arm, but John was not there. He was not in the kitchen either. The children were still asleep when she tiptoed out to the shop with a handful of change for milk and bread. Within minutes she came back without either.

She darted round the room, packing up the pieces that were theirs: pillows, sheets, knives and forks, the rickety kitchen chair, the children's paintbox.

As usual Ossie was crying. Rosaleen ran round after her mother, picking up things as she was ordered.

'Now Rosie, sweetheart, sit by the window, and tell me when you see Jack Fazak and his horse coming up the street.'

Half an hour later Catherine, her two children and all their goods and chattels were stacked up on the back of the coal cart.

'I need a pawn shop, Jack.'

'Right-ho. Where to, then, Mrs Morgan?'

'Do you know of a flat to rent? Anywhere? One that'll take children.'

'And Irish!' chuckled Jack.

'Oh yes, and Irish.'

They clopped along the streets in silence, until Jack broke the ice. 'Doing a moonlight, then, Mrs Morgan?'

Catherine held her head high. 'I am doing no such thing, Mr Edwards. I am simply finding new accommodation for myself and my children, as my husband seems incapable.'

'Oh!' Jack raised his eyebrows and decided to keep quiet until he could offload his cargo in a suitable place.

By lunchtime Catherine and her children were setting up home in a small flat in a court off the Stanley Road. When they had settled in and she had paid the first instalment of rent with the money from the pawned hat, Catherine piled the children on to a tram to the Pier Head and they spent the afternoon riding the ferry.

Over tea, as the darkness fell, Rosaleen asked after her father. Catherine changed the subject.

Later, although the flat had two rooms, one designated as bedroom, Catherine ended up sleeping with the children to keep warm.

Two nights later Catherine was awoken by a tapping on the door. From the letterbox flap she heard a sort of whistling.

She crouched down and tried to peer through, without being seen herself.

'Who is it?' she whispered. 'My husband will be home any minute. I'd advise you to go on your way, whoever you are.'

A pair of dark eyes glinted back at her.

'He's here sooner than you think, acushla.'

Catherine smashed the flap down. 'Get out of here, you pig,' she ordered. She strode away from the door.

'Hist! Hist! You have to open up. I have something for you.'

'And who told you I was here? That rat Jack Fazak, no doubt.'

'Catherine, please open up. I have to give you this. Please be serious.'

He crinkled a piece of fawn paper through the crack.

'Well just leave it then, and be gone, won't you.'

'I can't,' whispered John. 'You don't understand. I have to come in.'

'Oh, yes, that's right. You go off on your drunken revels, and get arrested and have me the laughing stock of the whole street and think you can just come crawling back and I'll take you. Well I'll tell you something. I'm not that easy a conquest, John Morgan, you twister.'

'For dear God's sake, Catherine, I'm not on a twist. I have to bring you some important news. Don't make it a row, for your own sake. Lookit, if you don't want me here I can just go, as I came. But you must read this first, and then decide.'

Catherine did not reply at first, just drew up a chair and sat on it staring at the letter flap.

'Look!' he pressed on. 'You're my wife. The mother of my two beautiful children, and another on the way. I love you. God knows that should be enough. I did wrong. I had a sore head from your accusations, so I went out for a wee drink.'

260

'The pubs were shut by that time and you know it . . .'

'Yes. Of course. But for an Irishman there's always somewhere'll open their doors. And wasn't it just my luck that the police chose that night to raid the joint? Sure I almost cracked me skull open trying to jump from the roof to escape.'

'A husband of mine spending the night in a police cell! I was mortified when I walked into the shop and found them all chirruping about it. I don't like being the subject of gossip, John Morgan. And I won't have you a-making me one.'

'You must let me in. I have news for you. It's not good news, I'm afraid.'

'Agh, you've been and gone and got the sack too I suppose.'

John crunched up the piece of paper and fed it through the letterbox. 'This is not the way I would be wanting to do it, but . . .' the telegram floated down on to the mat. Catherine snatched it up.

'It's from me brother,' said John. 'I'm so very sorry.'

Catherine read the small piece of paper and collapsed on the floor. The wiry form of Rosaleen crept round the corner into the hall. 'Who's there? Mammy, is that you? Are you all right?' she asked.

John hissed through the slit in the door. 'It's me, darling. It's Dadda.'

Rosaleen sprang across to the door, and stretched up towards the bolt.

'Oh, Dadda. Sure, we've been waiting for you to come, Mammy and me and little Ossie.'

'Just pass me the key under the door, would you darling. Your mammy's not so well, and I have to get in and help her.'

When he was inside the flat, John locked the door behind him, carried his wife to the bed, wiped away her tears

261

and sat with her, his daughter on his lap, his son asleep in bed, until she slept.

Rosaleen had no intention of going to sleep. Instead she plied her father with questions. He told her that her mother had had a nasty shock, for she'd had bad news about her daddy in Ireland, who had died.

'You won't die, will you, Daddy? Don't leave us alone again, please.'

John held the child to his chest and sang to her. He sang the song that he had sung to Catherine's dying mother, which she had loved so much.

> *'Over hills and through dales,*
> *Have I roam'd for your sake;*
> *All yesterday I sail'd with sails*
> *On river and on lake.'*

The child stretched up her arm and touched John's chin. 'It tickles when you sing. It tickles in my ears.'

'Agh, love, it's a special song for you, listen.'

> *'I dash'd across unseen*
> *For there was lightning in my blood,*
> *My Dark Rosaleen!*
> *My own Rosaleen!'*

Rosaleen sighed. 'A special song! Will Mammy be all right?'

'Yes, sure she will. When she wakes up she'll most likely have to go away for a while, but I'll stay here and take care of you.'

'And will you tell me the whole story of the song, Dadda?'

'Sure, that I will.'

Thus it was that Catherine went back alone to Ireland, to her father's funeral. Afterwards, as she left the churchyard, she was handed a small box, by a solicitor from Newcastle.

262

'It's been left to you in your father's will; well, your mother's will really, the items were, uh, held in trust for you.'

'Oh,' replied Catherine, numb. 'I hadn't really thought of things like wills.' It was being reminded of her mother at such a time that made her eyes brim full of tears.

'No. Well, one doesn't, at such a time.' The solicitor shifted from foot to foot. 'But as I heard you were returning to England tonight, I thought it would be more convenient to give it you now.'

'Well, thank you.' Catherine slipped the box into her bag, and nodded politely at the young man, who was already moving away from her.

'There's an obnoxious little swine if ever I saw one. I hope he didn't go upsetting you now,' said Cassie, threading her arm through Catherine's. They ambled along the country road.

'I'm so sorry, little one, that your father never made it up with you, but if I could get my hands on that Alan, Lord I'd shake the bones out of him. Still, there's plenty of chaps in this world can't take rejection, eh!'

They walked on in silence for a while, the clatter of their shoes echoing on the grey stone walls.

'I'm moving down to Dublin. There's nothing for me here now that I'm out of a job,' Cassie told her.

Catherine stopped and turned to her old nurse.

'Why are you out of a job? It's our family farm. You can stay on as long as you like.'

Cassie shrugged.

'Ah, so the little skunk didn't fill you in on the whole picture then.' She paused. Catherine signalled her to continue.

'Well, the truth of it is, your father has gone and done something very stupid and pig-headed. I'm sorry to speak ill of the dead, but that's about the level of it, and when I think of your lovely mother, and you skeetering about the place with old Cuchullin, and how that big lad of yours sang to her and worked so hard on the farm, and he's a good soul Lord knows everyone can see that, so how your father could have lived with himself those last weeks knowing what he was doing, I don't know.'

She bit her lip, and blinked away the threatening tears. Catherine smiled weakly at her. 'Sure but there's nothing that could happen . . . I don't understand, sure I don't.'

Cassie hung her head as she spoke, as though the shame was her own. 'He's gone and left the house, the farm, and everything to Alan. There's nothing for you.'

'Oh, Cassie, what does that matter? I never really thought about it, you know, till now. I never thought of owning it. I suppose I just thought it would all carry on on its own, with or without me.' She laughed. 'I could never have run a farm. Just think of it, will you!'

She paused and stroked Cassie's arm. 'It's only land. What does land matter to anyone? The only thing that worries me is what it'll do to you. You're sure you've got somewhere to go, now? With people to look after you?'

'Oh, sure, I'll be all right. I've a cousin in Dublin. She's a bit younger than me. Oh we'll paint the town red, the two of us!'

Catherine boarded her train to Dublin as dusk drew a curtain down over the blue mountains. She peered into the darkness, trying to make out the shapes of the hills where she had roamed as a child. She could see nothing but an impenetrable black.

Sitting alone in a ladies' compartment, she unwrapped the parcel the solicitor had given her. It contained a tortoiseshell box. This she opened gently. Inside were her mother's silver brush and comb. She held the box to her face and filled her lungs with the long-lost scent of her mother. As the train slowed to stop at a station, she snapped the box shut, and her thoughts flew from the bitter-sweet memories of her past, ahead to her children waiting for her in Liverpool, and as she tenderly stroked her belly, to the baby that moved gently inside her.

## August 1940
## Liverpool

'Ere, you, get yerself ter the back of the queue, you pushy cow!'

'I've been here for hours,' the woman bristled.

'Ay, we've all been here for hours, love, and we've been round the corner and all, at the grocer's, and before that at the baker's, so get yerself ter the back of the queue, before we chop yer up, and share yers out to supplement our meat rations.'

The whole queue squealed with delight at their success against the interloper. Catherine leaned back against a stack of sandbags as the woman was manhandled to the back of the crowd. It was hot, steamy weather, with the sun beating down on the dusty streets keeping everyone's temper short.

At last the door opened and the women shuffled slowly inside, clutching their ration books.

Armed with a bundle of sausages for her family, Catherine strode down the main road, to the corner baker's where she picked up her youngest son, Leo.

'Why's the Capellis' shop all boarded up, Mammy?' Catherine looked up and sighed. She had heard that all Italians had been rounded up when Mussolini's forces had joined the war, a few weeks before, but it had never occurred to her that they meant any Italians, like the Capellis.

'Because they're Italian, darling. It's the law.'

'Were they spies, Mammy?'

She shook her head; they were no more enemy spies than she was – the mere idea was ridiculous.

'No, darling. They'll come back soon. It's just a silly law, that's all. Look!' she twitched the boy's hand. 'There's your favourite pal.'

They slowed down as they came to the cinema. Hanging in a cage under the awning was a large grey parrot. 'Hello, there, Jake,' cried Leo. 'Hello there, Jake.'

The parrot replied with a squawked 'Hello there, wack!' Prim Mrs Carey was out on the pavement next door, as usual, scrubbing her front steps. Every time Catherine passed this house she had to struggle to keep a straight face, for where everyone else in Liverpool had used masking tape or pieces of glued-on net curtain to protect their windows from blast damage, Mrs Carey had made safe her windows with paper doilies.

'Keeping hot then, Mrs Morgan, isn't it?'

Catherine nodded and was caught.

'Sweltering,' she replied.

'Jerry won't like the hot weather. It probably does things to their steering equipment, you know. Those bombers, they'll never make it over the Pennines, not with the heat. I don't know why the Liverpool people make such a fuss about everything. Hitler wouldn't be bothered with such a filthy, grimy city as this. What's in it for him? That's what I ask.'

Catherine shifted from foot to foot, attempting to move off.

'I mean, we've seen a few planes. They've dropped a couple of bombs, but what did they get? Two budgies and a cemetery. Well, what's the point in that, I say. What's the point in blowing up a lot of skellingtons. No, no. Jerry's not serious about Liverpool, or we'd have had it good and proper by now. Look at London!'

Catherine nodded, shifted again slightly and motioned Leo to come along. But Mrs Carey was not to be deterred. 'And another thing. I think we should raise a petition against the cinema. It's not right their keeping a parrot out on the street.'

'Cruel you mean?' asked Catherine.

'Oh yes cruel to us as live next door. You can't get a moment's peace with it screeching out its rubbish day in day out.'

The wailing sound which at that moment struck up a groan that filled the evening sky was not the parrot but a siren warning of an air raid.

'And that thing. Too loud. Too much fuss altogether.'

Catherine yanked Leo past the Carey house. 'Must rush, Mrs Carey. Got to get the child home, you know.'


The air raid started about an hour after sunset. In the blacked-out front hall, Catherine and her children lay under the stairs and under the kitchen table, which had been pulled into the hall, and tried to sleep while the house shook with blasts from bombs landing on the nearby docks, and the streets all around. John worked as a docker in the day and an auxiliary fireman by night. He came in in the smoky darkness of the early morning, the brass buttons of his uniform twinkling in the flicker of the candle kept alight all night in a bowl on the stairs.

'Well, Liverpool got it right and proper last night, acushla. Wallasey mainly. But that won't be the end of it.'

Catherine sat against the stairs, stroking Leo's hair. The boy lay sprawled across the hall, his head in her lap. Ossie was tucked right under the stairwell, and Rosaleen had gone up to her bed in the room she shared with the two boys the moment the all-clear sounded.

'Why don't you go over to Ireland, to my brother? It's too dangerous here,' he urged.

Catherine shook her head.

'Impossible. I'd die of fright every minute I was away. And, lookit, when the boys were evacuated they simply got on the next train back home. Rosaleen would have to stay too. I couldn't do it.'

John stooped and lifted his younger son's limp body. 'Let's all get some sleep, eh, gal. Only three hours and I'm back at work.'

He carried the boy up the stairs, while Catherine shook Ossie and told him that the raid was over.

During August the night raids continued intermittently. Towards the end of the month Rosaleen swung in one evening after work, when the family was gathered round the kitchen table, and announced she had signed up for voluntary work. 'You're under-age,' John replied.

'Only by a few months. Anyway, I don't mean the services or anything. It's just me and Clarice have agreed to do fire-watching on Blacklers' roof. It makes pretty good sense to me, we work downstairs in the shop all day.'

John stood up. 'I say you don't do it but come back here and help look after your mother and your brothers.'

Rosaleen stood on the kitchen step and faced her father. 'I shall do as I like,' she glowered, then turned on her heel and marched up the stairs. John strode after her. Catherine tried to keep the boys talking, but a few minutes later footsteps clattered down the hall, and the front door slammed.

John came back into the kitchen and sat down as though nothing had happened. Rosaleen did not come home for a fortnight, and then she too behaved as though she had not been away.

One day Catherine came in after hours spent in a bread queue to find her daughter sitting in the kitchen regaling the boys with tales of the night raids.

'So do you have lots of equipment, hoses and stuff, like Daddo?'

'Are you kidding?' Rosaleen laughed. 'We're officially issued with a brush, a shovel and a bucket.'

Ossie leaned forward. 'So what can you do with them?'

'Well, the theory is – if an incendiary lands on the roof we have to sweep it off with the brush, and if it's managed to catch fire we chuck it into the bucket, and if it's set the roof alight we throw the bucket over it.'

'What about the shovel?'

'God alone knows!'

'Is it dead frightening?' piped up Leo.

'At first it was. But Clarice and me have a fine time of it nowadays. We lie under the awning that covers the water tank and gaze up at the stars most nights. The roof is so huge. It's like a vast ballroom with no walls. And it's so warm and lovely up there. Really peaceful. And when the bombers go past, you feel you could touch them. And they let off their flares and the whole sky lights up in a mass of colours, better than the Blackpool lights. Then the colours float down so quietly and slowly, like a rainbow melting in the heat of the summer night sky. It's like the most magical place in the universe.'

Catherine plonked the bread and powdered milk down on the table. 'Well now that you're back on the planet earth, would you like to put the kettle on?' she said.

While Catherine was laying the table, John came in through the back door, and Rosaleen started telling him her tales from Blacklers' roof.

'. . . And there's this lad called Jimmy, who's from the *Post*, and he's taken me out for tea at the Adelphi and everything, and he wants to write an article about the women of Liverpool and he's picked me and Clarice as his sample fire-watchers.'

Catherine turned to Ossie. 'Switch the wireless on would you, Ossie. Let's hear the news.'

'You're just not interested in my life, are you?' Rosaleen looked at her parents. 'Either of you.'

Leo looked up from his bread-slicing. 'It's broken anyhow, Mammy.'

John walked in from the scullery, deliberately ignoring Rosaleen's outburst. 'Probably the battery. Just nip yourself down to Halliday's, Leo and pick up a charged one.'

'No point. I got a new one this afternoon. I think it's a valve.'

'Then go out and get a valve,' said John, giving Leo a look.

Rosaleen pushed past him out of the kitchen and into the scullery where her mother was drying the dishes.

'And anyway, what would you be knowing about it? You're a thirteen-year-old lad,' asked John.

'I like taking things to bits, and making them work.'

'Like when you unpicked the back of your teddy bear to find out how he growled,' smirked Ossie, 'and then couldn't fit all the stuffing back, and cried for a week.'

Angrily, Leo kicked Ossie in the shin. Ossie pulled his hair and shook him. John grabbed them by the back of their shirts and pulled them apart, still kicking and squalling.

In the scullery Catherine tried to strike up conversation with Rosaleen over the dishes.

'I wandered out into the yard myself last week during a raid and saw the flares. My word, it was bright enough to read a book by.'

Rosaleen looked up. 'And when have you ever read a book? I doubt you could even read a tram ticket.'

Catherine whirled round and slapped her daughter's face. Rosaleen stood still for a second then hissed, 'I hate you all!'

John was in the scullery in a split-second. 'Don't you

cheek your mother, you little vixen. You're too young to be going out with men and you're too young to be playing silly buggers on a rooftop during the blitz. This is a war, you know, not a game of jacks.'

'Jimmy is a gentleman, and a very well-educated one at that. He went to boarding-school and everything. At least I get a turn better conversation than I'm ever likely to see in this place.' With this she turned on her heel and marched through the back door, slamming the entry gate behind her.

Everyone was silent for a second and then John bellowed, 'What in God's name is going on here? You're her mother. Has nobody got any control over the girl?'

Catherine cried in frustration, 'Don't look at me. It's not my fault.'

In the kitchen Leo let out a shriek as Ossie pulled out a handful of his hair, and, from the yard, shimmering through the heavy August air, the air-raid siren struck up its steady drone.


In the morning Catherine and Leo took a walk out and felt they might as well have landed on the moon. Huge craters in the once familiar roads, now lined with shells of houses and mounds of smoking debris, made the local streets unrecognisable. On the corner a wall, complete with pictures, windows and curtains, stood open to everyone's view. All that remained of one house was the front door, standing defiantly red within its frame, the only vertical structure for a hundred yards.

Leo held hard to his mother's hand and said timidly, 'We were lucky, weren't we? I hope everyone's all right.'

'Yes. Let's hope.'

'I've got a sore throat, Mammy.'

Catherine nodded. 'Me too. It's all very sad.'

272

They passed Mrs Carey's house. The doilies held firm. As usual she was out applying Cardinal polish to the front step. 'Mrs Morgan!' she tutted. 'Did I not warn you that Jerry had it in for Liverpool. Oh, it's a scandal. What have we poor people done to deserve this? Look at the mess they've made of my front door.'

'Oh yes, Mrs Carey, you should nip round the corner. There's a front door there Jerry missed. It would make you sick.'

Catherine yanked Leo and marched off towards the cinema, muttering under her breath. She took a few breadcrumbs from her pocket and squeezed them through the parrot's cage. 'Here you are boy. Now you just scream all night at that bitch next door, do you hear?'

Leo stood on tiptoe and whispered through the bars, 'Hello, there, Jake. Hello there!' At that moment a van driver, trying to manoeuvre round piles of bricks and great holes in the cobbles, put his hand down hard on the horn to scare some children on to the remains of the pavement. The parrot cocked its head and bawled 'Oh no, it's those bloody planes again. Down with Hitler! Down with Hitler!' Catherine smiled at the bird. 'He thinks the sirens are going off.'

John was washing down at the sink in the scullery when they got home.

'I've got the afternoon off, so I thought I'd take the lads out,' he said.

'Where to?'

Leo looked up eagerly. Ossie was outside in the yard playing with his toy plane. John whispered in his wife's ear. 'The pictures.'

'What's this, more Charlie Chaplin stuff?' Catherine asked sourly.

'Don't be silly. Laurel and Hardy, actually.'

When they'd gone, Catherine took the tram into town and went into Blacklers' to find Rosaleen. The shop was on many floors and Catherine didn't know which department to look for. After an hour's fruitless wandering she went up to the personnel department and found that Rosaleen served behind the tea bar.

She joined the queue and when her turn came asked her daughter whether she could talk for a few moments. Rosaleen got permission from the supervisor and stood beside her mother's chair.

'Can't sit down, I'm afraid, it's the regulations. I have to look as though I'm taking an order.' Rosaleen held out her notepad.

'You must come home,' Catherine said gently. 'All families quarrel, you know, but you mustn't let it go on for so long that it's impossible to mend the rift.'

'And do you have your coupons on you, madam,' Rosaleen announced to the room. Under her breath she added, 'I will not be bullied by my father. I am quite old enough to have a boyfriend of my own choosing, whether he likes it or not.'

Catherine grabbed her daughter's wrist. 'Have your boyfriends. Do whatever you like, but don't turn your back on us. I know what I'm talking about. Don't for God's sake, darling, live a life you might regret.'

From an adjacent table came gales of laughter. 'And they blew up the cold store up Stanley Road way, you know the one, and the whole bloody street was showered in chickens, and this wag was standing on the corner with a huge pile of them, bawling "Get your Christmas chickens early this year – ready roasted by Jerrys of Germany".'

Rosaleen bent down and kissed her mother on the cheek. 'I'm sorry.' She paused. 'I'll come home soon, Mammy, I promise.'

274

Catherine sat in silence sipping her tea, while Rosaleen went back to work behind the counter.

'Silly buggers! The ice rink got it too,' the nearby women continued.

'Oh no, that's old news, love, they got that last week.'

'No they got it again last night. This time good and proper.'

'Oh, no. So it's not true lightning doesn't strike twice then.'

'I hope they all got their skates on, and got the hell out in time.'

The women cackled and slurped their tea. Catherine looked up at her daughter, her black hair tied tight in a little cloth cap, smiling as she served another customer. She clipped her handbag shut, and stood up to leave.

'The best one was the morgue, though. Direct hit, it was. Blew all these dead bodies out all over the street. Hitler's a bloody stupid bastard. You can only kill people once, you know.'

They howled with laughter. Catherine looked at them and wondered how they could take such a ghoulish delight in these tales.

'And I hear a high explosive blew a huge lump out of Walton jail.'

'Oh great, that's all we bloody need. I suppose the streets are all crawling with mass-murderers. And me without a brick to lay me head under.'

'There's plenty of bricks for grabs, love. It's your roof you'll be missing.'

'Where the hell have you been?' John was standing waiting in the kitchen when she came in.

'Why? What's the matter?'

'It's the boy. He's sick. Burning up like a fever. Shivering. He's in our bed. Ossie's with him.'

Catherine pushed past and dashed up the stairs. She only needed to take one look at Leo. 'Get the doctor. Now, John. It's serious. He can't breathe, look.'

John looked over her shoulder.

'Get the doctor, John. Now.'

'But where'll I find a doctor now?'

'Somewhere. Anywhere. Try at the ARP post. Just hurry.'

Catherine sent Ossie down to boil some water, while she mopped at Leo's face with her handkerchief. She heard the front door slam. Feet bounded up the stairs.

'That was quick.' She ran out on to the landing, to meet Rosaleen, grinning from ear to ear.

'I said I'd be back, and look here, here's the piece about me and Clarice in the *Post*.' She spread the newspaper wide to display the centre pages, covered in photos. Catherine swiped the paper out of the way.

'Now's not the time. Your brother's very ill. I think it's diphtheria.'

Ossie ran up the stairs with the hot kettle. 'What shall I do with it?' he asked.

Catherine shrugged helplessly. 'I don't know. Wait till your father gets back.'

'Wait till your father gets back; wait till your father gets back!' mimicked Rosaleen. 'Can't you do anything on your own?' She turned to Ossie. 'Take it back and put it on the stove. Drop a few knives into it. The vegetable knife. Something sharp. And the apple corer. Come on, Mother. I need some towels, sheets anything. And something anti-septic.' She raised her voice. 'Come on. Hurry.'

Leo lay still on the bed making a strange croaking sound. He was blue in the face. Rosaleen pulled his clothes away from his neck and wiped it down with the antiseptic.

'Give me a fork.'

Ossie passed her one, and she used it to fish the knife out of the steaming kettle.

276

'What are you doing?' Catherine screamed as Rosaleen brought the knife down on the child's throat.

'Saving his life,' murmured the dark girl, as she pressed the blade into his windpipe.

The doctor, when he eventually arrived, replaced the apple corer, which Rosaleen had used to hold open the breathing hole in Leo's throat, with a piece of sterile tubing from his case.

'Where did you learn how to do all that?' he asked her.

'First aid. At work. I'm a fire-watcher.'

'Well done, girl! I like people who take the initiative.'

'Well, something's got to be done during this war, or we'll all go down,' she said.

He patted her on the back. 'Of course you're right. But not everyone does something about it. And look how useful it's been. You've saved your brother's life.' He turned and nodded at Catherine. 'Keep him warm, now, won't you Mrs Morgan, I'll get an ambulance round for him as soon as I can.'

The next morning Catherine called in at the British Restaurant under the nearby railway arches, and offered her services. She rolled up her sleeves and spent the afternoons from then on washing dishes for the homeless.

Night after night the raids continued. Different areas took a beating. Everton was not badly hit for a few nights, but on the last two days of September the area was devastated.

The family slept in the hall, Rosaleen with them most nights, taking it in turns to watch Leo.

One afternoon John came home and declared he had a present for Leo, who was now walking about in his every-day clothes, with a large dressing still wrapped round his throat. He leapt up excitedly.

'Where is it, Daddo, let me have it, please! Is it sweets?'

Leo tried to dive his hands into John's jacket pockets.

'Patience, kid. Now sit down and I'll tell you all about it.' They sat on the low chairs by the kitchen fire.

'As you know, three days ago Maybrick Road was hit.'

'Even Mrs Carey's with the doilies?'

John nodded. 'Oh yes. Even our Mrs Carey's.'

'Is she all right?' exclaimed Catherine.

'Patience, patience. Would you let a fellah finish his story in peace.

'So, early this morning the lads and I are called out to put out a fire that's started up when some incendiaries landed on the three-day-old rubble and set fire to a pile of doors and stuff. So I'm standing there pointing my hose at this fire when I hear a voice, distant like. But coming from the highest pile of bricks in the street.

' "Hello there. Hello there, wack," it goes. "Did you hear that?" I called to Fred, my partner. "There's some ould feller, been stuck in this mess for three days." "Hello there!" he goes again. "Hello there!" "Hold on, we're coming!" I cry. "We'll have you out of there in no time." And Fred and I pull at these blocks of bricks with our bare hands. We get down three feet. Nothing. Silence. Another two. "How could anyone survive under this lot," says Fred. And I shake my head. Then he goes again, "Hello there wack!", only much nearer. We grab at the bricks and chuck them over our shoulders and what do we find? Fred peers down into the dust and muck. "It's a bloody parrot," he says and he whips it out of the hole. The bird gives his feathers a quick ruffle and cries out, "Down with Hitler!" which got a bloody great cheer from the crowd, I can tell you. But that's not quite the end, you see. For when we'd pulled out the cage, under it was a shoe, and attached to that shoe was a leg, and so we went on digging and we pulled out Mrs Carey.'

Catherine gasped. 'Was she alive?'

278

'Just. They say we got her just in time. She's in the hospital. She'd told her neighbours she was going to stay with her friends in Cheshire, so everyone thought she'd already gone.' John shook his head. 'It's odd, isn't it. Just as you can be betrayed by your friends, so, it seems, you can be saved by your enemies.'

'Enemies?'

'She hated that parrot. Anyhow, the cinema's down and so he's homeless, and he's sitting out in the yard, so I thought we'd take him in as a refugee.'

Leo answered the door. A tall thin youth in glasses and a thick brown coat peered at him from the dark street. 'Is Rosaleen in?' he asked. His breath came out in white puffs.

'No. She'll be back soon, though, unless there's another raid.'

'That's unlikely, isn't it? Hasn't been one for over a month now. Jerry's given up on Liverpool.'

Leo pursed his lips. 'How d'you know that? Has Hitler written to you?'

The young man laughed. 'Ever the wag, eh? Could I come in and wait?'

'I don't know. I'd better ask my mam. Who are you?'

'Jimmy. I wrote a thing about your sister for the *Post*.'

Leo slouched along the hall, but by the time he'd reached his mother in the scullery Jimmy had already shut the front door and followed him into the kitchen.

'Hullo!' He held out his hand. 'You must be Rosaleen's mother, Mrs Morgan. I'm Jimmy, a friend of hers. I was hoping to take her out for a cocktail at the Adelphi.' He looked around, rubbing his hands together. 'My word what a cosy little house. Lovely warm fire. It's perishing out. Where's a good place for me to sit? Here at the table?'

Leo dashed in front of him. 'Don't move any of those

things. I'm just fitting a new speaker in the wireless.'

'I can do that for you if you like.'

Leo swept the screws and coils over to his side of the table. 'No, it's my job. I always do it. I studied it when I was ill. I'm good at machines. I've made my own Morse code machine, and it works. I'm going to be a wireless operator on a ship when I'm old enough.'

'And how old are you now then, lad?'

Catherine came into the kitchen with a pot of tea. 'He's thirteen,' she told him. 'It'll be a while yet.'

'Fourteen in a few months. I've had diphtheria,' he added proudly.

'And Rosaleen's too young for cocktails as well, I'm afraid,' said Catherine.

'Of course, Mrs Morgan. She's seventeen, isn't she? Ah well it'll have to be tea then. But I can't think even the Adelphi could make as good tea as this.' He lifted his cup and took a sip.

'So where's the rest of the family?'

'Oh, my husband is a fireman by night. He'll be out on watch. And Ossie's gone up the road to get some vegetables for our supper.'

'Lots of nice books.' He nodded towards a shelf of books in the dresser.

'Oh, they're all Rosaleen's.'

'She's a bookworm,' added Leo.

Catherine lifted the pot to pour a second cup, and the familiar wail of the sirens struck up. She put down the teapot. 'Oh dear. We'll have to move all this into the hall. Leo, clear up your bits,' she ordered.

As the boy brushed his wireless screws and coils on to a tray, Catherine and Jimmy carried the table into the hall.

'Sorry about this,' he said. 'Do you mind if I sit in and wait this one out with you?'

Ossie clattered in and joined them before the raid began.

The house shook repeatedly as bombs fell all around.

'That was a near one!' cried Leo, time after time. Only the parrot, in his covered cage, slept.

After five hours the barrage was not letting up. The windows had all gone, and great lumps of masonry had fallen in the yard. 'Shall we sing?' said Catherine. 'Come on. Hold hands and sing.'

'Sing the one about Rosaleen, Mammy. Daddo's song.'

Catherine looked down at her son. 'Not that one now, I think. Too sad. Let's think of something a bit more cheerful, eh?'

'What's the song, Mrs Morgan?' asked Jimmy.

'Oh, just an old Irish thing, you know, "My Dark Rosaleen". So what'll it be? "It's a Lovely Day Tomorrow"?' She licked her lips and went on, 'Sure, I've no voice on me like your father, but we'll all have a go, eh?'

Half-way through the song an enormous blast shook the house so that the walls moved. The ceilings came down, filling the air with grit and dust, and leaving them sitting in six inches of smashed plaster.

When the dust had settled, everyone laughed with relief. Leo spoke. 'I was just thinking how hungry I was, and now I've got a mouthful of ceiling to chew on.'

A rustling came from the kitchen.

'Hello there, wack!'

'Oh, God, now he's off,' laughed Ossie.

Catherine stood up and swept the plaster from her dress. 'I'll get the sarsaparilla from the scullery. I think we need a drink.'

The raid continued for another four hours. Shortly before dawn the front door opened and a voice called down the hall, 'Everyone all right in here?'

Catherine swept her hair back with a grimy hand and went to meet the warden.

'Yes. We're fine.'

'Catherine Morgan, the wandering wife, if I'm not mistaken!' The warden pointed his torch up at his face. 'Jack Fazak, ARP, coal man, removals a speciality.'

'Jack! No we're fine.'

'Well you're the only house in the street that is. Come on, love, I'm here to take you all down to the rest centre for breakfast, while we check out the buildings.'

'I'll be off now,' said Jimmy, wrapping his overcoat tightly around him as he stepped out into the smoky morning. 'Thanks for the shelter, Mrs Morgan. Happy Christmas.' He walked off, whistling in the dark.

Ossie came dutifully along, while Catherine wrote a note to leave on the kitchen table for John and Rosaleen. Leo dashed back for the parrot. 'I'll just wash me face, Mam. I hate having a crunchy face.'

As Leo closed the front door behind him, parrot cage in one hand, towel in the other, Jack shone the torch in his face. 'Like to give us a song, lad?'

'No, Jake can't sing,' said Leo. 'But he's a good talker.'

'Not the bird. I'm talking to you, Al Jolson. What'll it be? "Climb upon my knee, Sonny Boy"?'

When they walked into the brightly lit rest centre, everyone smiled and pointed at Leo. Catherine looked down at her son. 'Oh, dear. You'd better find a mirror. I think years of soot from the chimney landed on that towel before you wiped your face on it.'

'Down with Hitler!' crowed the parrot, and everyone in the shelter cheered the black-faced boy and his pet.


'But I told him I was on duty last night,' sighed Rosaleen. 'What's he think he's playing at? He just won't take no for an answer.'

'But there's nothing wrong with the boy. He seemed very pleasant to me.'

282

Rosaleen had been directed to the rest centre by wardens patrolling their street.

'Very pleasant indeed,' she whispered, 'if you like that sort of thing. I personally can't stand him.'

'A few months ago you were all over him. It was Jimmy this and Jimmy that.'

'Well, things have changed, haven't they. I won't go out with him. I don't trust him.'

'I thought you liked him.'

'Look. I went out with him twice. That's all. But he's too smarmy, and I don't want you snooing up to him when I'm not around, all right?'

'Hallo there, Mrs M. We live to see another day, eh!'

Catherine smiled at a woman she frequently saw in the butcher's queue, who now stood over their table. 'You bombed out, love?'

Catherine shook her head. 'No, thank goodness, Mrs Whaley. Just a near-miss. All the ceilings down, you know, and the children didn't get any sleep.' Ossie was roaring around the rest centre with some of his friends, but Leo leaned convincingly sleepy at her side. Mrs Whaley spied another dust-covered woman coming in through the main door and picked her way over to her.

'I just wish you wouldn't encourage him, that's all, Mamma.'

'He wanted to know about some writing you were doing. Maybe as you like writing and reading so much and he works for the newspaper he could give you an introduction . . .'

Rosaleen hissed, 'My writing's my own business. I wish I'd never told him that I write. It's just some poems and my journal. It's not for publication.'

'I'm sorry, dote, I thought he might be able to help you, that's all.'

'I don't need his help. It's none of his business.' Rosaleen

283

tore at the roll she had been given, and shredded it into small pieces which she dropped on her plate. 'When can we go home, anyway?'

Raised voices were coming from the street, and a shuffling, which sounded like a fight. The door was flung open. John, evidently drunk, staggered in, his fireman's jacket and boots almost white with dust, his black helmet askew.

'Where's the slattern?' he yelled. Two wardens came up behind him and held him.

'Steady on there, old fellah. We've all had a hard night of it. Easy does it, eh?'

John twisted himself free and took some unsteady steps towards the table where Catherine and Rosaleen were gathering up their things. He grabbed Catherine by the arm and hit her cheek with the back of his hand. She fell to the floor, where Leo crouched over her like a cat.

'You leave her alone,' he whispered. 'You leave my mother alone.'

The whole shelter had gone quiet, and scores of faces turned their way.

'When the cat's away, the mice will play,' howled John.

Jack Fazak scuttled into the hall and joined the two wardens trying to steady John.

' 'Ere, 'ere. I think you've had a drop or two to drink, eh? Come along there, me lad.' Jack dodged under his armpit and took John's weight on his shoulders. 'God, 'e's 'alf seas over all right! Let's get you home.'

Catherine and her children followed the men outside. Daylight showed how little of the surrounding streets was left standing. Smoke billowed from the railway sidings behind the rest centre.

'A bomb blew a barge right out of the canal, you know,' said one of the wardens. 'It's sitting over there, proud as punch, on the railway line.' The three men laughed as they dragged the drunken John Morgan along the rubble-strewn road.

'The barge now standing at platform three is for Crewe and stations south. . .'

'How embarrassing this is,' muttered Rosaleen. 'Having a father who's a drunk.'

Catherine sobbed and held her handkerchief to her eyes. 'I don't know what's happening any more. I do my best. I don't know what to do.'

'Can you lads manage?' Jack let go of John, and walked next to Rosaleen. 'Look here, gal,' he said. 'Your dad's as daft as soft Mick at the moment. He's up all hours, down the docks in the day, putting out fires all night. And how old is 'e now, eh? Forty-eight I should think, nearing fifty anyhow. And there 'e is gallivanting around like a lad of eighteen, dashing into fires as high as the Liver Building, lifting beams off people that'd normally take four men to budge. 'E's a bloody 'ero. And 'e doesn't know Thursday from breakfast time. I think if anyone ever needed a drink or two it's him. So leave it out, eh, lass.'

He turned to Catherine. 'I think some dozy warden told 'im 'e saw that young Jack-the-laddo in the fancy coat skulking off at the end of the raid, and 'e put two and two together and made forty-five. Don't you worry. I'll put 'im straight.'

Rosaleen huffed, and turned to her mother. 'Jimmy! You see! He makes trouble wherever he goes. God I hate him.'

'And I gather the big lad had a pretty traumatic night of it.' Jack lowered his voice so that the boys, traipsing along behind them, would not hear. 'Found a whole family of people 'e knew – dead. The house 'ad come down on them, and they'd survived, but the gas burst and they all got suffocated under the rubble. John 'elped to dig them out.'

'D'you know who — '

Jack took Catherine's hand. 'It was a lady who lived next

285

to St Silvester's, she came to your wedding, I think. That's what 'e was saying.'

'Gertie York. But she had two boys off in the services . . .'

'They were 'ome on leave. The whole lot were there. It being Christmas, you know.' Jack paused. 'That's what they call luck, isn't it. Spend two years safe in a trench only to come 'ome for Christmas, and die by your own fireside.'

Catherine squeezed Jack's hand. 'What do we do, Jack? You try and fill your heart with hope. Over and over you do it. And your life keeps speeding up, and it never works out how you want it, only ever for the worst.' She blinked her tears away and held her head up. 'Oh, God, I hate this war. I hate our false cheeriness while we're gazing into the teeth of hell. What's it all for, Jack? This war. What on earth's the point of it?'

Jack put his arm round her and nodded his head towards Rosaleen and the two boys.

'It's for them, isn't it? It's for the children.'

## May 1941
### Liverpool

'I've only had one hot meal since Sunday before last!'
announced the woman at the head of the queue. 'Horse-
radish and a rissole.'

'Been bombed out?' enquired her neighbour in the
queue.

'Oh, ay,' replied the woman with a shrug. 'Mind you,
they should have bombed those bloody houses years ago.
They were bleedin' cold.'

Catherine slopped a steaming pile of stew on to her
plate. While the children were in school she still spent her
days serving up at the British Restaurant in Athol Street.
Spring was in the air, and outside, the sun was shining.

'Ere, girls, come and 'ave a squint at this.' One of the
wardens eating his lunch on a trestle table in the street
outside the restaurant put his head through the door. 'It's
the kiddies' May parade.'

Monica, the supervisor, an imposing woman from
Blundellsands, in a well-tailored uniform, raised her
hands. 'I trust you will all honestly remember your place
in the line if we go out and have a look.'

Everyone squeezed through the door and watched the
children file past. The May Queen, a little girl of five in her
mother's dress frilled up with the remains of some net
curtains, was carried along on a fireman's shoulders.

'Oooh, chook, it's lovely to see the little ones looking

happy isn't it, love?' One of the customers beamed. 'It can't have been much of a life for them so far, eh?' She patted Catherine's arm. 'Did you 'ear about the little lad whose dad came back from two years away and said to 'is mam, "Why do we 'ave to take 'im everywhere we go?" '

Catherine laughed, grateful at least that John was too old for active service abroad.

'It looks almost normal doesn't it?' said the woman. 'If it wasn't for the backdrop.'

Catherine scanned the horizon. The dark city she had got to know in 1921 was gone, and in its place everywhere was sky and the skeletal remains of people's houses. She looked up at the blue, cloudless sky. What a way to let in the light, she thought.

'Back to work everyone.' Monica clapped her hands and they dutifully filed back into the restaurant. 'What's on today?' a newcomer to the queue yelled.

'Blind scouse,' cackled an old woman, walking past him to a table with her full plate.

'Blind?'

'Well it's what youse might call scouse, but you'd go blind looking for the meat in it.'

Monica gave them a stern look. 'It's Irish stew.'

'I'm not touching it if it's Irish,' hissed an old man in the corner. 'Irish indeed. The buggers are neutral. I ask you.'

The old woman rounded on him. 'Don't you start your sedition, you fifth columnist. You're worse than bloody Lord Haw-Haw, you are. It's a well-known fact that Liverpool is the capital of Ireland.'

The man hissed his disapproval.

'Listen here, Joe Soap,' the old woman continued. 'There's more of us Irish people in this city doing their bit than English, so put a sock in it, won't you. Anyhow, I haven't seen you out there manning the ack-acks.'

'I'm an old man.'

'Mmm. So's Churchill. It's not stopped him doing his bit. You're a bloody communist anyway, so shut it.'

She marched past him and plonked her tray down on a nearby table. Monica clapped her hands again. 'Come along, now, come along. I think we should remember who the real enemy is, don't you?'

Catherine, fascinated by the argument, had not noticed Rosaleen work her way up the queue.

'Hello, Mammy, surprise, surprise.'

'That's all right, Mrs Morgan,' nodded Monica. 'You take your break now.'

They sat out on the street, in the sun. 'Ah Mammy,' Rosaleen said stretching her arms out. 'Isn't it lovely.'

They ate their stew in tranquil silence.

'I saw the funniest thing happen on the way here,' said Rosaleen. 'The gate had blown off the dairy, and all these cows were wandering down Lambeth Road. Some wag said they must have come from the Grosvenor picture house, cos they're showing a cowboy film!'

'Isn't Clarice having lunch with you today?' asked Catherine. 'You're usually inseparable.'

'No.' Rosaleen paused. 'I'll see her later at work.'

'She's a nice girl.'

'Yes.'

'I should think when the pair of you are out together you turn the boys' heads.'

Rosaleen looked at her mother. 'What do you mean by that?'

Catherine shrugged. 'Well, just what I said. You're both very good-looking. I should think between you you could rustle up a boy or two.'

Rosaleen fell silent for a moment, gazing ahead at the debris-strewn streets and wrecked houses. 'I'm glad we've got that new house. It'll be safer, won't it, not being round here and right next to the docks.'

289

'Yes.' Catherine sighed. It made you feel as though you'd done your bit, she thought, having been bombed out. But it was odd how it had worked out: the family had been given a commandeered house in a tree-lined lane off Queens Drive. A bigger, nicer house.

'It'll be a pity, though, won't it? Clarice still lives in Everton, doesn't she? I do think she's a nice girl. Sensitive. I think your father's got quite a crush on her.'

Rosaleen stood up. 'Clarice, Clarice, Clarice! Why can't you just shut up about her. I have to see enough of her at work, don't you understand? I came all the way out here for my lunch so that I could escape, but I see there's no peace to be had anywhere.'

She bent down to pick up her handbag. Catherine put out her hand to calm her daughter. 'I'm sorry. I didn't know you'd quarrelled. It'll be all right again, you'll see.'

'Platitudes, platitudes, that's all we'll ever get from you, isn't it. I'm off. I'll be late.'

'See you later,' Catherine called after her, but there was no reply.


Leo rubbed his eyes. Ossie peered down at him.

'Good morning, Sonny Boy. Sleep well?'

As Leo clambered upright, stretching himself after another night spent under the stairs, an explosion shook the house. 'Oh no!' he moaned. 'It's not *still* going on. It's morning now. It's always over by morning. I heard the all-clear.'

'Correct, clever-clogs,' said Ossie. 'I don't know how you slept. It was the worst night of the war. Everyone says so. Jerry hit a munitions ship in Huskisson Dock, and what's going off now is the cargo on board. They reckon it'll go on exploding for days.'

'But the docks are miles away.'

'Correct again. But this particular ship is holding thousands of tons of high explosive.'

Leo bit his cheek. 'How do you know everything, anyway?'

'Easy. Everyone knows, except you, sleepyhead. The anchor was blown a hundred yards away. The overhead railway's gone. All the dock sheds too. They tried to scuttle it but it was too late and the whole of the docks're like an inferno.'

Leo swallowed. 'Where's Daddo?'

'Oh, he's all right. He came back earlier and told us all about it.'

'That's how you know!' Leo shuffled into the kitchen as Ossie continued, 'And there was a big explosion on the railway embankment and it blew away the garage over the road, and you didn't even stir, Dozy.'

Leo called in from the scullery. 'Where's Mammy?'

'Gone to work.'

'And Rosaleen?'

'Not back yet. She was on roof duty. Lucky she works at Blacklers. Daddo says Jerry got Lewis's last night.'

'Oh, it's all Jerry this and Jerry that. Why are you so funny today?' Leo peered at Ossie.

'I'm not. It's just that there's more. Come and look out the front door.'

The two boys crept out and walked along the front path to the street. 'What is it?' blinked Leo, squinting up at the white trees.

'Snow, of course,' laughed Ossie.

'But it's May.'

'Well?'

'But it's hot, and sunny.' He bent down and scooped up a handful of white stuff from the pavement. 'Is it cotton wool? Is it? Why's it all over our street?'

'Oh, it's our street now, is it?' sneered Ossie. 'I thought you thought it was too posh for us.'

Leo chucked the cotton wool at his brother and they had a snowball fight with scoops of cotton wadding from the front garden.

'Look at the time,' screamed Leo. 'We'd better get a move on. We'll both get detention.'

The two boys ran back into the house, spread some bread with margarine, slopped lukewarm tea into cups and poured seed into the parrot's cage. As they raced to see who could swallow their mouthful first, swollen-cheeked, giggling and spluttering, there was a rap on the front door.

The police fetched Catherine from Athol Street to identify the body, which lay crushed and broken on the railway line high up on the embankment above the back of the house.

John arrived at the house shortly afterwards. 'But why was she up on the lines? How could she have been? It must be a mistake,' he insisted.

Catherine took his arm.

'No mistake, John.' She sat him down and stroked his sooted and grimy hair. 'She must have heard the shouting. There was a trainload of mines and wagonloads of gun-cotton. An incendiary landed on it. The train started going up, carriage by carriage. The house was shaken to its foundations. We all thought we were so lucky to have escaped without a scratch, not even a broken window. And Leo slept right through it.'

She stopped for a moment, her throat choked with emotion, then went on, 'The railwaymen told me they unhooked the flaming carriages and rolled the others away. It was dark. You know you can't see the end of your nose in the blackout. She must have rushed up to help. They say she ran to the nearest wagon to the fire and managed to unhook it, but it went up before she could get away.'

John let out a dry sob.

'But, acushla, she was only a baby.'

'I can't bear it, John. We argued at lunchtime yesterday.'

She let a tear roll down her soft cheek. 'Her last words were in anger. And now I can't say sorry. I can't say sorry.'

Leo and Ossie fidgeted at the doorway. 'Is there anything can we do?' said Leo, his face blotched with crying.

John looked up at them. 'It's too late for us to do anything now,' he said grimly, 'but look after each other, as best we can. And hold her in our hearts.'

'She saved my life,' whimpered Leo. 'And now she's dead herself.'

# 1947
## Liverpool


'Oh she's a bobby-dazzler, that Mary. Your Leo's a lucky boy.'

Catherine glanced across the room at the young couple, smiling happily at each other as they divided the cake for the guests.

'They're very young aren't they? But I suppose that's the war for you. No one who lived through the war wants to wait till tomorrow any more, do they?'

'He's nineteen,' said Catherine. 'She's eighteen.'

The woman nudged her elbow. 'Oh, chooks, doesn't it make you wish you were young again, eh, and 'ave all of life stretching out before you, you know. Not like us old-ies.'

At forty-six, Catherine did not relish this conversation. 'Let's get ourselves some cake, shall we, Mrs . . . '

'MacIver, Doris MacIver ' She winked her fat red face. 'Well, seein' as 'ow you're twistin' me arm.'

Catherine steered the woman to the trestle table, beautifully decorated with lace and flowers, that stood at the end of the church hall to display the wedding cake.

'So that's both your lads accounted for now then, isn't it?' Catherine handed Mrs MacIver a large slice of cake, hoping she might fill her mouth so full she would be unable to talk, but to no avail. The mouth was full, but still talked on.

'Your elder son married a girl from Birmingham, that's right isn't it? And they moved south.'

'To the Midlands, yes,' Catherine replied politely.

'And have today's young couple, as you might say, found themselves some married quarters?'

Catherine tried to flash her eyes across the room to get John to rescue her. 'My son and his wife will be living with us, for the time being,' she said.

'Oh, shame! You'd 'ave thought the army could have come up with somewhere, wouldn't you, chooks?'

'He's in the navy, actually. Telegraphy.'

'Oooh,' said Mrs MacIver with a tone which implied she had never heard the word 'telegraphy' before. 'Very young, though eh?'

Catherine sighed. 'When his brother was called up in '44, Leo went along, and managed to join up too. I knew nothing about it. He altered his birth certificate, you see, and went off to sea six months before his seventeenth birthday. He met his wife through it. She was a nurse on board.'

A fat bald man arrived at Mrs MacIver's side. 'Come along, frilly lips, we'd better be pushing off, now, love.' He thrust his hand out towards Catherine. 'Joe MacIver, master icer.'

Catherine beamed at him. 'Oh, thank you Mr MacIver. You made a beautiful job of the cake, beautiful.'

Mr MacIver pulled himself up to his full height. 'Not bad, not bad, Mrs Morgan. But I shall be glad when sugar goes off the ration and I'll be able to work on a proper royal icing base again. Cardboard has its limitations, you know.'

Mrs MacIver tugged at her husband's arm. 'Oh come along Joe, do. 'E'll be telling you what they use for cochineal in a moment. Mrs Morgan's not interested, chooks. Ta for a lovely do, Mrs Morgan. You must be very proud.'

The two little fat people moved off towards the door.

Catherine turned to Leo and Mary, who were just behind her.

'Mother!' Leo stepped forward and kissed her on the cheek. 'Thank you for all this. It's been a wonderful day.' On his arm, Mary nodded heartily.

'We'd better go up the road and get changed,' Leo went on. 'I'm taking Mary out for a honeymoon drink. We'll see you later.'

Catherine held up her hands. 'No, no. One minute. Where's your father?'

She made her way into a corner where John was holding forth with a gang of his old friends from the docks. She paused for a moment to let him finish his story.

Shortly after Rosaleen's death John had performed some startling acts of heroism which many thought verged on stupidity. It had been his way of conquering his grief over his daughter's death. As a result, in one rescue attempt he had lost a hand and an eye, and damaged a foot. He let his sleeve hang long, wore a patch across his eye and limped badly.

The group of men laughed, and Catherine stepped forward. 'If I might borrow the father of the groom?' The men shuffled their chairs out of the way, but John rose without help. He was still a formidable figure, though his thick curly hair was now grey. He searched his inside pockets with his hand and pulled out a large buff envelope, then held out the elbow of his handless arm to his wife. 'Come, acushla!' They strode forward. 'Son!' – he looked roguishly down through his eyebrows – 'Daughter!' He held up the envelope. 'A little present from your mother and me.' Leo took the gift, and handed it to Mary to open.

'As a honeymoon was out of the question, we both thought a night of luxury at the Adelphi would be the next-best thing,' said Catherine with a smile.

296

'Off you go then,' beamed John. 'We'll see you tomorrow. You've both got keys haven't you?'

John came down early to get in the coal and light the fire while Catherine stayed upstairs preparing the bedroom for the newly-weds' return.

John picked up the morning newspaper from the mat. He chuckled to himself, wondering if the wedding photographs might have made it into today's edition, and how his boy would look.

'Good morning, Jake.' He poured some seed into the parrot's cage. Jake tilted his head and winked a hooded eye. 'Hello there, wack! It's that man again! Ahoy there!' he squawked. John laughed at the bird as he put on the kettle and waited for it to boil. 'Yo ho ho and a barrel of rum!' he replied, sitting down at the kitchen table. He spread out the paper on the oilcloth surface and smoothed it out with his hand. 'FIFTH COLUMNISTS REVEALED,' he read. He tutted to himself and read on.

'The *Liverpool Post* has uncovered a cell of anarchists in Liverpool who worked against the country during the war.' His eyes skimmed down the article.

A crash and a clatter in the hall made him jump up. A lump of what looked like brick lay on the doormat.

'Are you all right?' Catherine called from the landing. 'Yes, yes, fine,' said John. 'Just dropped something.' He limped into the hall, opened the door and went out into the front garden. He could hear footsteps running away, but saw no one. He came back in and looked at the broken pane in the door. After sweeping up the mess he returned to the paper.

His eyes were captured by a word half-way down the column. He jumped to that point: 'Rosaleen Morgan, a supporter of the Irish Nationalist Party, wrote poems espousing the destruction of England, and passed them around the staff of the Liverpool departmental store in which she worked.'

John's eyes raced over the whole article, his breath heaving in and out in tight gasps.

'Tea ready yet, John?' called Catherine, coming down the stairs.

John leapt up and with difficulty tore the front page from the paper and thrust it into the grate. Flames jumped up and consumed it within seconds.

Catherine sat down and pulled the paper towards her. 'Where's the front page?' she asked.

John faced the fire, breathing heavily. 'That was the problem. It, erm, got in the way when I broke the cup.' He turned to her and flung his bad arm out. 'This damned hand. I can't get used to it. It keeps getting in the way. I'm sorry.'

Catherine was pouring water into the teapot. 'Oh, don't worry, darling. It doesn't matter at all. Come sit down and drink your tea.'

'I won't, because I'm afraid I did a foolish thing, acushla, and when I'd broken the cup I was so cross with meself I tossed the saucer down the hall, and it went and broke one of the lights in the front door. And I want all to be nice for Leo when he gets back, so I'll just pop along to the glazier's and see if I can get it done this morning.'

He limped to his coat which hung on a rack by the door, and, flinging it across his shoulders, called back. 'You take care. I'll not be long.'

John walked straight past the girl at the desk and up the stairs to the newsroom. Secretaries moved forward to stop him, but stepped smartly back when they read the look on his face.

'Where is he?' he hissed to a young woman protecting
298

herself with a stack of paperwork. 'Where's the scum called Jimmy Bickerstaff?'

He spun round to face the whole room and spoke in a firm, tight voice. 'Too much of a coward to show his face, even before a feller with only one hand and one eye – their pairs being lost in service to this country.' He turned slowly and took in the whole room. Some cringed behind their desks, others were half up, poised to make a getaway.

'Well?' glowered John. The journalists' faces slowly twisted towards one corner of the room, not far from where John stood, where a young man sat serenely behind his paper-strewn desk. He rose and held out his hand. 'Mr Morgan, I presume? I never have had the pleasure.'

John let forth a growl and dashed at him, his clenched fist raised. Jimmy was knocked to the floor, where he sat holding his jaw. Others inched towards John, but he turned, his eye flashing, and they backed off.

'We may talk with a bit of a brogue and have a different way of going about things, but we pay our taxes here in England and it's England we've been serving during this last war. And that girl, my dead daughter, who he's slandered this morning, was no more a spy than is Mr Churchill. She was just a little girl with her head in the stars, who didn't want to go out with a man who had no tenderness in his heart, that's all.'

Jimmy had struggled to his feet and was mopping at his mouth with a handkerchief. 'She knew quite enough about Fenian history. I saw all the propaganda on your kitchen shelves,' he replied.

'To know Irish history, my lad, is to know that a heart full of poetry cannot hope to challenge a body armed with a rifle. If your soul sings you're better to sit on a mountain-side and look pensively down on life, not bustle down in with the throng. And that's what's been wrong with the Irish since the days of Saint Patrick. If we British had sat wistfully dreaming about our troubled past we'd never have wiped out the Nazis and sent them packing. Would we?' He turned and looked around. 'Would we?'

Someone at the back of the room started to clap.

Jimmy stepped forward. 'Very convincing, I must say. Well your precious daughter may not have actually been a spy, but she certainly wasn't as pure and innocent as you make her out to be. You don't know the half of it! You make any more trouble here and I can write another article about her and that Clarice Kersey that'd make your hair curl.'

John lunged at Jimmy again, but two men held him back. 'Steady on, old chap. We'll deal with the lad. Just go now,' one of them said. They walked him towards the door. He glanced back, trying to fathom Jimmy's meaning. The young man put his handkerchief away and stood leering, his hands plunged into his trouser pockets.

The door was opened by a little woman in an overall.

John stooped to speak. 'Mrs Kersey?'

The woman nodded.

'I've come to talk to your daughter, Clarice.'

The woman held tightly to the door handle. 'My daughter is dead, Mr . . . ?

'John Morgan.'

Mrs Kersey hesitantly looked up before addressing him. 'Are you Rosaleen's father?'

John nodded. Mrs Kersey opened the door fully. 'You'd better come in.'

She ushered him into the front parlour, a chilly dark room with a clock that ticked loudly. John stood nervously, holding his hat in his hand. 'I'm sorry to hear about your daughter.' He paused. 'Was it the war?'

Mrs Kersey sank down into an armchair. 'You'd better sit down, Mr Morgan,' she said.

John sat. The woman wrung her hands in her lap. 'My daughter hanged herself.'

'I'm sorry,' John muttered.

'She left a note. I burned it, I'm afraid. I wish now that I hadn't. It wasn't a bad thing she'd done.' She was trying not to let her voice betray her emotions as she went on. 'She hanged herself because your daughter was dead. She couldn't go on living without her, she said. She loved her, you see. She felt it was her fault that Rosaleen had gone to her death. They were going to stay together that night, but they quarrelled, and Rosaleen went home.'

John was silent.

'I saw the paper this morning. It must be terrible for you. That journalist was always hanging round them, he wouldn't see, just like I wouldn't see. We didn't want to see. Rosaleen loved Clarice. Clarice loved Rosaleen. Not a natural love, you understand.'

Mrs Kersey looked at John. 'Would you like a drink? Some tea? Something stronger?'

John shook his head.

'That evening Clarice told her she didn't want to be odd. She told your daughter that if she didn't want to go out with that Jimmy, then *she* was going to, to put an end to the rumours. Rosaleen said she would kill herself if Clarice went out with him. That, with the war, there was plenty of opportunity. Clarice told her to go ahead, if she wanted to be so stupid. She wouldn't be bullied by anyone, Mr Morgan.' Mrs Kersey wiped away a tear. The clock ticked monotonously on the mantelpiece.

'When Clarice got the news next morning at the shop that Rosaleen was dead she came straight home. Didn't speak to anyone. She knew I was out all day. I found her when I came in that night. The sirens had already gone, and bombs were shaking the pictures on the wall and rattling the shades on the gasoliers while I cut her down. I tried desperately to revive her. But she was cold. She'd been dead for hours.'

Catherine lay in the dark. She couldn't sleep, despite the time and the busy, turmoiled day she had spent. John had left before nine this morning, and now, three hours after midnight, he had still not returned. During the day she had had mixed callers, strangers yelling abuse, and friends and neighbours coming to express their disbelief in the *Post* article. She realised pretty soon that John had removed the offending article to protect her, and she in turn had tried to keep the news from Leo, when he returned with his new wife.

When John had not returned by lunchtime she felt worried and upset that he was attempting to take the burden of the whole affair upon his shoulders. By suppertime she began to think him ridiculous. When something is on the front page of a newspaper there is no question of keeping it to yourself. Rather than mooning off, he would have served the family better by being there at her side to ward off the insults and help keep the atmosphere light for Leo's return. Now, with Leo and Mary tucked up in their bed hours earlier, and she lying sleeplessly in hers, she knew he must be out on one of his binges.

Birds were singing outside the window when she heard the key turn in the latch and John's heavy tread stagger unevenly up the stairs.

He flopped down on the bed and pulled his boots off. Catherine could smell the whiskey fumes from where she lay. When he was undressed he climbed roughly under the cover.

Catherine spoke quietly. 'How could you do this? How could you leave us alone on a day like today, when we needed you?'

John grunted. 'I did what I had to do.'

302

'Getting drunk, that's the order of the day, is it?' snapped Catherine. 'God, John Morgan, sometimes you revolt me. Wasn't it you who said Rosaleen was an innocent, a baby, and we should hold her in our hearts? And so is this how you behave when even her memory is under attack from some sensation-seeking villain?'

'What is a villain? What is an innocent? I don't want to talk about her,' hissed John.

'What on earth are you talking about? This is the time we have to talk about her, to protect her memory . . .'

John seized Catherine's arm and held it roughly against the mattress. 'I don't want to talk about her,' he repeated. 'She did it out of spite. Got herself killed out of spite and jealousy. She went to her death with a cold heart, and sucked that little girlie in with her. Don't talk to me about her. I don't want to hear.'

Catherine slapped him hard. He pushed her down. She spat into his face. 'How can you? How can you? She had nothing to do with the INP,' Catherine blazed.

'No, that's something to be said in her favour.'

Catherine wrestled with him and he fought back hard, his lips tight set. 'Don't you touch me like this, when you're drunk!' she cried.

'You're my wife,' he shouted. 'I shall do what I like.' And he rolled on to her, tearing at her nightgown, trying to find peace within his own drunken violence.


Trains were rattling past the back window as she quietly climbed out of bed, tiptoed around the room and gathered her things. John lay sprawled across the bed, asleep at last, perspiration dripping from his face.

Catherine crept out on to the landing, clicking the door shut behind her. The wooden stairs creaked beneath her leather shoes. When she reached the kitchen she wrote a note for Leo. She put it into an envelope, licked it shut and propped it up on the kitchen mantelpiece. Then, wrapping her coat around her, she let herself out of the back door.

Leo was waiting for his father in the kitchen.

'What have you done now?'

John stumbled down the step. 'I don't know, lad. I've done wrong. Where's your mother? I have to say sorry. I was drunk. But it's no excuse. I shouldn't have done it.'

Leo picked up her letter and waved it at him. 'Bit late for that now, isn't it?'

John slumped into a wooden chair and dropped his head into his hands. 'Where's she gone?'

Leo laughed. 'You know Mam. She's not going to leave an address for you to just rush over and find her now, is she?'

John sobbed into his palms. 'I don't know what to do. I don't know what to do.' Leo looked down at his father and felt pity. 'God, what a mess this all is.'

John wiped his face and rose. Leo thought he looked small. Once he had seemed to him a giant, now he saw a stooped, ageing man, with lank grey hair.

'I'd better go. Your mother won't come back while she knows I'm still around. Just tell her I'm sorry. Everything's gone so wrong. I don't think I can ever make it better. Take care of her, lad. And your little Mary.'

'Aren't you going to take your things?' asked Leo, not knowing how to react.

'No. What're things to me now? Everything that was mine is hers. You see, she's the only thing I ever wanted.' He stepped into the scullery and unhooked the latch. 'I'll be in touch, kid. Take care of her for me when you find her, won't you?'

The door closed behind him with a rattle, and his footsteps clattered up the yard, out into the jigger, and away.

## 1948
## Liverpool

Catherine held Mary's hand as she lay on the bed panting. 'That's it child. Keep breathing nice and deep. It won't last for long.'

The windows were open to catch some of the humid afternoon air. Catherine wiped a bead of sweat from her brow. 'Lord, it's hot. I tell you, I'm feeling quite peculiar myself.'

Mary reached out and held her hand. 'Please don't let it last for ever. Were all your children easy to bear?'

Catherine laughed. 'To tell you the truth, the first time I was so green I didn't even know I was carrying a child until it was born.'

Mary laughed, then winced and gripped tight to the towel that was tied to the top of the brass bed. 'That's right darling,' said Catherine encouragingly. 'Pull on the towel. Sure you'll be fine. The midwife will be here in a short while. Everything will be wonderful and tomorrow you can sleep it all off.'

Mary relaxed again, and turned her head on the pillow to look out of the window. 'It's lovely to see the leaves on the trees, and the light spill in so green.'

'The place where I was born it was all green. Everything for as far as the eye can see. Not just one tree in a dark red-brick street.' Catherine sighed and brushed her hands down her skirt.

305

'But aren't we lucky,' said Mary, 'that the tree is outside our window.'

Soon after Leo had tracked his mother down he found them all a new house. No different from the old one, but it didn't have a railway embankment behind it which would always remind them of Rosaleen. It also gave them a chance to escape from the repercussions of the article in the *Post*.

Catherine smiled down at Mary. 'It'll be wonderful to have a child around the house again after all these years.'

'I hope I get my figure back,' said Mary. 'People tell me terrible tales of how fat you get.'

Catherine laughed. 'You shouldn't worry. Since I've had the change I've piled on weight. I'm huge. I can hardly get into any of my old skirts. My waist is now twice the size it was after I'd had the babies.'

'If it's a girl, Leo says he wants to call her Rosaleen, after his sister.'

Catherine smiled.

Darkness fell, and Catherine kept her bedside vigil. The midwife came and went. 'Oh, she'll be ages yet,' she told them, clicking shut her bag and making her way down the stairs. 'I'll be back later, a few hours at least.'

When she returned Mary was very hot and writhing around the sodden sheets. 'Isn't there something we should do?' asked Catherine in a whisper. 'This can't be right, can it?'

'Oh,' shrugged the midwife. 'This is nothing. You should see the sights I've seen in me time, dear. There's no need to go making a fuss about nothing. She's only having a baby, you know, not digging the second Mersey tunnel.'

Mystified Catherine offered to go downstairs to prepare more hot water.

'Not necessary, dear.' The midwife opened her bag and

pulled out a large paper bag containing her knitting. 'Make yourself comfortable, dear. There's a long wait yet.' She flopped down into the armchair. Catherine went next door to her own bedroom to fetch another chair.

'No men around?' asked the midwife.

'Mary's husband is at sea.'

The midwife cackled. 'Like us, you mean, dear.' Her needles clicked furiously. 'You've no husband, then? Lose him in the war did you, dear?'

Catherine hesitated, then said yes for the sake of peace and quiet.

'All right?' the midwife called over to the bed. Mary lay quiet and did not reply.

'There you are,' she nodded. 'Asleep!'

Shortly after dawn Catherine shook the midwife awake where she was slumped, snoring, in her armchair. 'I think it might be near,' she said quietly.

'I'll be the best judge of that,' she said, struggling to her feet. 'All right, dear?' she hollered at Mary.

'I didn't realise it was such hard work,' said Mary, her voice thick and croaky.

'Oh, anyone will tell you it's no picnic, won't they Mrs Morgan?' She rolled up her sleeves and felt Mary's abdomen. 'Men don't know what a pain threshold is.' Her hands moved clumsily around Mary's body. 'I think it's time for a kettle now Mrs Morgan, if you don't mind.'

Catherine nodded. 'Shall I bring it up here?'

Mary was keening loudly.

'No, dear. I was just thinking a nice cup of tea might be in order.'

Mary shrieked, and Catherine scuttled down the stairs to the kettle.

The little girl was born at midday. The midwife shut her bag and left immediately. While Mary lay in a sleep of exhaustion, Catherine sat looking down at the child, touching her cheeks and staring at her tiny hands and perfect white nails.

The heat was unbearable. A fly buzzed busily around the bedroom. Catherine got up and tried to swat it. She was feeling very unwell, but maybe, she thought, it was just the heat on top of the sleepless night and the tension. She tucked the blanket under the baby's chin and went downstairs to the scullery for some water. Leaning against the square white sink, her breath coming in gasps, she heard the latch on the gate, and footsteps coming up the yard. Please, she prayed, don't let this be that damned midwife back because she's forgotten something. As she stepped forward to open the back door a pain seared through her and she slumped against the kitchen doorway, sliding down to the floor.

The door rattled; a demanding rap came again and again. She tried to call out, but her voice would not come. Tentatively the door opened a few inches.

'Hello there? Is anyone home. Is this the Morgan household?'

Catherine stretched out her arms, and her voice came in a short burst. 'Help me, help me please.'

The back door opened and a hand took her firmly by the shoulder.

'Well now, me ould darling, if you aren't in need of a little assistance from an old leprechaun pal.'

Hughie helped her to the dark front room, and laid her down on the sofa. She was flushed and breathing shallowly. 'I don't know what's wrong, I feel awful.'

Half an hour later Hughie delivered Catherine of a baby girl. He cut the cord and placed the child on her mother's breast. 'You're beginning to make a habit of this,' he said quietly. 'And I was after coming here to enquire about another baby.'

Catherine stared at the baby's head. 'But I've had the

change. This is all a dream. I'm exhausted after helping Mary all night.'

Hughie stood up and ran his hand over her brow. 'Afraid not, darlin'. That's a beautiful girlie of your own. If you're all right for the minute, I'll just pop upstairs to see the others and I'll be down here to look after you all in a flash.'

Catherine stretched out her arm. 'Hughie . . .'

Hughie stopped in the doorway.

'Please don't tell anyone about this. Not just yet. I have to have time to think.'

Hughie nodded and left the room.


Mary's baby began to be unwell a few days later. The midwife called and said she looked fine to her. Nice rosy cheeks, of course she was hot, look at the weather. Hughie dealt with her and she left. Catherine stayed in her room with her own baby.

A week later Hughie came down from the boxroom where he was sleeping to find Mary sitting in the armchair by the kitchen fire. The fire was blazing in the hearth, although the sun was shining. She held her baby in her arms and rocked her.

'I can't get it hot enough,' she whispered to Hughie. He glanced at the fire. The coals were stacked so high they were in danger of tumbling down into the tiled hearth.

She rocked frantically back and forth, back and forth. 'She's so cold, so cold. Help me, help me. Put that big lump on, that one in the scuttle. That'll do it.'

He bent down and picked up the coal, and while laying it carefully on the scarlet bed of cinders, tilted his head to get a glimpse of the baby, held so closely to her mother's breast.

'That's right now, darlin'. Just be giving her to me now for a while. I'll just hold her for a little minute for you now.

Would you let me do that?' He spoke quietly as though he was coaxing something tiny like a mouse.

'No. No,' snapped Mary, rocking faster in her chair and clutching the baby tighter. 'Too cold. Too cold. Got to keep her warm. Get me a water bottle. That'll do the trick.'

Hughie rose. 'That's the thing, Mary.' He made towards the hall.

'No no, hot water! You'll need the kettle in the scullery.' He slapped his forehead with his hand. 'Sure aren't I the silly one? I'll put on the kettle, and then I'll be going upstairs to fetch my bottle.'

He went in to Catherine, who was feeding her own child, and told her. The baby girl gasped as though the news had transmitted itself through her mother's breast.

By nightfall they had still not coaxed Mary into giving them the dead baby. They sat together in the stifling kitchen, their light summer clothes too heavy to deal with the steaming heat. But still Mary rocked back and forth, mumbling and muttering to herself and to the grey body in her arms.

Hughie signalled Catherine to come to the hall.

'Lookit, I'm going to see if I can fetch someone in to help us,' he said softly.

Quietly Catherine let him out of the front door. She heard his footsteps clicking up the narrow street. An hour later, around midnight, the letterbox of the front door rattled. Catherine crept along the dark hall and opened the door. Her husband stood in the shadow of the yellow streetlight, his head bowed, his eyes lowered. Hughie pushed him forward. 'Come along there, wee boy, don't stand there dandering about like a goose.'

Catherine squeezed herself back until she felt the hard wood of the dado press into her spine, as Hughie led his brother down the corridor into the kitchen. She stayed for a moment or two in the relative cool of the doorway. She felt awfully tired, as though she could lie down in the hall and sleep, if only she didn't feel so hot.

She pulled herself up the stairs, holding tightly to the banisters, to check on her own child. When she came down into the kitchen, John was holding the dead baby in one arm, and had the other gently round Mary's shoulder. Mary, sobbing hard, had squeezed her face into his shirt front.

He was dressed in a suit, with a tie tightly knotted at his throat. Sunday-best clothes, hurriedly put on.

'How are you, acushla?' he whispered. 'I've missed you.'

Catherine's face was grey. She gripped the chair-back. Hot and cold waves of nausea swept her body. 'I'm sorry,' she gasped and pushed past Hughie, through the scullery and into the yard. Out in the sultry night air she fell to her knees, heaving. Sweat dripped from her chin on to the red tiles of the yard. She felt cold. She crawled towards the wooden lavatory door and slumped herself inside, where she was violently sick. She rested her swimming head on the seat, her teeth chattering like a typewriter. It was foggy now. She could hardly see the walls of the lavatory for curling mists.

She heard a distant voice. Was it singing, swirling through the night? 'Well, my little angel, what're you doing on the slopes of Luke's Mountain on such a wretched night? Come along now, let's get you warm.'

She felt peaceful. It was lovely to be young again. A strong pair of arms lifted her. She struggled. She could see no one. Through the fog, another voice, distant, sang. A male voice, clear and strong.

> 'All day long, in unrest,
>     To and fro, do I move.
> The very soul within my breast
>     Is wasted for you, love!'

She kept her mouth shut, but her eyes peered sharply through the fog. Still she could see no sign of either voice's owner. 'You've cut your hand too. And where's your wee shoe? Ah, dear me, what a sad, dotey, lost little thing you are. Don't be frightened, I'm only small meself, and these mountains are awful big for the likes of us. Hold tight round me neck, and we'll be home in no time.'

Still she struggled. Her mouth didn't seem to work any more. She tried to enunciate clearly, but her lips just curled around and her throat let forth groaning sounds. 'What's a wee thing like yourself doing on your own up the mountains on a foggy night in November?'

> *I could scale the blue air,*
> *I could plough the high hills,*
> *O, I could kneel all night in prayer,*
> *To heal your many ills!*
> *And one beamy smile from you*
> *Would float like light between*
> *My toils and me, my own, my true,*
> *My Dark Rosaleen!*
> *My fond Rosaleen!'*

She was being held down. Tied up. Bound. She could not move, however hard she struggled. All her limbs were weighed down. 'Ah, for goodness sakes, leave off,' came the voice in her ear. 'I'll tell you what. You calm down a wee bit, and when we get home I'll show you me crock o' gold.'

In the hospital Hughie sat on a wooden chair in a long, dimly lit corridor painted shiny brown and green. He had left John behind to take care of Mary.

'I'm going to take the wee body with me to the doctor,'

312

he had whispered to John before he helped carry Catherine, unconscious, into the back of the ambulance. Nurses rushed past him with trolleys, and men in white coats swished along the corridor into the operating theatre where they had taken Catherine.

After about an hour a young doctor came out and sat beside him. 'It's not looking good, I'm afraid,' he said. 'We have sent for a specialist. He's on his way. What appears to have happened is that she conceived twins. One foetus was very small, underdeveloped. It died in the womb. For some reason the womb did not expel it. Of course, carrying something dead inside you does no good. Dead things rot. She has blood poisoning, and septic infections. She may pull through, she may not, I must warn you. And there is a danger of mental complications. Her brain may have been affected. We can't know anything for sure.'

Hughie fiddled with the cap in his lap. 'Could anything have been done earlier?'

The doctor nodded. 'If she had been seen during her pregnancy and come in for the birth it would have been preventable.'

Hughie clenched his hands into fists and pressed them down on his knees.

'It's strange that she didn't come in earlier. A woman of her age . . .'

Hughie shook his head. 'I know, I know. It was all very complicated.'

The doctor patted Hughie on the knee as he rose. 'What happened to her baby? The one which managed to be born. Is it at home? It should be looked at too.'

Hughie stood up.

'What's the best prognosis, doctor?' he asked.

'Well, *if* she pulls through this, she'll be very weak. She'll never be quite herself again, I'm afraid.'

Hughie looked him in the eye. 'The baby died. I brought in the body.'

The doctor sighed. 'Ah well, Mr Morgan, that's probably the best thing all round, in the circumstances.'

When Hughie returned to the house in the early hours he found John sitting in the kitchen beside the dying embers of the fire, the windows open to let some of the heat out.

'Where's Mary?' he asked.

John tossed his head upwards. 'Gone to bed at last, the poor lass.'

'I'll just go and check on her.' Hughie rushed up the stairs and into Catherine's room. Her baby lay, quietly sleeping, in the wooden box they had made into a cradle. Gently he picked up the box and carried it downstairs to the kitchen.

He laid the baby girl at her father's feet. 'Now Johnnie, boy, we've got some serious talking to do.'

# ROSALEEN

I never did get into the Irish team on St Patrick's Day, but I did manage to score for the English side in the hockey match the year after my friend Anne wet herself at the concert. I was awarded a Saint George Medal, which I could wear on my school beret when I went out.

I wonder if the nuns would have been so generous if they'd seen me behind their backs, leading groups of girls into the school chapel.

'Come on, you'll see, there's nothing to it.'

'But what if we're caught?' squeaked one, full of trepidation.

'Doing what? It's me doing the doing. You just watch.'

They shuffled into the front pews and I strode up the marble steps to the altar.

'Oh,' cried one, 'you can't do that. Even the nuns aren't allowed up to the altar.'

I turned, like an actor in a rep production of *Richard III*. 'Oh yes they are, how else do the flowers get there?' I said. I reached the high altar and clambered clumsily up on to it. My audience gasped.

I sat and faced them, my legs swinging freely, the lace cloth tickling my calves. 'Come on, God, where are you?' I cooed coyly to the rafters. 'Come and join us, why don't you?'

One of the girls burst into tears and rushed up the aisle and out of the chapel. The others shuffled about uneasily.

I stood, legs apart, on the high altar. I pulled a flower from a tall vase, and raised its petals to my nose. 'Exquisite,' I sighed. 'Hello? No one at home? Not even the creator of such beauty as this simple rose.' I stooped and knocked on the tabernacle. 'Hello? Hello? Anyone in?' I stood and surveyed the rafters again. 'Why do you do it? Hey? If you're God, why can't you behave decently, and not like a bloody bastard?'

A riffle of sound passed through the pews, but I am not certain whether this was because of my sentiments or my use of language.

'Why don't you strike down the murderers, the dictators, the torturers? Why do you only punish the poor with your plagues? Why do you starve little defenceless black babies? Why play such silly-bugger games with the hearts and minds of people who are full of love for you?'

I paused, as though awaiting a reply. There was none. I surveyed my rapt congregation. I stretched out my arms and pointed them upwards, my face lifted towards the heavens. 'You see, I *know* you, God. There are only two possibilities here. Either you don't exist or you're the cruellest, most callous swine that ever breathed.'

The chapel was silent. In the distance a car on the main road hooted; the sound sifted in through the stained-glass windows, and seemed to rest there on the brightly coloured air. I climbed quietly down and brushed my hands together dismissively.

'See?'

Some of the girls moved quickly out of the chapel, avoiding my look. I have frightened them, at least, even if I have not convinced them. The others file out behind me, deep in thought. They are mine.

It wasn't long after that that I was expelled. The letter I brought home simply said I did not fit in. But the reference, unseen even by my parents, which passed from school to school meant that no convent, no Catholic school, would touch me. To my parents' horror, after the summer break I was to be sent to a Protestant boarding-school.


'You'll never plough a field by turning it over in your mind.' My uncle agreed to look after me while my parents recovered from the shock. So I was packed off to County Down to spend the holidays with him. He hated my black and inconsolable moods, when I couldn't speak for unhappiness.

'What're you after thinking about, eh?'

'I wish I could be good.'

'Why, sure you are good.'

'But I'm no good at school, Uncle Hughie. It's not just this recent trouble. I've always got the most awful reports.'

'Agh, go on. What did a school report ever do for anyone? Sure I never went within a mile of a school and what harm did it do me? I can read and write, and the rest.'

I looked at him as though he was an idiot. How cruel we are. How invincible it feels to be a child.

'But if I worked harder or something I could *be* somebody, not like you.'

He laughed his cackly laugh. 'And what are you now, if I might ask? You look like somebody to me, and from what I've been told you're as smart as a carrot, though you could do something about your manners, in my opinion.'

I sighed in response.

'Is it famous you want to be?'

I sighed again.

'Sure when you're dead and about eighty with plastic flowers on yer grave, then you'll be famous. Like that Van Gogh feller. Lot of good it did him.'

When I smiled at him he just quipped, 'I bet your lips are cracked,' pulled out a book from the shelf over the stove and quietly read to himself.

One day I asked him if he really was a leprechaun. He looked up from the basket he was weaving. 'Is it after making a fool of me you'd be?'

'It was my grandmother. She hauled me in when she heard I was coming over here for the holidays. She told me you were one, and that I should ask you.'

'Well, I'm withered, old and solitary and have a crock of gold. Make of that what you will. And I've been told I'm irascible. Mind you, that was by your . . .' and here he paused, 'dear grandmother.'

He then got up and quickly left the house. I heard him rooting about in the lean-to shed. I think I also heard a sound like a sob. But this is only now, when I look back. At the time I was too wrapped up in my own business, not realising that my great-uncle's unhappiness was very much my business.

Life at the new school was quite different. We slept later, as we did not have to attend daily mass, nor was the day broken by afternoon benediction. We had what they called a service, which was just a couple of readings and a lot of sloppy songs (like 'All Things Bright and Beautiful', ghastly baa-lamb stuff, but a doddle compared to a sung mass by Palestrina). There was no St Patrick's Day either. Or St Peter and Paul's, or Corpus Christi with all those endless processions, where we had to wander around the school grounds strewing flowers and carrying large plaster statues. There were no strict silence laws either.

Instead we had Bonfire Night (a celebration which was forbidden at convent – though we were never told why – so that after lights out on 5 November we would all silently creep from our beds and watch the rockets exploding in the navy blue sky, never understanding their significance, never knowing that they were lit to remind us that we Catholics were still the underdogs).

Bonfire Night celebrations were a hoot. A puny fire was lit in the playing field and we all stood around with sparklers while the teachers organised a firework display. Actually the teachers' husbands seemed to do all the actual firework-lighting, as back in those days everyone thought women were incapable of striking a match without masculine assistance. My friends and I had a whale of a time lurking in the shadows, and if we were lucky we'd have bribed a day-girl to smuggle us in some cider and really made a night of it.

At first the girls at the new school seemed stupider to me, knew less about books, art, music. They did know how to apply mascara and how to hitch their uniforms up to be in fashion, and kept scrap-books of pop stars.

I found that I was odd at this school in that I did not come from a broken home. All the other girls seemed to have either more or less parents than are strictly necessary. Many, for one reason or another, had just a mother, or just a father. These girls I felt rather sorry for. But others had mothers and stepmothers, fathers and 'uncles' who were not related to them, parents who seemed to prefer racing around nightclubbing in Paris and South Africa to bringing up their children. At first I looked down my nose at these pathetic children, who, for all their home experience, still spent their energy planning ways to snare a husband.

There were many lengthy conversations which defined the term 'husband material'. A suitable candidate must be handsome and rich. He should work in medicine, law, the services (commissioned officers only), the Stock Exchange, Lloyd's, property or have a private income.

Those girls were of course reinventing their own fathers. No dockers, miners, bus conductors or shop assistants need apply. It's funny, but if you hear something often enough it worms its way into your mind until you are convinced without ever having thought about it.

If I hadn't lolled on the tennis court, when the games mistress was off seeing to the other girls in the swimming pool and on the rounders pitch, and listened to this rubbish would I have married my own husband? Did I do it just to please those silly girls whom I secretly pitied and, once I had left school, was never likely to see again?

I'd been a year at the new school when Alma and I made the most of the rare summer holiday Liverpool sun and went out sunbathing together. The trip down to the Pier Head and a ferry to New Brighton was too much of a bother. We'd tried Southport, but it was too crowded and the sands were depressing, the way they stretched out for ever and ever with no sight of the sea except at high tide.

We took a bus to Crosby sands once but it was filthy. Tar had stained the sand dark grey, and given it a treacly consistency.

'We can't lie down here,' I sneered. 'Look at all these jellyfish. We'll get stung to death.'

'What are you on about now,' replied Alma happily.

'Look!' I exclaimed. 'Just look.'

'At what?' She was peering down along the tideline.

'Come here.' I pulled her skirt and pointed down to the patch of sand round my feet. Alma squealed and held her hand to her mouth. 'That's not jellyfish, you fool.'

I stooped to pick one up.

'No!' she screamed, 'don't touch them.'

Half-way down I turned and faced her. 'Why? If they're not jellyfish, where's the harm?'

'Well, they're thingies. You know.' She nodded at me knowingly.

'What thingies? What are you on about?'

'Johnnies. Rubbers. Contraceptives.'

I leapt back in a reflex action, then bent down, and
322

keeping a decent distance squinted at them.

'Eeeeuuurggghhh,' I said with conviction. 'What're they doing here?'

'They've come out with the sewage. People flush them down the lavvies when they've used them.'

'They never,' I said, examining the wares even more closely. 'You don't think we could get pregnant if we lay down on them, do you?'

Alma laughed freely. 'Course not, silly.'

I scrutinised her face almost as closely as I had inspected the spent condoms. 'And how do you know all this, anyway, Alma Braddock?'

She giggled and walked back towards the bikes. 'Wouldn't you like to know.'

We spent that glorious sunny afternoon talking of sex, and rubbing oil on our bodies, lying in our bras and pants on adjoining Chinese graves in Anfield cemetery. The place was a perfect sun-trap, and the polished marble was wonderfully relaxing to lie upon.

'So did you go all the way?' I lay on my side to read her face for the answer.

'Oh no, of course not. But I went pretty far. But you should talk anyhow!'

'What do you mean? I've been locked up at school with a load of girls, you know, not in Walton jail with a pack of sex-hungry men.'

'But what about Father Songster? Didn't you do it with him?' I jumped into a sitting position. 'I most certainly did not. He was a perve.'

'Oooh, you're a terrible girl.' Alma crossed herself. 'How can you say such things? No wonder they sent you to a Protestant school.'

'Cos it's true. He was a perve.'

'But he's a priest!' Alma's face was stricken with shock.

'So what. I don't believe in God any more anyhow.'

'Oh Rosaleen, go wash your mouth out with Sanilav.'

We lay in silence for a minute or two, the heat making the air palpable, and wavy. Alma broke the spell. 'What do you think happens when we die? Don't we go to Heaven?'

'I don't think so. Nor hell neither. I think we just go.'

'Go?'

'Out. Like a light. One day here; next day nowhere. More's the pity.'

Alma made no comment.

'If they were around I bet they all wish they could come up here and join us.'

'Who?' asked Alma.

'Dong Kee, and his friends in these graves. Pity to be lying under the sod on a day like today.'

The sun passed behind the upper branches of a yew tree and we were thrown into a goose-pimpling patch of cool air.

'I can't believe you say such awful things,' said Alma quietly, as though the chill had passed right through her soul. 'You're lucky. You're at a good school and everything, even if it is full of heathens and pagans.'

The sun burst out again and we closed our eyes and enjoyed the feeling as the oil picked up the heat. In silence another shadow passed across us.

'And what have we here, then?' It was a man. We both opened our eyes to see a policeman looking down at us with his hands on his hips.

Alma wiggled childishly. 'Just sunbathing, officer.'

'Constable, actually. It's illegal you know, defacing graves.'

'We're doing no such thing.' I stood up, pulling my clothes from the dry grass and holding them up to cover myself. 'We're just sunbathing.'

'And would you like me to pull you into the station to argue it out with the Super? Or maybe you'd like me to accompany you back to your homes and I can explain it all to your parents.'

Alma sidled up to him. 'I'm sure that won't be necessary, constable. We're just on our way.'

He grabbed her by the wrist. 'You could do me a favour, love, and it'll go no farther.'

I was struggling to pull my T-shirt on when he pushed Alma down on to the grass and unzipped his flies.

I assure you the scream I let forth could have woken Dong Kee, Chung Ma and all the adjoining inhabitants of Anfield cemetery. Alma scrambled to her feet. 'Run for it!' I yelled. And we did.

When we got home we sat on the bins in our entry and talked, as flies buzzed lazily around us. Just as, until that day on the East Lancs Road, I had believed that a priest could not have a sex drive, Alma had had similar faith in the police force. She now accepted the truth about the singing priest.

I think I already knew that Authority stood for nothing. This episode was just a gentle reminder.


It's afternoon again. The dynamic duo have just delivered my mug of tea. Lukewarm and grey. Undrinkable. What would I do for a nice strong copper-coloured brew? Or, preferably, a large whisky. Splash of soda, no ice.

My husband always drank vodka, the alcoholic's drink. Mind you, he said that whisky was the alcoholic's drink. I'd say that vodka is for alcoholics, whisky for drunks. Drunks are quite a different thing.

My Great-Uncle Hughie told me that the pirate my grandfather, John Morgan, was a drunk. I never saw that side of him myself. There was one time when I arrived at his flat unannounced and found him there in the bedsit alone, and he smelt funny. I know now that it was the surgical smell of alcohol on the breath. He pulled himself up to his full height when he saw me standing in the doorway and gasped very quietly. Then he turned and shuffled back in. 'Dandelion and burdock?' he enquired, heading for the cool cupboard. He came back with two fizzing brown glasses.

'Are you all right, Cap'n? You look all funny,' I said.

'I'm fine.' He rubbed his eyes and sat down. 'Promise me one thing, Bos'n. When you grow up don't turn to drink to solve your problems, it only makes them worse.'

'Should we not drink your dandelion and burdock then?'

He laughed. 'Oh this stuff's all right. Just don't hit the hard stuff, gal. Promise me?'

So that's another promise I didn't keep.

Oh, Captain, Captain, why did I hurt you so? How did I let you go among all those hissing snob cat-people, and deny to them that you were mine.

I never told you I loved you either.

Funny when you think, because I told my husband, that bastard Robert, over and over and over that I loved him.

Thump, as his fist hits my jaw. 'I love you.' Crack, as he pulls my thumbs back until the joints come out of their sockets. 'I love you.' Smash, as he breaks the bedroom door down, when I have locked him out because he is drunk and has obviously just had a row with one of his women and I am afraid. 'I love you.'

The more he hated me the more I said it. 'I love you, I love you, I love you.'

'Love's a game for fools,' said my Uncle Hughie. 'Love and politics, avoid them both at all costs.'

I yearned for the school holidays and my trips over the water to stay with my uncle, when my parents thought I was too much too handle. Beats me why they thought that they couldn't cope and yet a tiny little man of over seventy, who lived half-way up a mountain and didn't even have electric light, could.

326

'How's the world abusin' you?' he'd enquire as I climbed out of the taxi which carried me from the railway station to his front door.

'Not so bad,' I'd yell, pulling my case from the boot. 'And yourself?'

'Agh, mustn't complain. Everything's roses in the garden.' Then we'd both turn and look at his rough patch of cabbages and laugh together. 'I'm awfully glad I'm here,' I'd grin.

'The pleasure's yours,' he'd grin back.

Why did I resent every chore I was expected to do back in Liverpool? I'd do anything to avoid the washing up, fetching the coal from the box in the yard, brushing the mat, polishing the lino. And yet here in this hovel I'd gladly rush out into the snow and bring in armfuls of turf for the fire, chop wood, clean dishes in water that you had to smash the ice to get to.

'So how are you doing, yourself?' He sat me by the fire and quizzed me on my life at the new school and back at home. I paraded my list of exam failures and successes, my moments of sporting triumph, my attempts at creative writing for his scrutiny.

'Oh, oh, oh,' he gasped. 'Slow down to a gallop, would yer? Now what's that I see twinkling on your jacket?'

I proudly raised my Saint George's medal.

He buffed it up with his fist.

'I got it for playing hockey.'

He nodded, his eyebrows raised. 'Is that right, yeah?'

'It's a Saint George killing the dragon.'

'Yes, yes,' he whispered, looking at it closely. 'I see that.'

I sat before the flickering fire, swelling with pride.

'You're a nice little girl, whatever they might say about you. I just beg you to do one thing for me.' He paused solemnly before going on. 'Every now and then spare a thought for the poor old dragon.'

At the time I didn't know what he was on about. It just

327

seemed to be part of his quaint way of talking. Some years later I understood, but went too far in my interpretation, for after all, doesn't the dragon become as bad if it kills George? I see that now. But we can all look back and see our mistakes. It's just hard to do it when you're face to face with them, hugging your choices close to you as new friends.

Rattle rattle rattle. In come Laurel and Hardy.

'Solicitor's waiting for you.'

I stare at them. There is no arrangement for me to see him today.

'Chop, chop,' snaps Bug-eyes. 'We've other things to do than sit around awaiting your pleasure.'

I haul myself up from the bed, and slop along the corridor behind them, ignoring the howls of abuse from cells I pass. My solicitor can do what he wants. I don't trust anything that goes on in a courtroom. I am frightened by the whole system. It failed me once. Maybe next time it will give me what I deserve.

The little man sits and waits for me. He takes out a large pad and a fountain pen and fires questions —

'Where were you born?'

'Where did you go to school?'

'Where did you go to university?'

'How did you meet your husband?'

'Do you believe you had a fair hearing at your divorce?'

I draw the line at answering this one.

'I know what happened. I've read the transcript. Why can't you talk to me about this?'

'I already have.' I feel the defiance rising in my breast. 'What the hell relevance has it to anything?'

'Did you do what you did as vengeance against your husband for what he did to you there in court?' He taps his pen on the Formica top. 'Well?'

'It was an act of terrorism. Can't you read? Like all the others.'

'You have no need to support Patrick O'Shea. He knows the truth. He has told us all about these "others" you keep referring to.' His little ferrety face is a white wall. His black eyes bore through me. Tap, tap, tap. 'Oh yes, I know about the others; to me they are an irrelevance. It's the bombing of your family that bothers me.'

'I lost my children in that courtroom. What am I meant to say? That because I lost them I killed them? I'd do anything, *anything*, to bring them back.'

'Back?' He is glaring at me now. His eyes searching my face, penetrating my soul.

'From the dead. Even I can't do that.'

He opens his mouth, then hesitates. He lays the pen down, and slowly rubs his face in his hands. He takes a deep breath and starts the inquisition anew.

'You lost a lot more in that courtroom, didn't you? You lost your whole life. It had been methodically filched from you since the day you were born, and that day your husband used a terrible fact, till then unknown to you, to immobilise you. Am I right?'

I leap up and stride to the door. 'Let me out!' I yell at the woman with the keys. 'I can't listen to this.' I can feel my face burning. Tears are not far behind. I hear his voice, quiet and greasy. 'It was the first you ever knew of it, wasn't it? Someone might have had the decency to tell you before.'

The keys shake in the lock and the door finally creaks open. When I'm back in my cell I lie face down on the bed. I don't cry. It all hurts too much. The beat of my heart shakes the solid bed. I can imagine Patrick trying to help me out. He has only ever shown kindness for me. The least I can do in return is be true to him.


07.15, 23 June. Awoken by alarm call in a hotel room in Manchester. I wash, take in a tray of continental breakfast,

329

and read the complimentary newspaper. At 9.30 I am in a large computer superstore buying circuits, solder, discs. I take lunch in the hotel dining room, then retire to my freshly valeted bedroom.

I unscrew the covering plates of the portable computer and survey the works. I unplug the hair-drier and push my soldering iron into the socket. While it warms up, I open the window. I don't want the smoke alarms going off. I put on my special jewellers' glasses and set to work, rewiring circuits, fitting fuses and timers and detonators. An hour later the job is complete, but for the wad of high explosive which must be inserted into a newly created space under the battery.

Before I have a chance to switch on the television the phone burrs.

Reception tells me there is a parcel and a bouquet of flowers. 'That'll be my husband,' I laugh. 'Some champagne and flowers to brighten up my days away from home. Please send them up.' The girl asks if I would like it unwrapped and opened, with a glass and ice?

'No, no,' I say. 'Sun's not quite over the yardarm yet, for me, I'm afraid. I'll put it in the fridge up here and open it later tonight. Thanks for the thought.'

A few minutes later I open my door and receive the gifts. I make sure the bellboy sees my overwhelming happiness as I tip him.

When he is gone I dump the flowers in the waste-paper basket and unwrap the parcel. A long wine box inside contains the packet of explosive.

I pack my belongings into my large briefcase, and put the computer into a separate bag.

I swing merrily past the girl at reception.

'No rest for the wicked,' I call, and leave the hotel through the revolving doors.

The bomb goes off at the central police headquarters at

six, while they are changing shift and twice as many people are in. A repaired computer had been delivered to the heart of the building by a smartly dressed, well-spoken, middle-aged woman with an RP English accent.

By then I am already back at the hotel sitting in the cocktail bar sipping a gin and tonic, a drink I loathe. I check out of the hotel early in the morning and take the London train. In the ladies' room at Euston I change back into myself, let my hair down, pull on a jumper and jeans. I drop my smart suit in at a branch of Oxfam on my way back to my flat. There I clean up as well as I can, pack what I need into a big holdall and lock up. I take the midday boat-train for Paris, where I make my way to the airport and am on the first flight to Dublin.

Due not only to the number but also the occupation of my victims, I am now the most wanted woman in Britain. I am also the most hated, not really for the violence or callousness of my crime, but because I am English, and respectable and middle class. No longer 'common', no 'Paddy' or 'soft Mick' am I. 'Bog Irish' I am not. I am one of them. I am English.


Darkness never comes in this cell. The light goes down but never out. How I would love to sit in the black, or lie again with my back on the dew-soaked grass and gaze up at the stars. If you ever read science books you will know that nothing matters. It's not just that we are like ants; we are so small that we are invisible, like microbes, squirming busily around for an infinitely short moment of time. I terrified myself at school, reading in an introduction to physics all about light years, and stars so far away that the light that we see now was actually radiated to us when Elizabeth I sat on the throne of England.

'That wicked woman' she was called at convent, 'bastard

daughter of a hero turned bad'. Later, after I was expelled and landed up at an ordinary school she became 'the Virgin Queen, the greatest ruler we have ever had'.

You see, even in history there is no such thing as truth. There is only opinion.

Maybe because they'd only just got rid of the virgin mother, Protestants felt they had to invent the virgin queen. Virginity! I don't see why any of them should have got so excited about such a thing. Catholics are wrong anyway. In the unlikely event that she did conceive a child without penetration, she would certainly have lost any traces of virginity when the baby came out of her. Babies do not come out of your belly button, as anyone who has given birth will point out.

My babies.

Change the subject.

The lights have gone down. Did they forget to bring my supper tray, or did they think it best to let me cool my heels after the visit from my legal adviser?

'Poetry is something more philosophic and of graver import than history.' So said Harry Stootle.

But then it was he who also said, 'Man is by nature a political animal.'

It's history and politics have got me where I am today – a nice square cell with a horrible flickering light in the ceiling.

If only I had a screwdriver I would disconnect it altogether. I would be happier in the dark, like my grandmother. That's funny, isn't it. For we were both utterly in the dark, while everyone whispered around us and behind our backs.

'Give me a slewsther, agrah,' she said to me one day when I brought in her tray, 'a sweet one now.'

I was puzzled.

'A kiss, darlin' dote, a slewsther.'

332

Was it the very Irishness of the word that revolted me, or was it its onomatopoeia, the sloppy wetness it conjures up? Anyhow I backed away, wincing.

My children backed away from me when I came upon them fresh from a beating. It's instinct, I suppose. They saw the crumpled face, the mascara in lines down my cheeks, blood drying around my nostrils. I smiled, then they backed away. I suppose there was blood in my mouth too, on my teeth. I smiled so they would not be frightened. I was appalled that they should see me like that. Every other time I had the opportunity to wash myself, put on dark glasses, whatever was needed to make me look like a normal mother.

When I was beaten after my arrest, by mad guards and other women, it was all right. The terrible thing is to be beaten by someone you love. While it's going on your mind races, trying to work out why. You search the face of the man you love, and find you don't recognise him. It is as though he is in a trance, and you can't get through to him, no matter how loud you scream.

The prison beatings were almost a religious experience. I understood for the first time all that bunk they'd fed us in religious knowledge lessons at the convent, all about St Theresa of Avila and her ecstasy, Saint Catherine of Siena and the stigmata, Saint Catherine of Alexandria and the beatings she took and her torture on the wheel (which gave its name to a firework), and my own name-saint, Rose of Lima, who put broken glass in her shoes, brambles in her vest and rubbed chili pepper in her eyes, slept each night strapped to a crucifix and offered it all up. That action of offering it up takes you out of the pain, and you watch your own body breaking and rending as though it were a doll's, while your mind remains free.

It was my mind that my husband broke really, not my fingers or my nose.

He drank, of course. But many people drink and never lay a finger on anyone.

I didn't mention it in the divorce proceedings. I didn't want to damage his career. I didn't want to damage his career! God how funny.

'What've you got to be laughing about?' The Bob peers through the grille. I'm waiting for her to tell me my lips must be cracked. It's the Irish accent, I suppose.

The levity of the moment catches me unawares and I find myself replying, ' 'Tis just a thought full of whim and inoffensive mirth.' An Uncle-Hughie-ism. A crowbar couldn't crack her face. Her eyes tighten and move up as her thin lips press against the grille. 'God curse you to hell,' she hisses, and slams the thing shut.

'Damn these eggs.' I was frying them on a rough griddle over the fire and the fat kept leaping up and burning my hand. 'Now a curse is a very dangerous sort of thing,' said my uncle. 'It has an anatomy of its own. There is cursing and cursing, of course. There is the witty curse: "Six eggs to you and half a dozen of them rotten", or the malicious curse: "Go die and give the crows a puddin' ". But no curse is safe, in my opinion.'

I pulled my stool closer to the fire.

'Because it's against religion you mean?'

'Agh, no, no. Sure didn't Jesus Christ himself curse a poor harmless tree because it bore no figs for him to eat when he wanted one.' He paused and twinkled. 'And look what happened to him.'

I gasped in horror.

'You see a curse doesn't necessarily land on target. True, a curse will hover for seven years in the air ready to alight upon the head of the person who provoked the malediction,' he whispered. 'It hovers over him, like a kite over his prey, watching for the moment when he may be abandoned by his guardian angel.'

'And then?'

'If it doesn't make it, it turns homeward and searches out its original owner.'

I gasped. 'How horrible.'

'Oh, yes,' he said, shaking his head. 'It's a shame really. Some Irish curses are very beautiful things, full of poetry.' My rapt silence encouraged him to go on.

'May you melt off the earth like snow off a ditch,' he crooned. 'May you melt away like butter in a summer sun.'

I'm talking to myself again. Saying these things out loud. It would be nice to have a cat in here in this cell with me, or a dog, to stroke in this electric twilight. The magnolia walls stare blankly back: they never argue, never laugh, never sleep.

I love to be alone. But just now, just tonight, it would be nice to have someone who'd tell me their story. I'd like to listen. To talk in that way that's like tennis. Not just turn it all over and over with myself.

At university we all played mind games. That's what everyone called them then, anyhow. I suppose they'd have a more clinical name for them now. The obvious ones of course, like 'you walk through a field (what's the field like?), cross some water (what's the water like?) and find a key (what's that like?), and then there's a house and you're inside it with a bear in the garden, what do you do?' The field, water, key, house and bear all represented something. I think the house was yourself and the water was sex. Something like that anyway.

There was a more obscure one. I can't actually remember the rules but you had to recall the best and worst moments in your life, without thinking for longer than five seconds. And always after that one you'd lie in your bed that night and suddenly realise you'd said things that were utterly trivial compared to the *really* best and worst moments.

So, best moment? One, two, should be giving birth to the twins, but that was mixed up with such awful things, four, five. Help! The summer of 1969, coming down from university in the Midlands to the Isle of Wight to see the pop festival. Bob Dylan, the Byrds. Being in love with Bill. He was big, had long wavy hair and a beard, and cooked his own bread. Sounds ridiculous now, doesn't it? But he stroked my hair so softly, and whispered lovely things to me, lying in that stubble field in the sun with the music pumping out all day and night from the platform. Running out of money, and him getting a row of bottles and playing tunes with them in between the acts, there at the back of the litter-strewn field, to beg so that we could eat. People painting each other's bodies. Everyone kissing and smiling and holding each other so tenderly and kindly. Peace and love. Peace and love. And we loved it all so much we stayed down, sleeping on the beaches. We dangled our legs off the end of Shanklin Pier and watched the sunrise, and walked to the top of Tennyson Down yelling poetry to the wind:

> *'You have driven me mad, fickle girl – may it do you no good!*
> *My soul is in thrall, not just yesterday nor today.*
> *You have left me weary and weak in body and mind*
> *O deceive not the one who loves you, my Roisin Dubh.'*

Then, when autumn dragged us back to our studies, I did deceive him. I still don't understand why. I loved him. I felt safe with him. Ah yes, that must be it. I never could stand to feel safe for too long. I was too accustomed to a life of unpredictable ups and downs even then.

And there was Robert: a few bunches of flowers, notes

on beautiful writing paper inviting me to dinner in a romantic and expensive Italian restaurant, the sight of a man of our age in a suit with short hair – it all seemed very attractive, very dashing. So, excusing myself to Bill, pretending I have research to do, essays to write, practical work to set up, I start accepting Robert's invitations, buying different clothes, turning into another person. Like a performance, losing myself in my new character, just like Marlon Brando, or Jane Fonda going to live with prostitutes in order to do her film role in *Klute*.

Bill laughed at my new look. He thought I was having a joke, standing there in my sensible skirt and jacket, my hair brushed and tied back, and the sound of his laugh killed my love for him. Just like that, in an instant. I looked at the man I had adored for two years, and couldn't imagine how I had ever even liked him.

The wall in this cell is so cold and rough against my cheek. How did I make such a mistake? I can see myself with Bill today. Instead of sprawled on a solid bed in this miserable cell I would be sitting by a fire, holding out forks of toast to the orange coals, in a cosy house up a mountain with four children.

Not children. Not children again.


My Received Pronunciation is impeccable. When I was at university proud northerners dismissed me as smugly bourgeois, middle-class and southern. I laughed inside as they 'bathed' and 'pathed', and 'working-classed' with their short A's. They spouted their inverted snobbery and I quietly hugged my roots. I've always liked secrets. Robert was a figurehead of RP on campus. So tall, and smart, and supercilious. I have always been unaccountably attracted by the enemy.

I had never known anything like his snide wit. It

shocked me into irrepressible laughter. Our affair lasted for six months. He would come round to the terraced house I shared with three other girls and, standing in the garden in his long navy blue overcoat, toss stones up to my bedroom window when everyone was safely in bed. Then I would sneak down the stairs and let him in through the kitchen door. Sometimes we'd meet on Sundays, loitering on street corners in the shelter of the locked doors to fish and chip shops, and kiss. We kissed for hours sometimes as the grey Midland skies steadily drizzled until the litter-strewn gutters gurgled.

We went to a 'news cinema' together. The days of real news cinemas had long gone. We saw a pornographic film called *My Swedish Meatball*, then stood in a dark dusty alley off Digbeth and had sex ourselves.

The affair finished when I invited him to a party in our house to celebrate one of the girls' birthdays. There was a large bonfire in the garden, though it was summer. The living room was crammed with students, drinking Hirondelle and smoking joints. Outside the window sparks flew into the royal blue sky and couples sprawled around the fire in the ragged grass. Bill had turned up, with another girl, a short earnest little thing. It only took a few plastic cups of the foul-tasting wine and she was three sheets to the wind. I was fussing about being hostess of the year when Bill asked me to dance. I was happy to see him, as any friend is to see another after a separation.

The lights were low, and the music was saccharine. I think it was Fleetwood Mac's 'Albatross'. He put his arm around my waist. I put mine around his. We shuffled clumsily from foot to foot in time with the music. We got no closer. I don't think we could have then, even if we'd wanted to. There was too much left unsaid.

A hiss in my ear. It was Robert: 'Stop it.'

I turned and faced him, still holding Bill.

'Hands off, or else,' he whispered.

I faced Bill. 'Excuse me for one minute, Bill.'

I turned to Robert. 'I dance with who I want to dance with. All right? I am only *dancing* with him.'

Robert looked down at me, his lips tight, his eyes hooded. 'Do what you want,' he said. 'And I'll do what I want.'

'Good!' I glared, turning back to Bill and holding him in a full embrace.

When the record came to an end I excused myself and went out into the garden for some fresh air, and to fork through the ashes for a baked potato. I sat on the damp grass and the red of the cinders burned my cheeks. I dug greedily into the charred skin, chatting absently to others. That potato was one of the most delicious things I have ever tasted.

When I'd finished I went back into the house. People had passed out on the sofa and in shadowy corners. I scanned the dancers. Bill was shimmying with a tall blonde in a miniskirt little bigger than a belt. No sign of Robert. He had obviously left in a huff.

I pulled open the door to the staircase and made my way up. I could hear giggling from my bedroom. 'Robert?' I called softly. As I pushed the door gently I caught a glimpse of his dark hair and the drunken pint-pot friend of Bill's, naked and grunting as he pumped at her. He threw out an arm and slammed the door in my face.

I clattered down the stairs again and shook one of the sleepers, a homosexual boy curled up against the fireplace. 'Julian? Julian, wake up.'

He opened his eyes. 'Oh hello darling, I'm sorry, did I fall asleep?'

'Take me away,' I begged.

'Where to?' he groaned. 'You live here.'

'I know I do. There's an all-night café by the station. I want to have a lorry-driver's breakfast.'

'Ooooh! Sounds fun to me,' he smiled. 'Doesn't sound your scene, though.'

'It's Robert,' I whispered. 'He's upstairs with some grubby little girl.'

He lifted his eyebrows. 'Enough said,' he grimaced, as he got up.

I should have learned my lesson about Robert that night. That was the end of our affair, as I said. But it was not the end of our story together, for eight years later I married him.

My husband, Robert, was a lawyer. He would proudly crow, after a few vodkas, that he could get anyone off, however guilty. He would smugly sit in court and watch his reasoning persuade a magistrate or a judge to let off with a warning a drunk driver who had left his victim paralysed. 'There's always some mud to be slung,' he boasted. 'I just make sure it hits the victims, not my clients.'

It was odd, really. He was so handsome, like Gregory Peck, or Robert Taylor, his namesake, that in Hollywood he would have been the hero for the defence of the inno-cent. In life handsome people are rarely friends to the innocent. He seemed to get better-looking with the years, and when I met him after the eight-year gap, his beauty almost took my breath away.

After graduation I had gone through a rough patch. I had got a first, and was thought to be the brightest person in my year. But in 1970 being a woman was tantamount to having an IQ of 43. Work was hell to get. I signed my letters with an initial, and was always granted an interview by return of post. Then, once they set eyes on me, the vacancy was suddenly filled, the person was staying on, any excuse they could dredge up.

I moved to London and took a small flat in Highgate. The unemployment exchange made me fill in the Professional and Executive Register, then told me I was over-qualified, and would I like a job waitressing in a wine bar?

Poverty knocked, and I answered. I did a few temp jobs in laboratories, and the nearest I got to acknowledging my qualifications was the fortnight I spent answering the phone in a computer shop in Watford.

One evening, as I slopped trayloads of lager around a wine bar in Covent Garden, I received a pinch on my bottom that made me spin around to accost the person who had delivered it.

'Hello, beautiful,' said Robert, his teeth so shiny and white, his eyes sparkling in the candlelight. 'Is this a mirage, or is it my child genius lover from my wicked past?'

When the bar closed at midnight he came home with me. He brought with him a bottle of whisky and we sat on the rug and drank and talked until the sky lightened and birds sang in the trees outside the window. He was warm and charming and funny. When I stretched forward to switch on the gas fire he knelt behind me and kissed me gently on the neck. His arms slid round my waist and he pulled me towards his taut body. 'Don't bother with the heat,' he whispered.

I twisted round within the circle of his arms and raised my face to take his firm kiss. Our lips remained locked together as we slid to the floor. There was no nostalgia in this coupling. It was as though I had found a new, passionate lover, and we explored each other's bodies as if for the first time. His satin-soft fingers traced a line from my cheek, down my taut neck and across my nipples. His palms cupped my breasts as he slid down and gently kissed them. His hands moved down, along the sides of my waist, riding up across my hips, tracing the arch of my

341

pelvis with his forefinger. As our tongues wrestled together, his hand slid down the outside of my thigh, then, passing across my knee, started the slow, tantalising move up the soft skin of my inner thigh. I opened my legs wide, and he lay between them. His fingertips were teasing the swollen, wet lips of my vagina and I thrust towards him. He pulled away and my nails dug into his buttocks pulling him back, to enter me.

We made love over and over, as the milk van rattled in the street outside, as the postman wearily climbed the stairs and dropped a bill through my letterbox, as the traffic on the main road built up and declined, as the sun burst out and streamed through the open window, projecting green leaf shadows on our nakedness.

At noon, lying there on my floor, Robert invited me to lunch. 'I'm not rich, I'm afraid, Robert,' I replied. 'My qualifications went for nothing, you know.'

'Who cares?' he grinned. 'I've enough for us both. Let's have a bath together, then we'll go out in style.'

While I prepared the bath, Robert booked us a table. In the bath he kissed me with a dark longing. 'You must stop,' I whispered. 'I can't resist you.'

'Good,' he murmured, pushing my body back and gently thrusting again between my thighs. 'Let's work up an appetite.'

When we were dressed we took a taxi to the Hyde Park Hotel and sat at a small table looking out on to the park.

'I can't eat,' I confessed, sliding the delicious food round the china plate with my fork. 'All I want is you.'

'I feel the same,' he said. And I believed him, although his plate was empty.

We married a few weeks later. I adored him. He had swept me off my feet all over again. But, looking back, I suppose the warm feeling which seeped through me that day was not unrelated to those silly conversations with

342

those idiot girls at school. I'd 'hooked' someone who was
'quite a catch', 'real husband material'.

I never knew why the nuns had not allowed us the annual
pleasure of Bonfire Night until the evening when Robert
took me to the firework display of my life.

'It's the most English of them all,' he said as we climbed
into the Jaguar and raced down the M23. 'Very traditional,
very exciting.'

The town of Lewes was buzzing as we parked the car.
The streets were thronged with people. There were to be
five processions by different firework societies, and from
various points in the main street you could witness them
all before choosing your favourite and following it to its
own field and fire.

We'd been married for a few years now. But at last I was
pregnant. Only four months, not showing or anything, but
after a solid month's throwing up I was not yet feeling A1.
We made our way to a small hotel on the high street and
had a drink in the low timbered bar-room. Robert had the
local Armada ale.

'This is what it's all about you see, fighting off the
enemy, like we did to Spain.' A local know-all had collared
us and was giving us a potted history of the Lewes festival.

'Spain?' asked Robert.

' "Far on the deep the Spaniard saw
  Along each southern shire
  Cape beyond cape in endless range
  Those twinkling points of fire."

The beacons, warning of the Spanish Inquisition.'

I had to hold my face in one hand to disguise the
mounting laughter.

343

'I didn't know the Inquisition made it to Britain,' said Robert seriously, leading the fellow on.

'No, they didn't make it because of the beacons. That's what the Armada was for, you know. But we beat them hollow.'

I managed to speak, my stomach muscles still clenched against the rising tide of hysteria.

'But I thought all this was about Guy Fawkes?'

'Oh, yes, Guy Fawkes of course,' nodded the man, sagaciously. 'And also the landing of Good King Billy at Torbay in 1688. That was November 5th too, you see. And he was a great king. He fought for the famous British tradition of toleration and understanding, and brought freedom of worship to England.'

'Ah,' Robert nodded. 'Oh, dear!' He looked at his watch and winked at me. 'Come along, we'll be late for Michael.' We linked arms as we rolled along the street.

'I thought we'd never get free of him, didn't you?' Robert laughed.

Far behind us a number of fire-crackers rattled glass in the shop windows.

'Can you smell the tar?'

Already there was a smoky tang to the air. We pressed back into a doorway which was up a few steps and waited for the processions to pass.

First a lot of bored and tired-looking children strolled by dressed as Vikings, followed by some women decked out as wenches. It was like any small-town carnival procession. People carried banners announcing the name of their group, and behind them came more Vikings holding burning crosses.

'I didn't know that they had Vikings in the Ku-Klux-Klan,' hissed Robert.

Then came a gang of sailors, boys in striped shirts and flat hats pulling flaming tar barrels in little carts. The heat

344

of the flames warmed our faces as they passed. Then came the banners.

'Remember remember the fifth of November,' said the first. 'Lest we forget,' said the next, 'the Battle of the Boyne.' Next came a huge effigy of the Pope, with a noose round his neck and painted blood spilling from his mouth. Close behind, more banners and more flaming crosses, then a chanting crowd dressed as monks, all with blood smeared around their mouths and nooses hanging from their necks: 'I see no reason why gunpowder treason, Should ever be forgot.'

'I'm frightened,' I shouted to Robert above the din of snapping fire-crackers and yelling crowds. I don't know whether he heard me or not.

> *'A farthing loaf to feed old Pope,*
> *A penn'orth o' cheese to choke him,*
> *A pint o' beer to rinse it down,*
> *An' a faggot o' wood to burn him.'*

I looked hard at the people who sang out these words. They grinned maniacally.

> *'Burn him in a tub o' tar,*
> *Burn him like a blazing star,*
> *Burn his body from his head*
> *Then we'll say the Pope is dead!*
> *Hip! Hip! Hoooorrraaahhhh!'*

The crowd burst into spontaneous applause as a burning tableau marched past. 'No Popery here,' it read, 'Death to all Catholics.'

The heat from more barrels and crosses burned our faces like a hot summer's day, and the smoke-filled air was acrid and heavy. I tugged at Robert's arm. 'Let's go,' I said. 'I've had enough.'

'Don't be ridiculous,' he yelled. 'It hasn't even begun yet. We've got to see the bonfires and the fireworks.'

A woman turned and added, 'And when they explode the Pope and all the bishops.'

'It's hideous,' I said to my husband. 'It's frightening, isn't it?'

He turned to me and sighed. 'Oh, for God's sake . . .'

'Really. I can't stand any more. Please let's go home.'

He started laughing. I looked at him in the light of the passing flames and he seemed like a devil, and I remembered that his children were in my belly.

'I suppose you think that they're coming to get you,' he sneered. 'So it's true what they say, "Once a Catholic . . ." '

'Don't be ridiculous,' I snapped. 'But it's not right. They couldn't march around with banners saying "Death to all Jews" or "Death to all Blacks" could they?'

'Well, they bloody should be able to,' hollered my husband. 'I thought this country stood for free speech.'

I tried to breathe in the charred air, looked at this man, whom I loved, and felt sick to the pit of my stomach.

When I think of the divorce I suppose I was to blame, really. From that moment it is certain I was unable to love him as I had done before.

He always said that I started the rot. In court at the divorce hearing he told the whole assembly that I was frigid and cruel and didn't understand a man's natural needs. I should have stood up and said, 'Like fucking a prostitute the night I was in labour giving birth to our children; like refusing to sleep with him for weeks after he advised me I should see the doctor for some antibiotics as he'd picked up a dose of the clap and may have passed it on to me.' I didn't speak at all. I felt too humiliated, looking up at the tourists and students in the public gallery, all weighing me up and seeming to scrutinise my face for signs of sexual inadequacy.

I hate to think about the divorce. That hellish grey day when my life collapsed.

I had no money, I lived in a rented room, had no job and no prospects. I knew that Robert could put a better face on the whole procedure than I, but still I believed that the law favoured the mother in cases of child custody. Miss Pelham, his 'personal assistant', a busty little Kensington slut in designer clothes, wore glasses for the occasion, and a tailored grey suit. Her usually bouffant hair was pulled tightly back into a bun, and she smiled the sickly sweet smile so well appreciated by men, so universally distrusted by women.

'Lucinda is devoted to the children,' he declared.

For months Daddy had brought home gifts – books, toys, the latest clothes, all beautifully wrapped – and presented them to my children. I marvelled at his generosity. It was only when emptying a waste-paper basket that I found the card from one of them. 'Best wishes on your birthday, Lucinda (XXX).' They were expensive gifts, and brilliantly chosen. Always things that the children had been yearning for and talking about. Whenever I had suggested we buy any of them, Robert had countered that we would spoil the children. After finding the card I kept an eye out for the next gift, and like a grubby private detective, searched the bins next day. 'Heard you were looking for one of these! Love Luce XXXX.'

I rowed with Robert. He told me I was a hysteric, and there was no need for me to be jealous of my children's gifts. She bought them for him, he argued. On his behalf. That's why she signed the cards.

When we are young I suppose it is easy to be bought. When I found myself in the hideous position of trying to poison them against her, I realised the only person who came out of it badly was me. In their innocence they believed she bought presents for them because she loved

347

them. When you are little it is impossible to believe that everyone does not love you. Lucinda Pelham, as fresh as an advert, as young as spring, would tut at me with pity when we met, her gimlet eyes scanning my jeans and jumper as though I was standing there covered from head to toe in horse-shit. 'You should get him to give you a better clothing allowance,' she sighed, running her fingers down her own tailored silk jacket.

For some weeks after the divorce I sat, usually in the rain, on some church steps across the Common and watched the house, hoping to get a glimpse of my children. I saw her come in and out, always impeccably dressed. Her face boasted no bruises. I can't believe that he stopped seeing other women, visiting prostitutes, going home with clients, so maybe Lucinda simply didn't mind; after all she had an enviable clothing allowance.


'Your solicitor is here again.'

Ah, it's the large dyky one back. Bug-eyes and the Bob are obviously on another rota.

'I don't want to see him.' I turn away from her and face the wall.

'I don't think it's a question of what you want or don't want,' she snaps. 'He's come all this way for you and my orders are to escort you to the interview room.'

He's there, briefcase bulging. I sit opposite him. 'Do you want another confession? That's all I'm willing to give you,' I tell him.

He smiles at me. 'That will be lovely.' He pulls the top off his fountain pen and scratches away as I tell my stories. Five pounds of explosive; eight dead. Two pounds; one dead. It's like the football results.

'I'd have gone for the nitrate fertiliser and icing sugar;
348

so easy and available but rather bulky for one working alone. You'd need a navvy really, to get it into the car, or on to the back of the lorry.'

He looks up. 'So you always worked alone?'

I nod. 'It's me you want to lock up, not Patrick.'

'Where exactly did you live at that point?'

I hesitate, then tell him the Muswell Hill address.

'You did not live in your Irish property at all?'

I search his face. 'You know I didn't have a property in Ireland.'

'Ah no, of course,' he fumbles with his papers. 'That belonged to your husband.'

It was shortly after I was expelled that my uncle first offered it to me. Not long after the Pirate died.

'Do you like me farm, Titch?' asked Uncle Hughie as we strolled across the stony fields poking at cabbages to find one for our dinner.

'No,' I answered truthfully. 'I hate it.'

'Well now, is that a fact? You're not lying to me now?'

'No.'

'So will you explain me this: why do you choose to come here for your school holidays, and not spend the time with your parents?'

'Oh, I see them. I'm there some of the time. But it's so dark in that house. I hate it.'

'Wisha! A minute ago you hated it here. I'd have thought that you'd prefer Liverpool. The Beatles and all that. Yeah, yeah, yeah.' He shook his head in the mopheaded way of all Beatles impersonators. 'Oooooooh!' he squealed, most unconvincingly.

'How do you know about the Beatles?'

'Doesn't everybody the world over know about them, to be sure.'

'You don't have a television, though.'

'Agh, the goggle-box isn't the beginning and end of life,

you know. I have me own version, anyhows. It's called a window.'

I sighed at him. He was impossible.

'So you don't want me to leave you the ould place then, when I'm pushing up the daisies?'

I was horrified. How could he talk like this about dying, he the most vital person I knew?

'No, no, no!' I shouted and held my hands to my ears. 'You won't die. You're not going to die. I won't have it.'

He stood shaking with laughter, a little wispy man, his hands on his hips, his legs slightly bent at the knee.

'Agh, stop your humbugging talk. In the big world the old people do go a-dying and leaving things after them.'

'But not you. You're a leprechaun, remember. You can live to be a thousand years old if you want to.'

'Ay,' he sighed. 'And when the sky falls, then we'll all catch larks.' He leaned against a post and said, 'So who shall I leave it to then? The dogs' home? Sure they'll not want it. It's not worth a thing anyhows, it's the sentimental value really. We Morgans have been here for centuries.'

'Then leave it to Uncle Oswald, he's a Morgan. If I get married I won't even be one.'

'That cold rogue? Not another red ha'penny will he get from me. He's as tight as a drum, that one.'

'What do you mean?'

He stroked my hair, then stood with his hand on my shoulder. 'Sure didn't you give up your pocket money to be sending me the batteries for that old torch? To my mind that was a richer present by far than all the crown jewels of England.'

I laughed. 'Don't be silly.'

'No, no, I talk the truth. What would I be doing digging in me turf in a ruddy great crown? It was a rich thought of yours to bring a prehistoric into the modern age. Your uncle never ever even sent me a birthday card in all his life.

You'd think I didn't exist. He never turned up to Leo's wedding. He never had a good word to say about your mother.'

His hand tightened on my shoulder, then relaxed.

'No. He's the type'd offer you an egg if you promised not to break the shell.'

I turned and faced him. 'Well that's sorted then. You can leave it to my father.'

No one would have thought that he'd outlive both my parents and still have the choice to make again many years later, when I was married.

Oh.

> 'If I had six horses I would plough against the hill –
> I'd make Roisin Dubh my gospel in the middle of mass –
> I'd kiss the young girl who would grant me her maidenhead,
> And do deeds behind the raths with my Roisin Dubh.'

'What is that?' enquires the solicitor.

'It's an old Irish poem. Someone told it me at university.'

'And what is "Roisin Dubh"?'

'Dark Rose. *Dubh* is dark, you know, like *bawn* is blonde.'

'Ah, yes of course. *The Colleen Bawn*. I believe I saw that play at the National Theatre, some years ago. So you are a colleen dubh?'

We sat in silence for a few moments.

'So if the farm was not yours, why were you there that day?'

I felt my whole face flinch as though he was moving to hit me. 'I won't talk about that. I won't talk about that day.'

'No, no, of course.' He put his pen in its cap and into his briefcase. 'Tell me more about that poem. Do you know any more of it?'

I searched his face. He appeared to be genuinely

intrigued. It was certainly a less painful subject, and more interesting to talk to someone than sit in my cell conversing with the creamy walls.

> 'Roisin, have no sorrow for what has happened you:
> The friars are out on the brine, they are travelling the sea,
> Your pardon from the Pope will come, from Rome in the East.
> And we won't spare the Spanish wine for my Roisin Dubh.'

He leaned on the table and held his eyebrow up with one finger. 'So tell me. This poem is about Ireland, yes? It is like another, is it not? A poem that bears your own name?'

'Yes.'

'Fascinating,' he said. 'How many innocent people do you estimate you have cold-bloodedly murdered for this Dark Rose of yours?'

I faced him out.

'Thirty or so.'

'Ah,' he sighed knowingly. 'We don't count family, then.'

'Give me some paper,' I hiss. 'I'll write it all down in my own handwriting. Whatever you want.'

The wardress shifts slightly at the door. He turns. 'Yes?' he says.

'It's not my business, but are you her defence counsel?' She is smiling.

'Oh yes,' he says, 'believe me, I am.'

Although the Moustache hauls me off to take what is laughingly called lunch in my cell, the solicitor is there again in the afternoon, raring to go.

'Tell me about the Christmas bombing. Give me the details.' My man stabs down at his notepad with a newly sharpened pencil, leaving crumbs of graphite jumping like fleas upon the yellow pad.

'You know all about that,' I sigh.

'I know a bit. You can give me the details if you would be so kind. Where did you sleep the night before? What did you wear? How did you travel? Paint me a picture.'

I am determined to convince him, this strange ferrety fellow, that I deserve to rot in hell. He can have it.

21 December, London. Muswell Hill. Suitcase packed. Clothes, mostly bought yesterday at Oxfam. Old rubbish which I wouldn't be seen dead in. Even me. The woman who let her husband down by not dressing smartly enough. The clothes are neatly packed, the suitcase full but not crammed. None of that sitting on top of it while trying to press down the front catches, like we had to do at school.

I pull on an old coat and wrap a scarf round my head then march out of the flat and wait at the bus stop. I am heading for Victoria coach station. It's raining. Not very hard, but a steady and icy drizzle. Perfect weather for a bombing. I put the case under the stairs and sit happily staring out at the damp streets.

People are rushing around desperately buying presents for people they don't like because it's Christmas and they feel they have to. No one wants anyone to think of them as Scrooge. The street lights are on, and most shops have pretty coloured lights in their windows. The misty windows on the bus, with trickles of rain running down the outsides in jagged stripes, mix up the colours and the whole effect is as though we are looking at the world through a kaleidoscope.

I go into a daydream, sitting there, and think of Christmases past, sitting near the fire, the well-dressed tree blinking behind me, watching the twins tear the paper from their presents. Their faces light up. We all laugh, even Robert, who I know is tense and miserable. Today, because Lucinda has gone home to her own family, he won't be finding any extra work to drag him into the office.

I've bought him something I know he wants. I hope it will please him. He opens it, smiles contentedly and moves over to gently kiss my cheek. 'Look what Mummy's bought me.' He holds the present up for the children who don't care much; they've too many more of their own to explore.

The doorbell rings. 'Oh, God,' I get up wearily. 'Must be carol singers. Anyone got 50p?'

I open the door and find Lucinda in the doorway, mascara running down her cheeks.

'Is Robert in?'

I call my husband out. He comes reluctantly, but his face lights up when he sees who it is. I go back to the children. Lucinda has missed the train. Lucinda has nowhere to go. Her flatmate has gone home. She has lost her keys.

I don't believe a word of it, but it is Christmas after all. I make up the bed in the spare room.

Lucinda shares our Christmas lunch and stays. When the children have gone exhausted to their beds we are left together, the three of us. Robert offers to take us both out for a drink.

'And who's going to look after the children?' I ask.

'I will,' volunteers Miss Martyr, with a winsome look at my husband.

I'd rather leave them alone with Lady Macbeth as a babysitter.

'You go,' I say. It is a *fait accompli* anyhow. When they have gone, after I hear them laughing together conspiratorially in the street as they climb into the Jag, I sit in front of the television and watch 'Golden Xmas hits of Morecambe and Wise' or some-such. Eventually I go to bed. My husband does not join me, although they are both up bright and early together at the breakfast table.

'The bombing?' My solicitor drags me back.

'Tyres squeal and the bus shudders to a halt at some lights. Where am I? Oh my God, miles past the stop. I start to panic. What is the time? How much time have I left? Will it be quicker to walk back? Shall I just leave the case here? I wrench the case out of the luggage hold and leap from the bus platform. I walk very fast. I fancy I can hear the case ticking away. Five minutes. What if the clock is fast? Oh my God, but it's heavy. Five pounds of industrial and bags and bags of four-inch nails.

'Panting, I reach the station, put the case down beside a queue and run for it. A street or two away I hear the blast, and make my way back to Muswell Hill.'

'Next?' The solicitor is drawing cartoon wardresses on his pad. He hasn't written any of it down.

'I don't remember,' I say. 'If you spend long enough on your own, time just merges into one long faceless blob.'

'What happened after the Christmas when Miss Pelham came to stay?'

'Oh that?' I wince. 'I put up with everything, the way wives do. They think if they ignore it it'll go away. But it gets worse.'

'So that was not the occasion you deserted the matrimonial home?'

'I never deserted anything. I just couldn't stand it any more. Something terrible happened. Involving my children. I wanted someone to advise me. I went to Ireland. I ran away. It was a mistake. I wanted to see my uncle.'

'Did you see him?' He squints at me over his specs. His eyes are scanning me again, as though he is trying to super-suction my thoughts up and out of me.

'Yes. I was lucky that time.'

I had found Hughie in the red carved bed, coughing and wheezing. He looked terrible. As soon as I saw him I forgot my own problems. He lifted his head from the pillow and flopped it back down again.

'Oh, it's you is it?' he said. 'What's up with you now, not get enough milk for your Cornflakes this morning?'

355

'You're ill,' I said.

'Not really,' he coughed. 'Divil of a thing it is, but a complaint they call an all-overness ails me.'

'Flu,' I said.

'No, no. It's just a cold. I didn't have enough whiskey this morning, that's all.'

I rolled up my sleeves and set to work on a stew, bringing him in a hot toddy while I peeled. He croaked at me through the door: 'So what are you after doing, being here, when you should be at home tending your husband and children? When will you bring the little dotes over here so I can corrupt them too?'

'Why don't you get heating in here? It's ridiculous a man of your age – what are you now, eighty? – living in this Neanderthal style.'

'Neanderthal,' he mumbled. 'I'm too young to die and too old to change. Just leave me in peace, won't you.'

'I'm surprised you didn't get pneumonia years ago.'

'Oh no,' he groaned. 'There you go again, round and round on your hobby horse. Go away, leave me alone. It's worse than having a radio set.'

When he'd cooled down, and was feeling better I sat by his bed and told him why I was there. How my husband was due to go away on a long weekend over some work, and I had turned up at four, as usual, to pick up the children from the nursery school they'd been at for a few months.

'No, sorry, I'm afraid they've gone,' a pinched-faced teacher greeted me. 'Their mother picked them up. The family were going away for the weekend. They wanted to beat the traffic. Quite understandable. Fridays are always hell.'

I thought I had misheard.

'Who picked them up?'

The woman looked at me blankly. 'Their mother, Mrs Taylor.'

I took a deep breath.

'I am Mrs Taylor,' I said, through clenched teeth. 'Who has taken them? It was not their mother, for I am their mother.'

She looked at me now as though I was mad. 'No, their mother is a short blonde lady, always very smartly dressed.' She paused. I suppose I had gone white.

'You're the children's auntie, aren't you? I understood from Mrs Taylor that you were their auntie. Don't worry, they're quite safe. Pity they've worried you like this. They should have warned you.'

When I got home I phoned the hotel and asked reception to put me through to Mrs Taylor.

'Sorry,' she sang down the line in that tone exclusively used by hotel receptionists. 'Mr and Mrs Taylor have gone out to the adventure park with the children. They shouldn't be long. It closes soon, they're only going for a look. Would you like to leave a message?'

I put the phone down.

Uncle Hughie lay in silence.

'You know it feels as though I'm dead, standing there watching my own funeral,' I said. He stretched out his bony hand and stroked my hair. Just like he used to do when I was young.

'Should I go up to the school with my marriage certificate, prove it to them?'

He sighed. 'It's no use carrying an umbrella if your shoes are leaking.'

He looked at me and knew I didn't understand, so he changed tack.

'Why did you marry him in the first place? It was always a mystery to me.'

'I loved him.'

'Agh, yes of course, of course. But I should think you've loved a few people in your time, and you didn't marry them, did you?'

'Maybe they didn't ask me.'

'And I shouldn't think you'd be scared of asking them.'

'My parents thought it was a very good marriage.'

'Then maybe your parents should have married him, not you.'

I began to lose my temper with him.

'So I suppose you're on his side,' I snapped.

'It's not a question of sides. And anyhow it's impossible to chose between two blind goats.' He paused to change tack. 'This sex business. Do you ever talk to him about it, at all?'

'No. The sex was always fine. That's why I thought everything would be all right. I wonder sometimes if the sex wasn't best when he hated me most.' I shrugged. 'I've tried very hard never to be a shrew, a clock-watcher, standing there in the hall tapping my feet when he comes in late, yelling "Your dinner's in the oven", and all that stuff. Even when I knew he was off with other women, smelt their perfume on his clothes, saw his exasperated face because it was me he was coming home to.'

He shook his head. 'I apologise in advance, but just tell me what will a man not do to get a rub of the ould relic?'

'Well I never made a fuss about it.'

'You let him walk all over you, is that what you're telling me?'

As I did not, could not, answer, he plucked a while at the bedclothes before asking again very gently, 'Tell me, gal, why did you marry him?'

I looked up. 'I'll leave him. I'll take the children and we can run away from him together.'

'Leave him to the concupiscence of Miss Pelham?'

'Why not?' I said with confidence. 'If it wasn't her it'd be any one of a thousand others.'

'Where will you go?' he asked quietly.

358

'Anywhere. As far away from them as I can get. Somewhere where he'll never find us.'

'That rules out this place then.'

'I know. I'll go to the West, as far as you can get. County Mayo.'

'Aren't you the great woman for the plans?'

'Achill Island. That's where we'll go.'

'Lord, you don't want to go to Achill. Why, that's just two thousand alcoholics clinging to a rock in the Atlantic, where on a quiet night you can hear the dogs bark in America. You'd go mental in a week. And the children would be fighting to get away from you and back to the whips of money they get from their papa. You've thought of that aspect, I'm sure.'

'I wish I was dead,' I sobbed.

'Agh, there you go again. One foot in the grave, and the other on a banana skin.'

In a few days he was much better. He wanted a walk around the hill he said, to get a glimpse of the sea.

'I used to wander out here with pretty little Catherine Tate, my sister-in-law to be, when she'd run away from home. What a beautiful woman she was. I miss her so much.' He wiped a tear from his eye.

'Agh lookit, that idiot wind has blown some dust up and half blinded me.'

We sat down. He seemed very weak still.

'These hills are teeming with ghosts,' he said. 'Don't you feel them brushing past your skin?'

I held my face up to the sun, and felt a cool breeze stir the down on my cheeks. 'I feel something,' I said. 'But I can't quite catch it.'

'It's a funny ould country, isn't it? It's peaceful enough up here, I suppose, but down in those villages there are soldiers patrolling the street with machine guns. Absurd, isn't it?' He pointed down to the rich swathes of

359

green below. 'Those fields are made from the richest earth in the world. Because for centuries we Irish have used the best fertiliser of them all. Human blood. The bodies of men, women and children.' He stood up and turned to face the other way, before sitting down again.

'I can't bear to look at it. To see the green and know it sits upon the red below. Lookit!' He pointed down towards the sea. 'There's a pretty sight.'

There was an old Middle Eastern dhow just offshore, with maroon sails slopping loosely in the stillness of the bay. 'It's a pity I'm such an old fellah now. I'd have liked for you to to bring your children here for a few days or so, with your husband's permission though, you understand. And if I'd been young and sprightly again, I would have walked them down the coastal path and showed them the flora and fauna, the witches' hares, the magpies, the seals howling on the shore.'

'There seem to be lots of robins around. And wrens.'

Hughie gasped in horror. 'Oh, my dear, that's a bird you don't be wanting to mention around these parts.'

'A wren?' I was mystified.

'Oh yes. The Dreolin. The little blackguards loved the Irishmen so much that they perched on their drums as they were lining up to fight that rogue Cromwell and his men. And the rascals made so much noise that it alerted the Cromwellians, and they fell on the Irish and it ended in mass slaughter. That's the tale, anyhows. Don't think much of it meself, now, do you?'

'Do you have many squirrels round here?' I asked, trying to make better my *faux pas*.

He spat. 'Agh, no, what are squirrels but rats in drag? I've no time for such creatures, meself. I hate the rats, you know. They come snooping around me ould place searching for a morsel o' food. I have to shoo them out with a broom.'

'Why don't you put down poison?' I suggested.

'Good God, I couldn't be doing anything like that. They've as much right to live as I have. I just don't want to share a house with them, that's all. I'm not that strapped for company.'

'You should move,' I said.

He ignored me.

'Did you ever go to Australia?' he asked. 'Now there's a funny country for you. I'd like to see that before I die. All those weird animals, mice as big as dogs, furry things with webbed feet, kangaroos hopping all over the place.'

I looked at him and saw what a contradiction he was, so old, so young.

'It's like the opposite of Ireland, Australia. They've got all those extra animals and we've lost a few,' he went on.

'Like snakes, you mean.'

'Snakes, woodpeckers, roe deer, moles, weasels, toads, newts.' He sighed as though the loss was his own personal worry, then perked up again. 'Did you ever see Maggie's Leap?' he asked.

I shook my head.

'Agh, it's just down the way. It's a deep deep cleft in the rock, called after a young girl called Maggie. One day, on her way home from market she was running from a young man of evil intent, and as he neared her and neared her, her only chance was to jump and risk tumbling down four hundred feet of sheer rock into the sea, or stay put and be ravished on the spot. Anyhow you must have worked out the rest. She made it safely to the other side, and not one of the eggs in her basket broken.' He smiled at me. 'And if you believe that you'd believe anything.'

'And Bloody Bridge,' I asked, 'further along. Does that have a story too?'

His face tightened as he replied, 'It's a story no one round here tells that much. You'd get a bomb in your morning post if you went round talking about it.'

361

'Tell me.'

'It happened way back, 1641. Some mad Irishmen, and madder Catholics, including the old English Catholics mind you, rose up and slaughtered hundreds of poor Protestants in their beds. Then they set fire to their meagre dwellings. Those that escaped they stripped of their clothing and left to wander the hills in the freezing October night air.

'They rounded up about eighty women and children and drove them off the bridge and laughed to see them drown. Some wags used these poor floundering creatures for target practice, and as they came up for air, shot at them. Those that the madmen missed, well, they waited for them to clamber out, gasping for breath, before beating their brains out on the banks.'

We sat together in silence.

'Your, er, the Pirate, me brother, used to sing a song. I've not the voice, meself, of the big laddo, but it was like this:

'O, the Erne shall run red,
   With redundance of blood,
The earth shall rock beneath our tread,
   And flames wrap hill and wood,
And gun-peal and slogan-cry,
   Wake many a glen serene,
Ere you shall fade, ere you shall die,
   My Dark Rosaleen!
   My own Rosaleen!
The Judgment Hour must first be nigh,
Ere you can fade, ere you can die,
   My Dark Rosaleen!'

'It's a sentimental version of a very old Irish poem. Strange how they knew even back then that it would never end.' He looked at me very steadily.

'God help me, ideas jump around my head like frogs in

362

a bucket. I don't know where to start on this, but, please, don't even think of coming to live here with your children. I manage all right, because it's easy for me to keep myself to myself. You're altogether a more sociable sort. You'd be in trouble in half a minute.

'I worry for you, my little dote. You go by the name of that song, and so did another of my nieces, a quiet dark, misunderstood little girl, who lived in her own secret world, unable to share it with anyone. She was a bit of a hero, but they branded her for a villain when she was in her grave and unable to defend herself, because she kept a secret and she was, like all of us poor benighted Irish people, sentimental.'

'My Auntie Rosaleen. I was called after her. She died before I was born.'

He took my hand and squeezed it as he said, 'We've all had it over here in the North. This business has touched our family for generations. Get free. You're English now. Go back to your husband. Go home.'

The solicitor is staring at me across the Formica table. His eyes are soft, dewy.

'Did you go back to him? Did you follow the old man's advice?'

'Yes. Now that I think back on it, what other advice could he have given me? And even if he'd given me wonderful advice, would I have taken it? I doubt it. I was always stubborn. I always knew best. I think I'd already made up my own mind to go back to Robert before he said anything.'

I went home and tried to make a go of my marriage. I cooked things from recipe books, and dressed up, and wore make-up and perfume in bed. If Robert had something to say I sat and listened and 'oohed' and 'aaahed' in

363

all the appropriate places. I became interested in rugby and cricket. I reminded him how clever he was, how handsome, how sexy. When this procedure – which I read of frequently in women's magazines, where it is called 'working at your marriage' – was at its zenith I had a letter from Uncle Hughie asking me to come over to Ireland; he had important things to discuss with me. It was a tranquil time in my marriage. The trouble seemed to have calmed down, Lucinda was away on some course, Robert smiled, the children were happy, everything was sublime.

I knew my uncle. He'd be wanting to discuss the migration of the pipit, to sit by the fire in the close of the evening and read me poems. He could wait.

Robert had suggested that I take the children to afternoon sessions called Mother and Child at the local pool, which had just been modernised with wave machines, a *trompe-l'oeil* beach with plastic palm trees, lots of slides. Everything a child could wish. I felt it made up for the lost weekend at the adventure park. He gave us enough money to go next door afterwards and have fish and chips, another favourite of the twins.

These afternoons were like paradise. He had a heavy divorce case on that fortnight, but at five o'clock, when we were finished, he'd drive over from work, and pick us all up in the Jag. Wet swimming things were flung into the boot and the children jabbered away in the back, almost sick with happiness.

We'd gone regularly for two weeks when one day we arrived to find a large blackboard outside the centre which read: 'Sorry! Pool closed due to heating failure'. Not wanting to ruin the day altogether we piled into the fish and chip shop, for a fish supper wrapped up in paper, and then caught the bus home.

'Daddy will miss us,' they chanted at me as we rode along on the front top seats, their favourite place.

364

'It's all right,' I assured them. 'I'll phone him when we get in.'

The children raced through to the kitchen to get out plates, ketchup and salt and vinegar ready for our takeaway feast. I went into the living room to phone my husband and warn him that we were already home.

I need not have bothered.

He was there, on the sofa, stark naked, in the midst of the sexual act with a dark-haired woman I had never set eyes on before.

'I'm not surprised she's getting a divorce,' I said from the doorway, 'if this is how she spends her afternoons.'

He leapt up, grasping round on the floor for his clothes. 'Mummy, where's the ketchup?' The voice came from the hallway.

My husband's face blackened. 'Get them out of here!' he yelled, kicking the door shut in my face.

I packed up the fish and chips, grabbed a weekend bag and ordered a taxi.

By eight o'clock we were in Belfast. We spent the night in a hotel. The next morning we took a train down to Newry. We arrived by taxi at Hughie's place at midday.

The door was flung open. I was shocked when I walked in. The place was wrecked. The ceiling had been smashed through, and rafters could be seen. Slates had even been pulled off. From the living room you could see the sky.

'Wait outside,' I said to the children.

The bedroom was also pulled to bits, the elegant carved red and gold bed was hacked to pieces, the drawers pulled out of the dresser, contents strewn over the floor.

My heart beat in my mouth.

Going back through the living room I noticed great hunks of the bed were lying charred on the fire. The house had been ransacked.

365

I took hold of the children's hands and marched them down the hill to the village.

'Where're we going, Mummy? Why can't we go home?' The words echoed around my racing mind.

I found us a small café and sat the children down, before quietly asking the lady behind the counter if she knew what had happened to my uncle, where was he?

Her face clouded. She glanced towards the children and said, 'They'll be all right in here. You'd best come through to the back.'

She poured a cup of tea and sat me down in her sitting room. 'He was a nice old chap,' she said. 'Always on the grin. Always kind and quiet, like.'

'Is he dead then?' I asked, my mouth blotting-paper dry. 'I'm sorry. Yes.'

I sat as though in a dream while she told me what had happened.

'There are some rogues around this place who imagined the ould fellah was loaded. This story that he had a crock of gold coins. Spanish gold, they called it. But I knew that was all blether, just a tale to keep the kids all going, passing himself off as a leprechaun. Well it was easy to believe, him being so small and all. With those pointy transparent ears of his, well, it was good crack for the ould boy, that's all.

'I'd not seen him around the place for a few days, I must say. I wish now that I'd gone up there to enquire after him, but it's such a stiff walk and all, well, you just don't, do you?' She looked down at me.

'I'd drink your tea, lass, you need a bit of sugar, I should think, what with the shock and all.' She went on.

'He must have been ill for a few weeks I think. He'd been lying there anyhows, without a morsel to eat, and his skin as thin as paper, for some time before he died, they say. The lady at the post office said he'd sent off a letter to England and was confident he'd a friend or something was

366

coming over to look after him. Well, it seems they never turned up. Didn't even reply, or the postman would have found him earlier. Have another cup, dear, you're awful pale.'

She went through the strip curtain to the shop. I took out a handkerchief and wiped my face. There were no tears. She came back and sat next to me.

'Those two little darlings are enjoying themselves out there. I'm just after giving them an extra slice of cake. I hope you don't mind. Are you sure you want to hear all this?'

'Oh yes,' I said. 'I have to know everything.'

'Old Michael O'Shea found him. They used to play dominoes together sometimes at the pub. Michael had been a bit poorly himself, you know, but when he felt better he staggered up the hill and found him. Dead.'

'Why is the place all smashed up?' I asked, numb with horror.

'Oh that's these terrible people round here. When his body had been taken off and buried, they all fancied they'd go find his crock of gold. I ask you. Well, they searched the place, pulled it to bits. But, what did I tell you, nobody found a thing. If he'd had a bit of money he'd have got himself the electricity put in years ago, an ould soul like him. He'd have given himself a few more comforts if he'd had the cash.'

'How did he die, do you know?'

'He was very old, darlin'. When Michael found him he was lying in that queer bed of his. And the weird thing was, Michael says the ould chap was holding a dead rat in his hand. I suppose the rats had got in. They're terrible creatures you know. Great little climbers. The poor ould thing couldn't move I suppose, and was trying to catch them with his bare hands. Well, there's that to be said for it, I suppose. He probably died happy, for with his last breath he'd got hold of one of the little divils and squeezed the life out of it.'

The solicitor is now scribbling madly. The yellow pages covered in his scratchy writing pile up on one side of the table.

'Is this man Michael O'Shea any relative to Patrick O'Shea?' he asks, not looking up from his notes.

'I met Patrick O'Shea the morning after the terrible discovery of Hughie's death. He came into the bar where I was talking to his father Michael, who had found my uncle's body. His father introduced us and Patrick immediately sat down and talked of Hughie, what a nice man he had been, how he'd be missed down in the village.

' "Are you a relation?" Patrick asked.

'When I told him, he said I should call in on a solicitor's office in Newcastle. He then took me to a small and cheerful day nursery run by a friend of his, where they kindly allowed me to leave the children for the afternoon. Then he took me to the graveyard to see Hughie's grave. "It's a beautiful stone," I said. "Who was responsible for that?"

'He shook his boyish blond hair. "Oh, it's nothing. Me Da and I just organised a whip round. I mean it's the least we could do. I just wish we'd realised the straits the old boy was in a bit earlier, that's all."

'We called in at the solicitor's office on the way home. A dapper little fellow rose and shook me warmly by the hand. "Well, I don't know what sort of news you'll be finding this, but you've inherited Mr Hugh Morgan's farm. There are all the usual checks to be made of course, but he has named you sole beneficiary." '

My own solicitor makes an 'aaah' sound, and nods to himself. 'Go on, please,' he murmurs. 'What happened next?'

'I took the children back home, but after a few weeks found it impossible to stay with my husband. When I had challenged Robert with the scene I witnessed on the day that the swimming pool was closed his face had blackened, and he fought me physically and at last slammed my fingers shut in the door. I didn't scream. I didn't want the children to hear. But I knew that while I was in the house, this sort of thing would carry on.

'When I saw the children afterwards, my nails already red and black, they were frantic. They could smell my fear, feel the atmosphere.

' "What's happening, Mummy," they whimpered. "Are you and Daddy fighting again?" Their little faces gazed up at me in a sort of horror, and I knew the only way I could protect them was to separate from Robert.

'I packed myself a small case, kissed the children goodbye, and told them I had to go back to Ireland on business. "About that horrible house on the hill?" one of them asked.

'I told them I was going to turn it into a nice house again, and left. My plan was to get my uncle's house into some order so that I could take them there with me to live, away from Robert and his floozies and drunken bouts of violence. It was a stupid move. For by leaving the marital home I had as good as relinquished my claim on my children.'

'Am I right to presume that you had further contact with Patrick O'Shea at this stage?' The solicitor has removed his jacket, and rolled his sleeves up.

I start to tell him how I got to know my partner in crime.

'Roisin have no sorrow for all that has happened to you:
The friars are out on the brine, they are travelling at sea,
Your pardon from the Pope will come from Rome in the East,
And we won't spare the Spanish wine for my Roisin Dubh.'

When Patrick had started to recite this poem to me, up there on that sunny hillside, my mind flew back to Bill, my first real boyfriend, whom I had dumped for Robert on our first time round. Bill had yelled the poem to me time after time from clifftops, on beaches, on downs and in vales. 'The Little Black Rose' it was called, the original of the rhymed version by the Victorian poet Mangan, the favourite song of the Pirate.

Patrick seemed to have the same spirit as Bill, the same *joie de vivre*, a sparkling kind of youth. He shinned up on to the roof and tapped away until all the broken or absent pieces of slate were fixed. He screwed chunks of wood to the damaged rafters until they were firm. Then he skimmed the ceiling with plaster.

Meanwhile I was clearing the floor, sorting out books, mementoes, the odd swatches of glittering fabric my uncle had hoarded.

'What about the bed?' I asked him. 'Any hope at all?'

He stared down at the charred pieces of timber all laid out like a giant Airfix kit on the field outside. 'It's quite hopeless,' he said shaking his head. His eyes swivelled up and scanned my face. 'But I think we should try, don't you?'

All day we would work in the house, slopping on paint, screwing shelves back into place, building the chimney breast back up (the looters had practically torn it away brick by brick in their quest for the crock of gold). Clearly Hughie had sold off his Spanish pieces of eight long ago, for cash. There was no trace of them here.

'Now this chimneypiece is even bigger and better than it was before,' Patrick crowed. 'Much better updraught you'll be getting now. There's a bit of space inside.'

In the evening we would stroll back down to the village and share a glass of Guinness and a whiskey.

I had a little money in the bank. I had never touched the

370

money my grandmother had left me. Now I knew she would approve of my use of it. I paid Patrick for his work, but after the first week he declined any more payment for his services. 'I've nothing else to do with me time, after all,' was all he said. 'And I was awful fond of the old boy, and let's face it I'm awful fond of you.'

I knew all about Irish blarney, so I chose not to hear the last remark.

I phoned the children every evening from a pay phone in the street. If I was lucky one of them answered and we spoke. Other times I got him or, worse, Lucinda, who had reappeared on the scene, and the phone was slammed down on me.

When Patrick saw how unhappy I was on the nights I had wasted my phone money on an insult from either of those two he'd be very tender and kind, treat me to supper, sit and listen to me for hours, while I searched for a solution to this intolerable situation.

'Strikes me you should be there, not here,' he said quietly one evening. 'I'll keep an eye on Hughie's old place for you; and look, I've a small flat in Muswell Hill. Why don't you stay there? It's lying empty as it is.' He handed me the keys there and then. Next morning I flew back to London. When I next called at our Clapham home I was presented with a roll of papers by my husband. 'I'm divorcing you,' he announced. 'You'd better find yourself a solicitor.'

I always suffered from an irrepressible desire to fulfil everyone's prophecies of me. When I was called a trouble-maker I became one, so when Robert had accused me of coldness I suppose I became colder. That's what is odd about it. If I was generous and someone accused me of being mean, I would become mean, almost to please them. The day that Robert said I was like a dog, always following him around whimpering, I turned into a snivelling, dewy-eyed mutt.

And the day we met in the solicitor's office to start divorce proceedings I did the opposite.

We sat at either end of a large desk, solicitors between us. My man was a cheap and cheerful chap I'd got through legal aid. I had no job now. I'd been a wife for years. I could have worked during the marriage. God knows we had enough money for a nanny. But Robert said it wouldn't look good for him if I was out at work. It would look as though we were strapped for cash. So I stayed at home. I arranged dinner parties. I played with the children. I cooked.

His solicitor smelt of a very exclusive eau de cologne. Musky, and foreign. His suit was elegantly cut, bespoke. He wore a carnation in his buttonhole.

At a certain point in the proceedings the two solicitors left us alone together to see if there was any chance of reconciliation.

'It's just procedure, don't worry,' Robert said, when they had gone. 'You're looking good.'

I looked at him. Images of Flush, Greyfriars Bobby, Argos, Lassie and Rin Tin Tin flashed through my mind. 'I miss you,' I say, despite myself.

'You left home,' he snaps. 'Not me.'

I am stunned into silence. Of course he is right. But I'd go back home tomorrow, if only, if only . . .

'I still love you, you know.' It's out of my mouth before I have a chance to stop it. I glance at him. I know my eyes are begging for a reply.

'The trouble with you,' he sighs, 'is that you've no sense of loyalty. You're incapable of being true to anyone.'

I don't answer him.

'You're always asking questions, and then you're so quick with the accusations. And after that it's chip, chip,

chip. You're always chipping away at people. It's why you're so unpopular.'

I thought of all the friends I'd had before I married him. The people he said bored him. The people he practically banned from the house, or from my company. I'd always been popular. Loyal.

'When you're in law you have to think in strong lines. When I fight a case I don't really care if my clients are innocent or guilty. My brief is simply to get them off. To work like hell on their behalf. Total strangers. And there's you. Can't even be loyal to those you *say* you love.'

'I . . .' I opened my mouth to speak, but my throat closed tight. I thought of the Pirate. I thought of Uncle Hughie. It was true. I was disloyal. I had betrayed two of the dearest people in my life. I swallowed and made a decision to keep a watch on myself. And I decided at that moment that the next person who was kind to me I would be loyal to until the day of my death.

That person was Patrick O'Shea.

After my divorce I moved from Muswell Hill into a smart London flat, bought by my husband. It was all part of some legal skulduggery called the property settlement in which he got everything and in exchange provided me with a flat in lieu of alimony.

It was a maisonette, the lower floor of a nice Victorian terraced house. For the first few days I sat there in the back room and stared out at the windswept garden. I didn't move, didn't eat, didn't sleep. I was in shock.

One night I heard the sound of a woman sobbing in the room above me. The upstairs flat was clearly owned by someone else who felt that their world had collapsed.

Next day I bought a spade and went out into the garden and dug. I turned over every square inch, remembering Uncle Hughie's remarks about land being a thing you must take care of.

I had no idea what my future held. I had to find the present. Get to grips with it. For the moment I would dig. I'd make this garden into a triumph of inner city beauty, maybe even grow carrots and cabbages and peas; plant an apple tree, gooseberry bushes, raspberries, strawberries. On the weekends allocated for the children to see me, they would would love to come here and feast on the home-grown fruits.

I dug until I ached, turning over each sod, tugging at yards of bindweed, matted rye-grass. After a while, I stood with my foot on the spade and wiped the sweat from my brow. As I looked up I saw a sad-eyed women staring bleakly out of the window. I smiled and grimaced as though to say, 'Tough work!' She nodded in reply. We held each other's glance for a moment and then went our own ways. A few days later we met on the front doorstep, fumbling in our bags for our keys. It was late afternoon. On impulse I invited her in for a coffee.

We talked pleasantries for some time. Nice neighbourhood. Nice house. Nice shops. Nice and near the tube. That sort of thing.

'As the sun's gone over the yardarm,' I said, thinking immediately of the Pirate, and pulling out another piece of phoney sea-talk. 'Let's splice the mainbrace.'

She looked at me as though I was cracked, and I shuddered, remembering what the judge had said of me in that hellish courtroom. I dropped the levity.

'Would you care for a drink? Whisky, wine, martini?'

'Some wine would be nice,' she said, pulling a cigarette from her bag.

After a few drinks she started to loosen up and told me she'd only moved in a few days before I had. Her lover had told her that an affair they'd been having for years must come to an end. He wanted her to keep out of his way so that he could 'try to make a go of it' with his new wife.

I tutted vehemently. Her chin was shaking, her lips tight.

'I did everything for that bastard,' she said. 'All the things his wife refused to do. I did everything for him. Everything. I helped him on the papers for his divorce. Researched among dusty files in registries for him. Cooked for him. Everything.'

She explained that as compensation for ending the affair he'd bought her the flat. ' "Just so there'd be no hard feelings," he said. But I ask you, how can a silly flat compensate me for all those years of devotion and the loss of his love for me?'

He'd evidently been well off, I thought, and she was such a mousy little type. I asked what he did for a living, how they met.

'He was in law,' she said. 'I was a legal secretary. Typing, filling out forms. Not very important things, really. But I stuck by him over some very sticky times.'

'Oh, my husband was a lawyer,' I said in sympathy.

'Oh well you know the shenanigans that go on then.' She quivered into her glass as she drained the last dregs from the bottle into it. My glass was empty so I went over to the sideboard to open a new bottle. I twisted the corkscrew down through the foil into the cork, gripping the bottle in my other hand.

'My mother always said to me I was a fool. "Who'd ever trust a man that handsome?" she'd say. "Girls like you are two a penny to them." But I really thought he meant it when he said he'd marry me when he'd got rid of his wife, who was a bit of a grasping shrew, from all accounts.'

I tugged at the cork. It was very stiff.

' "And not only the looks," my mother'd say. Mr Fancy-pants, she called him. "And that film star name!" she'd say. "Robert Taylor! I ask you, what sort of a fool does he take you for?" '

The cork came out of the bottleneck with a crack. The bottle slipped through my hands and bounced once on the floor, before rolling on to its side. Wine sopped into the new cream-coloured carpet in a red puddle. I fell to my knees, gasping for air.

My husband had bought this house lock, stock and barrel and used it to fob me off and to fob off his obliging little secretary too.

She was suddenly on her knees beside me. 'Oh dear, what a mess. I'll get a cloth,' she offered.

I sat hunched up on the floor my head in my hands, sobbing. She handed me the cloth and then hovered by the door. 'Oh dear,' she said. 'I'm so sorry you're upset. Life's awful isn't it. So cruel.'

I hadn't moved. She shifted about uneasily and said, 'I'd best go back upstairs I think. I've brought it all back with my going on. I'm terribly sorry.'

When she'd gone I flung around the flat, packing all my things. Nothing in the world would convince me to spend one more night there.

In court the gift of this flat had been blown up as a magnanimous, kind and gracious move of his, a fair balance, considering he was to stay on in the family home. He would stay there because it was better for the children, who would be living with him.

My children, my children!

The stack of yellow pages fall to the floor of the interview room. My solicitor stoops to recover them.

'Just one more thing, and then I think we're through.' He puts the notes into his briefcase and asks, 'Presumably you left this maisonette and went back to Patrick O'Shea's bedsit in Muswell Hill?'

'Yes.'

'He was there with you?'

'On and off.'

'That December. The run-up to Christmas. You were in London?'

I nod. Trying to remember everything.

'Tell me about it.'

'Patrick comes and goes. It is Christmas. I am depressed because I will not see my children. Not unless I take a taxi to the end of the street where they live, a scarf wrapped high to cover my mouth, my hat pulled low over my eyes, and stroll casually past the house, glancing through the window, hoping that at that moment they might come out of the front door. But not with him. Not with her. With whom, then? They will not come out on their own. Not be left alone to cross that web of roads to the Common. Please God not.'

'The night of the bombing. Where were you? Where did you go?'

'I don't remember,' I mutter, lying.

'You must remember something,' he snaps. 'It was hardly just an ordinary day. For you or the victims.'

I hesitate.

'I went home. I turned on the television. Hideous adverts with snow and singing Father Christmases asking you to buy records, toys, books, perfume, furniture. A row of turkeys doing the can-can and suggesting you buy a frozen turkey for Christmas dinner. Next they'll be getting a row of goose-stepping Nazis to advertise British Gas. Eventually the news came on. A stern news-reader announced that two bombs had gone off at Victoria Coach Station. Seven dead, over thirty injured, some seriously.'

'Did you feel satisfied with yourself?' He appears to be searching his briefcase, not really interested in my reply.

'I turned over and watched a discussion on funding and museums. I felt nothing. Nothing.'

'Good,' he snaps, rising from the table. 'See you in court.' He nods at the wardress and is shown out.

I've been tarted up this morning. Given my best clothes, a bag of make-up.

I learned at my last court case, the divorce, that make-up was not a good idea. I was not used to wearing it, and slapped it on: blusher, mascara, lipstick, the lot. I also rollered my hair, backcombed it. I was aiming at the kind of power dressing that was a hallmark of Miss Pelham. I did not want the judge to think I was a slob, and I knew that Robert would use the casualness of my dress to make a point. However, I misjudged the moment.

Miss Pelham turned up looking rather like Jane Eyre, while I was like a character from a Jackie Collins novel. Appearances were certainly in her favour that day. So this morning I sweep back my hair into a tight bun, and slick down the rest. I apply the tiniest trace of mascara, and that is it.

I am then trotted briskly from my now familiar magnolia cell, bundled into the back of a high-security van, and raced across London to the accompaniment of wailing sirens.

After the initial questions – name, age, 'will you swear', and the rest – a lot of legal wrangling goes on with Queen's Counsel and my own barrister standing up at the bar and having intense whispered conversations.

I was given to believe that Patrick and I would be on trial together, that I would see him today. I was told on my arrival that this was not to be: we are to be tried separately. I think the whispering concerns some new evidence my solicitor has told me will be brought out. I don't know what it will be, but with any luck it will damn me.

I told him he knew my feelings about the matter. I was not interested.

This courtroom is rather bright and airy. I was expecting something out of one of those old black and white films, with Michael Dennison in a little horsehair wig. I feel very much calmer today than I did for the divorce. But then, today I have nothing to lose except my freedom, which I have no use for anyhow.

378

I wish Patrick was here.

They are listing dates now, and events. They all talk in strangely monotonous voices. It is hard to follow what they say for any length of time.

I followed the divorce all right. I listened while my husband's man described me as a money-grabbing social climber, desperately trying to cover up her working-class roots. They passed *me* off as a floozy and a trollop while little Miss Pure Pelham sat there in her scrubbed innocence beside my husband.

'And what relationship is the defendant to Patrick Michael O'Shea?'

'No blood relation, my lord,' drones my defence. 'They have an emotional and sexual relationship.'

The judge scribbles. The jury look at me as though I am still that same floozy I was during the divorce. A cough from the public gallery ricochets around the courtroom like a gunshot.

'And the defendant owned the small cottage on Luke's Mountain? Is that correct?'

My counsel rises to reply.

'No my lord. She was willed the property by her late uncle, Mr Hugh Morgan, but lost possession five years ago.'

'So she was in effect trespassing on the day concerned.'

My counsel waved this off. 'Technically, yes.'


We walked up the hill, Patrick and I, that first day I owned my uncle's little house on the Ulster hillside. 'I can organise some men to repair the roof properly,' he said. 'And clear the place out for you, if that's what you want.'

'I don't know what to do.' I sank down on to one of the fireside chairs, now a skeleton, its innards spilling out, the dry brown horsehair stuffing lying in obscene tangles all over the stone floor.

379

'I don't believe it. I should have flown over when he asked me. I thought he would be pleased I stayed at home. I was trying to make a go of my marriage.'

Patrick stood there in the moted beam of evening sunlight streaming in through the little stable door.

'It was a waste of time anyway,' I went on. 'My husband isn't interested, you see.'

'So will you be moving in, at all? Or selling up?'

I stooped and picked up a pile of books lying on the floor, some with pages torn out, most just flung down however they happened to land.

'I don't know. It depends on the children. I'll go wherever is best for them. Hughie told me I wasn't to bring them here to live.'

'So you'll be selling, then. Well, me Da and I can help you find a buyer, I would think.'

I was trying to piece the lost pages together, slipping them back into their rightful books. There is a sentence underlined in old red ink on the page in my hand: 'Poetry is something more philosophic and of graver import than history,' I read. I look at the top of the page: 'Poetics'. I scrape around on the floor until I find the book. '*Poetics*. Aristotle.' I laugh. 'Harry Stootle! I've got it! Aristotle!'

I smooth the page into place and laugh more brightly than I have done for years. 'Aristotle!'

At my divorce the judge described me as mentally unbalanced and suggested I receive psychiatric help. In the courtroom now I realise that I am laughing aloud, and freeze. No one is looking my way, thankfully. A heated discussion is going on about dates and addresses.

A funny wizened little woman whom I have never seen in my life is in the witness-box talking about some flat she owns in north London. She rents it out, she says. It must be our flat in Muswell Hill. Patrick's flat. Wigged men are presenting local-government lists, electoral rolls.

My counsel is now telling everyone about my husband. How he called the police to have me taken away from his doorstep on various occasions, and got a court order to prevent me coming near his house.

It wasn't his house I was interested in, the fool. It was the children. I only wanted to see my own children. I realise now that I must have looked like a madwoman the night he had me physically removed by the police, my hair straggled across my face from standing out there on the Common for hours in the wind and rain, water streaming from my soggy clothing into a puddle on his doorstep.

I even caught a glimpse, well, no, I didn't actually see them that day through the open door, but I heard a tiny voice calling out from the kitchen: 'Who's that. It's a cold wind.'

And Miss Pelham briskly swept across the hallway, singing sweetly, 'It's nothing, darlings, just a mad old tramp, begging Daddy for some money.'

I screamed then and rushed in, struggling with Robert, who bundled me out on to the step and slammed the door on me before going to phone the police. It wasn't a good idea, for the children saw me, and I suppose I *must* have looked pretty mad.

The judge is scribbling frantically. He looks much stricter than the other one. This one is wrinkly and thin with huge sandy eyebrows. I should think painters always want to draw him. His face looks as though it's been hung in a thousand galleries over the centuries.

The divorce judge was portly and jolly-looking, like someone out of a Dickens musical. When he announced the end of our marriage and awarded my uncle's house and my children to the care of my husband he looked as though he was about to leap up on to the bench and burst into a verse or two of 'If I ruled the World'.

I'd had too many shocks that day to really take anything in. I was on the verge of recovering from the announcement that Miss Pelham, his pure-as-driven-snow companion, was merely a friend and colleague who was supporting him through this difficult time, and helped take his mind off his marital difficulties by partnering him in games of chess (games of chess!) when they dropped the real bombshell.

I don't know why all my life it had been kept from me, but to hear the news in a public court from the barrister of a man who had made my life a living hell was insupportable. He had known all the time, of course. They all had. The whole family: the Pirate, Uncle Hughie, my mother, my father. Probably not my grandmother, I suppose, but I imagine that she knew somewhere in her bones, and that is why she was so mad all my life.

My husband had found out when he'd searched out the birth certificates for our impending wedding. It was there written quite clearly in a large copperplate hand on my birth certificate. No one had done anything to hide the information, legally speaking. It was just a silent conspiracy within the family circle.

I am not my parents' child. I am really the daughter of the Pirate and his wife, mad Catherine Tate. Conceived after a drinking bout which had stemmed somehow from the death of the woman I always thought was my Aunt Rosaleen.

My father Leo was my eldest brother. My mother was simply his wife. My parents were those two Irish lost souls whom I had separately insulted and betrayed.

My husband put it to the divorce court in a simpler way: 'Her mother has been locked up within the family home for years, a hopeless case, a sort of modern-day Grace Pool; while her father, a drunken Irish navvy, staggered round the streets of Liverpool dressed eccentrically and making out he was an escapee from *Treasure Island*. You can see that with such a background my wife is bound to be unbalanced mentally.'

I had sat there in the divorce court, my mind spinning back, replaying scenes from my childhood, trying to make sense of it all.

'So that is why she has conjured up these fantasies about my relationship with Miss Pelham, and why the children would be safer, I'm sure you agree, my lord, in my care, being given the education that they deserve in suitable surroundings, without these lowering influences.'

I smiled to think that I *could* have joined the Irish team on Saint Patrick's Day, and been given the shamrock, and taken part in that concert where the girl sitting next to me had wet herself laughing at the poem 'My Dark Rosaleen'.

'And Patrick Michael O'Shea rented the flat. Mrs Taylor stayed there with him occasionally, I understand.' The judge scribbles away. The jury look bored.

'So how long had this, er, relationship with Mr O'Shea been going on?'

'Since the death of her uncle, Mr Hugh Morgan, my lord, a period of approximately five years.'

'And the bombing campaign allegedly organised by this O'Shea, this occurred over the same period, correct?'

'Yes, my lord.'

When the solicitor I had engaged to divorce me told me I had a strong case, I believed him. 'No problems,' he said in the confident manner of legal people. 'You have a little property of your own, and your husband is bound to provide a decent alimony on his income. No problem at all.'

So I went back to Hughie's house to wait out the time. I

was digging round the side of the house when I came across the large tin drums.

'Did you bring these up?' I asked Patrick, next time he called.

'Oh, that stuff. Yes. It's fertiliser. I thought we should try and get the ground going again. It's a bit exhausted isn't it?'

I looked at the giant drums. 'That's enough to fertilise half of Ulster, isn't it, not four tiny stony squares of earth.'

He laughed. 'Got it off the back of a lorry,' he said. 'We'll use what we need and I'll get rid of the rest. Don't worry.'

After having done all this work, loving this place, because it tied me to the people I loved most and had lost, it was a terrible blow to lose it to a man like my husband. I was in car-crash shock in that courtroom after finding out who I really was, and hearing the judge announce that Robert had custody of the children, and that I could only see them 'at his discretion'.

So when they came to the property settlement I simply sat numb, not hearing the grand debate going on all around me. Only when I left the house which I shared with another of Robert's cast-offs did I really understand that Hughie's house was no longer anything to do with me. I knew Robert wouldn't be interested in living there. He hated Ireland and everything Irish. Or so I understood whenever he raised his fist at me, for it usually fell with a volley of 'you Bog-Irish bitch, with your stupid Paddy relations' type insults. I presumed he would sell it.

Whenever I was in Ireland I went back to look at the place. I walked past most days. Whatever the weather I kept my eye on it. I had relinquished my key, but Patrick proudly presented his. Like two naughty schoolchildren we let ourselves in and sat in the little living room in the summer evenings.

When winter approached I suggested we light a fire in the empty hearth.

'No,' he said sharply. 'Too much evidence against us. The ashes and all. And we don't know how safe the chimney is now. Best not.'

'Oh come on!' I was getting up to find some firewood.

He gripped my arm. 'No. Believe me. No. You mustn't think of lighting the fire, d'you hear me.'

Only when he was so firm did I think that what we were doing was illegal. Till then Patrick's philosophy had made it seem all right. 'We did all the work, after all,' he'd said. 'It would be a crime to just leave the old place empty.'

'It'll never be empty,' I had replied. 'It's full of ghosts.'

But from that day we agreed not to go back to the house until we could do so legally. When Robert put it up for sale, as he surely would do soon, and I would buy it.

'And the infatuation occurred in the period shortly after the divorce.' The judge is making this point clear, either to himself or to the jury, I'm not sure which.

'The man Patrick O'Shea gave her comfort at a time of great distress. But how involved was he in the stake-out of Mr Taylor's Clapham house, if at all?'

Patrick and I had barely ever been in London at the same time. He never accompanied me on those terrible painful trips to Clapham. He agreed to keep an eye on the hillside farm, to contact me if it was put up for sale, while I sat in London, trying to arrange the elusive contact with my children which had been promised by the divorce judge.

Whenever I saw my children Robert made sure that either he or Miss Pelham was always there too. When I made a scene about that he simply withdrew permission for me to visit. That was when I started haunting the Common, and he got the injunction out against me.

385

I remember coming home very late one spring night when my husband had had me carted off in a police car, and finding Patrick there in the Muswell Hill flat with two of his friends. Two young men in leathers, who pulled on balaclavas as they left.

Patrick was always the one for turning up like that without a warning.

Next morning I was up and out before he woke, as I had to appear in court to answer the charges of causing an affray, or whatever Robert had accused me of.

He was gone when I got back, so I returned to Clapham Common to watch. I kept up my vigil for months, unseen. It was only a few days before Christmas that I was spotted. This time the police gave me a warning, but as I had seen the whole gang, Robert, Lucinda and my children, pile into a car and drive away I knew they were going to his parents in Cambridge, or, horror, perhaps to hers. But from the pile of gift-wrapped boxes in the back of the newly acquired Range Rover, it was clear they would be away for the whole Christmas period, and my vigil would stop. A policeman saw me on to a plane to Northern Ireland, where I treated myself to a few days off in a posh hotel in Newcastle. Late on Christmas Eve Patrick arrived to join me and we had a lovely time together until I returned to England in the New Year.

Another great time we had was on St John's Eve. His father Michael had told us how in the old days they'd burned fires up the hill and people had come from near and far to celebrate the equinox and the feast of St John the Baptist.

We planned to have a picnic up the hill, with as many of the locals as would like to join us. Patrick himself was away most of the day, but the women of the village and I cooked a boxful of cakes and other good lightweight food, carried it to the top of the hill and made a vast bonfire from pieces of driftwood and any rubbish we could lay our

hands on. At dusk everyone trailed up the hill and we lit
the fire. I sat with Michael O'Shea, running to fetch him
glasses of beer and baked potatoes from the fire. I was
worried that Patrick wouldn't turn up, but when the fire
was at its highest he rolled up pulling a cartful of biscuits,
and beer and spices in a huge pot. 'When the fire goes
down to cinders we'll put this on and have a warm cup to
see the dawn in,' he said, as he went over to his father and
kissed his forehead.

Some soldiers had stormed up the hill in a Land Rover,
thinking there was trouble going on, but they just took our
names and were soon calmed with a mug of ale and a cake.
They went on their way peacefully enough.

The jury shuffle restlessly, and murmur. The judge is
holding his forehead now, and shaking his head. 'So that
accounts for all the dates, bar one. Mr Carter,' he glares at
my barrister, 'what surprises have you got up your sleeve
for this one? Surely the evidence is incontrovertible that
the accused was present and active upon the night of 15
August. She was arrested at the scene of the crime, was she
not, and taken straight from there to Belfast where extra-
dition orders brought her to London to face these charges?'

August the 15th. The most terrible day of my life.

I turned up unexpectedly in Ireland having watched my
husband pack children and mistress into the Range Rover
with lots of camping gear and boxes of food and the usual
items for a holiday. My London vigil now had no purpose.
Soon after I arrived I searched the village for Patrick,
hoping we could have dinner together or share a drink at
the pub, where I would be staying as usual. Everyone
seemed to think he'd gone up to Belfast on business and
would be back later in the evening.

While I was waiting I took a walk. I strolled out of the

village in the hazy close afternoon sun and walked inland, down the valley. After a mile or so I turned down a gravel lane and ended up outside a magnificent farmhouse, with a paved courtyard, stables large enough to hold a string of racehorses, a dairy block and thick white gateposts. While I stood and admired the beauty of the building, nestling in the verdant and lush dappled light, rays of sunshine flecked with dancing insects, tyres crushed the gravel behind me and I stepped back into a ditch to avoid the shiny black hearse which swept into the courtyard.

An old woman dressed in black came out and shook hands with the undertaker. They had a short conversation, both shaking their heads, then went into the main door, together with two assistants from the hearse.

I sat on a flowery bank outside the gates for a while intoxicated by the magical stillness and beauty of the place. After about half an hour the men came out with a coffin and slid it into the back, in the lower compartment, so that it was not visible through the glass windows. Then the hearse turned in the yard and drove out past me and back along the lane.

A few moments later Mrs Murphy, the lady who ran the café in the village, came out of the front door, wrapping her headscarf round her neck and saying goodbye to the woman in black. I greeted her as she walked out through the gates.

'What're you doing out here?' she asked.

'Just walking,' I replied. 'Killing time till Patrick comes back home.'

'Why,' she said, 'amn't I just after passing him on me way out here. He was heading up the hill.'

'Might I catch him, do you think?'

'Oh, it was a while ago now. He's probably taking a look at ould Hughie's place. He's often up there.'

'I shouldn't think so,' I said, rather worried, but then,

388

perhaps she had not heard that I had lost the place, and Patrick was only taking a walk up the hill to look for me.

As we walked together to the end of the gravel lane she told me how she'd been brought in to help wash down the corpse of the gentleman who owned that huge farm. 'He would have been a hundred if he'd only lasted the year out,' she shrugged. 'That's life for you. Sad though, really. He was all alone in life, you know. No friends. No relations. Didn't mix at all with us locals, thought he was above us all.'

'Was that his widow, in black?' I asked.

'Morag! God, no. She's been his housekeeper for years. She was just there to pick him up whenever he fell down the stairs, and cook his gruel, you know the kind of thing!' She laughed as she turned out into the main road. I left her cackling away to herself, and started the stiff walk up the hill to Hughie's house.

I came up behind the house, in its shadow. As I neared the window I saw that Patrick was inside, and not alone. I saw a woman's hair. I crouched down and hid myself behind a gorse bush some distance away, but with a perfect view of the door. After only a quarter of an hour or so the door opened and out came two men I had never seen before. One of them linked arms with the woman and laughed. I was relieved that the woman was not there with Patrick alone.

Patrick was last out. He turned and locked the door, then slipped round the side of the house and slid the keys under one of the oil-drums of fertiliser.

I was going to jump up from behind the bush, but some inquisitive devil in me kept me there.

'So it's on for Tuesday, then,' said the woman. 'I'll pick up the sugar on Monday from Cash and Carry.'

Patrick looked at the oil-drums. 'I'll fetch them down in the Land Rover after I've picked you up. And Santa's goodies from the shelf, of course. And then . . .'

They all looked at each other and laughed.

'Firework night!' grinned one of the men.

I lay flat on the ground under the gorse as they passed me on their way down the hill. I stayed there until I felt sure they were all out of sight, then retrieved the key and let myself in.

The place was empty. There was nothing left behind, no proof that they had been there at all. I opened all the cupboards. They were bare.

The dusky light was failing. There was still no electricity in the house.

What did they mean by 'Santa's goodies'?

Up the chimney, I thought. The new, widened chimney breast. I peered up. I could see nothing, for the light was failing fast. I stood in the fireplace, my head up behind the chimney breast, and reached up. There were shelves inside the hollow of the chimney! No soot. We had never lit a fire since the rebuilding.

My hands felt along the shelves. I fumbled with a squashy plastic bag. It felt like mozzarella cheese. I pulled the package down and took it to the window to inspect it in the failing light: 'Super Ajax. Industrial explosive.' The packet was illuminated for me by a shaft of moving light which swept past the window.

It was a car.

Quickly I shoved the packet back on to the shelf up the chimney and let myself out. There was no time to replace the keys, so I crept round the back of the building and threw them along the far side where they pinged as they hit the oil-drums and clattered to the ground beside them. Then I scampered back to the gorse bush. It was a Range Rover. Maybe they had changed plans and were coming to pick up the oil-drums now. The car pulled up right outside the front door. The driver's door opened and my husband got out and stretched himself.

'Well, if we don't like it, we can always go down and stay at the Slieve Donard,' he said. 'Come on, you lot. Let's get sorted.'

Miss Pelham was already opening the front door. 'Oooh, stuffy!' she cried. 'You can tell it's been empty for ages.'

She came back and pulled out some boxes from the rear door of the car; the same boxes I had watched her pack only yesterday.

'Ah,' sighed my husband. 'Just breathe in that pure air. We'll all sleep well tonight.'

My twins jumped out and stood admiring the wildness of the place. The moon shone down. They looked beautiful standing there in the blue light. Only yards away from me at last. I decided to stay in my lair. Eventually they would come out without him or her, and I could talk to them alone.

'Come on, you pair of shirkers,' my husband yelled. 'Let's have some help here, or we'll never get settled in in time to go down to town for dinner.'

They all trekked in and out of the house until the car was empty.

Miss Pelham came out alone. She peered round the sides of the house. I was very frightened that she'd see me. So I dug in, and laid my face flat in the dusty soil. I could hear her footsteps clattering around, then the door shut again. There was a lot of animated chat, then Robert came out with a small blow-up tent and a foot pedal. He drove the pegs in, the children looking on in awe, then started pumping it up.

'We can do that!'

'Oh please let us do it, Daddy. We can do it.'

He shrugged. 'Good. You want it. You do it. I don't know why the house isn't good enough for you.'

'We just want an adventure, Daddy, that's all.'

He strolled back inside. 'And to get away from the Wicked Witch of the West End,' giggled my daughter.

My son was stamping away at the pedal. 'I'm pretending this is her face,' he said. They both laughed, holding their lower lips tightly with their top teeth so that no noise came out.

My daughter sighed, standing with her hands on her hips like a little slave-driver. 'I wish Mummy could come back. I want to go on holiday with Mummy.'

My heart beat so I thought they would be able to hear it. My mouth was dry. I shifted position and was going to whistle or hiss to them, something that wouldn't frighten them too much, but the door burst open and Miss Pelham stood there glaring out into the dark.

'Come on, for God's sake. We haven't got all night. Come inside now for a moment and get dressed for dinner. Your father's just lit the fire, come and look.' She turned on her heel.

A fire!

The explosive.

I threw myself out of the bush as my children trotted meekly towards the house.

'STOP!' I yelled, grabbing my son by the arm, tugging at my daughter's dress as the explosion blew us back through the air. The blast felt as though it sucked my cheeks from my face, my clothes from my body.

When we fell to earth a second roar burst from the house. Parts of the roof flew up in the orange air. Flying slate, and brick pounded down on us. All three together at last. I pulled their limp bodies towards me, and wiped their faces. Blood dripped from my son's scalp, and soaked into the dust. My daughter lay still against my bosom.

'Live!' I cried. 'Oh, God, please, please let them live.' My hands were shaking and sticky with blood. Time seemed to stop. I lay still, holding my children close to me.

Before me, the house was a raging inferno. The gutted, twisted wreckage of the car lay in a heap where the oil-drums had stood.

I started rocking back and forth. 'Don't die!' I cried. 'Don't leave me now that we've found each other again.'

I was shaking violently now. I stretched my hand out beside me to keep my balance. My fingers dug into the dust. Something cold. I looked down. Gold pieces glinting at me, fragments of a wooden chest jutting up out of the earth where it had lain buried. Pieces of eight. Spanish gold. I scooped them up and piled them into my children's pockets. I put my ear to their lips. I could not feel their breath. Lights were coming up the hill. White lights. Blue lights. Flashing against the yellowing sky.

'I have nothing more to add, my lord, than to point out to the jury and yourself that a woman who had for so long gone to such lengths to be near her children is hardly likely to wish to kill them.'

The judge shifts in his chair. 'And Mr O'Shea?'

'Mr O'Shea, my lord, is an entirely different case. He made use of the vulnerable situation my client found herself in, to ingratiate himself with her to gain access to the secluded house which he needed as an arsenal. The connection between them is very slight. I have no reason to think that my client had any involvement with his pseudo-political mission. You will see that Mr O'Shea's statements, however vague on behalf of himself, vehemently deny that Mrs Taylor, now Miss Rosaleen Morgan, had any part in his terrorist activity. Her own statements, I think you can see, are not worth much as evidence. She was simply at the wrong place at the wrong time. Or, should I say, at the right time. For without her swift action it is certain that her children would have been killed in the blast as well as the two adults.'

I sit up.

'My children are alive?'

All faces turn to me in the dock. I leap up. 'You mean my children are alive? Why has no one told me this? The wardresses told me they were dead, that I had killed them. Oh, my God, oh my God.'

I hear the words: 'Drop all charges.' The policeman behind me has for some reason forced me back into my seat. Someone is yelling, 'Silence in court! Silence in court!'

'The time spent in remand more than accounts for any period I would suggest she serve for wasting police time.'

I can hardly breathe. 'My children are alive!' I announce to everyone. 'Alive!'

I bring up the palms of my hands to cover my face, and my cheeks are warm and wet from the tears rolling down them.


The mousy solicitor is with me as we are driven to the foster home where my children have been cared for during my imprisonment.

'Why didn't you tell me?' I demand.

He shrugs. 'For a long time I thought you knew. It never occurred to me that no one had told you, or worse that those frightful women had misinformed you.' He tuts quietly to himself. 'I shall see that they are put on a charge for that. The moment I realised, I was going to tell you. I opened my mouth. But something in your eyes made me think it would be better for you in the long run, if you were kept in the dark, once again, for just a little while. I knew you were innocent, incapable of all those awful things, but you've a strong personality for a woman. I thought while you were looking so browbeaten you would be a better witness for your true self. I am very sorry, but I hope you see I did it to help you. And them.'

He turns to me and pats my hands on my lap. 'It's the most fascinating case I've ever worked on,' he says, smiling. 'Quite the most satisfying case I could ever hope to get. There are some other things, too, that I've not had a chance to tell you in all the excitement,' he says. He pulls his briefcase on to his knee and snaps it open.

'The smallholding on the hill in Ulster is, as you know, practically worthless. But on the death of your husband possession of this has naturally passed to your children.'

I nod. Could I ever bear to return to that place?

'The most amazing news, though, I'm sure you'll agree, comes from the same locality. While I was over there doing my research, the local man told me that a large property there had been left to a Mrs Catherine Morgan, née Tate, of Liverpool. He was placing adverts in the Liverpool papers to trace this lady or any of her descendants.

'The fellow who lived there, a Mr Alan Bird, had written the will years ago. He'd been spurned at the altar by her, apparently. All very romantic stuff. Her father had given the place to him, it seems, because he was furious that his daughter – your mother, that is – had run off with his groom! Just like a novel, isn't it?' He grins. 'Anyhow, as her daughter, that means the place is yours.'

'What about the gold coins? The Spanish coins. My children had them. They were meant for them.'

He tutted.

'Difficult one that. Do they constitute treasure trove? Officially I'm told they all belong to the Queen.'

'But they were my uncle's. I know he would have wanted the children to have them.'

'Armada gold,' he says in a dreamy voice. 'Going back

to another Queen Elizabeth, and through all these centuries of history between.'

He sucks in air between his teeth with a hiss and says, 'What a challenge, Miss Morgan!' He twists in his seat to face me. 'Would you like me to fight it?'

'Agh,' I say with a wink. 'Why the divil not?'

# My Dark Rosaleen

I am the sum total of centuries. I am my
family. I am history. I am geography. I
am phonetics, grammar, style. It all ends
in a bare cell. Once it would have
finished at the end of a rope. No more,
unfortunately for me. Where did it all
begin? How many centuries has it taken
to lock me in these four walls, with only
the odd fly for company?

Fidelis Morgan is the daughter of
Liverpool Irish parents. She works as an
actress and is the author of ten books,
including several on 17th and 18th
century theatre history, plays,
adaptations and articles. She lives in
London. *My Dark Rosaleen* is her first
novel.